The literature and information ⦚⦚⦚⦚⦚⦚⦚⦚⦚⦚⦚⦚⦚⦚⦚⦚⦚⦚

Health Resource W9-AFY-643

is not intended to be a substitute for consulting
with your physician or other health care provider.
Your physician's medical advice is critical.
Only your physician can render a definite diagnosis
and recommend appropriate treatment.

Hudson Hospital & Clinics

HealthPartners Family of Care

405 Stageline Road • Hudson, Wisconsin 54016
715-531-6250 or 1-800-993-2325
www.hudsonhospital.org

LAUGHING
Sickness
A Medical Mystery

LAUGHING
Sickness
A Medical Mystery

Anne Black Gray

BridgewayBooks

Laughing Sickness: A Medical Mystery
Published by Bridgeway Books
P.O. Box 80107
Austin, Texas 78758

For more information about our books, please write to us, call
512.478.2028, or visit our website at www.bridgewaybooks.net.

Library of Congress Control Number: 2007927790

ISBN-13: 978-1-933538-93-8
ISBN-10: 1-933538-93-7

ACKNOWLEDGMENTS

I want to thank all those who helped me through the various stages of writing this book. First, my writing group—Scott Edwards, Sharon Holmin, Cat Hulbert, Robyn Joy Leff, Pat Lohr-Williams and Roark Whitehead—for offering much valued advice as they combed over early versions of many of the chapters. My appreciation for their support and valuable comments go to my novel-reading friends—Trudy Armer, Shirley Friedman-Chase, Louise Hoare, Mary Kummer, Ethel Schwartz and Charlotte Weiss. Virginia and Ira Teller and Renee and Jim Copes offered thoughtful commentary and Cheryl Woodruff provided an insightful review of every aspect of this work. Finally, I appreciate the devotion and dogged dedication of my husband, Ed Gray, who has read every page of the manuscript and its revisions almost as many times as I have.

Although this is a work of fiction, much of it has a factual basis. The medical success claimed by the fictional Las Flores University as described in this book was actually accomplished at UCLA and Stanford in research I did not have space to adequately describe and praise.

I wish respect, kindness and success for all those with hard-to-diagnose, debilitating diseases looking for ways to improve their lives.

CHAPTER 1

On a normal day Jessica could have sprinted, hopped or even turned cartwheels across this floor. She could have climbed fingerhold by fingerhold, toehold by toehold, over a boulder if one had been in the way. She was not normally, could never remember being, sprawled flat on her face with her cheek pressed to cold tile.

She peered across the gray and white floor glistening with the immaculate shine of a first-rate hospital. There was nothing to trip or stumble on. Like one of those large, inflatable lawn Santas after the air pump is turned off, she'd simply failed to stay upright—sagging, wilting, then collapsing in a limp heap.

A clown's absurd fall. She giggled at the thought and felt better. Laughing always distanced her from whatever mess she was in. Not that she'd call her situation today a mess. Drunks, overdosed druggies, frail senior citizens and very sick people who fell on the floor were in a mess. She was just tired, very tired. Her sprawl was comic, not pathetic, and unlike the addicts and sick people, she could get back on her feet.

Rolling onto one side, she tried pushing to a squat as if she'd fallen while skiing, putting all her physical and mental energy into the effort. Nothing happened. Her arms were useless. She tried folding her knees under her to gain leverage, but only managed to curl into a fetal position.

This shouldn't be happening. At twenty-five, she was in great condition—ate vegetarian, exercised daily, hardly drank any alcohol and never touched drugs. For her to be spread out like melted jello, even as tired as she was, was crazy. And frightening.

Could it be that she'd finally gone over the top and completely exhausted herself? She had to admit, she habitually ignored advice about sleep and rest. Fernando, for one, had warned her she'd drive herself to exhaustion, but she'd never believed that could really happen. She tried to picture herself grudgingly acknowledging he was right, that some aerobics workout on top of a ten-hour workday had pushed her over the edge.

Of course, he would never hear that admission. To say she was wrong and Fernando was right, especially at a time like this when not listening to him was probably a mistake he wouldn't let her forget, would be impossible. He always made such a big deal out of it when she didn't take his advice. So she wouldn't tell him about today's collapse. And she wouldn't tell her mother, who'd be sure to point out that she had a habit of bringing trouble on herself. They didn't need to know about this ridiculous, self-inflicted exhaustion, or that over the past few days she'd ignored warning signs. She hoped she hadn't done herself permanent damage.

"You okay?" a woman's voice called out. "Do you need help?" Another woman.

Jessica felt embarrassed. People were getting all worked up just because she was on the floor. "I'll be up in a minute." Her cheek scraped on the tile each time she moved her mouth.

"Why don't they call somebody? She can't just lay there." An old man this time.

"Hey! How about listening to me!" Jessica shouted as best she could with throat and mouth feeling as tired as her arms and legs. "I have the floor here."

The jabbering stopped. Someone with a high voice began to giggle. The man guffawed, and a woman gasped, then tittered.

That was more like it. Laughter was a whole lot better than pity or nervous fright. "Just give me a minute. Okay?" There'd rarely been a predicament she couldn't relieve with a little humor. If she could get people to laugh, she didn't have to worry about being smart or stupid, capable or incapable. It was enough to get a laugh.

She'd never been so afraid.

"You don't think I should call the paramedics?" Jessica was pretty sure the voice belonged to the mid-fortyish receptionist who'd hunched myopically over the forms when checking her in.

"No! Please don't." Call the paramedics! Like she'd had a heart attack or something. Nearsighted or not, the woman was in charge of a waiting room in one of Southern California's finest hospitals and should have the insight and experience to recognize a person in basically good health.

The tappety-tap of high heels approached. A pair of shiny black pumps appeared in front of her face. "I'm going to call for help." It was the receptionist again. Her shoes twisting against the tile betrayed her nervousness.

"Just give me a minute and I'll get up. I'm not drunk or anything." Maybe all she had to do was gather a little strength. She'd always been able to overcome exhaustion by pushing herself.

Breathing deeply, she tried channeling all her energy into her arms and legs.

No use. She felt as if she weighed as much as an elephant.

What had she done to herself?

The receptionist knelt down and put a hand on Jessica's shoulder. "I'm going to call for a wheelchair." Jessica heard the shoes retreat, then the sing-song sound of phone buttons being pushed. "I need a wheelchair up front. Stat."

Jessica shuddered. A wheelchair. For her. This couldn't be.

From far down a long corridor she saw two black-tired wheels approaching, clicking like a pair of hungry insects. When they were almost on top of her, she glimpsed a young man in a green orderly's uniform behind the chair. His worn, low-top sneakers with ragged shoe laces appeared inches from her face.

"How ya doin'?" His voice was flat and gravelly.

"Super."

"Terrific. Can you stand if I help you?" He took her arm.

"I'm a bit weak. You'll have to lift me."

He put his arms under her armpits, clasped his hands under her ribs and easily raised the upper part of her body off the floor. "This okay?"

It was humiliating to be hauled around like this, but the sooner it was over the better. "Let's go."

He dragged her—she was horrified at how limp and helpless she was—onto the flimsy-looking plastic seat of the wheelchair, picked up her purse and laid it on her lap. "There you go. Do you need to be taken somewhere?"

"No, I'll be fine. Have to wait my turn to be seen." By the time her turn came, she certainly hoped she wouldn't need a wheelchair.

He nodded, and Jessica watched him amble off down the hall whistling.

She tried to brush off the blue wool dress she'd worn to the office, but with little success. Incredibly, her arms were too weak. She couldn't even open her purse to get the pack of towelettes she kept for cleaning emergencies.

As she glanced around the room now, people averted their eyes. One minute she'd been worrying people were staring at her, the next she was worrying why they wouldn't even look.

She struggled to swing her head backward against the plastic back-rest so it didn't sag to her chest like a drunk's and so she could see the others and correct any wrong impression they might have about her. She picked out two young women in sweaters and short, tight skirts sitting a few feet away.

"Normally, I'm a champion slalom skier," she improvised. "You know, downhill, zigzagging like mad around those little poles."

One responded with a wan smile.

Come on, these ladies could do better than that. She wasn't exactly a slalom skier, although she was pretty good, and her quip wasn't exactly hilarious, although it wasn't terrible either. They might have done her a favor and laughed a little bit.

She spotted a stiff, flat-footed shoe strapped with Velcro to the foot of the woman who'd smiled. "Been doing some heavy racing yourself?"

"No." The young woman grimaced. "Stubbed my stupid toe in my own bedroom. But I'm doing fine. This thing's supposed to come off today." Her voice sounded cheerful, but her eyes were almost apologetic as they traveled over Jessica's limp form.

The verdict in those eyes! Jessica couldn't let it pass. "You think you did a stupid thing? Just look at me. This is what working ten hours a day, seven days a week can do to you."

The eyes looked down at the floor.

Jessica stifled a shriek that she didn't want to be judged by her appearance at this moment. She was fumbling for a comeback when an old man, no doubt the one who'd spoken out, took a seat close to her. He had thin, white hair and a cane he tapped lightly along the floor as though he didn't really need it. He leaned his hands on the head of the cane. "You're such a pretty young thing," he said in a voice she sensed he was forcing to sound cheerful. "I'm sure the doctors here will help you." He pulled a little plastic box from a jacket pocket and, eyes gleaming as if displaying priceless treasure, opened it to reveal several round pills nestled in compartments like miniature eggs. "Look what they did for me. Gave me Coumadin. Five years ago I had a stroke and not one since. Saved my life."

She was glad he was back to enjoying life. "Want to party when I've got my dancing feet back?" She winked at him.

He gaped at her.

She could diagnose this guy in a minute—broken funny bone. Same for the other six patients in this room. People were reluctant to laugh in a hospital for fear they'd be thought insensitive to the suffering around them. But they were wrong to be so somber. It was better to be daring, to clear the air of fear and dread. In her view hardly any of life's problems were really awful. Tough as they sometimes seemed, most came and went before any real harm was done. She'd always sailed through the rough waters she ran into on a sea of laughter. It would help to have someone laugh with her, but the people in this room weren't cooperating.

She could take encouragement from them anyway. The old man was spry and full of life. The lady with red shoes who'd gone back to her knitting didn't look sick. The pink-cheeked pregnant woman across the way, hands folded across a bulging belly, seemed really healthy.

Everyone here was living evidence that Gebauer doctors knew what they were doing, and Dr. Trumpower, whom she'd seen only once for a sprained ankle since she joined the HMO five years ago, was supposed to be one of the best GPs. He'd probably tell her to quit working such long hours.

Advice she didn't need. She'd already promised herself to never, never overwork herself this hard again.

CHAPTER 2

Only four days ago at work she'd had the first warning she was doing too much.

Before sitting down at the required Monday morning meeting, she'd stood in the back of the conference room, stalling. Crassly institutional, its beige, paint-chipped, windowless walls bare except for a plastic-rimmed clock, the room was totally cheerless. This was not a place Rank Aerospace's customers ever saw. This was a behind-the-scenes sweatshop.

Up front, in a hand-tailored Italian suit that glimmered with expensive sheen, stood Larry Armor, vice president and leader of the proposal effort she was working on. Eyebrows furrowed, mouth tight and grim, he faced a dozen rows of managers, engineers, bean counters, schedulers and technical writers pressed to the backs of their chairs, braced to withstand the storm they knew was coming. Armor was rumored to believe that without his screaming and yelling to drive his "peons" on, they'd be lazy and unproductive, and his ambitions would remain unrealized. His current goal was to win this contract, worth almost a billion dollars, for which he'd be rewarded with more power, money and prestige than anyone except the CEO. Jessica knew there was no use complaining. No one in Rank's top management would fault him for abusing subordinates as long as he won this proposal and brought in the big bucks.

Besides, she'd developed methods of handling a heavy workload and a killer boss—she was a coper. Stay focused on getting her work done, and she wouldn't be drawn into the energy-sapping, time-consuming anxieties she often saw embroiling others. Keep physically strong with aerobics, and she could take the pressure. Most importantly, find something to laugh at in this clown's rants that she could share with Whitney.

Near the back she spotted her friend's blond head. She'd saved a place beside her.

Hanging out with Whitney made any day, good or bad, a better day. Whitney was possibly the most agreeable person she knew. Too agreeable for her own good sometimes. And Whitney was possibly the prettiest person she knew. Her honey-colored hair spread smoothly to her shoulders. Her sea green pantsuit was spotless and flawlessly pressed. As usual, she looked like a million dollars.

Jessica glanced down at her own brown wool slacks. Cat hairs. She'd missed a few this morning. Picking them off as she went, she hurried over to take the saved seat. "Hi, Whit."

Whitney looked up from the notebook in which she was scribbling and raised an eyebrow.

Jessica recognized Whitney's "What are we doing in this awful place" look and raised both eyebrows to signal "Beats me."

Whitney lowered both eyebrows in a scowl, as if to say "I hate being here."

Jessica raised one eyebrow and simultaneously scowled with the other, a totally confusing message that caused Whitney to have a fit of giggles.

It made no difference how they felt. Much as she and Whitney despised Armor's Monday morning harangues, there was no cutting them if they wanted to stay on this job. And Jessica did want to stay. Working on this proposal was exciting. The stakes were high, the competition fierce, the race against time a challenge. Everyone put in long hours, working together as a team. No one wanted to let the others down in the effort to win. It was like playing on a baseball team in a pennant race or fighting alongside your buddies in a war.

And she wanted to prove she could do well in her first real post-college position and go for a pay boost and, if she was really lucky, a promotion.

Whitney was another story. She hated the way Armor and the rest of her management treated everyone so much she was on the verge of bolting off the job. Whitney was not a coper.

Lunatic Larry was strutting up and down, black- and gray-streaked hair tousled, chest out, chin raised. The man never stood still. He looked up at the clock. Seven thirty. Most Rank employees straggled in between eight and eight thirty, but on this proposal Armor demanded a seven-thirty start. Jessica and Whitney believed he thrived on demanding and dominating.

"Sometimes when I talk to you people, I sense a team, a powerful engine beneath my foot," he began, his voice a deep growl.

Jessica almost moaned aloud. Under his foot. What an image. She wondered if he ever really looked at any of them and saw the resentment he provoked.

"But sometimes I feel you working against me. This morning I'm getting bad vibes." Full lower lip protruding, Armor glared at the assemblage.

Jessica fixed her eyes on the ceiling above his head. She'd once overheard him call his tantrums "keeping the employees out of their comfort zone." Time to blot him out and go into her own zone. There was plenty to think about.

Like the mess of crudely typed and handwritten rambling thoughts on ground station antennas she'd been given Friday. Engineers, even the most proficient and inventive, were awful writers. Her job was to take their scribbles and make them clear, blend in the company's sales pitch, and see that the artwork and data supported the message. She liked the challenge of quickly grasping new technical concepts and writing them up in words with punch. Even the engineers were often surprised and pleased.

She heard a crescendo in Armor's already loud voice. "Where's the frequency plan? Five days before the executive review and there's no frequency plan."

Her stomach became a tight fist. Jim Stone was the manager and she was the technical writer for that section. Stone and his engineers hadn't yet given her anything to work with, saying they'd be lucky to have the design ready by Saturday and the write-ups would have to wait. Fine with her—she had enough other work to do without dealing with some humongous frequency plan. Until now, she hadn't given it a second thought.

Armor leaned forward and brought his palms down so hard on the back of a front row chair it shuddered, then glared right at Jessica.

"You've had six weeks to get that plan out."

She gasped and pressed back into her chair. She should have written something. Just to flake on the whole plan had been dumb. Armor sometimes fired people on the spot when he was really angry.

"And you've shown me nothing. Shame on you." Jessica felt her face grow hot and her pulse pound. "Join me, ladies and gentlemen, in saying 'shame on you' to Jim Stone. He has let you down."

She turned around to see a red-faced Jim Stone sitting right behind her. This was sick. Everyone knew Stone was capable and drove himself and those who worked for him hard. Still, it was a relief to know Armor wasn't attacking her.

On second thought, she realized she'd overreacted. She was so low down in the pecking order around here that Armor scarcely knew she existed, let alone what work she should have done.

"We had to rework the crosslinks," Stone answered. "No sense in picking a frequency plan until we know what the links are."

"Now, Jim." Armor sounded like a teacher addressing a wayward student. "You and I went over that crosslink design two weeks ago. You've had all this time to write that plan up. Get it on the wall."

Get it on the wall, indeed. Drafts for the proposal didn't go up on the wall until they were ready for review. Jessica would bet that if Stone was reworking the crosslinks they needed reworking.

As if he'd overheard her thoughts, Armor spoke up. "You people have got to stop improving things that work well enough. We've got cost and schedule to think of, not just performance. Never forget: 'Better is the enemy of good enough.'"

Jessica leaned toward Whitney and whispered in her ear. "Never forget: 'Mottoes are the crutch of the mindless manager.'" Whitney stifled a giggle and whispered "Shush." She was afraid Armor would catch them laughing.

Jessica felt a finger poke into her back and turned around to face Stone. "Stick around after this is over," he whispered. She nodded and turned forward again, wishing she could find a way to avoid him. She didn't have time to do any of his stuff by Saturday.

After Armor finished a forty-five minute diatribe and stalked out, Jessica made a lunch date with Whitney for the cafeteria. No time for the Parkview Café's spicy cheese quesadillas or sun-dried tomato pasta these days.

Before Jessica could scoot out the door, Stone caught up with her. "Come on. Let's go figure out what we're going to do."

She followed him, enjoying the view from behind. He had a rolling John Wayne swagger that was kind of sexy. Before going to engineering school, Stone had earned his living as sheriff of a small Texas town. Tall and sinewy, he was easy to picture twenty years younger with a gun belt slung below where he now had a pot belly.

He rated an office with a door and four walls that went to the ceiling, not a tiny cubicle like hers. Plopping himself into the leather chair behind his large wooden desk, he waved her to one of the four guest chairs. Jessica wondered how many Armors he'd had to endure to earn this office. She admired how well he coped with the pressure and made a mental note to observe his technique.

"I'm sorry, but I just don't know when I can fit your work in," she said. "I'm booked solid with meetings and other write-ups from now until late Friday."

Stone sat forward with a jerk and pointed a finger at her. "Look, if an old fart like me can keep up the pace around here, so can you." His voice rose from a growl to a shrill whine. "You're young. You can take it."

Jessica almost leapt out of her chair. "That's not fair. I pull my own weight. No one can do the impossible just because Armor demands it." Evidently one way he coped was by yelling at people working for him.

He glowered at her. "He's the boss. He wants the write-up Saturday—we get it done by Saturday."

He must have been a sheriff too long. Marching to orders was way too important to him. "I'll have to work late nights on top of the days I've already got filled."

"You'll be rewarded someday." He gave her a wink and a Will Rogers wide-mouthed grin.

"I certainly hope mine gets here soon and I can spend it. None of this hereafter stuff for me."

Stone picked up a pile of rumpled papers from his desk. "This is where Armor and I left the plan two weeks ago. See what kind of shape you can put it in."

She backed out of his office and pulled the door shut. For the foreseeable future, she'd have to work even more than her current ten hours a day. She could just forget about dinners out or relaxing at the piano. It'd be hard to get the laundry and grocery shopping done.

Armor would be on Stone's case day and night and he'd be on hers. She mamboed down the hall to her office cubicle the way they did at aerobics—one, two, three—kick Armor and punch Armor, and one, two, three—kick and punch.

At two thirty, Whitney stopped by Jessica's cubicle. "Got a minute?"

Jessica spun around and leaned back in her swivel chair—she couldn't lean very far back without bumping into the desk. "Only a minute. I'm trying to finish this write-up so I can start on Stone's work by five or six." She rubbed her tense, aching shoulder, wondering what it would feel like if she was still hunched over her computer at eight or nine tonight.

"I need to sound off. My boss has me programming an equation for calculating thermal gradients," she said, perching on Jessica's table, legs swinging in the air. "Any high school graduate can do that."

"Why not tell him that?" Sometimes she couldn't believe how totally incapable Whitney was of working out problems with her bosses. Whitney was sharp, a first-rate spacecraft engineer and deserved better treatment than she got. The problem was she always tried to please everyone. In the face of conflict, she was passive.

Whitney shrugged. "You know me."

"Come on, Whit. Don't be a wimp. That's how they get you. They count on you to take whatever they dish out."

"That's me—wimp of the workplace." Whitney grimaced.

"Write your boss a proposal," Jessica said. Her fingertips and hands had begun to tingle as if they'd fallen asleep. She rubbed her hands together to awaken them. But her arms were getting weak. "Tell him what you feel you're capable of." It seemed as if her throat and jaw wouldn't work right; her speech slowed. What the hell was going on?

"What's the matter?" Whitney asked.

"I don't know." Jessica felt her energy factory shutting down fast. She was weak and cold, starting to shiver. She felt like she was going to fly apart. Chilled and clammy, she began to sweat all over. She fell forward onto the table, arms spread out, head pressed flat to the cold surface. She struggled to sit up, but failed. She couldn't imagine what was happening.

"No kidding, Jessica." Whitney's voice had gone to a higher pitch. "What's wrong?"

"I don't know. I just don't know. I feel like I'm going to pass out. Don't leave me alone." She'd never felt like this in her life, not even when she'd had the flu and a temperature of 104.

She could see Curt Simons from down the hall standing in the cubicle entrance and two engineers she didn't even know by name peering over the wall. Feeling like an animal in a zoo, she tried to end the show by sitting up, but couldn't move.

"It's nothing," she said, the side of her face still pressed to the table.

"What?" Whitney's face was down near hers. "I can't understand you."

"No—thing." Jessica tried to say the word clearly. Actually, she felt quite good now—free of her body, as if she were drifting over the flowery alpine meadow in the poster on her wall. Even in her dazed condition, she knew this was strange. But why fight it.

Jim Stone's voice came from above. "What's the matter, Jess?" He put his hand on her back.

What was the matter? Something had to be wrong, but a part of her never felt happier. "Lupine." She tried to tell him about the lovely mountain flowers, but couldn't move her tongue and throat to form the words.

"Maybe you'd better go home," he said.

That would be nice. "Pretty soon."

"You're not ready yet?"

"In a minute," she managed to say. She could see his wristwatch. It was just after three. Now that her hands felt normal—they'd stopped tingling—everything was perfect. Except, for some reason, she was afraid she couldn't move. Maybe she could move a little bit if she found the mental strength to make the effort, but she couldn't find it. "A few minutes."

"Somebody better stay with her," Stone said. "She seems awfully weak."

"I will," Whitney replied. "Look, she's shivering."

Someone laid a heavy man's jacket over Jessica's back and shoulders. That was better, but she was still cold, suddenly chilled through. She wanted to drift off into sleep. A rational voice in her head rejected this idea—people didn't suddenly drift off into rapturous sleep in the middle of the day.

The next thing she knew, she roused from a stupor to see Whitney sitting in a chair in the cubicle entranceway. Slowly, Jessica sat upright. She looked at her watch—five o'clock. She'd been zonked for hours—a whole afternoon lost.

"I almost fell asleep," she said. With a start she realized Jim Stone had seen her sprawled on the table. Everyone had.

Whitney eyed her. "How do you feel?"

"Stronger. Better. But I'm way behind schedule now. I can't believe how tired I got."

"I never saw anyone sink as low as you did. We almost called the paramedics, but you said not to."

"I'm okay." Jessica remembered feeling strangely giddy with happiness and refusing the paramedics as if it had happened in a dream. Still a bit weak, she stood up slowly. "I just want to go home. I thought I could handle this job, but it must be getting to me. I guess I need a rest." Tomorrow she'd figure out how to catch up on her work.

When she pulled into the underground garage at her apartment building, she remembered Whitney walking her to her car. But the drive up the freeway to the Orange Grove exit and down the winding street to her place was disturbingly blank.

As soon as she got out of the car and onto her feet, her thighs began to tremble. It was going to be a tough haul from the garage up the steps to the courtyard; her apartment was on the second floor, all the way back. She focused on trudging up the first flight of gritty stone stairs, forcing her leaden feet to move. At the top she was exhausted and leaned against a rough stucco wall, clutching a manila envelope crammed with write-ups. Can't stop. Got to keep going. She crossed the courtyard and dragged herself up the second flight and along the walkway to her door where she fumbled for the key holder in the bottom of her purse.

After pushing the key into the lock and turning it, all she had to do was shove the door open. She couldn't do it. She tried to will herself to be strong, but had no more mental than physical vigor. Her calves trembled, her thighs crumpled, and she sank onto the rubbery doormat where she lay down, exhausted.

A short time later Fernando had found her there, still too tired to get up.

CHAPTER 3

The waiting room had grown quiet. No one seemed concerned about her now. The two young women were chatting, the pregnant woman was reading a magazine, another was knitting, the old man was dozing. Jessica was as weak as before, but as long as she was in a wheelchair instead of on the floor, the people around her seemed to think everything was under control.

She squirmed in the seat and tried to lift her arms. No use. A lot of good all that fitness training had done her. It had only created an arrogant confidence that her body didn't need rest and recuperation.

Closing her eyes, she tried recalling something other than the stress at work that might have done her in. Like last Friday, before her first spell of exhaustion, when she and Fernando had started to make love.

Hand in hand, they'd walked a fast-paced half mile in an exhilarating February breeze to Mario's, an Italian restaurant she'd found on a side street. They sat at a candlelit table with a red and white checkered cloth. She watched in fascination as the light from the sputtering candle reflected in Fernando's dark eyes when it flared, leaving a diffuse glow over his warm olive skin when it dimmed. She gazed as if seeing for the first time his finely drawn eyebrows, expressive deep brown eyes, thin nose, and straight, strong mouth. Her Spanish matador—her sensitive artist.

Well, actually, a new MD going for a specialty in oncology, his thoughtful, protective nature just as appealing as his sexiness.

The air in the restaurant was drenched in the aromas of cooking tomatoes, garlic, oregano and onions. Their table was close enough to the front door to get a blast of cold air every time it opened, but warmth quickly enveloped them the moment it closed, fanning her cold, hot, cold, hot like when she had a fever.

Soon the waiter set an antipasto platter loaded with onions, cheese and olives between them. Fernando poured Chianti into her nearly empty glass. She loved his attentiveness. She watched the movement of his hands over the surface of the bottle and picked up the sexual tension lurking in his eyes. She could almost feel his body pressed close and his arms around her.

Cool it, for heaven's sake, Jessica laughed at herself. You're lapsing into a sexual drool and it's only six o'clock.

"Mammoth would give us the most time on the slopes," Fernando said.

They'd been planning to go skiing as soon as his exams were over, but she wasn't sure she could even manage to take off a weekend from work.

"Let's try for it," she agreed. "But someday I want to go big time— Aspen or Steamboat Springs."

"Not enough thrills coming down from the top of Mammoth?" He smiled. "Your capacity for excitement never fails to astonish me."

She laid her hand on his arm and squeezed.

Their red-aproned waiter emerged from the steamy kitchen entrance with two plates of eggplant parmigiana. Since they'd started seeing each other, Fernando had begun to eat more and more like the vegetarian she was. "I think this guy's a mysterious alien," she whispered. "He magically materialized from that fog bank by the kitchen."

Fernando laughed as the waiter placed the hot dishes he'd gripped with thick, red-and-white napkins on the table.

She rolled her eyes. "I'm serious." She watched the man's back disappear back into the mist. "I hope you don't want dessert. They've just beamed him up to the mother ship."

"And what do they eat for dessert where he comes from?"

"Ambrosia. Nectar of the gods. They sip it from each other's lips." She let her gaze linger on his mouth.

Fernando leaned toward her. "I hope I get to sip mine from your lips, not his." His breath warmed her cheek, giving her tingles.

"Will you sip slowly at first or plunge right in?"

He squinted as though thinking hard. "It depends on which of us I want to give the greater pleasure to."

"Oh, me. Me. Give it to me."

Sucking in little gasps of air at every third or fourth giggle, he had to set his wine glass down.

She loved giving him the laughter he said he'd lacked growing up.

There's no such thing as a perfect match, she always told herself, but sometimes, like tonight, she and Fernando came close. They'd both spent their whole lives in Southern California and loved the out-of-doors, good food and classical music, especially piano and jazz. They put a high value on hard work and shared a passion for science, which hardly anyone their age cared about.

Religion wasn't a problem because they avoided the whole subject. And, although he was inclined to be bossy, he didn't annoy her very often.

Not a perfect match, but she was so happy with the positives, the negatives hardly mattered. Truth was, she looked forward to sex so much, and was so euphoric during and after it, that she could easily overlook a few imperfections.

She hadn't figured out yet whether she loved him or not. Love was such an unruly emotion. It could disrupt their relationship.

Outside after dinner, it was dark and the breeze had stiffened into a chill wind. Fernando grabbed her hand and urged her on until they were dashing down the sidewalk under streetlights flickering through wind-tossed tree leaves. Halfway down the hill a stronger blast struck them, unexpectedly fragrant with the scent of early blooming jasmine. They ran the length of the long block, past a row of apartment complexes, rushing through the perfumed air.

By the time they got to their building and raced through the courtyard where colored lights gleamed on palm trees and stucco walls, she felt like she was on a runner's high. Almost out of breath, they dashed past his downstairs place and up the steps to hers.

She unlocked the door and turned on a small desk lamp just inside, keeping the light dim. As they embraced and kissed urgently, caressing each other's lips, she felt the change begin: his strong arms grew pliant, his knees trembled. She ran her fingers over his face, chin, down his body. He began to breathe in deep gulps and his body shook, his self-control slipping from his hands into hers.

Wonderful. Perfect. She lingered over him, excited with anticipation of joys yet to come.

When she felt about to weaken too, she grasped his hand and led him past the blue couch and the grand piano that filled most of the living room into the short cupboard-lined hall and on into the darkened bedroom.

She turned on the lamp beside the bed, checking that the curtains were closed. She liked the light on so she could watch him undress and he could see her.

She pulled the soft, tan wool sweater over her head and flung it over the back of the cherrywood rocker by the bed. Her breasts weren't spectacular, but they were enough to draw Fernando's gaze. She flung her arms around his neck and kissed his ear as he reached around to unfasten her bra. With gentle hands, he caressed her back until she tingled all over.

He pulled away and began to remove his corduroy jacket and un-button his flannel shirt. Then he opened the shirt and yanked it off, the shape of his tennis-toned chest muscles and nipples showing through his undershirt.

Her turn. She slipped out of her jeans and thong, kicked off her flat-heeled shoes, and sat on the quilted bedspread.

He leaned over and pressed his fingertips lightly on her nipples, which had assumed lives of their own and grew erect at his touch. She felt as if she could fly around the room.

"Come on, Ferdie," she said and pulled him down onto the bed beside her, laughing as she kissed his neck, his soft fuzzy chest and threw herself half over him while he was still struggling to remove his shorts.

A low-pitched snarl came from the living room, followed by screeches and hisses.

She let go of the now-naked Fernando and sat up. "Elsa."

"What?" he mumbled.

"Something's wrong with Elsa." She jumped up from the bed and dashed across the bedroom.

"Can't it wait?" Fernando came running behind her.

Jessica turned on the living room light, blinking in the glare. Piano, desk, chair, couch, her own reflection in the mirror—nothing amiss here. A yowl and a low growl drew her eyes to the small end table beside the couch. A scruffy black tom, a stray she'd often seen in the canyon behind the apartment, was backing her cat under it. Elsa's back was arched, ears back, tawny, silky hair standing straight out from her body.

The tom must have gotten in earlier when she'd left the door open for Elsa. "Scat!" When she lunged at it, it scuttled behind the couch.

"Stay away from that filthy animal!" Fernando's voice rang out. He went to the kitchen pantry and came out brandishing a broom. "Open the door and I'll sweep it out."

She unlocked and slid open the glass balcony door and screen.

As she knelt and watched from the other end, Fernando, on hands and knees, poked the broom behind the couch.

The tom made a run for it, leaping straight at Jessica. Barely getting her hands in front of her face in time to protect herself, she grabbed the cat and stood up, staggering backward.

The cat yowled, all claws and teeth. She ran to the door and heaved the frantic beast out as it snarled and spit and slashed at her with its hind claws.

When she'd closed and locked the sliding door, a sharp pain in her left hand made her look down. "Shit! Look what that beast did to me!" Blood dripped from the thumb heel and red streaks were raked over the back of her hand.

Fernando thumped the broom handle on the floor. "Jess, you really shouldn't leave that door open. Anything can get in here—stray cats, squirrels, possums. Those things carry all kinds of nasty bacteria and viruses."

She'd been dating Fernando for six months now, long enough to recognize the shift in the tone of his voice from ordinary citizen to medical authority. But, even with the pain, she couldn't help giggling. He'd delivered his pronouncement standing naked with the broom, handle down, like a Biblical patriarch holding the staff of wisdom.

"And when the great Fernando smote the floor with his staff—Lo! Stray cats, possums, lizards and snakes sprang forth." She lifted her hands toward the ceiling.

His face reddened. "This is nothing to joke about. Wild animals carry all kinds of diseases."

What a prophet of doom. The scratch hurt a little bit, but so what. She'd had cats all her life, been scratched many times, and was never the worse for it.

"I leave the door open because I want Elsa to be free to come and go when she wants." One of the reasons she'd moved to this apartment on the rim of a canyon was so Elsa, named after the *Born Free* lioness, could roam the jungle-like wilds below.

"And look what happened! Let me see that." Fernando strode over, took her hand, and held up the palm where he could see the blood oozing and dripping. "Jesus, that's deep. Go run it under water for a good long while. Then put some Betadine on it to clean it out. Do you have any antibiotic ointment? You don't want to risk infection."

She wished he wouldn't fire orders at her like this, but she supposed he was right. She trudged obediently to the bathroom and picked out the bottle of Betadine from among the containers of shampoo, conditioner, tissues, hairspray and skin cream lined up on the counter—she checked to see that they were still lined up straight—then gingerly scrubbed her wound.

Fernando marched off to the bedroom and emerged in the white terrycloth robe she always thought of as his at home doctor's coat.

When she was done, he inspected her hand again. "When was the last time you had a tetanus shot?"

"I don't know. Almost five years ago, I guess. Right after graduation, just before I went to Nepal. I might have had one after that. I'm not sure."

"That recent? No worry then."

Who said she was worried?

He wasn't through. "There hasn't been a case of rabies in dogs or cats around here in years. And besides, that animal didn't attack you—we attacked it. So we can rule out rabies."

"Wow! What a relief."

Grabbing a sweatshirt from the bedroom, she went to the living room to see if Elsa was okay after her close encounter with a would-be rapist. Fernando followed and, as she plunked herself on the couch, stood with one foot on the blue upholstered arm, his hairy leg almost in her face, hands folded on the raised knee.

Elsa jumped onto the couch, then climbed onto Jessica's bare-legged lap. Jessica rubbed the long, silky fur. Elsa was beautiful. No wonder toms chased after her.

Fernando cleared his throat. "Cat scratch fever and toxoplasmosis—

they're always lurking around and can make you seriously sick, even if they're almost never fatal."

Oh, brother. She was going to get the full treatment over a stupid little cat scratch. She forced a smile. "I'm glad you were here to look after me." Of course, if he hadn't poked the broom at the cat, the cat wouldn't have leaped at her. "Anyway it's over now. Let's just forget about it, please."

An almost perfect relationship. The imperfection she was now experiencing she attributed more to his preachiness than to any mistake she'd made. The distinction was important, because in one case he would be in the wrong and in the other she would be.

He stretched forward and clutched her shoulder. "The important thing is for you to get an antibiotic in the morning. And promise me you won't let any more stray animals in here."

She pressed her face into Elsa's fur. It was her apartment, and she'd let in anything she wanted.

Before work the next day, she dropped by Gebauer and got a little bottle of an antibiotic called dicloxacillin. Just to be on the safe side the nurse also gave her a tetanus shot, combined with diphtheria and whooping cough.

No worry. She'd had lots of cat scratches in her life. The antibiotic seemed pointless, but she filled the prescription just in case. She didn't want an argument with Fernando when he asked. And he'd be sure to ask.

All day Friday she was fine. When she ran a 102° temperature on Saturday, she started the antibiotic. Sunday, her temperature was down to one hundred. By Monday the fever was gone. When Fernando, standing in her kitchen in his white robe, had pronounced her fit to return to work, she'd given him a big, happy hug.

CHAPTER 4

"Jessica."

A uniformed nurse, a tiny harried-looking woman with fine black hairs straggling from under a white cap, stood in the waiting room doorway. "Jessica Shephard." Her voice was high and as tiny as she was.

"Over there." The receptionist pointed. "In the wheelchair."

The words jarred Jessica. There were better ways to refer to her than "over there in the wheelchair." Like that young woman in the blue dress. Or that athletic-looking girl with the suntan.

She made an effort to stand and walk on her own, but was still too weak. Look at what a mess she, Miss I-can-cope-with-anything, had made of herself.

The nurse's smiling face was in hers. "Doctor's ready to see you." Trotting behind, she hurried the wheelchair along, stopping at a table to take Jessica's temperature, blood pressure and pulse rate. "Everything's fine," she said with a perky smile.

"Except for two little things. I can't walk or use my arms."

The woman looked away and pushed the wheelchair into a roomy, wood-paneled, sunlit office. "Temperature and blood pressure normal," she announced before leaving.

Backlit from a window behind his desk, a smiling Dr. Trumpower, his starched coat spotlessly white, projected a calm, confident air. Under a freshly styled head of dark, wavy hair, his broad, firm-fleshed face radiated the self-assurance of success. She glanced around the office— medical books and papers, computer, laser printer. His office was neat, always a good sign.

"I remember you, Miss Shephard. Sprained ankle, wasn't it? January, maybe February, 1997."

"Good memory!" Remarkable memory. She'd only seen him that one time a little over a year ago.

"Looks like you're having some problems." His eyes glowed like those of the fastest runners at the track where Jessica ran, eager for a new challenge.

Good that he was eager, but she hoped her case was no particular challenge. She wanted to get back to normal fast, change her behavior to keep this from happening again and put this episode into the past and forget it. "It's my job. I'm tired and stressed out." She laid out the scene at work and described the cat bite incident, in case it meant anything. "Basically, I'm in really good shape—eat vegetarian, work out, take care of myself. Probably all I need is a break from work, but I'm so exhausted I thought I'd better drop by and see you anyway."

He nodded, his expression now somber. "Healthy young people like you, especially here in Southern California, feel invincible."

"Right." Her own body was one of the things in life she'd always known she could count on. She took care of it. "I've never reacted to stress by collapsing before. I always thought that was an overweight, middle-aged man thing."

"Tell me what you've been experiencing." He scrutinized her in a way that made her feel like a riddle he was going to enjoy solving.

She positioned her head against the back of the wheelchair to look at him and talk more comfortably, feel more normal. "Every morning for the past five days, I get up, drive to work, start out fine. You wouldn't believe I had a problem in the world. Then, almost like clockwork, it comes on by three or four in the afternoon. First, my fingertips and toes tingle, kind of like my hands and feet are going to sleep. Then I get weak all over and feel like I'm falling apart, like I'm going to pass out. At work I slump over on my desk or table. Today I actually fell to the floor in your waiting room. Can you believe that?"

Said out loud, her symptoms sounded surprisingly severe. She watched Trumpower's face for a sign of shock or surprise.

Not a flicker of anxiety disturbed his smooth features. "Any pain?"

"No, thank heavens." She was encouraged by his lack of alarm, which she'd like to believe was a sign she hadn't exhausted herself past the point of no return.

"How weak do you get?"

"I feel like gravity's gone wrong and it's fifty times stronger than normal, so bad I can't move. The funny thing is, except for getting weak, I sometimes feel really great, like I'm on a runner's high." She searched Trumpower's face for a response in kind to her smile.

He cleared his throat. "Let's begin by eliminating the more common possibilities. I want to run blood tests for a few things. Like diabetes. And I want to look at your Vitamin Bs and electrolytes, especially since you're a vegetarian."

"I don't think that's necessary. I take B vitamins, especially B-12." She wasn't stupid about her vegetarianism.

"You may be right, but I want to make sure we're not overlooking anything. Let's see. Lyme disease—that's carried by ticks—and toxoplasmosis—that's carried by cats."

Jessica squirmed, remembering Fernando's lecture on keeping the balcony door shut. She should pay more attention to him, value his opinion. If only he weren't so preachy.

Trumpower picked up the phone. "Louise, I'll need you to draw blood." He hung up and then stared down at the desk, rolling a ballpoint pen over and over between his fingers. "You take any drugs?"

"You mean cocaine or marijuana or something? No! Just the opposite. Some people call me a health freak." What a nasty question.

"Okay, okay. I had to ask. Any multiple sclerosis or other disabling illness in the family?"

"My dad had systemic lupus erythematosus, but he died of heart failure."

"Your symptoms would be unusual for lupus, but I'll have a blood test run for it anyway. It does show a familial propensity for autoimmune disorder."

Jessica knew about autoimmune disorders like her father's—the body went haywire and attacked itself through its own immune system. It had never occurred to her that she could inherit lupus. Daddy's parents hadn't had it.

"It says here in your file you have hay fever and food allergies."

"Yes. But the worst of them pretty much went away by the time I was twenty-one." This seemed like a waste of time.

Or was it? She had an idea. "You know these attacks come around the same time every day after I've been at work a few hours. Maybe I'm getting exposed to something there I'm terribly allergic to." That could be it. Why hadn't she, with all her allergies, thought of this before? It was unusual for someone as young and healthy as she was to collapse from overwork or stress. But allergies, especially on top of stress? Who knew what troubles that combination could inflict?

Trumpower looked interested. "What's your work environment like?"

Jessica thought a minute. "They use a lot of chemicals in the art room and in repro. I think the ventilation system circulates the smells everywhere."

He looked even more interested. "There are such things as poison buildings. And if you're very sensitive..."

"Sensitive! I used to throw up every time I ate certain kinds of food. Once I got all twisted up and partly paralyzed when a doctor gave me Compazine to stop my vomiting. Turned out I was allergic to it. Maybe I should stay home one day and if nothing happens we'll know there's something I'm allergic to at work." Not tomorrow, the day of the big review. Sunday would be the first opportunity.

Trumpower nodded. "It's worth a try."

The nurse came in with a syringe, three small glass tubes, a pipette and a rubber tourniquet. Jessica watched her blood fill the tubes.

"You don't know how many allergic reactions I had as a child. Cherries, cantaloupe, onions, pollen, bee stings, Portuguese man-of-war—always something."

The nurse undid the tourniquet, stuck a Band-Aid over the needle's entry point, and left.

"I'll be damned," Trumpower said.

"No. I'm—the—one–that's–damned." Jessica's throat and jaw muscles were getting as weak as her arms, legs and neck so that she could barely choke out the words. What was going on?

Trumpower jerked forward and peered at her closely. "You're having difficulty speaking."

"My—throat—and—mouth." This was terrible. She could hardly get any action out of her vocal chords. "Hard to swal—low."

He stood up, staring down at her. "I think you should go downstairs to emergency."

She tried to lift her hand to his coat sleeve, but couldn't. "Emer—gen—cy?" Did he think she was having a life-threatening allergic reaction? Anaphylaxis?

"You're having difficulty speaking and swallowing. If your throat closes or the swallowing reflex fails—well, you could have Guillain-Barre. You've got to go to the ER."

Guillain-Barre! Fear caught in her throat and she nearly threw up. She'd read about that recently, maybe in *Scientific American*. It was terrible. "Guillain-Barre can completely paralyze you, can't it?" She couldn't believe how slurred her words were.

He was pacing around and waving both hands. "Some people get it following a tetanus shot—weakness, numbness, tingling and sometimes paralysis. I haven't got anything here to help you. You should get help fast."

"Tetanus shot! Like I had after that cat bit me?" She was frightened to hear her words sounding drawn out and mushy.

"I'll get a patient escort to take you." Trumpower reached for the phone.

After he hung up, he didn't even sit down as he scrawled on a sheet of paper. "You're lucky to be here. We can get you to emergency downstairs and have you on a respirator in minutes if we have to."

Lucky? Jessica began to shake with cold. Or was it fear? She grew light-headed and slumped over, weaker than ever.

In two or three minutes, the orderly who'd put her in the wheelchair appeared in the doorway.

Trumpower handed him the paperwork. "Take Miss Shephard downstairs to the ER. And hurry." He turned to Jessica. "They'll take good care of you down there." His distraught eyes seemed to express her own fear.

"What's wrong with me?" she managed to mumble. But too late. The orderly wheeled the chair out the office door. He moved fast, narrowly missing a doctor and a nurse as he raced down the hall.

CHAPTER 5

The automatic doors to the emergency facility opened with a whoosh to admit the speeding wheelchair. As they barreled past the registration window, a brittle-voiced woman leaned out and yelled, "Wait, come back!"

The orderly hesitated, and Jessica was trying to gather strength to tell him to keep going when, to her relief, he headed on down the hall to the security desk. "Her doctor just called," he said to the uniformed guard, holding out the papers Trumpower had given him.

"You have to register first." The guard pointed to the window they'd passed. "They need to know how to bill your insurance."

"Help—me," Jessica managed to say.

"Just go to the window, please."

The orderly shrugged and turned the wheelchair around.

Tears came to Jessica's eyes. They wanted money before they'd lift a finger to help her here.

At the window, the woman demanded that forms be filled out, identification and proof of insurance produced. Jessica had to get the orderly to ransack her purse until he came up with everything asked for. It seemed to take forever before she was back at the security desk.

"Is there a patient out there?" Jessica heard a woman's high-pitched, nasal voice, but couldn't see who was talking.

The orderly wheeled the chair around the desk to a little cubbyhole that was more like a closet than a room for seeing patients. Jessica was confused and frightened to find herself in this cramped place with no sign on it, no indication of what was supposed to happen here.

A fortyish blond woman in a white coat was perched on a straight-back chair behind a table. "Hi, I'm June." She sounded unaccountably, incongruously cheerful. She took Jessica's temperature and blood pressure, then filled out more forms as Jessica mumbled her vital statistics and symptoms. It seemed to Jessica the more she talked, the more her mouth and throat weakened. If June noticed, she never showed it, never asked Jessica if she was frightened. Maybe June ignored patients' fear because it got in the way of what she needed to do, or because she didn't want to know a patient was afraid. Or maybe she'd seen so many sick people that she was bored with their fear.

June wheeled Jessica back to the security desk. "Keep an eye on her. She's having trouble speaking and swallowing, and I don't want to leave her alone in the waiting room." She deserted Jessica and led a crying little boy and his parents back to her cubbyhole.

Jessica tried to call out that she needed help now, but managed only a gurgling sound.

Peering at her over the top of a magazine, the guard said, "You'll be going back there pretty soon." He pointed to double doors behind the desk.

Jessica tried to raise her chin from her chest to talk to him, but couldn't. The people here seemed to know the process and were putting her through the mill like soup at Campbell's. But soup doesn't need to know what's happening to it.

"Won't be long." The guard resumed reading.

Jessica sat and waited, the security desk radio sporadically blurting out incomprehensible messages, the guard slowly turning crackling pages. She heard the cubbyhole lady talking soothingly to the sobbing child. Two grubby, tired-looking men in blue jeans sauntered through a door with a sign that said "Waiting Room." Waiting seemed to be the ER's principal activity.

She rested her head against the back of the wheelchair—at least in this position her jaw didn't hang open—and tried to collect her thoughts. She'd always feared one of her allergies would become anaphylactic. In anaphylaxis, blood pressure drops precipitously and the throat closes, choking off the breath. Death could follow. Same for Guillain-Barre, only then the breathing muscles fail.

She was still breathing and could swallow. Maybe this wasn't anaphylaxis or Guillain-Barre. Maybe she'd get better later like the other times. Or maybe not. Fear began spreading from her toes and fingers, following the paths of numbness and tingling through her weakened arms and legs to her fluttery stomach.

She needed a doctor *now*. This was the Gebauer ER. *What was going on?*

Chill, she told herself. They have a triage system here; they take the most serious cases first. There's nothing you can do about that. And Fernando always said you couldn't die in the ER if you tried, what with the defibrillators, respirators and other contraptions. Trouble is, he'd also said, they might just let you wait until you were at death's door before treating you.

If they knew you were dying. Who was making these decisions? The guard? The lady in the cubbyhole?

She could get the guard's attention if she felt she was dying. Unless she passed out, in which case he might not notice. She swallowed. Still okay. She wondered if she'd know if she was dying. What did it feel like to die from asphyxiation? Like suffocating under a pillow? If she lost consciousness suddenly, she wouldn't be able to call for help.

She needed someone who could speak for her here and now. She should call Mom or Fernando. Digging into her purse, she pulled out what she thought was the cell phone. It was a hairbrush. She put it back and went back to groping through the purse.

She started to feel drowsy. Hard to focus. Her damned job. Poison. She dreamed about a hazmat team breaking down the locked door of the super-secret proposal area with axes and hauling Armor off to jail for endangering people's lives. The building was cracked open to the fresh air and she was saved, floating on soft, fluffy clouds of happiness.

The reverie ended when her wheelchair began rolling toward the double doors. Turning her head, she glimpsed a white sleeve and a man's hand. Was this a doctor at last? A gurney pushed by two uniformed paramedics and carrying someone covered with bloody sheets sped by toward the end of the hall. Jessica's heart went out to that person. To her relief she didn't follow him, but was pushed into one of many small rooms opening off the corridor.

"A nurse will be with you in a minute," the anonymous pusher said, and left. The room was furnished with a narrow padded bed, covered with a white paper sheet, white counters and cabinets, white walls and two steel chairs with white plastic seats. The place smelled of Lysol. Supercleanliness and sterility were necessary for any ER, but they'd be no help for her situation today. Strange-looking instruments with tubes, dials, and rubber bags hanging from shiny metal wall mounts must be useful for a wide range of emergencies, but she couldn't imagine what good any of them would do her. The only sounds were low voices and the pad-pad of rubber-soled shoes in the hall belonging to people who seemed to have a purpose disjoint from her.

After a few minutes, a young, white-coated woman, sturdily built, came bustling in and said, "How are you today?" Without waiting for an answer, she yanked off Jessica's dress and shoes, managing to put a starched, white cotton gown on her even though Jessica was no more help than a rag doll, then eased her out of the wheelchair onto the bed.

Jessica peered at the woman's badge. It had a long name and "RN" on it. Finally, someone she could identify—a nurse.

She flopped backward and the woman took a cotton sheet from a cabinet and put it over her. Through a haze Jessica felt her underarm temperature being taken, her wrist pulse counted, her blood pressure measured with an arm cuff. Blood was drawn. She wondered why they couldn't share the blood Trumpower had already taken but didn't have the strength to argue.

"Cold," she mumbled, shivering.

The nurse put a second sheet over her. "That better?"

By the time Jessica could mouth the words "still cold," the woman had left and she was alone again, listening to rubber-soled shoes passing by.

A white-coated figure with a badge that said "Vashti Rhundi, Resident, Gebauer University" was staring down at her. "What's the trouble?" He was chunky, brown-skinned, wore gold-rimmed spectacles and spoke with an accent—Indian or Pakistani, Jessica guessed.

A ray of hope. She'd heard some of the Indians and Pakistanis who came here were brilliant.

"Can't move. Arms. Legs." It was frightening to hear how soft and muffled her voice had become.

"Trouble talking?"

"Yes." She wanted to tell him about the pollutants at work and warn him about anaphylaxis and Guillain-Barre, but he didn't wait for her to struggle with the words.

He pulled on her upper eyelids to peer into her eyes. From the side, he lifted her head up and, when her jaw fell open, peered into her mouth.

"How long have you been like this?"

"Five days. Off and on."

"Use any drugs?"

"No!" Not this again.

Rhundi frowned and tapped his foot on the floor. "I want you to sit on the side of the bed."

He had to help her and hold her upright once he got her up. Jessica felt totally helpless. You'd just about hit bottom when you couldn't even sit up unaided.

He asked if she had blurred vision and then tested to see if she could visually follow a pencil he waved in front of her face. He said her eyes were fine. She could have told him that.

He tapped under her kneecaps. "Hmm." He tapped again several times. "No reflex." Then he dragged a pencil over the soles of her feet. "Reflexes okay here."

He asked her to step down and walk.

"I'll try." But when she had both feet down and eased her weight onto them, her thighs wouldn't hold and she crumpled to the floor, sprawling out the way she had in the waiting room upstairs. She couldn't imagine how she could be this weak this long.

Rhundi called out to a passing woman in the hall. "Nurse. In here." The nurse helped him drag her back onto the bed and spread the sheets over her again.

Standing by the bed, hands on hips, Rhundi muttered as if to himself. "Hmm. No pathology. None at all."

"Can't walk. Barely talk."

"I need objective symptoms."

Not walking, not talking—those weren't "objective symptoms"? This, she was beginning to think, was not the sharpest mind at Gebauer.

"Could I have Guillain-Barre?"

Rhundi shook his head. "I'll have to consult with Dr. Chapman, but I don't think so. Wouldn't come and go like this."

"Pollution," Jessica said again. He hadn't bothered to ask her about anything in her life that might be affecting her, and she was desperate to tell him. "What do you think—"

"Can't say. Dr. Chapman will talk to you."

She hadn't even been able to finish her question. "Chap—man?"

"The senior physician on duty tonight." Rhundi turned and left.

She was alone again. Wait until she told Fernando how scary this place was. They might have all kinds of fancy equipment here, but you could die before you got any real help.

Nix on the negative thoughts. Had to straighten her head out. Not give in to fear. She tried to remember how it felt loping around Gebauer's track, breathing cold morning air. Her body would tire, then surge strong with a second wind. An endorphin rush, Fernando called it; it always made her feel marvelously light and free of her body's normal limitations. That's what she needed—an endorphin rush. Closing her eyes and concentrating, she tried to will one.

At the sound of a smooth, mellow male voice, she opened her eyes. A man with graying brown hair and crow's feet at the corners of light hazel eyes, in which she thought she saw kindness and a spark of intelligence, was leaning over her.

"Hi, I'm Dr. Chapman, the physician on duty tonight. Dr. Rhundi tells me you're presenting some unusual symptoms."

"Yes, he was here." Jessica's throat and tongue muscles were working better. "But he didn't know anything."

Chapman looked as if he were trying to suppress a grin. "There's a neurologist on duty tonight. I'll ask her to come down and see you as soon as she's free. I'd rather not send you home without her looking at you."

Jessica liked and trusted this man right away for sharing her opinion of Rhundi. Also, Chapman was a real doctor, not just a doc-barely-out-of-the-box resident like Rhundi.

Chapman patted her arm. "Don't hesitate to ask for me if you need me." He disappeared out the door. She wished he'd stay.

She managed to lift her arm enough to look at her watch. Seven! Fernando must be pretty worried by now. She should phone him. Her cell phone was across the room in her purse on the counter.

If only someone would come by and get it for her. If only she didn't have to lie here and wait for someone to come by.

One thing was clear—she had to make the most of the times when she could do for herself. Once she got away from work, the more she moved the more the polluting chemicals she was allergic to were carried away by her blood, sweat and kidneys. She was always better by late evening and that had to be the reason why. She could almost convince herself allergies were her problem, a problem she assumed the ER would know how to deal with.

The nurse stuck her head in the door. "How you doing?"

"Could you get me my purse?" Jessica pointed to where it lay, relieved she could now make herself heard.

"Sure." The woman grabbed the purse, placed it carefully on Jessica's stomach and turned as if to leave.

"One more thing. I'm still cold," Jessica called out. "Two more sheets please."

The nurse hurried over to a cupboard above the counter and yanked open the door. Pressed and folded sheets piled there put Jessica in mind of the alcove outside her mother's bathroom with its floor-to-ceiling cupboards. As a little girl, she would pull open a cupboard door and stare with fear and admiration at the stacks of absolutely flat, ironed sheets and towels, all the items in each stack perfectly aligned, everything under perfect control.

The nurse pulled two from the top of the pile and spread them over Jessica. "Okay?" She smiled and was out the door before Jessica could answer.

But Jessica's situation was improving. She was warm and she could talk. She was even getting hungry.

She got the cell phone out of the purse and dialed her apartment. Fernando was bound to be waiting there by now.

He picked up after only one ring.

"I didn't want you to worry," she began.

"You're stuck at work again."

"No, I'm in the ER. At Gebauer. But don't worry." She'd reveal nothing about her falls so she wouldn't have to endure his fussing.

"In the ER? What the hell, Jessica! What's going on?"

"I've been kind of exhausted and run down. Remember, you found me on the doormat a few days ago." She chose her next words carefully to conceal, without lying, that she'd totally lost the use of her arms and legs. "So I went to see Dr. Trumpower. For all the good it did me. You'd have thought I had the plague, instead of just too much work on top of an allergy, the way he got all excited and sent me down here."

She heard Fernando's muffled footsteps over the phone. He must be pacing on the living room rug. "Tell me exactly what happened."

"I kind of ran out of energy. But I feel better now."

"I'm coming over as fast as I can to see what's going on."

"You don't need to." She hoped she'd be able to drive home. If not, she could always call him again.

"I'm coming."

"Then bring me a sandwich. And a banana out of the fruit bowl. I'm hungry."

Just after she hung up, a young woman in a white coat, with horn-rimmed glasses and cropped, glossy black hair, carrying a clipboard, appeared in the doorway. "Jessica Shephard?"

"That's me." Jessica immediately liked the way this woman's eyes met hers as squarely as her own in a mirror.

The woman stepped jauntily on white, rubber-soled shoes over to Jessica. "I'm Dr. Behrens." She reached out her hand.

Concentrating, Jessica managed to get her right hand high enough to briefly grasp the doctor's before it fell back onto her abdomen. She read the badge on the starched lapel: "Heidi Behrens, Resident, Neurology."

Shit, another resident. But Jessica liked the looks of this one. Not much older than she was and exuding an eager confidence. Probably had been a top student in med school.

"I know you're going to figure out what's going on with me."

"We're pretty good at diagnosis." Behrens flashed a quick smile and wrote something on a sheet attached to her clipboard. "Let's hear about you."

For the third time today, Jessica laid out her story while Behrens stood listening intently, occasionally pacing alongside the bed, interrupting often with questions. Sharp questions, Jessica thought. Like "Does the weakness begin in your hands and feet and spread to your arms and legs or does it attack everywhere at once?" And "Can you grasp an object in your hand during an attack?" The tingling always began in her hands and feet—the weakness always began in her arms and legs. She could usually grasp an object if someone put it in her hand. Behrens even asked questions about her work environment. "What chemicals are you exposed to?"

This was more like it. Behrens was the kind of doctor you'd expect here. She had Jessica sit on the edge of the bed and perform the same simple tasks Rhundi had. When Behrens tapped under her knee with a little hammer, the leg kicked forward. "Good reflex."

That idiot Rhundi hadn't even been able to do the knee-jerk reflex test right. Behrens added eye tests where Jessica had to stare at the ceiling without tilting up her head and open and close her eyelids. She asked for hand and foot motions, which Jessica could do easily. Then she picked up the clipboard where she checked off items on a list and made notes.

"What were those eye tests all about?" Jessica asked.

"Some rare neurological disorders interfere with the ability to fix the eyes on the ceiling or hold open the eyelids."

Jessica wanted to yell out a cheer. This woman was great. Thorough and recently trained, she knew what to do, unlike the clueless Rhundi and the panicky Trumpower.

"I don't have Guillain-Barre from that tetanus shot I had last week, do I?"

"I don't think so. Your condition fluctuates rapidly and Guillain-Barre's progressive. We could give you some tests, but they're kind of painful, and I don't think that's necessary."

"I'll bet this is some kind of allergic reaction." Jessica braced herself for the bad news—the building she was working in was poisoning her and she'd have to get out of it. No one quit in the middle of an important proposal like she was on. She could be fired.

Come on, Jessica. Chill out. Most likely there will be a medication to take that will solve everything.

"I have an idea. Let's see how you walk now."

An idea. Good news. She needed some good news. Feeling light as a feather, Jessica hopped down from the bed, folded and fell to the floor. Damn!

"Come on. Up." Behrens took Jessica's hands and pulled her to her feet. "See if you can walk a straight line, heel touching toe at each step." Holding her arm, she led Jessica slowly across the floor.

Although shivering in her bare feet and skimpy hospital gown, Jessica concentrated, almost keeping her feet aligned.

"Very good," Behrens said. "You're doing very well."

Jessica warmed to the praise. "I'm doing my best."

Behrens took a pad of paper from a counter top and began writing.

"May I ask what you're writing?"

"A prescription."

What a wonderful word! A prescription meant there was a pill or something for whatever she was allergic to. With the right medication she might not have to leave the proposal. She knew this woman was good the moment she first saw her.

"What for?" She could hardly wait to hear the name of the medicine that would make her well again.

"Valium."

"Valium?" Valium was a tranquilizer. "All I have to do is take valium?"

Behrens sat on a chair and crossed her hands on her lap, holding the prescription slip. "It's usually a big help in calming conversion disorder."

"Conversion disorder?" What on earth was that?

Behrens looked Jessica in the eye. "Conversion disorder is psychological—conscious knowledge of painful emotions is repressed and converted into physical symptoms. I want you to see a psychiatrist as soon as possible."

Jessica wanted to strangle this bitch.

"You." Jessica tried to point at her, but could only glare. "You have the nerve to tell me, after I've waited here for three hours, that this is all in my head?"

"You have good muscle strength, fine reflexes, and your eyes are fully under control. There's nothing physically wrong with you, yet you say you can't walk or lift your arms."

Jessica felt her face grow hot and tears welled in her eyes. "I say I can't walk because I can't. What the fuck else should I say?"

Behrens tapped the clipboard on her lap. "Undoubtedly, you're deriving some benefit from this—like gaining someone's sympathy, perhaps avoiding difficulties at home or work."

Jessica raised her voice almost to a scream. "How can you possibly think I want to be flopping around like this? Would you? Would anyone?"

Unperturbed, Behrens picked at the edge of the notepad in her lap. "You seem very excited."

"You're making some big mistakes. Valium's a relaxant. How can you prescribe it for me when I'm already so weak?" A chill passed up Jessica's spine and sliced into her brain. This woman was not going to help her.

"You exhibit no pathology. No physical problems."

"What you mean," Jessica said, "is that you can't find a physical cause for my problem."

"If you want to put it that way."

"That's the only way to put it. Do you always assume that if you—and I emphasize the word *you*—can't find a physical cause, there isn't one? Do you know how to test for every allergy there is? Any allergy? You didn't test for even one tonight."

Behrens didn't answer.

"Surely you can see the great big hole in your logic." Jessica was so upset her breath was coming in gasps. "You detect no physical problem, therefore my problem must be mental. What about the possibility you don't know how to test for what I have? Why didn't you test for any allergies?"

"All right." Behrens stood up. "I amend my statement. You have no detectable physical pathology."

"That's not good enough. I need help and you're just standing there babbling."

Behrens thrust a piece of paper at Jessica. "Your prescription."

Jessica snatched it from her, tore it in two and tossed it onto the floor.

Behrens' face reddened. For the first time she looked flustered. She scooped the trashed prescription off the floor and stormed out.

What arrogance! Behrens didn't find a physical pathology, so there wasn't one. How could she call herself a doctor in this world of modern medicine? Jessica couldn't wait to tell Chapman about her. He'd have to get someone else or help her himself.

She had to wait fifteen fuming minutes before Chapman shuffled in, looking harried and tired. He plopped into a chair, flipped through what looked to be Behrens' notes, took a couple of deep breaths, then spoke. "Busy evening. What can I do for you?"

"That neurology resident you sent was here. She said I have conversion disorder."

Chapman looked at her and rubbed his chin. "She's new. I don't know her very well."

"I don't think that woman's competent. She prescribed valium. For someone weak like me."

"I read Dr. Behrens' notes and I saw you earlier. If I were you, I wouldn't take valium."

This was crazy. Chapman barely knew and didn't trust Behrens, yet he'd wanted Behrens to see her. Jessica couldn't imagine how this place worked.

"Good thing you're checking up on your residents. I think it could be dangerous to take valium."

"I agree with you."

"I need to see someone else."

"I'd start lining up appointments with specialists if I were you. A neurologist to begin with. And come back here if you have any trouble breathing or swallowing."

"I mean someone here, now."

"You seem to be out of danger for the moment."

"What do you think's wrong with me? Best guess."

Chapman shook his head. "I have no idea."

Jessica could have screamed. After half an hour with Trumpower and nearly four hours in the ER, no one had a clue about what was wrong with her. No one had told her what she should do, how she should lead her life now or what she could hope for in the future. What was she supposed to do if she had more episodes? Was this as bad as it could get or was there worse to come? Who was going to answer all these questions?

CHAPTER 6

Who was going to come up with answers? Tonight Jessica had assigned that role to herself. She'd devised a treatment for her allergy and it had worked.

She glanced at the clock above the living room table. 2:00 a.m. Time to go to bed. Her laser printer spit out a final page with a swish and a beep.

In the ER parking garage she'd had a terrible fight with Fernando when she'd wanted to drive her car home. He'd insisted that driving after being so exhausted—he didn't know the half of that—would be a stupid mistake that, as a doctor, he could not permit her to make. She'd tried to make him understand that she had a second wind and wasn't exhausted now. And, even if neither Trumpower nor the ER had recognized it, she was probably just suffering from a combination of being tired and allergic reaction. They'd stood for a long time in the small, dank, dimly lit parking garage, arguing. In the end, he'd given in, but not before goading her with one last barb—if her illness *was* psychogenic, it wouldn't be surprising if she did crazy things.

She'd been shocked. It was a nasty kind of tactic she'd never known him to use before. And once they'd gotten home he'd had another fit when she'd taken out her laptop and begun working on write-ups she hadn't been able to finish because of time wasted at the hospital.

His deep breathing was uninterrupted from where he was stretched out on the living room couch with Elsa contentedly asleep on his stomach. She paused, charmed by the happy, tranquil pair. But, grateful as she was that Fernando cared enough to stay and watch over her, she still suspected he'd waited up just to see her overdo it and collapse as he'd predicted. He always had to be right and he didn't like it when his will was thwarted.

With no help from him or the doctors at Gebauer, she'd figured out how to take care of herself during the night. Every hour she stood up from the computer, jogged around the apartment and did pushups against a wall. Then she drank a tall glass of water and urinated to flush the poisons from her system. It had worked marvelously well, further proof that allergies were causing most, if not all, of her problems. When she got a chance, she'd ask Fernando to get her some Benadryl. It had helped her with allergies in the past.

She reread the introduction. Great clarity and not one typo. It looked terrific. She wasn't going to let the team down.

She'd like to go to the piano and play a triumphant work, like a big Beethoven sonata, but she didn't want to wake Fernando and have another argument. Or wake the neighbors. So she merely patted the shiny Steinway and played the opening measures of a sonata in her head as she headed off for bed.

After shutting off the 6:00 a.m. alarm, she showered and put on blue jeans and a large T-shirt with the Gebauer seal. Nobody dressed for work on weekends. In the full-length hall mirror, she scrutinized her reflection. Bright eyes, early morning rosiness to her cheeks, body vibrant with energy. Absolutely no sick person had ever looked this good.

Once more she was as healthy as ever after being away from Rank for several hours, even though she'd worked until two. It was hard to imagine an illness that invariably attacked on the job in the afternoon and vanished in the evening when she went home. As far as she could see, the only possible cause was an allergy to something at work. This weekend she'd test out her theory. Today she had to go in for the review, but she'd pay careful attention to irritating odors and leave by late morning or early afternoon. Tomorrow she'd stay away entirely.

Elsa looked up sleepily as Jessica placed a note on Fernando's chest—she'd gone to work and would call later. Laptop and envelope stuffed with printouts in hand, she snuck out the door.

At the corner, she bought bagels, cream cheese and orange juice. It was seven o'clock, and she had plenty of time to drive to Rank, get Stone to approve her work, then tack it up and leave before she was exposed very long to whatever was making her sick.

As soon as she got to work she headed for the cavernous war room. Windowless, its four white corkboard walls were entirely covered with the thumb-tacked pages of the proposal first draft. Most were neatly laser printed, but some were cut and taped together from earlier documents or scratched out and scribbled over. Scattered yellow post-its on which suggestions and critiques were scrawled stuck out here and there. In the center of the room, two Formica-topped tables like those in the cafeteria were cluttered with paper wads, boxes of thumb tacks and paper clips, scissors, tape, grimy coffee cups and candy bar wrappers. Four grubby-looking, unshaven engineers were huddled over a sheet of paper on the table in front of them. Probably a last-minute effort to settle an issue before the review began.

She liked the feel of this room where you could see the nitty-gritty work of the proposal getting done. She was proud to work here beside these tired, rumpled master craftsmen making plans for their spaceships. She liked this job, where she could use both her education in science and her infatuation with words, composing her write-ups carefully to feature whatever points she was trying to make.

She looked up and sucked in a breath. Above each major section, in huge letters, a banner proclaimed: "Better is the enemy of good enough." An arrogant Armor aphorism if she ever saw one.

Tempted to stand on a chair and yank down the atrocity from above Stone's section, she caught herself. It wouldn't be fair if Stone, tough on her as he was, was unjustly blamed for something she did. So, reluctantly, she thumbtacked her meticulously crafted pages below the insulting slogan.

Seven thirty, still early. She'd go see if Joe was finished with the artwork.

She headed across the main proposal area, a low-ceilinged room in which half a dozen engineers were working at computer stations. Most of the spacecraft design was done on computers these days. A cone-shaped, metal light fixture was suspended on an adjustable-length cord over a lone drafting table where a white-haired man was perched on a high stool, hard at work on a sheet of paper three or four feet long. Two secretaries at the far end of the room were already busy at word processors.

Managers' offices, one of them Jim Stone's, opened off the near wall. Through a door on her left she could see two artists hunched over their publishing workstations. On the other side of the room was a door that opened into the passageway where her cubicle was. Not one window, not even a skylight, opened to the outside world, a precaution against industrial espionage. Warranted or unwarranted, she didn't know. But the stakes were high and management was obsessed with secrecy.

She headed for the art room with high anticipation. To her, the artists, especially Joe DiCarlo, were magicians. If you wanted shapes that appeared to be three-dimensional, from any perspective, Joe could give them to you off his computer. If you wanted an exploded receiver, with all its parts spread over the page and arrows pointing to their true locations, he could produce it. In black and white or in color, on foldout sheets or small enough to tuck into the corner of a page. He could show you any of it instantly, then modify it as you watched. Good artwork like his eliminated the blindness in the leap of faith from a paper design to a huge, complex satellite. It made her job easier.

Joe had already arrived, or maybe had never left since last night. A muscular, dark-haired man in a Coors T-shirt, he looked more like a wrestler than an artist.

Jessica rolled a chair over to his workstation. "I'm here," she announced.

He looked up, eyes bloodshot but twinkling. "No, no. Not you." He held his hands over his face.

"No new artwork, I promise. How late were you here last night?"

Joe stood and flexed his arms back, then up. "Don't ask." He glanced down at a heap of wadded papers surrounding his chair. "I got kind of tired and made a few mistakes."

"I bet you never went home." She offered him a choice of bagels from her bag and set out cream cheese and a plastic knife. "How about some breakfast."

Joe kicked a couple of paper wads out of the way and sat down. After spreading cream cheese on a bagel, he peered at her. "You okay? A lot of us were worried you were sick."

"I'm doing just fine." From the looks of them, she was probably doing at least as well as anyone here.

Only, she was allergic to something the rest evidently weren't. She had to stop thinking of herself as invulnerable. "Maybe you should worry about yourselves too. I think my problem may be pollution in this building."

"No kidding." He sniffed the air. "Ammonia, acetone, printer toner. All that good stuff I've been inhaling for years."

The strongest odor was acetone, a sharp, chemical smell that seemed to come from a corner of the room, burning her nose and throat when she got a whiff. "This could be a killer building. You know that, Joe?"

"I'll worry about that when I have time." He turned to his computer and tapped in commands. "Got some pretty pictures for you." A display lit up with a multicolor view of a satellite switchboard in the sky, gathering up and routing phone messages from a multiplicity of ground stations and other satellites.

Jessica laid her hand on her chest. "You're a genius." Good as his work was, she still insisted on scrutinizing it, trying to be tactful about correcting spellings and straightening out fouled-up frequency band assignments. He looked awfully tired, and she wanted to be careful of his feelings.

One by one, the four full-color, finely detailed figures emerged from his printer, each one exuding a pungent chemical odor. She stood back from the printer and waited a couple of minutes for the smell to dissipate before offering profuse thanks and running with them to the war room. She got rid of the artwork fast, tacking it up in Stone's section. Ten of nine; all her work was in good shape and she was doing fine.

With time to spare, she loitered to see what the five members of the executive review team, in T-shirts and jeans and sitting around a table, were up to. One of them, a tall, big-boned man unaffectionately called Bigfoot by the employees, was an open rival of Armor's and liable to badmouth the work just because Armor was running the show. He wore a tent-sized shirt that said "Giants Hit Home Runs." Armor, gripping a table edge, was at manic intensity, delivering a monologue on the wonders of "his" system.

This was going to be a high-tension day—people's work could make them heroes or zeroes in the eyes of the reviewers.

It would be awful if she collapsed. For one thing, she wouldn't be able to drive home. For another, she was terrified of falling in front of some of the biggest executives in the company, especially Armor, who didn't tolerate weakness. And her boss, Fred Vole, didn't like dealing with people who had problems. He'd be the first to try to sweep her right out the door along with the other debris that had fallen to the floor.

Still, Jessica felt energetic and confident. Her work was done and in good shape.

Taking a slow walk past the wallboards on her way to Stone's office, she checked out the ground station antenna and transmitter sections, written in the spare, illuminating style she'd worked so hard to perfect. Whether she was going to be a technical writer forever or not, and she wasn't sure about that at all, she felt it was worth the effort to sharpen her skills. She especially liked choosing words that conveyed the exact message she needed, then stringing them across the page like notes in a musical score.

Suddenly she froze. Under the title "Summary and Conclusions" was an empty space. An engineer had given her a very rough draft Wednesday, but she'd gotten sick and forgotten about it. She was pretty sure the rough was in her office file. If Stone was satisfied with his section, she could start on the missing pages right away. But this hitch in her plan for finishing and leaving early was unsettling.

She dropped in on a blue-jeaned, khaki-shirted Stone going through a stack of computer printouts. "Come see your section." She couldn't help grinning.

"You okay?"

"I'm fine." That was no lie. "Come on." She led the way to the war room.

The review had begun. The five executives were huddled around the engineer who was captain of the executive summary, the first volume of the proposal. Nearby hovered Jessica's boss, manager of proposal operations, supervisor of a large pool of the company's writers, artists and editors. Hands shoved into pants pockets of his gray flannel slacks, his gray hair perfectly barbered and combed, Fred Vole was doing a nervous little dance about the reviewers. Unlike the engineers, he wouldn't be held accountable for the design, but he was vulnerable to criticism for poor writing, sloppy layouts and artwork that missed the point.

Fortunately, Vole had not witnessed any of Jessica's collapses. But she wondered if he'd heard about them.

Stone stood reading his section. A broad grin spread over his face, as though life had suddenly gotten better. "I was afraid you weren't going to have diddly-squat ready for me. But you came through, didn't you?"

She could have hugged him. Everything was going great, and all because she'd defied Fernando and stayed up last night.

They sauntered over to Vole. "What's the agenda?" Stone whispered.

"They're going to go through in order," Vole whispered back. "Executive summary to ground station. They'll break for lunch at noon and finish by five."

Jessica searched Vole's face, getting a small nod of recognition. No sign he knew of her troubles, but he normally hid his feelings. His secretiveness always made her feel uneasy, like he was lying in wait to ambush her.

It was only 9:30. She should have enough time to do the missing write-up and be out of here before noon.

She headed for the passageway leading past a row of cubicles to her own. With four-foot-high walls and no door, they didn't keep out other people's conversations and afforded no privacy for sensitive personal or work-related phone calls and discussions, raising the stress level for everyone working here. But cubicles were cheap and easily relocated and rearranged. That they also made the employees feel cheap and easily relocated—when they were already being asked to sacrifice so much of their own time—apparently didn't concern management. Some of those big shots ought to try getting the wording of a proposal write-up just right with other people's phone calls, squabbles and mumblings to themselves pouring into their ears.

She walked straight to her end cubicle, as usual looking neither left nor right. That was the best she could do to give her neighbors a bit of privacy.

Risking a deep breath, she sniffed the air. No detectable trace of art room odors back here. But she wouldn't be surprised if chemicals had seeped into every part of the building.

She plunked her purse and laptop down on her paper-cluttered, gray metal desk. A few books—Strunk and White's *Elements of Style*, a dictionary, a thesaurus and company handbooks for technical writers—were crammed into the metal bookcase attached to the wall above the desk, a fluorescent light bolted to its bottom. Behind the desk there was barely room for her swivel chair, and it was jammed next to a three-foot long gray metal table. There was not even space for a file cabinet, which she would have loved, to keep her papers in separate hanging folders instead of on top of the desk and table and stuffed into drawers. She'd considered bringing in pictures of her parents and Fernando and a vase of bright-colored, artificial flowers. But in this facility with no windows, she'd decided to paper every inch of wall space and one end of the bookcase with posters of mountain scenes—alpine lakes and meadows, panoramas of mountain tops and forests, and a snow-covered ski slope. She warily eyed the picture of the alpine meadow that had transfixed her to the point of eerie euphoria as she'd weakened and collapsed. Strange. Scary.

Rummaging through a desk drawer, she found a copy of the ground station electronics section and her notes on the summary and conclusion. After studying what she'd written, she decided the main points to be made were that Rank's design could transmit and simultaneously receive, without significant interference, signals from any of the system's overhead satellites using equipment that was reliable and not expensive to manufacture.

She opened her laptop. Then it occurred to her that this stuff was from Wednesday morning. What if there'd been changes since then?

She headed for the war room.

"This orbit's too fucking low!" Bigfoot was bellowing at Armor. "You'd need ten times the GNP in fucking satellites and ground stations to deal with it."

Armor's face reddened. "Just wait a damn minute. I didn't pick this orbit out of my ass. There were extensive trade-offs. If you'd shut up and listen, you'd see."

Bigfoot moved in close, forcing Armor to look into his Adam's apple. "You call this bullshit trade-offs? Your elevator isn't running to the top floor."

Jessica slipped over to the ground station section and began comparing it with Wednesday's version. She wanted to finish her business and get out of this room as fast as possible. She didn't need more stress.

It turned out the number of antennas and transmitters had been increased. Probably something to do with the low orbit they were arguing about. Good thing she'd read the posted write-up because she could no longer claim they could use a small, cost-saving number of ground antennas.

Staying close to the wall, she got to the door on the other side of the room and sidled out. What a bunch of junkyard dogs these guys were. There was so little intelligent content to their carryings-on and they were so full of attitude instead of ideas that she often wondered how they had gotten promoted to the highest positions. Worst of all, temperamental and capricious as they were, they could hire and fire.

Back at her cubicle she found Stone laying some pages on her desk. He looked up. "As long as you're here, you mind giving this a little of your time? It's something on signal multiplexing I just wrote up. But I don't think it's real clear."

It was almost ten and she didn't want to take on anything else, particularly if it was already messed up. "How long is it?"

"Page and a half."

"I guess that wouldn't be too bad." She waited for him to notice her reluctance and take his signal multiplexing write-up elsewhere. But he didn't.

The write-up turned out to be a snarl. It was almost noon by the time she took him what she'd rewritten. Good thing he liked it. Time was getting so short. She went back to her cubicle and started on the ground station summary and conclusions. She could hear voices in the war room yelling again.

It took a while to get the first paragraph rolling, but once she did the rest began to come. Typing to the edge of her ability, she managed to finish at one thirty. She grabbed up the papers and her purse, dashed to the war room and tacked up the summary pages.

Since she was still feeling good, she decided to risk sitting down at one of the tables to listen to Stone for just a minute or two. In the slow, deliberate manner of a lecturing college professor, he was Texas drawling his way through the capabilities and limitations of the design. She saw it was going well and began to relax. Everything was going well. She'd met the deadline for all her sections. Today was good. She felt good. She was good.

Electric tingles zapped her hands.

She should have left an hour ago.

The door was many steps away, but there were chairs to help her get there. She stood and, leaning on the back of first one chair and then another, was almost to the door, when her thighs gave way, forcing her to stumble into the chair she was leaning on. She tried to appear as though she'd just decided to sit down, but slumped face down onto the table, sending pens and pencils skittering.

The room grew quiet.

She knew Armor and Bigfoot and the others must be staring at her. They'd see how weak she was. This could be the end. They'd think she was useless, throw her off the proposal. She tried to sit up, but as usual it was no use.

A hand patted her gently on the back. "This young lady was up all night making sure my section was done just right," Jim Stone was saying. "She's exhausted."

Jessica wanted to laugh and cry. Sheriff Stone was coming to her rescue.

She sensed a shadow looming over her. "That's dedication." It was Armor. "Just the kind of employee I like on my team."

He was on her side!

"That's Jessica Shephard," Fred Vole piped up. "She works for me."

And Vole too!

"Armor, I've always heard you work your people to death and pay them peanuts." Bigfoot was having his say. "But this is pathetic."

"Maybe you've never seen a dedicated employee before," Armor retorted.

Jessica was glad her face was pressed to the table where they couldn't see her smirk.

"You go home now and get a well-earned rest," Armor said, his usually gruff voice vibrant with pride. "I'll call a company car to drive you."

That was nice. Jessica stopped fighting the pleasant fog that was drifting over her.

When the car arrived, she leaned on Jim Stone's arm on one side and Joe DiCarlo's on the other and was half carried outside.

"Thanks for covering for me, Jim," she said. "You made a heroine out of me, of all people."

"You must have put in a hell of a night last night."

It had to be plain to these guys that ordinary exhaustion couldn't account for this extreme weakness. She didn't want worry or pity from them.

"I did work pretty late. But this—well, it's allergies. My doctor says I must be allergic to something in this building." She paused to let them consider this. "I hate to say this—I know you're such a big fan of his— but I think it's Armor allergy."

DiCarlo squeezed her elbow. "A lot of us have a bit of that allergy."

"I may have to wear a mask when I'm around him."

Stone gave her a fishy look.

"Or maybe I'll need to be in a bubble-head, an astronaut's helmet."

She felt their giggles through the men's arms.

"You always make my day, Jessica," Stone said. "I never knew anyone who made me laugh more than you."

That was the reaction she was looking for. They wouldn't remember her collapse as anything but funny. That didn't mean she didn't have a problem. The allergy part had to be true. Go to work, stay until midafternoon, then collapse. It had happened that way every single one of the last six days. Something in this place was destroying her.

CHAPTER 7

Jessica planned to wait and talk to her mother when the priest was speaking and Mom would have a break from playing the organ. No one would hear them up here in the loft, and if they talked then they wouldn't have to listen to irritating instructions on what to think and believe. She wanted to ask Mom about her own and family allergies, their cures and consequences. Today was the big test, her first entire day away from work since the attacks had begun.

But first the music. On Sundays, when Mom played the organ, she always brought either Jessica or her stepfather, Richard, along to turn the pages.

Jessica scooted her folding chair up tight to the bench. There was just enough room in the loft for the organ and bench, her chair and a wooden coat tree. Her mother didn't like to share the bench with a page turner—she said having someone else right up against her was too restricting.

She watched her mother's small, strong, thick-veined hands reach out to set the organ stops, which peeked out like little white eyes from the edges of the organ. The four-level keyboard spread as far as Mom could reach on either side, with wooden pedals arrayed at her feet across the thick red carpet. The instrument, hulking a couple of feet higher than Jessica when she stood, seemed too large for a woman as small as her mother to manage. But Mom was a big musician in a small package.

Jessica scrutinized the back of her mother's head as Mom leaned forward to squint at the music on the rack. It was alarming how fast her dark, curly hair was graying. Then she looked down and smiled. Below the legs of a rose-colored pantsuit showed the old-womanish, flat-soled, black, laced oxfords Mom always wore to play the organ, insisting she couldn't work the foot pedals in high heels or anything that wasn't firmly tied to her feet.

Changes in pencil were scribbled on the music—organ stop and dynamics notations. Mom had an infallible instinct for tailoring sound to the acoustics of a particular church and to the level of simplicity or grandeur of the service. Jessica shared some of the congregation's happiness, enjoying the kaleidoscopic beauty of the stained glass windows, the majesty of the high-vaulted ceiling and the many voices that soared grandly from the organ.

But, as usual, her gaze eventually wandered to the glazed statues of woebegone, totally humorless saints haunting spooky little candlelit nooks. Fernando and his family put great faith in this pantheon, while she not only disliked their dour looks, but also had doubts about their usefulness. For one thing, they occupied niches not only in the church, but in a bureaucracy. When you wanted help, you first had to find the right saint to recommend you to Mary. Then, if you were worthy in her eyes, Mary would refer your case on to Jesus who, in deserving instances, would put in a word to God. If you got that far, you might get help. The process seemed very much like the rigmarole you had to go through to get your computer fixed or petty cash expenses reimbursed at Rank, with the end result just as uncertain.

When it came to religion, she preferred observing for herself how God functioned, what He did and did not concern Himself with, to taking it on someone else's authority. This, she felt, was evidence of her natural scientific mind, reinforced by education. For God to be revealed, she asked only for evidence of His activities.

One of the things she watched for was when or whether God answered individual prayers. From past randomness of the outcome of prayers to the niche-bound saints, she had deduced that God had chosen not to operate through this bureaucracy and it would be futile to ask any of its members to restore her health. Mom would be a more likely source of help.

Jessica looked at her watch—seven fifty. She stood up and peered down at the priest. He smiled and nodded. Time to start the music.

"Mom," she whispered.

Her mother looked up, hazel eyes large behind her glasses. "I'm ready."

Of course she was. Mom was never late for anything. She reached below the seat with both hands to turn the squeaky knobs that cranked the bench down low. She claimed to be five feet tall, but Jessica had long ago guessed she was at least an inch under.

Her mother flexed her fingers and thumbs ten times, rotated each ankle ten times. Then she began the Bach piece quietly, terracing a crescendo in the quantized steps appropriate for Baroque music. The sound gradually intensified to fill the church. No pillar shaking or window rattling for eight o'clock mass.

Jessica sniffed the air. A sharp, unsettling, acrid smell of smoke was drifting into the loft from the votive candles down below. Polluted air, here in the church. This could be as bad as going to work.

Panic.

Chill, she told herself. After all, she'd been exposed to this smoke for the last four or five years, since she'd finished college and been pressed into service as a page turner, and nothing bad had ever come of it.

Jessica didn't know exactly when it started, but sometime after she'd entered Gebauer University, where she'd lived on campus, her mother had begun taking organ engagements. In fact, Mom was doing a lot of things she hadn't done when Jessica was living at home. She'd always taught piano, but now she was also playing solo recitals at the library and accompanying the dancers at a dance studio. At Thanksgiving break her freshman year, Mom had introduced Jessica to Richard, who'd eventually become her stepfather. The two of them had destroyed all the grass in the backyard where Jessica had played as a little girl and were now growing tall, waving lilies and daisies, little border pansies and marigolds, and vegetables like tomatoes and beans, which they raised with such care you'd think they were children.

Today she wanted her mother's help. She needed to know about any childhood weaknesses caused by allergies and what had been done for them. Maybe there'd been an incident she'd forgotten.

Jessica reached her left hand across to grab a page corner and turned it just in time. Better pay attention. She watched Mom's hands work the keyboard, short fingers arched and the finger pads making full, sensitive contact with the keys. Perfect hand position for piano. Not necessary for getting the right organ tone, but Mom wasn't going to lapse into sloppy keyboard technique during organ performances.

After the Bach and the invocation, the priest began speaking.

Mom let her hands rest on her knees.

"I'm trying something new today. Not going to work at all," Jessica whispered. She'd ease into the subject.

Her mother glanced at her. "You shouldn't feel obliged to go in every day of the week. That place doesn't own you."

"I think that place is getting to me. I'm going to see if I feel better when I stay home today."

"It's like I told you," Mom said. "Your job pays well, good benefits. But you could have done better."

What did she mean by "done better"? Well, Jessica knew what and didn't want to hear it again. Mom had never gotten over not being able to pick a career for her. "I'm not talking about the kind of work I'm doing."

Her mother moved the Bach piece to the end of the rack and opened a thick, bright yellow music book. "You could have been a pianist. Playing or singing music is the most satisfying thing a human being can do. And you're lucky that's where your talents are."

Jessica had to restrain herself from talking more loudly. "The quality of the air at work and what it's doing to me is what I'm talking about."

It frightened her to even think about becoming a professional pianist. She would never be as good as her mother. Or as good as her mother wanted her to be. Sometimes, though, she thought if she'd at least tried to realize Mom's frustrated musical ambitions, Mom would have been happier.

But those choices were in the past. Early in college she'd become convinced that science was the only genuine, reliable way to know the universe, including humanity. She'd settled, despite her mother's dissatisfaction, on a history of science major. Today science and technology were influencing the course of humanity more than anything else in the world, and Mom couldn't appreciate either them or Jessica's choice of work on a communications system that would impact globalization of society and business.

Still, in spite of the challenge, scientific adventure and good pay, her job lacked something. But she didn't want to discuss her life's goals now.

"Mom, I've been having a little problem."

Her mother turned back to the organ and began playing a stodgy old hymn with grunty foot pedal sounds. The music took up only two facing pages and didn't demand any page turning.

Jessica decided they could discuss things better after the service.

After Mom finished with a gentle Bach prelude, Jessica gathered up the music books and put her purse strap over her shoulder. "We're going to breakfast at Barney's?" Her mother and stepfather always went to Barney's Coffee Shop for Sunday breakfast, instead of one of the fancier brunches in downtown Pasadena, because Mom couldn't see paying more for breakfast for the three of them than she'd just earned playing the organ.

"Not today. I have to run all the way across town to Santa Monica."

Jessica led the way down the flight of red-carpeted stairs from the loft to the nave. "I wanted to talk to you just a little bit, Mom. Did anything I was allergic to ever make me so sick I got weak or fell down when I was a kid?"

Jessica waited at the bottom of the stairs while Mom came down more slowly, clutching the handrail. "You fell. Plenty of times—all children do—but not from allergies. Even yours weren't that bad. Mostly you fell down when you laughed, now that I think of it."

Jessica remembered when a playmate tickled her or someone at a slumber party told a funny joke, down she'd go shrieking and giggling. People often say they fall down laughing when they're describing something hilarious, but she was the only person she'd ever known who actually did fall. Her whole mind would be consumed when she heard something funny, to the point where she lost self-control. Now her falls were no laughing matter.

In the car-filled lot, Jessica caught up with her mother. "I think I'm having a really bad allergy problem."

"Antihistamine. That'll help."

Jessica wanted to scream. "Do you think it's that simple? I've had some pretty bad symptoms." She heard her own voice go shrill.

Her mother stopped beside the red Toyota and began searching for the key in her purse. "What do you mean?"

"I don't know what I mean. Some afternoons I get so weak."

Her mother unlocked the car door. "Then you're working much too hard, Jessica." She pulled the car door open.

"Could we talk for just a minute?"

Mom looked at her watch. "Is it important? I have to be in Santa Monica an hour from now."

She handed Mom the music books. "Never mind."

"Call me this evening."

"Sure."

Jessica watched the car pull away, its smelly exhaust belching into her face. Mom was so wrapped up in activities that she didn't have time for her anymore. Some of her friends had told her how their parents had reacted after they'd gone away to school or moved out, but she never would have believed her mother would be like that. Once you leave the nest, don't try to come back.

CHAPTER 8

Getting home early without breakfast wasn't all bad—she could cook a treat for Fernando. He deserved a break from her problems. She made him a special breakfast of avocado huevos rancheros and hot buttered tortillas, one of the few really good recipes in her meager repertoire.

Another favor she'd do for him was lay off the religion humor, especially this morning after he'd gone to Mass. In the past, he'd made a few attempts to persuade her that Catholicism was a rare absolute a person could hang on to in an undependable world. Then, when she had told him what she thought of authoritarian religions, he'd stomped out of the room. Since then they'd had a tacit truce whose rules were that he wouldn't pressure her about Catholicism and going to Mass and she wouldn't dispute or poke fun at his beliefs.

Like condoms. She'd once quipped he used them religiously. And when he'd just about recovered from that remark, she'd asked him how a practicing Catholic like him could use a birth control device. He'd denied using condoms for that purpose. They were for disease prevention, sanctioned by the medical profession. "So the AMA outranks the Pope?" she'd blurted out. As his face had reddened, she'd regretted the remark.

"I prayed for you today," he said, looking up from his Sunday morning newspaper.

"Thanks for the thought." She stifled the urge to say she hoped he hadn't prayed to any saints because she doubted the message would ever reach its destination.

Today she'd keep her big mouth shut. He already had enough to put up with because of her spells without having to endure her wise-ass remarks. Most evenings, she had to be looked after like an invalid. They hadn't gone out all week long—not for a movie or a walk or even a pizza. And as for sex, well forget it. She'd had no interest at all. He hadn't said anything, but she knew it must be on his mind, bless his heart. He was the nicest, most tolerant man she'd ever dated. Whatever had made him this way, and religion may have had a hand in it, she prized the result.

And how devotedly he looked after her. Today he wanted her with him at the medical school library while he studied for his finals. She was happy with that. She could look up the adverse affects of the chemicals used in the art room at work and she wouldn't have to be alone, waiting to see whether she got weak when she was away from work.

Just after noon, they exited the shadowy parking garage behind the med school and plunged into bright sunlight splashing over well-groomed spring lawns and gardens. Jacaranda trees waved pale young leaves and promising lavender buds in the March breeze. Jonquils and tulips lined the walkway between buildings. White jasmine pitched over a brick wall, leaving behind its heavy, sweet scent. Even the buildings were light and bright—cement, white brick or fieldstone. Here and there, students sunbathed or read on stone benches. Jessica had known this place for a long time, ever since Mom had brought her here to play when she was small. To her the Gebauer campus was the epitome of Southern California life—warmth, sun, openness and young people bursting with good health. And Gebauer had a solid academic reputation and a world-class medical school. She'd never even considered attending another university and neither had Fernando.

It took him less than five minutes to bring up MedLine on one of the library's platoon of terminals and show Jessica how to query the system. Then he was off.

She felt right at home perched high on a stool in front of a terminal like this, having spent many college hours in the main library tracking down every little tidbit on Galileo's tricks for measuring time before there were reliable clocks, or how the first fossil specimens of Precambrian life were discovered, plugging a large gap in the evidence for evolution. She felt she had the right traits for a researcher—patience

But after a list of references on allergies revealed no symptoms like hers, she decided to investigate myasthenia gravis and periodic paralysis, just to relieve her mind. It didn't take long to find a neurology journal with a review article on periodic paralysis that described the disease as characterized by episodes of weakness or paralysis of the arms and legs that usually began in the morning. Usually. What if it didn't begin in the morning?

There were many strange terms she'd never encountered before—hyperkalemia, hypokalemia, myopathy, myasthenia, myotonia, cell wall potential, ion channels. She laid the journal in her lap. She badly needed a medical dictionary.

She decided to walk to the bookstore across from the library. A clerk showed her where the dictionaries were and recommended a thick one with a gold title on a black cover. Next to the dictionaries was an oversize book with an interesting title: *Current Medical Diagnosis and Treatment, 1995 Edition*—just three years ago. She scanned the table of contents—"Blood and Serum," "Reproductive System." Then she spotted "Diseases of Muscle and Neuromuscular Junction" with entries on periodic paralysis and myasthenia gravis.

Leaning against a shelf, she was surprised to feel her heart beating fast as she began reading the neuromuscular chapter. Frequently, she had to refer to a nearby dictionary. There were at least two types of periodic paralysis—hypo- and hyperkalemic. Hypokalemic meant too little potassium, hyper too much. Potassium levels must have something to do with paralysis. Maybe one of the art room chemicals was preventing her body from using potassium. She soon realized it was going to take a long time to plow through periodic paralysis alone, let alone any other diseases.

She checked the cost of the books. For a dictionary and diagnosis book together, she'd have to shell out nearly two hundred dollars, which would put her a little short when it came time to pay the rent and utilities this month. She'd have to load up her credit card again when she'd promised herself she wouldn't do that anymore. She took the books to the counter. "If I pay for these books and they aren't the right ones, can I return them?"

A woman on a stool behind the cash register looked up from painting her fingernails. "Three days. Bring the receipt."

"You've got a deal."

Back in a library armchair, she returned to potassium levels and periodic paralysis.

A shadow fell across the sunlit pages. Fernando's hand caressed the back of her neck. That felt really nice. She looked up into his beautiful, suntanned face, his long eyelashes forming a perfect canopy for his deep brown eyes. Fernando was so delicious he never looked like the student, the exam-time bookworm, he really was.

He was smiling, evidently not annoyed at losing study time to check up on her. "How are you feeling?"

"So far so good." She glanced at her watch—two o'clock.

He closed the book on her finger to look at its title. "Lange's *Diagnosis*. Where'd you get this?"

"I just bought it. This too." She handed him the dictionary. "You probably wouldn't need help reading this stuff, but I do."

"You bought these? They must have set you back a couple of hundred."

"Yes, but I can return them tomorrow. I hope you're impressed by my cleverness."

"I'd be even more impressed if you could understand them." He dragged over a well-worn leather armchair beside hers and sat down. She opened the book on the arm of his chair and leaned on his shoulder. "Here. Read this." She pointed to the part on periodic paralysis. "Then the section on myasthenia gravis."

He leafed through the two sections. "I remember those from a neurology course. Very rare. Allergies are much more likely to be your problem than these things."

"You're probably right." He must be right. He'd been an MD long enough to know what made sense and what didn't. "Nowhere does it say people with myasthenia gravis or periodic paralysis only get sick in the afternoon at work."

"And still you bought these books."

"Stick with me. I'm a big spender."

"You're supposed to spend money on your lover, not the damned book store," he whispered in her ear, nuzzling it. He snapped the book shut. "Why don't you go for a walk or read something more cheerful? Give yourself a break, Jessica."

"I will. See you in a couple of hours." She smiled and pressed a finger to his lips.

He returned to his carrel on the second floor.

Back to myasthenia gravis. It was an autoimmune disease. Like her father's lupus erythematosus. Her own immune system's reactions in the past to many foods and to bee stings had been hyperzealous to say the least. She shuddered. What if her immune system had gone haywire. A legacy from her father.

She remembered the hush around him. A tall, muscular figure, he was often stretched limply on the couch or hunched in the oversized recliner in the den, a glass of beer at his side. Mom said Daddy drank to ease the aches and pains of the lupus. She and Mom would tiptoe, trying not to wake him if he was managing to sleep a little.

Jessica would sometimes sneak up to scrutinize him. He had red blotches on his face. "Daddy, wake up," she'd said once. "Let's play croquet." Before he got so sick they all used to have a lot of fun playing croquet in the backyard. He'd feel better, she just knew it, if he'd come out and play the way he used to. But Daddy only took a sip of beer and said, "Later, maybe." He'd died before later came.

Jessica returned to the shelves and, with trembling fingers, picked up another neurology journal that compared myasthenia gravis and periodic paralysis. She read that both could strike at any age, but periodic paralysis most frequently hit teenagers, while myasthenia usually struck in the twenties.

So young. How old had her father been when he'd come down with lupus? He would have been thirty and already sick when she was four. She'd never thought of him as young. He'd been robbed of a great chunk of his youth.

Sometimes, the article went on, victims of either disorder become so flaccid they appear to be unconscious. In fact, they are actually awake and totally aware of what is going on around them. Both could involve the muscles of breathing and swallowing. Both are occasionally fatal.

Fatal! She remembered Trumpower's concerned look when she'd had problems with her throat. But the article said fatalities are rare. And the diseases themselves are rare. So fatalities are rarities piled on top of rarities. It'd be like being struck by lightning at the same time your house was being leveled by an earthquake.

Both illnesses are incurable, but treatable with varying degrees of success. She sat back and watched a young woman hurry along the flower-lined sidewalk. If she did have one or the other, it could be with her for life. Hurrying along a sidewalk might become a rare luxury. Or an impossibility. Forever.

She was only twenty-five. That would be so unfair.

And so unlikely.

Fernando checked on her every hour or so. By the time he was ready to go, it was late afternoon.

"Four o' clock and I'm fine," she said, picking up her books and the articles she'd photocopied. It was late in the afternoon and she was doing great. What an idiot she'd been to spend half the afternoon driving herself crazy with worry.

How had she let this happen? She never allowed herself to stew and churn with anxieties on the job. She was always the happy-go-lucky joker. Now that she was back to normal, she'd return to her beloved laughter.

Fernando took the books in one hand and her hand in the other. She squeezed his and smiled. Maybe they could go out and do something fun tonight.

At their apartment building, they stopped off to feed Fernando's Siamese cats. Bill and Hillary were neutered and spayed. She knew she should get Elsa spayed too, but hadn't gotten around to doing it. That was so irresponsible; there were already too many unwanted cats in the world. If she had, maybe that tom wouldn't have been in her apartment and she wouldn't have been bitten. Next week she'd take Elsa to the vet's.

The cats were all over Fernando, meowing with their almost human voices and rubbing against him. Bill came to Jessica and called to her as if to complain about Hillary hogging Fernando's attention.

She stroked the fat cat and grinned at Fernando. "Four thirty and look at me. I'm fine. I'm sure I'm allergic to something at work."

"And you wasted the afternoon buying books you don't need and worrying about diseases no one ever heard of," he chided.

"I should have gone for a walk and looked at the flowers." She imagined herself dancing through a field of flowers. This day was turning out wonderful.

"Just think." Fernando confronted her. "If you'd stayed home and rested this week, you would never have been put through all this."

It was almost a pleasure to hear him lecturing her again, like everything was back to normal. "If I'd stayed at home, I wouldn't have finished my work. Now I'm practically a company heroine. I worked until I keeled over. Literally." She might even get a pay raise out of this. She'd spend it on a big ski trip.

"You are so stubborn. You never admit when you're wrong." Fernando put his arms around her, hugged her tight and rocked back and forth. "And when I'm right."

"Heroines have a right to be stubborn if they want to." She nibbled sharply on his neck to avenge the uncalled for "I'm right" remark. Just as she felt him shiver, she felt electric tingles.

Tingles of sexual excitement? She giggled.

"Tonight you can be anything you want." He was still hugging her.

As her legs lost strength, his hugging turned into holding her up. She tried not to collapse but, with her thighs turning to rubber, was forced to free herself from him and sink onto the sofa.

Fernando's face turned grim. "What's happening?" He leaned over her.

She didn't want to think about what was happening. "You have nice furniture, Fernando." The sofa cover was flowered and embedded with cat hairs. She sniffed the sofa, enjoying the cat aromas.

He gaped at her. "I have nice furniture! What are you talking about?"

"Look at those stripes—black and gold and sunshine yellow. Don't you just love sunshine?" How lucky she was to have a boyfriend who owned such beautiful, nice-smelling furniture.

"You're acting funny. I've never seen you like this."

"What do you mean?" She felt the tug of despondency threatening her euphoria.

"Jess!" He tugged at her shoulder. "Tell me what's going on. What should I do?"

She tried to clear the fog from her mind.

"Feed Elsa? And check my phone messages?"

"I mean for you—now. Do you need to go to the ER?"

"I don't think so." It was hard to deal with all these questions.

Fernando was stroking her hand. "I ordered pizza. It should be here in a few minutes."

"Oh good." She rubbed her eyes. "What time is it?"

"Six thirty."

She was weak and had lost a couple of hours in a haze again. How could this have happened when she'd spent the whole day away from work?

"Are you okay?" He looked so worried.

"Yes. Just tired." She struggled to a sitting position.

"You had a message on your phone. Dr. Chapman called again."

The ER doctor. He'd called yesterday too, to see how she was. He must be worried. That made two of them.

But she didn't want to think about that. Not now. She asked him what kind of pizza he'd ordered.

"Gourmet vegetable. Your favorite."

After eating, Fernando wanted to discuss her condition, but she wanted distraction. They snuggled up together on the couch and watched an old Star Trek episode, where the good guys fought a terrible alien enemy and won. She began to feel stronger. "I want to stay with you tonight."

"All right. I'll sleep on the couch."

"No." She squeezed his hand. "I mean with you." If they were going to be like normal people, and she was determined they would, they had to do what normal people did.

Fernando withdrew his hand. "I thought I'd just look after you tonight."

"You would be looking after me."

He jumped to his feet. "I'd better clean up the kitchen."

She picked up the pizza cutter and the two water glasses, took them into the kitchen and put them into the dishwasher. He wadded the pizza box and stuffed it into the plastic trash can.

"There." Jessica brushed her hands together. "Kitchen cleaned."

"I'll take the trash out to the dumpster. Old pizza boxes can get pretty smelly."

She was waiting for him at the front door when he came back. "Fernando, I can see you're squeamish. I need to feel good. And going to bed with you would make me feel good."

He was standing rigidly against the closed door. "I think I should take care of you, not take advantage of you."

She reached out and took his hand. "Come on, Fernando. Take care of me. Make me feel better."

When they reached his bedroom and embraced, he pressed his mouth to hers. She wished she felt excited by his kiss. He usually excited her. This should be exciting.

Maybe she could arouse Fernando, cause him to tremble and come under her spell. But how could she control his reactions when she had no control at all over herself anymore. She failed to even venture her tongue toward his. She was calculating that if one in every 20,000 people has periodic paralysis, then there were about 400 of them in Los Angeles County and she could be one of them.

As she pulled her shirt over her head and removed her bra she wondered if it might be possible to die in bed from what she had without even being able to call for help. She kicked off her shoes and sat on the edge of the bed. They had to go through the motions of the sex they'd always enjoyed to keep the sickness from destroying her.

CHAPTER 9

It was premature to give up on allergies, Jessica told herself and Fernando. Only allergies fit the way these attacks struck every afternoon, then vanished in the evening.

Fernando agreed. He considered getting her some Benadryl, but decided against it because Benadryl makes patients sleepy and slow, which he feared would make Jessica's unknown problem worse. Even though that sounded right, she wished he'd left the decision to her.

In her cubicle at work, she put an air filter on the desk and wore a smaller, battery-powered one on a cord around her neck. She hung another from the car rearview mirror and had a large air purifier delivered to her apartment.

In the past, she'd had some allergies to chemicals in makeup and nail polish. So she threw out anything that wasn't hypoallergenic, including bath soap, shampoo and conditioner. She pulled down shower curtains that had been polluted by soap and hair care liquids and hung new ones. She replaced the bath towels and bath mat.

She spent two entire days, watched over by Fernando, in the med school library away from home, church, car or work and any exposure to pollutants and chemicals.

On days when her attacks were mild she was encouraged. When they were severe she was discouraged. But no matter where she was, every single afternoon, somewhere between two and five thirty, she lost all or partial use of the muscles in her arms, legs, neck, jaws, tongue and throat. The symptoms might go away in a few minutes or last a few hours.

At work, she was still normal all morning. In the afternoons she'd become adept at hiding her collapses, which wasn't easy since passersby could see into her cubicle. She put her chair against the door, leaned her head back where it could nestle in a little corner formed by the door and its frame, and held some papers on her lap. No one just passing by could see whether she was working. Someone in the next cubicle would have to stand up and stare at her to see what was going on, but no one ever did because of a tacit agreement to grant each other some privacy.

After a week, she was forced to give up on her allergy theory despite the fact that she could think of no other reason for the attacks to strike only in the afternoon. Having to give up what had seemed like a good idea for no idea at all was a huge loss.

Fernando told her not to be discouraged—she'd only been sick a few days. He told her to make an appointment with a neurologist.

"Then you think it's time to think about periodic paralysis or myasthenia gravis."

"It's time." He tried to smile with confidence, but his smile was shaky.

CHAPTER 10

Behind her, Fernando dogged her every step from the parking garage to the plaza she was slouching across, at a pace she thought would irritate a snail. He was observing Jessica's hips, knees, ankles—everything that should be articulating. Walking wasn't fun this chilly, soggy morning.

"I'm beginning to favor periodic paralysis," he called out. "It's mostly confined to the arms and legs, like you. Myasthenia gravis usually affects the eyes more."

Jessica was too consumed with her struggle toward the medical building to reply or even think about what he'd just said.

He took her hand as they entered the building, its hallways full of doctors, nurses, ambulatory and wheelchair patients, all moving faster than Jessica. It was as if everyone else was living in a world with one set of physical laws and she was in another where gravity was stronger and the atmosphere more viscous.

She stopped for a moment, appalled at how far down the corridor the elevators were. Fernando must have sensed her distress because he put his hand under her elbow so she could lean on him. She pulled her arm away. "I know you're trying to help me, Fernando, but I want to do this myself."

She began muttering internal mantras. Mind over matter, where there's a will there's a way, never say die. All of that. She took a deep breath and ordered herself to take a normal step. Success. One step, two strides, three, four, five, six—she could do it! Right in the middle of seven her mind lost its grip, her thighs lost tone, her feet groped for support. She was lucky to land on a stretch of carpet because she fell hard on her knees and elbows, the pain a reminder that she couldn't escape the laws of her new world, no matter how cruel and absurd.

Fernando's hand was on her back almost as soon as she landed. "Are you all right?"

"I tried to rely on mental strength, but that must not be my strong point."

"Why did you let go of me? I would never have let you fall."

"I appreciate that. I needed to try." It seemed like he wanted her to think she'd failed when she wanted to be congratulated for the effort.

He left for a minute, bringing back a chubby little woman with a wheelchair who called herself "patient transportation." Fernando lifted Jessica gently under the arms and lowered her into the seat.

"Will you be okay now? I could skip class and come with you."

"You go ahead." She knew he was anxious to see his exam grades.

"Be sure to get a referral to a neurologist." He kissed her on the forehead and watched as she was wheeled away.

By the time her name was called, Jessica's knees were sore and throbbing, but she was able to trudge across the floor—the same spotless tile she'd fallen on over a week ago—to Trumpower's office. The pseudo-leather chair across the desk from him let out a sigh when she plopped herself into it. She'd only glanced around his office before, but now scrutinized it for signs that he had the right stuff to help her. His desktop was well-organized—a folder in the center, two stacks of journals at one side that must mean he kept current, a framed picture of him being awarded a plaque, and another of what she guessed were himself with his wife and two teenaged sons resting on a stone outcropping with Yosemite's El Capitan in the distant background. To his left, on a table matching the desk, were a new Aggravon 1998 laptop, laser printer and fax machine. A diploma from Washington University Medical School shared wall space with documents and awards with gold seals on them. All signs were positive that this man was well-educated, well-equipped and up-to-date.

Trumpower's broad, substantial face looked confident, not shaken as it had been when he'd sent her to the ER. "What happened after you left here the other day? I was a bit worried about you."

Worried? Hysterical was more like it. Now his voice was so relaxed, she got the sense all his other patients must be doing well. She told him about the conversion disorder diagnosis and Chapman agreeing that she shouldn't take valium.

Trumpower shook his head and grimaced with dismay. "Their specialties down there are first aid and saving lives. As for the rest..." He spread his hands out on the desk.

But hadn't he sent her there? If he believed the ER was only good for first aid and saving lives, he must have feared for her life, a fear apparently shared by Dr. Chapman.

The fear was catching, creeping up her arms and legs to her fluttering heart.

"I no longer think allergies are my problem. I used air filters and purifiers and spent a couple of days in a library away from all my normal haunts. Yet every afternoon I was weak. I'm worried about periodic paralysis and myasthenia gravis."

Trumpower opened a folder on his desk. "Here's some good news. You tested negative for diabetes, lupus, toxoplasmosis and Lyme disease."

He wasn't even going to address what she'd just said. "Then you still don't know what's wrong with me. Only a few things that aren't." She felt a tightness in her throat.

He clasped his hands over a flab-free midsection. "Be patient. You've only had this a few days. This is just the second time I've seen you and my first look at your test results."

Only a few days! They'd been the most frightening days she'd ever experienced. "I've been looking into those things you tested for and none of them is episodic. But I did find some neurological disorders—hypo- and hyperkalemic periodic paralysis, myasthenia gravis, myasthenic syndrome, Lambert-Eaton syndrome. Possibly Addison's disease. Why don't we look at those?" She hoped he'd see that she was knowledgeable and could be of great help to him.

Trumpower erected a steeple with his fingers in front of his face. "You sound as if you spent your weekend getting a medical degree."

"I've been spending a lot of time in the medical library."

He pointed the steeple at her. "I'm delighted you're interested enough to do some reading. But why don't you leave the doctoring to me?"

"I'm trained in research. I have a degree in history of science from Gebauer. I can help."

"I want you to get an MRI of your brain. Make sure there's no tumor."

"That sounds constructive." Another awful possibility to worry about. "And I think it would be a good idea for a neurologist to examine me, especially for periodic paralysis and myasthenia gravis."

"A bit premature. We don't want to get involved in things like that until we've investigated the more common possibilities."

"Why let some investigations wait on others? Isn't that risky?" Since no one knew what she had or what damage it could do if left untreated, she urgently needed help now before something awful and irreversible happened. "I'll get the MRI, but please just give me a referral to a neurologist." She felt the beginning of a headache clamping down on her temples.

He sighed and reached for the Medical Center directory next to the phone. "Neurology. Robert McDonald," he mumbled, filling out the required referral form and shoving it across the desk at her.

She thanked Trumpower and left him, hands folded on his desk, shaking his head. She hoped she hadn't totally alienated him.

McDonald was balding, with fringes of white hair and tired-looking, watery gray eyes. His office was small and windowless. Model military airplanes filled the bookshelves, while books and papers were strewn over his desk and piled on the floor. He spent a few minutes on her file, muttering to himself. Then, after quickly running her through the now familiar stare at the ceiling and follow-the-moving-pencil tests, he sat back and declared he didn't think she had myasthenia gravis.

She was shocked. How could he possibly come to a conclusion so fast? And with so little information.

McDonald's sleepy-eyed explanation was that the first symptoms of MG were usually blurred vision and droopy eyelids, and her eyes were fine. On the faint chance she had periodic paralysis, he suggested lots of bananas and orange juice to raise her potassium level. "Go home, relax, eat bananas and come back in a week if you aren't feeling better," he advised. "Don't worry yourself. These things are very rare. You're not likely to have one. When I was in medical school they taught us that when you hear hoofbeats, think horses, not zebras."

"Take a look at me. I have stripes all over." With her strange and severe symptoms, she felt he should be concerned enough to look for stripes. She might have a rare serious illness. Someone had to have them. She understood how a doctor might employ a statistical strategy—consider common things first, then rare ones. But this didn't take into account that rare symptoms fit her better.

He dismissed her after exactly fifteen minutes.

She headed down a maze of hallways to meet Fernando at the med school cafeteria. By now she understood her new world a little better. A basic rule was you only got fuel for your life's business at a rate that whoever or whatever was in charge saw fit. She could stride rapidly for six paces before she fell or she could trudge very slowly almost indefinitely. Or there were in-between cases where she could push herself a little. She'd gotten so she could match effort to distance so she wouldn't fall before she got where she was going. Usually. Unless the masters of her world got stingy with fuel.

She found Fernando waiting for her at the entrance to the packed and noisy cafeteria. They sat at the end of one of the long, gray, scarred Formica-topped tables where they could have a little privacy. He was so aglow because he'd learned he'd aced his finals that he was shoveling the paste-taste cafeteria macaroni and cheese down without complaining.

She was happy for him. "You deserve it, Fernando. I wish all doctors cared as much about their profession and worked as hard as you do."

As she described her visit to McDonald, finishing with the banana edict and the fifteen minute dismissal time, Fernando scowled. "That's HMOs for you. The ideal patient is allotted fifteen minutes of the doctor's time, no more. I may have to confront that someday in my practice."

"You'll install Jessica's patient removal system in your office. At exactly fifteen minutes, your door will open, a large sucking noise will be heard and your patient will be vacuumed out and deposited in the lobby. It'll be the next breakthrough in medical technology."

Fernando turned red as he tried not to choke on a mouthful of macaroni while giggling.

Jessica felt a little better when she got him to laugh. "I'm zonked. It takes a lot out of me going to these doctors. I thought they'd help me."

"I wonder if Trumpower and McDonald are taking you seriously. They might believe your problem is psychiatric."

"Why do these doctors think I'm nuts or on drugs? What kind of attitude is that, Fernando?"

He shrugged. "They can't find anything they can quantify. No abnormalities in your blood or blood pressure, no fever, no inflammation, no measurable symptoms of any kind. Makes them suspicious."

"Primitive thinking." She shoved away a side dish of coleslaw drowning in watery mayonnaise. "Of course, I can guess where it comes from. In the seventeenth century, when Descartes insisted on experimental proof as a foundation of science, he divided the world into the rational and the irrational, the provable and the unprovable. A good scientist had to come up with a well-defined output he could measure. That way of thinking evolved and got carried to extremes. Now it's if you can't measure it, it doesn't exist. But that's wrong. Lack of evidence of a physical problem is not evidence for a lack of a physical problem. It's simply lack of evidence." The words came streaming out of a file her beleaguered mind must have spent the past few days constructing on its own.

"Very logical. I have no objection to logic. But if I had a patient and couldn't find a physical cause for his complaints, I'd at least suspect a psychological cause."

"That doesn't sound much different from suspecting your patient's inhabited by demons. Why not add exorcisms to your treatment list?"

Fernando grimaced. "No matter what you think, if doctors have no test evidence to convince them you're sick, a lot of them won't want to be bothered with you. And the only way you can get competent treatment is through a doctor."

"That idiot resident in the ER wanted to dose me up with valium, of all things."

"I asked around about her. The neurology staff is not proud of this year's crop of residents. They call them the 007 class—licensed to kill."

"Licensed to kill! But they're working in the ER."

Fernando nodded to a couple of men in white coats passing by with loaded trays as though they were members of a close-knit fraternal group. "My guess is that woman you saw won't be asked to stay after her residency."

"She could kill someone. She could have killed me."

"Unfortunately, there's no getting rid of her until her residency is over. Gebauer could be sued for a whole lifetime's loss of income as a physician if she was fired."

"How about a suit for death by malpractice? How would the med school like that?" She slapped the table weakly in an effort to bang on it.

"Who'd testify against her? Not another resident, that's for sure. Management tries to cover themselves by having senior physicians supervising the ER."

"Like Chapman. He's a good guy. Told me not to take the valium and he called me at home for several days to see how I was." She barely finished her sentence before she fell forward.

Fernando yanked her plate from in front of her just before she sprawled onto the table. He checked his watch. "Twenty-five minutes. You have an attack twenty or twenty-five minutes after you start eating. The higher the carbohydrate level, the harder you fall."

Some boyfriends would have been turned off by a sickness like hers. But the more symptoms she got and the weirder they were, the more fascinated and involved she realized Fernando became.

With nothing better to try, over the next few days she ate a banana at every meal, carried them in her purse and stashed some in her desk drawer at work for snacks. She thought her symptoms were getting worse, or at best staying the same. So much for the banana theory.

Back at Trumpower's she asked for a better neurology referral, but he wanted to explore the possibility that she might have contracted an unusual infection from her encounter with the cat.

The cat again. What if she'd gotten some cat thing like the mad cow disease that she'd read about. In England it had passed from cows to people. She shuddered.

The appointment with the infectious disease physician was brief—she had no idea what Jessica had. As far as she knew, cats couldn't transmit anything but cat scratch fever or toxoplasmosis. Never heard of a mad cat version of mad cow disease. On a scrap of paper she wrote the name of a Gebauer neurologist who did research on neuromuscular disorders in addition to running a clinical practice.

When Jessica next saw Trumpower, she told him she'd gotten diddly-squat from the infectious disease doctor, except for the name of a research neurologist.

A wisp of annoyance flitted over his face "Well we tried. Have to cover all the bases."

"I've seen seven doctors, counting those pathetic ER residents, and still no one has any idea what's wrong with me." Jessica's chest was so tight from trying to stifle her fear and frustration she could barely get out the words.

Trumpower formed a steeple with his hands, the way he had when she'd told him of her medical journal reading. "Some people think doctors are gods. But we don't know everything."

Jessica stared at his steepled fingers. He may not believe he was God, but he apparently had aspirations.

Trumpower kept the steeple in place. "My dear, I appreciate your anxiety. But you're going to have to allow me to be your doctor. We could waste a lot of time on stray ideas. I'm sure you don't want to do that." His voice was maddeningly calm, as though he were trying to reason with a mental patient.

She took a deep breath and dove into dangerous waters. "Do you trust me? Do you believe I'm sick or do you think I'm nuts? Or malingering?"

"I intend to do everything I can to determine what's wrong with you."

With empathy, she recalled TV interviewers trying to get straight answers out of politicians on *The Lehrer News Hour* and *Face the Nation*. They almost never succeeded. She shared what must be their unbearable frustration. It wasn't likely they shared her desperation.

"I'd like to see this man." She slapped the scrap of paper with the neurologist's name on it on Trumpower's desk.

Trumpower folded his arms across his chest. "Another neurologist? You already saw McDonald."

"He must have mistaken me for a chimpanzee. He told me to eat bananas."

Trumpower sighed, reached for a pad of forms and wrote her a referral.

She had begun to wonder what characteristics a doctor who could help her would have. Trumpower had a great reputation among Gebauer's staff and had graduated from a first-rate medical school. She gazed at the family picture on his desk. In the photograph, his head was the highest, higher even than El Capitan.

CHAPTER 11

Clinging to Mom as she lurched into the dimly lit parking garage outside the ER, from which she had just been discharged, Jessica prayed they didn't have to walk far to the car. She could talk and hold her head up and use her arms, but her legs were buckling, whether more from illness or from terror she didn't know. There was a lot she didn't know these days—what was making her sick, how sick she was going to get, how to get the care she so desperately needed.

Even though it had started only a few hours ago, the memory of the worst attack she'd had yet was like a bad dream—vivid images interspersed with intervals of haziness. Jim Stone had been in her cubicle when it struck. "I need to go to emergency." She'd managed to get out the slurred and muffled words. He'd rolled her right out of the building in her desk chair to his car. She remembered a wild ride over city streets.

At the ER security desk, he'd called Mom and must have waited until she arrived. For six hours Jessica had remained in the ER, under observation, traumatized with fear her throat would close up. What a jolt for Mom who'd never, until now, heard about her attacks.

"Now where did I park the car?" Mom mumbled. A car door slammed in the distance.

Signs hung above aisles lined solidly with cars read, informatively, "Parking" and "Additional Parking." Since it was only eight in the evening, Jessica expected there'd be people coming and going. But she saw no one.

"I walked down some stairways. Then down a long aisle. Probably this one." Mom nodded straight ahead.

By the time they'd groped their way to the end of the aisle, Jessica had to lean into Mom's arm near the elbow. She felt the arm begin to quiver. "That's too much weight on you, isn't it?"

"Let's catch our breath for a minute and see where we are." Mom stopped.

Jessica tried to stand alone but swayed, lost her balance and staggered to one side.

"Don't do that." Mom grabbed her arm. "Look, the stairs are right here."

Trying not to lean so heavily on her mother this time, Jessica grasped her around the waist and they slithered sideways like attached Siamese crabs. She hadn't held onto Mom's body like this in a long time and it caught her by surprise that her mother's flesh now hung so loosely on her bones.

They came to a door that said "Stairs" and opened it. "Look familiar?" Jessica said.

Mom's shoulders twitched and trembled. "I was in such a panic when I got here I can't remember. But this could be it."

They struggled up one floor to "B Level," on to "Plaza Parking" and past a door to "Level 3." Mom was panting for breath. "I don't remember this."

Jessica felt as lost as Alice down the rabbit hole, reading mysterious doorway signs that all seemed to want to be chosen, but offering no clue as to what was beyond them. She was weakening so fast she knew she didn't have much time left to pick the right one. How could the ER have discharged her in this condition? "Could we have come the wrong way?" Her mother was too small and old to be dragging a grown daughter around.

"I think we'd better go back the way we came," Mom said.

"In a minute." Jessica leaned against a cold, concrete block wall and her mother leaned beside her. They saw two people get out of a car far down the aisle and walk the other way.

"Why didn't you tell me you'd been sick before?" Mom's voice had an accusing edge to it.

"I tried to. Last Sunday at church. You were in too big a hurry to listen."

"You'd been to the ER! You should have told me right away."

"Sorry." There was no way to come out ahead. If she asked Mom for help, she was ignored. If she didn't, she was criticized. "I have to handle my life myself, not always be a burden to you. You didn't call your mother every time you had a problem. Did you?"

"Why hasn't anyone in this great big place figured out what's wrong with you?"

"I wish I knew." Jessica gripped the handrail and dragged her absurdly heavy feet up the stairs. On the way toward the Plaza Level, she leaned into Mom's arm near the elbow again. They passed the entrance to a brightly lit hallway where a sign said "Pediatric Hospital."

"Don't remember that," Mom muttered.

Her usually meticulously careful mother hadn't remembered or written down the route she'd taken to the ER because Jessica's condition had literally scared the wits out of her. Poor Mom. Poor Jessica too. What would come of them if she became completely flaccid in this huge garage?

Soon they stumbled into an area labeled "Lot B."

"I just remembered something," Mom said, looking around at all the lettered and numbered support posts with red stripes. "Where I parked, the posts had blue stripes."

They leaned against each other and peered down the aisles to the right and left. Red stripes everywhere.

"I see a driveway heading into another garage." Jessica stared ahead, unable to lift her arm to point. With her fuel supply for the evening about to give out, the dark car-lined aisle ahead would take an eternity to traverse. But she was frightened of giving up and struggled down the aisle anyway, gripping Mom's hand, then propping herself on Mom's arm and finally hanging onto her shoulder. After several minutes they were only halfway to the end of the aisle and her mother's whole body began shaking. They couldn't go on.

Jessica staggered over, slumped onto the hood of a car, then slid to the pavement between cars. With no control over any part of her body, she was no longer human, but like an earth-bound plant.

Mom leaned over her and tugged on her hand.

"Don't. I can't move and it hurts when you pull." The pavement was gritty and smelled like motor oil.

"Someone has to come along soon."

They waited for long minutes. Except for Jessica's fear-driven heartbeat pounding in her ears, they waited in silence. "Help, someone, help,"

Mom called out. Not even an echo answered as her voice dissipated into the void.

Jessica didn't know what would become of them if they didn't get help soon. "You go ahead and leave me here. You can look faster without me."

"I can't leave you. Someone could step on you."

"I'll be okay." Mom was probably right. No one going to their car would expect to find a person lying beside it. But she just couldn't burden her mother anymore, and they had to get out of here somehow.

"I can't go without you."

"Mom, I don't want to stay here all night."

"Then I'll put you over my shoulder and carry you."

"Take a look. I'm not a baby anymore, Mom. I got big." Mom wasn't being rational.

Jessica heard tires rolling on concrete and a kind of squeaky-creaky noise. It didn't sound like a car. "What's that?"

Mom turned around. "It's one of those parking enforcement golf cart type thingies. Coming this way. Thank God."

The vehicle stopped close enough that Jessica could hear its little engine hum. "Please help us," Mom pleaded.

It took several minutes for Mom and the driver to drag Jessica onto the cart and several more minutes of driving the cart up and down aisles on two floors before they found the car.

"Thanks so much," Jessica said when the driver, holding her securely by the waist, half carried her to the car. She was embarrassed at importuning a stranger and having him go to all this trouble for her.

But embarrassment was nothing compared to her guilt over the ordeal she'd just put her mother through. Mom was too old for this. And there were still older threats to their relationship. Entangled with her dreads for Mom and herself was the fear that helplessness might drive her to need her mother as she hadn't since she was a child.

At home Mom dropped onto the couch, while Jessica collapsed into the cherrywood rocking chair. That left only the piano bench or one of the three uncomfortable wood-backed, antique chairs with knobby embroidered cushions for her stepfather, Richard, the only entity new to the room since Jessica's childhood. He perched on the piano bench where a floor lamp lit his seamed, weathered face and crown of thick white hair. He was handsome, a dead ringer for the old-time movie actor, Eddie Albert, Mom admired so much.

"I don't remember what I'd planned for dinner," Mom said, rubbing her forehead. "I'm too exhausted to make it if I did remember."

"I don't really care," Jessica mumbled.

"I've never seen anything as confusing as that parking garage." Mom put the back of her hand to her forehead as if to fend off an unseen danger.

"You should have called me to come get you," Richard said.

Jessica nodded. "I wish we had."

"I would have carried her if that cart hadn't come," Mom said.

"No way!" Richard's voice was gruff with emotion.

"Mom, you could have had a heart attack dragging me." It was time her mother stopped thinking of herself as indestructible.

"We both could have died there and no one would have found us until it was too late. Shipwreck victims set adrift to founder in ocean-sized garages." Mom waved her hand as though shoving an imaginary boat out to sea.

"How about I take care of dinner?" Richard offered.

"I was hoping you would," Mom said.

Richard's one cooking utensil was his wallet. The only question was whether it would be Marie Callender's or Chinese takeout.

"Vegetable soup and lemon meringue pie okay?"

Marie Callender's.

They had the soup, corn bread and pie on TV trays Richard set up in the den, where they usually ate if there was no company so the dining room tablecloth wouldn't get soiled. More casual than the living room, the den was furnished with a super-soft sofa, armchair and recliner, all decked out in old mail-order slipcovers. An inexpensive, scratched-up wooden coffee table where Jessica had used scissors and crayons as a little girl stood in front of the sofa. Across the room were windowsill-high bookcases that had held children's books on the lowest level when she was a child. On a higher shelf was a TV, behind which she'd often surreptitiously poured bowls of Cream of Wheat Mom had insisted she eat for breakfast. For years, she'd been afraid to look behind that shelf.

Hands shaking, Mom leaned over and fumbled until she managed to unscrew the lid to Jessica's soup and open the Styrofoam container of cornbread and butter. "Now let's hear what's been going on with you. And don't you dare leave out anything just to spare your mother."

Jessica stalled by blowing on the hot soup. She couldn't recall ever seeing her mother tremble like this. "It's hard to describe. Every afternoon for the past ten days, it seems like gravity's gotten a lot stronger. But only for me." She went through the history of mysterious collapses, visits to doctors and negative test results.

The room got quiet, the only sound the faint one of Jessica chewing soft corn bread. Mom's face muscles went flaccid, the corners of her mouth down, so that she appeared to age before Jessica's eyes.

Richard looked stunned. "How on earth have you been getting to work?"

"When I wake up I'm fine and I can drive. My attacks come in the afternoon." She wouldn't tell them that lately she'd been feeling a little weak by midmorning and didn't know what she'd do about driving if she got bad really early. "I get better in the evening."

"Have you been taking care of yourself?" Mom peered over her glasses.

"Like always—you should know by now—I eat right, take vitamins, run, do aerobics. It doesn't make sense for me to be sick. For a while I thought I must be allergic to something at work, the way it comes on at the same time every day."

"If I know you, and I do, you're trying to do too much. Wearing yourself out." Her mother shook a soup spoon in Jessica's direction.

That spoon! It was as though Mom's shaken finger had grown grotesquely. "I'm careful." She almost cried. She was being treated like a child. "I don't try to walk to the cafeteria anymore. I pack a lunch or buy yogurt and bananas from the roach coach that comes to the front of the building." On her worst days she couldn't chew food like apples or celery. "I don't work more than eight or ten hours a day." At least not every day.

"What does Fernando think of all this?" Her mother was enchanted by Fernando's Latin charm and sought his medical advice on everything from ginkgo biloba to dizziness and headaches. And every time Mom looked at him, Jessica just knew she was seeing smart, good-looking grandchildren.

"Fernando doesn't think I have a brain tumor. He thinks I might have an autoimmune problem like myasthenia gravis."

Mom's shoulders twitched.

Jessica knew what that twitch was all about. "If my father had an autoimmune illness, I'm much more likely to have one—the same or another—than most people."

"Have you been tested for lupus?" Mom asked.

"Yes. I don't have it."

"You need to come and stay with us so we can take care of you." Mom's voice had lost its tentative, questioning timbre and taken on a ring of certainty.

"No!" Jessica shook her head. "I don't want to be a burden on you. You've got your own life." She sneaked a glance to see if Mom's hands were still trembling.

"At least stay home from work for a while. Rest." Mom was getting strident.

"Mom, it's my life. I'm not walking off my job. I can't and I don't want to." She didn't want to give up living on her own. She could still see her father lying on the couch, right in this house, drinking beer while Mom padded around, tending to him and everything else that needed doing while he'd lain there helpless. She dreaded the idea of becoming like a child, dependent on her mother again.

"Maybe you're worried about your insurance." Richard ran a local office for a big insurance company. "Even if you have to quit, they'll give you ninety more days on your insurance at Rank. Then they have to let you buy that same coverage for a reasonable cost for the next eighteen months if you want it."

"I'm not quitting. And I'm not staying home."

"I'll drop the organ recitals and the ballet school," Mom said. "Just teach at home like I used to when you were little."

"I'm not little anymore. Haven't you noticed?" Jessica heard her voice rise in pitch.

"Don't get huffy." Mom pushed her glasses to the end of her nose and peered over them.

"I need to live as normally as I can. So do you. A grown woman being taken care of by her mother is not normal."

"I don't need you to decide what I should and should not do."

"And I don't need you to tell me what to do," Jessica snapped. To her surprise she had tears in her eyes. "I want to live on my own in my own place. Can't you understand?" And she never again wanted to feel her mother's body shaking under her weight.

"Want me to search on the Web for myasthenia gravis?" Richard asked.

"That would be nice."

"You'll at least stay the night," Mom said.

"Sure." She didn't have the strength to argue anymore.

CHAPTER 12

"Mom was on the phone again," Jessica said as Fernando lugged the heavy, screened wooden cat carrier into the apartment. "Trying to talk me into moving back home. I just can't do that." Even as Jessica heard the words come out of her mouth, she feared she might end up doing exactly that. If she got as weak as she had in the hospital parking garage again—none of the doctors she'd seen would venture a guess as to how often that might happen—she didn't want to be alone.

"You're only four days out of the ER. She wants you where she can watch over you. I can understand that." Fernando set the rocking and jiggling carrier on the carpet between the couch and piano bench.

A couple of days ago, using leather workman's gloves, he'd caught the feral tom that had bitten Jessica, taken it to the vet and had it tested for toxoplasmosis and other feline diseases. Amazingly, the creature got a clean bill of health. "Great shape," the vet had said. "But he's filthy." He'd convinced Fernando to do the world a favor and have the cat neutered, de-fleaed, cleaned up and given a precautionary antibiotic. The bill came to over two hundred dollars, but Jessica was now free of mad cat disease worries.

"I can understand your Mom. But she doesn't need to worry," Fernando said. "I'll look after you."

"I wish you'd tell her that. She wants to do everything for me, like I was a baby. She's too old for that and so am I."

The tom let out a deep, mournful howl. Elsa ran out from the bedroom and stopped, crouched in the hallway just outside the living room, eyes riveted on the carrier.

Jessica knelt, with more dread than made sense to her, and peeked through the wire screen into the cage. The devil cat glowered at her through slitty yellow eyes. "He's not a bit friendly. Just cleaner. I don't want him in here."

"We can't very well dump him back in the canyon with all those wild animals and vermin." Fernando's voice was querulous.

She stood up slowly and with difficulty. "He's not going to live here. It scares me to think what he might do if I was alone and he saw me fall."

"He can't stay in my place either. You know how Bill and Hillary are about other cats."

"Then it's back to the canyon with him."

"I spent all that money cleaning him up. Stay back and I'll see how he behaves." Fernando unlatched and slowly opened the carrier door. Elsa turned halfway around, ready to scurry back into the bedroom.

The tom remained in the back of the carrier.

"Come to think of it, I could partition my apartment," Fernando said. "Close the door to the back where the bedroom and bathroom are. Give him that and give Bill and Hillary the kitchen and living room. No problem for me since I'll be staying with you all the time anyway."

All the time? True, he'd been staying at her place the past two weeks, doing the vacuuming and dishwashing and scrubbing down the bathroom, while she was often too helpless to do much. But they'd never discussed anything permanent. Although the help he'd given her had been wonderful, she wasn't sure she wanted him to live with her permanently.

"Why couldn't he stay out there on the balcony?" She glanced over the dining table at the sliding glass door that was always closed these days.

Fernando squatted beside the carrier and laid a protective hand on it. "That's the same as dumping him back into the canyon. We can't do that."

This was his doctor's tone of voice she was hearing. For a cat. The nasty one that had bitten her. "Why can't we? Before I was sick I wasn't afraid of him, but I am now."

Fernando put his finger to his lips. "Shh." He stood up and backed away from the carrier.

The tom's black nose and whiskers were inching out. His head, low with chin almost to the floor, swiveled back and forth as he surveyed his surroundings. To Jessica he looked satanic.

From the hallway, Elsa hissed, fangs bared.

That did it. Jessica dashed into the kitchen, got the broom and shoved the snarling tom back into the carrier. "Get him out of here, Fernando. Put him back in the canyon. He's used to it."

"I would rather see him properly cared for."

"Fernando, this is a feral cat. Why don't you just let him go?"

He leaned down and lifted the heavy carrier, which began rocking violently back and forth as the cat heaved itself from side to side. "I'll take him downstairs, make him at home. Then I'll go to the market and get some more cat food and litter. What do you want for dinner?"

He was nuts, but the thing would be in his apartment, not hers. She thought a minute. He almost always fixed pizza or pasta. "How about cheese enchiladas?"

He grimaced. "Too tough."

"You get the ingredients and I'll make them. I have Mom's recipe."

"You're always weak at dinnertime."

"You're right. I forgot for a minute." It amazed her that every now and then she forgot she was sick.

"Give me the recipe and a little advice and I'll try to make them."

"You're so good to me." She owed him so much.

"See, you don't need your parents."

It was true. She was happy—she could live on her own without Mom's help. Independent and self-sufficient.

CHAPTER 13

Arriving at work the next day, Jessica was tense. She had to attend a meeting small enough that everyone would see if she was having trouble. She'd always treasured the respect for her work and the light in peoples' eyes when she was kidding around with them. Now she feared she'd see attitude changes, frightened faces and freaked out stares, signs of pity and low regard.

No sooner had she slipped through the door and into a chair in the crowded, windowless conference room than her concern shifted. About twenty men had their attention riveted on Tim Dunmar standing at a flip chart draped over an easel. Armor was presiding at a table at the front, head swiveling back and forth, glowering. Rapid-fire exchanges rifled between Dunmar and the engineers as they debated a spacecraft antenna issue.

Whitney, in a black, scoop-necked dress and matching gold-buttoned jacket, her blonde hair pulled up into a shimmering bun, looked especially stunning at the front table. But Whitney was not participating in the meeting—she was taking notes, her long red fingernails flashing as they moved under the overhead fluorescent lights. As Jessica watched the meeting progress, she saw no one was asking Whitney's opinion on anything. Jessica could barely stifle a cry of rage.

"Paul said to try thirty-seven ohm resistive loads." Dunmar, his voice nasal with a bad cold, tapped Whitney's notepad with a wooden pointer. "Write that down—thirty-seven ohms. O-H-Ms." He spelled it out.

Jessica wanted to cry with hurt and shame for Whitney. Not one of these men seemed the least bit embarrassed at how they were treating her, apparently didn't even care whether she knew what an ohm was, only whether she spelled it right. Worse yet, Whitney appeared unconcerned. A good reputation in an aerospace engineering company like Rank was too hard to come by for Whitney to let it slip through her fingers like this. And Whitney's attitude could siphon off hard-won momentum from other women's careers. Jessica felt like crying for everyone this morning.

Now that she thought about it, she became suspicious of why she'd been summoned here. This seemed to be a technical issues meeting writers didn't ordinarily attend. Maybe they had some "women's work" for her too. Maybe the bosses expected her, like Whitney, to accept whatever odds and ends they deigned to toss at her now that she was sick.

Dunmar covered nitty-gritty detail after detail. Whitney kept writing, showing not the slightest sign of irritation in the careful way she occasionally turned to a new page of the notepad.

It seemed to Jessica that she, not Whitney, was being observed by Armor with some interest. Possibly he remembered her as the devoted, but exhausted, employee who'd collapsed at the review. Or was he doubting her ability to keep up the pace on his proposal? Thankfully, she wasn't slumping and her head wasn't drooping or mouth hanging open.

"Jessica, I want you to see that these changes are incorporated in every part of the write-up," Dunmar said. "Antennas, structures, weights and measures, everywhere."

"Do I get to carry a gun?" Jessica shot back. "The guys'll respond a heck of a lot faster if I do."

Whitney looked at her wide-eyed, horrified at her brazenness, Jessica was sure.

But Whitney had the wrong take on this. After today she, Jessica, would be remembered as brazen, which was a lot better than weak or servile.

An hour later she emerged from Dunmar's office. Complaining constantly of his stuffy head and raw sore throat, he'd given her a list of areas where changes were needed. Jessica had felt like letting him know he had nothing much to gripe about, but remembered she too had once thought of a mere cold, with its small discomforts and diminished energy, as a major burden.

She began in the warren of cubicles assigned to the antenna section. First Jack Murray, the lead design engineer. Jessica knew him as a buddy whose dark eyes would sparkle when they shared a good joke. She liked the way he laughed, as though it rippled through his whole body. Tall and wiry, Jack looked a bit cramped and folded up in his little one-size-doesn't-fit-all cubicle. While she took notes he told her the changes needed in his write-up.

When she attempted to leave his office, she was so weak she could scarcely lift her leaden feet.

"You're walking like you're on the high seas," Jack said. "This is no cruise ship, in case you haven't noticed."

As Jessica started to giggle, switches flipped in her brain. Her attacks no longer started with a hazy euphoria, but were now beginning with what felt like flipping switches that preceded her falls by as much as half an hour or as little as a few seconds. She had the distinct impression that Jack's joke had just now set the switches off. Maybe her system was so overwrought that the least little thing, like giggling, could push her over the edge. She'd always gone overboard in the laughing department. Maybe she'd have to cool it in the future, try to be more serious so she wouldn't collapse. "I've been working with Jim Stone so long I'm getting a Texas swagger."

With a lot of mental effort she could sometimes delay the switch action. Concentrating, she managed to gain the few seconds she needed to back up to the cubicle wall and slither down it to a squat. It was no easy trick to slide her legs out from under herself until her back was against the wall, legs straight out on the rough industrial carpet. Jack wasn't laughing anymore. He jumped to his feet. "What's wrong?" His black, wing-tip shoes and gray flannel pant legs appeared in front of her.

"I'm having a little spell. I get these now and then."

"A spell? You mean a seizure? You're having a seizure?" His voice was urgent, almost a whisper.

His tone frightened her. "No, not a seizure." Too bad she wasn't as certain as she tried to sound. How did she know "seizure" wasn't a reasonable term for what was happening to her?

"You can't stay on the floor. I'll help you up." He leaned over and tugged at her elbow.

Floor fright again. No one could see her on the floor without going into a panic. "Just let me sit here a minute." She knew she was still too weak to get up.

"I better call the paramedics. You're having a seizure, I know it. In my high school there was a guy that had seizures." His feet headed toward his desk.

"No paramedics! I'll be okay." If the paramedics were called, Armor or someone else in management would hear about it. "I'm just having a little allergy trouble." Even if she no longer believed this, she had to say something.

Jack plunked himself in his chair. "I hope you know what you're doing."

After a few minutes of painful silence on both their parts, she felt gravity letting go its ferocious grip. When she struggled to her feet, he wouldn't look her in the eye.

Wobbling out the door, purse over one shoulder, notebook in hand, she didn't feel like Jack's joking buddy anymore. She felt isolated.

After a few hours she was exhausted from the strain of trying to control and hide her weakness from all the people she'd had to question. Whenever she'd felt switches go off in her brain, she'd had to concentrate so hard on stalling them that she was often unable to speak or write for a short time and feared it must have looked like she'd spaced out. Then, when the switches and weakness let up, she had to ask questions fast and write answers frantically, never knowing when she might be struck again. She worried rumors would spread about her after today. Would they reach Armor? Vole?

When she finally got back to her cubicle, she returned to Jim Stone's work. By leaning into a wedge formed by the back of her chair and a wall, she was able to prop herself semi-upright above the computer keyboard. At first Stone had had fits of anxiety over the impact her condition would have on her job, but after three weeks he now seemed convinced she could keep up. She didn't know where his confidence would go if she got worse.

It was six o'clock before she felt recovered enough to stand. Funny, Whitney hadn't come by yet. They usually got their sack dinners out of the refrigerator and took a break in Jessica's cubicle at six.

She headed for the main project room at an unhurried pace compatible with what she estimated to be the amount of fuel she'd been allotted tonight. At the refrigerator, she found her lunch—soft, easy to chew cottage cheese, applesauce, dinner roll and butterscotch pudding.

Sack in hand, she was trudging down a hall between cubicles when she recoiled at the sight of Kyle Bumpers lounging in Whitney's doorway. Decked out in a stylish suit with flared trousers and a jacket tucked at the waist, the man was a living satyr—a tall, muscular thirtysomething with black curly hair, a short goatee and a nearly perpetual leer. Time for Jessica Shephard to rescue damsel-in-distress Whitney.

"Hello, Kyle. Got any intel for us?"

As a marketing rep, part of Bumpers' job was to scout out the competition.

"Not a thing." Bumpers shook his head as though saddened. "Pretty dull."

"Really, Kyle. You give new meaning to the expression 'being in a rut at work,'" Jessica quipped.

He paused and, when he seemed unable to hold back a glimmer of a grin, Jessica congratulated herself for scoring a point off him.

"Been concentrating on counter-espionage lately." His grin broadened into a schmoozy smile. "I just dropped by to see what Whitney could do for me in that department."

Behind Kyle, Whitney winked. "I can't do a thing for you, Kyle."

Blocking her way into the cubicle, Bumpers pressed close to Jessica. "You're on the front lines here, you and Whitney. Anyone from our competitors approach you? Ask you out?"

She stepped back enough to get him out of her face. "No such luck."

Unlike most marketeers at Rank, Bumpers seldom traveled to prospective customers or made up advertising brochures. No one seemed to know exactly what he did. Rumor was he obtained proprietary designs and marketing plans from competitors by seducing their secretaries and finding ways to blackmail their engineers. A couple of weeks earlier he'd made the newspapers when he was found locked inside the trunk of his own car in a supermarket parking lot. The lot happened to be next door to a competitor's facility. Bumpers had claimed he'd been robbed at gunpoint, then shoved into the trunk.

Jessica, like everyone else at work, couldn't get enough of the urban legends of his lurid life. But she got enough of the snake himself in a hurry.

"See you later, babe." Bumpers let his gaze fall to Jessica's mouth where it lingered a moment before he left. She felt like washing her contaminated mouth.

Jessica plopped herself onto Whitney's only guest chair. "What have you and Mr. Pulp Fiction been up to?"

Whitney tittered. Her laughter was never boisterous. "He wanted me to go out for drinks and dinner with him at some restaurant where a lot of Aerojet people hang out. He said we'd see what loose talk we could pick up—I'd be the technical ears and he'd listen for marketing info."

"And Dave?"

"He said there was no reason to tell my husband. This would just be a company private thing between the two of us."

"I bet you're thrilled." She opened her lunch sack and took out the cottage cheese. "Whit, I couldn't believe that meeting this morning."

"I knew it." Whitney raised her hands, red nails gleaming under the overhead lights, as if in surrender. "I knew you were going to get on my case the minute I saw you sitting there."

"I felt bad for you. They wouldn't treat a man like they treated you. If I were you, I'd have said I didn't suffer through four years of engineering school so I could take meeting minutes." She didn't like being so pushy with Whitney, but Whitney needed somebody to push her.

"Well, you're not me." There was a trace of sarcasm in Whitney's voice. "We can't all be like you, Jessica."

"Be like me?" Jessica sighed. That was a good one. "Who'd want to be like me? I'm the joke that isn't funny." She told how she'd collapsed in Jack Murray's office. "I tried to get him to see the humor in it, but he got all weird."

"It's hard for people to laugh when they see you fall. It seems so cruel."

"I don't like the idea of people thinking I'm too freakish to laugh with. Next thing they won't want to work with me."

"You're not going to convince anyone by clowning around while you're on the floor."

"I have to let people know I'm still me."

"By making wisecracks about carrying guns?"

"At least I'm not passive."

"You're you and I'm me. You want to get a laugh from people and I like to please them. Everyone's not the same, Jessica, and we don't want to be. There's more than one way to skin a cat."

"Whitney!"

"Sorry. Bad choice. I didn't mean that."

"Cats should be pampered, not skinned."

Whitney smiled. "There's more than one way to pamper a cat."

"You're not abject enough. Let's hear more pathos."

A couple of passing engineers stared over the top of the cubicle at the two of them giggling away, Jessica's head sinking onto the table as though she'd had a sudden need for a daytime nap. "Whitney, I think I actually get weaker when I laugh."

"How can you tell? You're always laughing."

CHAPTER 14

Always laughing. That was a reputation Jessica doubted she'd live up to today.

Holding her umbrella at an angle against the chilly, wet wind, she hopped over puddles in the red-bricked plaza in front of the medical building. Hopping was easy in flats. Pumps, even with small heels, made walking nearly impossible when she was weak and wobbly. She'd almost quit wearing them.

Today she was going for a Tensilon test, the latest in a nerve-racking series ordered by the diligent and thorough Dr. Cowan, the neurologist she'd badgered Dr. Trumpower into letting her see. Each test had soaked up a few hours or even an entire day, which had made the struggle to keep up with her workload harder than ever. Six weeks into her illness, she was using her last day of sick leave.

So far the tests had yielded absolutely no clue as to what was wrong with her. Earlier in the week, she'd lain for most of an hour in a confining metal tube, strapped to a narrow, padded board, deafened despite ear plugs by the smash-bangs of an MRI scanner. The results had been cheering—no brain tumor, no sign of multiple sclerosis, nothing missing from her brain. By measuring the response of her muscles to painful electrical stimuli, Cowan had also ruled out a bunch of neuropathies. Blood tests eliminated periodic paralysis and antibody-positive myasthenia gravis.

Cowan had concluded she might be suffering from antibody-negative myasthenia gravis, like fifteen percent of MG patients. An uncommon type of an already rare illness, he said. He wanted her to take the Tensilon test, which often enabled a definitive diagnosis. He'd also told her of reading about a few episodic paralysis cases of unknown origin where the patient, though undiagnosed and untreated, recovered spontaneously in two months. She half believed he was trying to hold out a thin strand of hope for her to cling to.

With a lucky draw in the disease lottery she might end up with a short-term disorder, but she was increasingly certain that her symptoms fit myasthenia gravis.

She'd studied every piece of information she could get her hands on about MG. Richard had downloaded articles from PubMed and Fernando had copied others at the med school library. Since she still went to work every day, she had to squeeze reading times into non-working remnants of evenings and weekends. The medical dictionary and diagnostics book she'd loaded her credit card down with were becoming thumb-worn.

Thanks to all the reading, she now understood how muscles normally worked and how they failed with MG. Voluntary muscles are controlled by nerve impulses sent from the brain to a neuromuscular junction. The problem is a nerve fiber doesn't directly connect with a muscle—it has to send a substance called acetylcholine across the junction to receptors on the muscle. When enough acetylcholine is received, the muscle activates and a person can walk. Like she could this morning, with ease.

In an antibody-positive MG onslaught, antibodies attack the receptors and knock them out. Acetylcholine can't get across the synapse to the muscle. If enough sites are knocked out—bam, on the floor. No more walking. Maybe no more talking or swallowing or breathing.

The blood tests showed she did not have these antibodies. In antibody-negative MG, which she was suspected of having, an unknown substance attacks the receptors and causes the same MG symptoms. An antibody-positive patient is fortunate in that a simple blood test for antibodies confirms a diagnosis. With no known substance to test for, the antibody-negative diagnosis is not so simple. Myasthenia gravis was autoimmune, and so was her father's lupus. The disease fit her in every way from symptoms to science to genetics. During an attack she'd fit right into the gallery of suffering myasthenics pictured in medical journals with drooping heads, slack jaws and open mouths.

There was a good side to MG—it was usually treatable. Most patients did well on a medication called Mestinon, which, along with surgical and blood cleansing procedures, had increased the odds of survival from fifteen to eighty-five percent. Myasthenics would never be athletes or concert pianists—she was certainly glad she hadn't tried to be a pianist—but on Mestinon they could usually lead active, productive lives. They could work, drive, dress and bathe unaided. She had to try it.

She closed the umbrella and dripped through the swinging glass door into a long, poorly lit hall with many closed doors behind which she imagined interrogations of the bodies of frightened and hopeful patients were being conducted. At a bank of elevators she pushed the up button. She couldn't possibly climb the stairs to the sixth floor.

When the elevator came, she braced herself against the back wall, hoping to mitigate the impact of the acceleration. But as the elevator came to a stomach-dropping stop on six and the door opened, her brain switches got zapped so fast she hadn't an instant to stall them off. She was barely able to force herself out of the elevator and walk three wobbly thigh-weakening steps, sinking lower at each one, until she crumpled in a helpless heap. Her umbrella fell to the tile beside her, its clatter resounding in the long corridor.

Despite the noise, no one appeared—her good luck. The elevator effect, which had wiped her out every time she'd gone up one at work this week, was usually over fast unless people came and got all excited. Other people's excitement always prolonged her symptoms, possibly because she couldn't concentrate on getting her brain to switch back to normal.

She waited, motionless, stripping her mind from thought. This was what it took—turning off her mind to reset to normal. In only a minute she was able to push herself to a sitting position. Another minute and she was on her feet again, a bit shaky but nearly as strong as she'd been when she'd entered the building. She could bend over and scoop her purse and umbrella from the floor.

There had to be a clue here. Acceleration caused something very abnormal to happen to her, but she and Fernando couldn't see how either the elevator effect or the after-meal collapses fit into the acetylcholine theory.

In today's test Dr. Cowan would inject Tensilon into her arm and she would quickly, but temporarily, be freed of all her symptoms if she had MG because the Tensilon would keep the level of acetylcholine artificially high for a short time. If she didn't have MG the symptoms would not go away. At least not entirely.

At the diagnostic facility a receptionist ushered her into a brightly lit room lined with shelves stocked with bottles and vials. A white-uniformed nurse—young, with a warm, confident smile—brought in Jessica's file.

"Hi. I'm a bit nervous." Jessica felt her jaw slacken, her mouth hang open.

"Not to worry. Doctor and I will both be watching, and if there's any problem, the atropine's right here." The nurse picked up a little stoppered vial from the counter and waggled it. Her attitude seemed to say no one needed to worry about this test, it was so routine.

"Atropine?"

"In case you stop breathing. Don't worry, we hardly ever have to use it."

"Stop breathing?" No one had mentioned not breathing. What kind of deadhead wouldn't worry about not breathing? The nurse rolled a table up to Jessica, then a pole on wheels from which hung a clear plastic bag of liquid with a tube attached. Tubes and bags, morbidity and death. Was it too late to get the hell out of this place?

Her legs went weak. She plopped into a chair. "What do you mean by 'stop breathing'?"

"I shouldn't have put it that way."

"Then what did you mean?"

"I should have said in case you need a little help. I'm going to start an IV in your hand. It's only a saline solution." Before Jessica could protest that she didn't know if she wanted to go through with this, the back of her hand had been swabbed with alcohol and a needle inserted into a vein. She felt a prick, then warm liquid entering her bloodstream.

"Are you weak right now?" the nurse asked.

"A little." What if she stopped breathing during the test? Would this woman or Cowan act fast enough to save her?

"Can you do anything to bring out the symptoms?"

"Walk around, wave my arms." Maybe she didn't want to know if she had MG badly enough to take this test. Maybe she should just leave before things got really bad.

"Okay, but not too vigorous. I don't want your IV pulling out."

Jessica did stumbling, clownish aerobic dance steps around the room, barely able to raise her legs for kicks, slouching from foot to foot. "One, two, three—kick," she counted, with slow mambo arm motions like an electric fan that was failing. Soon she and the nurse were laughing so hard Jessica had to sit down.

Incredible. This was the third time this week laughing had added to her flaccidity. It was beginning to look as though in her condition she could no longer afford to laugh. One more pleasure lost.

Dr. Cowan, a shortish man whose spareness of body was evident under his white coat, bustled in with a manila folder, two small bottles of liquid and a box of vials and arranged them meticulously on the counter. Fernando had said Cowan's first-rate reputation as a researcher partly derived from his meticulousness. A doctor who would miss no detail, leave no stone unturned, might be just what she needed.

He peered at Jessica, now a sodden heap in the chair, over the top of his narrow, slitty glasses. "Still want to go through with this?"

"Of course. Don't you?" Jessica wondered if Cowan sensed she was ninety percent bluff, that a large part of her was ready to bail out of this test.

"Walk around. Let's see how you're doing."

She dragged herself to her feet and goose-stepped past him in slow motion—head drooping, arms hanging and barely swinging. "I always wanted to march in a parade."

"Clear neck and limb weakness," he said as he wrote in the folder.

"My mind's still going strong. You probably can't see that."

"Here." Cowan held out the two bottles and two empty vials to the nurse. "Would you please go out of the room and put Tensilon in one vial and saline in the other. Don't let me know which is which. We're going to do this double blind."

Giving in to the weakness in her leg and back muscles, Jessica crumpled into a chair. "You mean you think if I knew I had Tensilon, I might jump up and run around the room? Skew the test? That's a joke." Clearly this man didn't understand the limitations imposed by her world. But he was running things and there was probably no point in arguing.

The nurse brought back two identical looking vials of colorless liquid and offered them to Cowan.

He chose one. "I'm going to put this in a little at a time. As I do, tell me how you feel."

Jessica felt butterflies in her stomach and immediately lost muscle tone. Now she had something else to worry about. What if her symptoms became so strong they overpowered the Tensilon?

Cowan inserted the vial into a valve plug in the IV tube. "How's that?"

"I feel something. Hard to say what." But she was sure something fundamental was happening inside her.

Cowan took a deep breath and pushed a little more of the liquid into the IV. Jessica barely had time to think about its effect when her eyeballs began jerking and slewing every which way independently of each other. Her breathing came hard and fast. She was sucking for air.

Gripping her wrist, Cowan asked "Are you okay?"

She wanted to talk, but could only gasp. The room around her was slowly being blown to pieces, shattering into thousands of kaleidoscopic fragments.

"Are you okay?" He was shouting as though she were deaf.

She wanted to yell "Help," but couldn't. She couldn't even look at him, couldn't find the shards of him among the shining colored pieces. She couldn't gulp enough air.

Cowan yelled again. "Are you okay?"

No, she wasn't. She was dying.

"Hand me the atropine," Cowan said.

Spikes of hot air unsuccessfully tried to force their jagged way into Jessica's lungs. She felt faint. They had to hurry or she would die right in front of them.

"Help is on the way." The nurse's voice.

On the way wasn't fast enough.

"I'm going to inject the atropine." Cowan was still holding her wrist.

Jessica caught her breath in a gasp. A few of the kaleidoscope pieces began to coalesce. "No," she squeaked.

"You're coming back?"

She was still hungry for air, but her breathing was normalizing. "Tensilon?" she gasped.

"Can you walk?"

She stood and wobbled slowly across the room. She felt strange, but much better. "Gravity's almost back to normal. I feel free and light."

"You're still moving slowly," Cowan observed.

"But what an improvement!" Jessica lifted her arms. They no longer felt as if they were weighed down with lead.

The nurse gently pulled out the IV. Trailed by Cowan, Jessica walked almost normally down a long corridor, then turned and, head high, promenaded back to the examining room. "This must be what it feels like to be resurrected from the dead. How long will I feel this good?"

"I don't see huge changes in how you're walking. You were very slow before, and you're slow now."

"She doesn't have to move one foot at a time like a baby," the nurse said.

Jessica glanced furtively at Cowan. Evidently he wasn't upset by being contradicted. In fact, he seemed not to have heard his nurse at all.

Cowan observed Jessica take a few more steps into the examining room. "You still have a hitch. As if your joints have ratchets."

In control of herself, Jessica eased, rather than fell, into a chair. "I feel so much better." In a way. Behind the feeling better loomed the specter of myasthenia gravis.

Cowan stood before her, rubbing his chin. "I was reading last night. Some undiagnosed cases of short-term paralysis have shown improvement with Tensilon."

"Whatever I have, if Tensilon makes me momentarily better I should benefit from Mestinon. They both increase acetylcholine in the junction. Right?" She would count the day a success if she could get that medication.

Cowan picked up a manila folder and scribbled something on it. "Your test wasn't definitive."

No matter how exhausted or strung out she was, she always had to find the strength to plead her case with some doctor. "I'm clearly better. The Tensilon worked."

"Going from strong symptoms to no symptoms would be definitive. You're not symptom-free."

He wasn't going to take her word on her improvement even though she had firsthand knowledge and he didn't. But since she needed him, she suppressed her frustration. "Could we try a quantitatively controlled schedule—a little Mestinon this week, a little more next week and so on? If it has a bad effect on me, couldn't we see it in time to stop?"

"I'd rather you had a single-fiber EMG—single-fiber electromyogram—first. That test accesses one muscle fiber at a time and isolates the malfunctioning ones even if they're in the minority. It's much more refined than the EMG you had the other day."

One more test. Would there never be an end? Would she ever get help? "Fine. Then schedule me, please."

"I don't give those. Only Dr. Hatfield does, and he's very popular. It can take months to get on his calendar."

"Look. So far, I'm not measurable, certifiable, quantifiable. I can't help that. I need help anyway because my mouth is always hanging open, I can't hold my arm up long enough to brush my hair and I fall on the floor at work."

Cowan leaned back against a cabinet. "It's hell, I know."

She wondered if he'd admit to knowing anything he couldn't measure. "Hell is the right word." She felt like crying.

He looked at the floor in front of her feet.

"All I'm asking for is a little Mestinon—a little of my life back." She wished Cowan wouldn't sink into his chair and hold his head in his hands like that. To look at him, you'd think he was the sick one, not her.

He raised his head. "I guess I'd be willing to start you with the beginning MG dose."

"Thank you. Thank you." Jessica got up, picked up his hand and clasped it.

He pressed her hand weakly. "I hope I'm not going to be sorry I did this."

CHAPTER 15

"I'm sorry I ever did it," Jessica leaned back from her computer to rest and sobbed. "Sorry I ever signed up for this damned proposal." Any job at Rank would be less demanding and less stressful than this one.

It was two o'clock and she was working on borrowed time. Cowan had allowed her only thirty milligrams of Mestinon daily, enough so far to keep her out of the ER, but not enough to get rid of the weakness all day. Yesterday by three, she hadn't been able to hold her hands above the keyboard for more than a few minutes at a time. By tomorrow morning she was supposed to come up with interesting, compelling words about tables and tables of data on amplitude ripple, phase noise intermodulation products, and image rejection when she couldn't care less about any of it.

Although she tried to fight them back, tears welled up and trickled down her cheeks. Without the health insurance that came with her job, she would soon be broke and on Medi-Cal, which Gebauer doctors did not take. She had to keep working to pay the medical bills. If she lost her job, she didn't know what she'd do.

She sobbed, then put her hand over her mouth. Someone might hear her and come to see what was wrong. These days people were always coming to see what was wrong with her.

Sorry, sorry, sorry. She was sorry she'd ever agreed to work on this proposal.

She inhaled and exhaled, forcing out every bit of air. Enough, Jessica. Stop fretting over how much you still have to do. Take one piece of data at a time. You can handle one piece.

In a cubicle across the passageway, two engineers were arguing whether front end losses or noisy mixers were the worst contributors to channel noise and therefore most urgently in need of redesign. Behind her, she could hear Tom Quinn telling his wife over the phone "No" she could not have her charge card back for even a day because she just couldn't control her spending. Somewhere a desk drawer scraped open and a swivel chair squeaked.

Community life in cubicle land.

It took a while, but once she managed to concentrate, she waded through the receiver section, focusing on phase and amplitude ripples. They caused telephone channel distortions and had to be kept small. She could deal with that. She began writing how Rank would reduce distortions by tightly controlling satellite receiver quality.

Whitney appeared in the doorway. "How are you doing?" She usually checked on Jessica three or four times a day.

"So far so good." Jessica glanced at her watch—three thirty.

"That's great."

"These days a great day is when I get paralyzed later rather than earlier."

Whitney grimaced. "Myasthenia gravis sucks."

"Yeah, Whit." Jessica managed a grin. She loved Whitney. Unlike a lot of others, Whitney understood that meeting MG head on with sarcasm and humor made the disease feel a lot less frightening than when people pussyfooted, used euphemisms or tried to avoid discussing her problems altogether.

After Whitney left, Jessica dove back into receiver performance and by five o'clock had completed the write-up. She walked over to the war room, where she tacked her work up without any problems, bending for the low pages and stretching for the high ones.

It was time for the decision about driving home. Depending on how bad off she was, she either drove on the freeway or slowly on surface streets or, if she had to, got a ride with someone. With the flipping of switches in her brain as a guide to warn her, she was convinced she could make good, safe driving decisions for every situation.

Tonight, with her brain completely free of funny signals, she drove home on the freeway, parked in her new handicapped space in the underground garage at the base of the stairs, and easily climbed the two flights to her apartment.

Fernando was there, preparing dinner. He gave her a warm embrace and a gentle kiss on the mouth, so warm and tingly she wanted more. But she held off. She never felt passionate after the paralysis hit and didn't want to start anything she might not want to finish.

Elsa rubbed against her legs, meowing and purring for attention. Fernando had set a green salad on the table and was chopping tomatoes, basil and mushrooms to sauté and spread over the pasta he was about to cook. Her home, her Fernando, her Elsa, her piano.

She sat down on the bench and riffled through a pile of music stacked on the piano. A happy, frilly Mozart sonata—that's what she wanted. She warmed up with a few scales, then began playing. Her fingers were strong and limber. The upper register of the piano responded beautifully, producing lacy passages of clean, sparkling high notes. She hadn't played so well since she'd gotten sick.

After a while, Fernando called that dinner was ready. She sat upright at the table, an unusual achievement for her these days, and left her little lacquered, Peruvian handcrafted pill box closed. She had the feeling she didn't need any medication right now.

"Time for your Mestinon," Fernando observed. "It's been helping a lot. Pretty much confirms an MG diagnosis."

"I don't think I need it tonight."

"You don't need it? Has MG destroyed your brain?"

Jessica twisted her napkin. So far her brain switch theory had been a hard sell when it came to Fernando. "Like I told you, as much as half an hour before I'm going to get weak, unless it's something quick like an elevator, I always feel my brain circuits flipping around. Always. Never any different. Right now I don't feel anything."

Fernando gave her a skeptical squint. "I'd feel better if you took your Mestinon. I have study group at school tonight."

"How about if I take it later if I need to. Why worry about a short medication gap since I'll just be sitting in the apartment?"

Fernando picked up their dishes and carried them to the sink. When he came back, he leaned over and kissed her cheek. "Just be careful."

"Good thing you warned me. I might have tried vine swinging over the canyon if you hadn't."

After he left, Jessica thought momentarily of getting out the articles on MG she'd photocopied. Instead she cleaned the bathroom for the first time in weeks. At nine, she watched her favorite science fiction show, *X-Files*. Then she undressed like a normal person, brushed her hair like a normal person, climbed into bed and snuggled under the covers.

In the morning, she woke up happy and rolled over to look at Fernando. He was awake. When his eyes met hers, she smiled. This was going to be a good day and she wanted to share it.

"You aren't going to skip your medication again this morning, are you?" he said.

She was.

She got out of bed, pulled her clothes out of the closet and drawers and headed for the bathroom.

By the time she got to work at seven thirty she was in a good mood again because she felt so normal. Some people were already on the job when she walked past their cubicles.

Right away she discovered her printer was out of toner. Now she'd have to fill out a requisition form, chase down her boss in the executive building, get him to sign it, then pick up a cartridge from central stores. Damn! What a stupid waste of time. She called Fred Vole's office and verified he was in.

Heading out the door, she started across the parking lot. These days she usually drove to other buildings because if she got weak she could drive slowly back over the lightly traveled roads between Rank's buildings even when she couldn't walk the distance.

Today she felt strong and vigorous. The April morning had a green freshness even the asphalt roads and cement sidewalks couldn't entirely hide.

Forget the car.

She hurried along a walkway edged by oleander bushes on one side and an antenna test range with instruments and antennas on high wooden towers on the other. She loped down a sidewalk to the executive building snuggled against a steep sand and stone escarpment believed to be an earthquake fault line that snaked along the San Gabriel Mountains.

A uniformed guard admitted her to the glassed-in lobby, beyond which wound labyrinths of narrow, white-walled, indoor-outdoor carpeted corridors. Three-foot high, glossy color photos of satellites showcased Rank's commercial success.

Once in Vole's lavishly furnished, windowed office, she explained that she needed a new toner cartridge for her printer as soon as possible. Vole pressed his fingers together as if pondering a momentous decision before signing the form with a bright-eyed smile, as Jessica thought he would. She knew his fondness for situations, preferably inconsequential, where it was clear what he should do, and his distaste for those where he risked making a mistake.

Then he cleared his throat. "I've been looking over the staff's vacation and sick leave. You've used up all you have for the year and it's only April." His gaze was directed toward the wall behind her.

Jessica felt a chill. For weeks she'd been expecting this, but today she'd been blindsided. "I've been having a little health problem."

"My secretary tells me she's heard you've been very sick."

Jessica felt her jaw tighten and her face grow hot. "I'm not sick now."

"You've been out a lot."

"I think I've got things under control. And I'm keeping up with my work." She pasted a big smile on her face—see how great I feel—and stifled the urge to hit him with a smart remark.

He glanced down and fingered the edge of his desk blotter. "For your sake, I hope so. If I have to pull you off the proposal, I don't know where I could use you."

"Thanks for your concern." Jessica took the form and left.

By midmorning, she'd installed the cartridge and was back writing.

At noon she hiked to the cafeteria with Whitney. At seven o'clock, she walked to her car, scarcely able to believe she was still mobile. And no Mestinon all day.

She had to think of what to say to Fernando, while being careful not to get him prematurely excited over how well she was doing. But she was beginning to hope.

Driving down the freeway, she went over Cowan's words in her mind. He'd read of a few undiagnosed, clinically observed, cases of episodic paralysis that simply went away after a couple of months. Why shouldn't she be lucky enough to be one of those? She gripped the steering wheel and laughed out loud.

At her apartment she opened the front windows so she could hear Fernando's cats, who always meowed a screechy duet when he came home.

Right now she'd call her mother.

As soon as Mom said hello, Jessica blurted out, "I'm beginning to think I might be well." She jumped up and down—ka-boing, ka-boing—like she had when she was a child with good news she couldn't wait to tell.

"Jessica!" Mom's voice burst through the phone.

"I've had no weakness all today or yesterday. And no Mestinon." Ka-boing, ka-boing.

"I'm stunned."

"Remember me telling you about those two-month cases? I think I'm one of them."

"Why couldn't you be? Wait 'til I tell Richard."

She'd known Mom would be thrilled. "I hope there's still snow somewhere near Los Angeles. I want to go skiing."

Mom laughed. "That's my Jessica." She paused. "It's a bit soon to think of skiing. You ought to work up to it slowly."

Since Mom couldn't see her, Jessica rolled her eyes.

An hour later, Jessica heard a door open downstairs, followed by a chorus of meows.

She dashed outside, bounded down the stone steps and ran the last few feet to Fernando's door. It was ajar, yielding to a push. She stepped inside, ready to throw herself at him. "I feel great!"

He eyed her thoughtfully. "Describe great."

She'd wanted to run into Fernando's arms, not be interrogated by Dr. Munoz. She reminded him how strong she'd been at work and at dinner yesterday and told him all she'd done today without a trace of weakness.

"And no Mestinon," she finished.

"Walk around the room."

She complied as he watched closely.

"Now faster."

She trotted and flapped her arms like a hummingbird's wings. "Isn't this great?"

He nodded. "A big improvement. No drooping. Good joint articulation."

His clinical demeanor was getting on her nerves. "Aren't you happy for me, Fernando?"

"Of course."

She trotted up to him and stopped. "It'll be so much better for both of us. We can go for long walks. We can go skiing. You won't have to do everything for me."

He looked down at her, dark eyes full of tenderness. "I like taking care of you."

She considered adding that she'd once again be more energetic in other ways. But he seemed a lot more compassionate than passionate.

After an eggplant dinner at Mario's, just before they started for home, he asked her again how she felt. Tugging on his hand, she led him across Orange Grove Avenue and down the street to their apartment building. She dragged him on, racing across the lighted patio and up the steps to her place. After unlocking the door, she turned on the desk lamp just inside the living room and reached out with her arms.

"Are you okay?" he asked. "That was a long run."

She embraced him and kissed him urgently until his mouth responded to hers. She let her fingers wander over his body until she felt his knees go weak.

Grabbing his hand, she pulled him past the couch and looming piano into the hallway and on to her bedroom. When she shut the door behind her, she heard Elsa meow plaintively from the living room. Elsa could stay where she was.

The next morning, after Fernando left to play tennis for the first time in a couple of months, Jessica decided to skip going in to work just this one Saturday. She needed to erase unhappy memories of struggling with her job while she was weak, get a clean start on Monday. And Monday she'd call Dr. Cowan's office to cancel her next appointment. No more visits to Trumpower, either. No more wheedling him for referrals.

She went out on the balcony where Elsa and the tom, now named Ishmael, lay basking in the sunshine. After it had shredded a bed pillow and refused to use the litter box, Fernando had been forced to let the old reprobate run free. To their surprise it hung around on Jessica's balcony most of the time. She had banished it from inside her apartment.

For a while she sat on the balcony, leaning her arms on the wrought-iron railing, reveling in the chaos below. Nothing in the canyon grew in any pattern or order. A eucalyptus tree rose next to a live oak, both towering above the balcony. Swordlike green spikes of yucca trees slashed their way across and up the canyon. Leaning over the balcony railing, she could see the top of an orange tree clustered with ripe fruit. Lavender-flowered vines climbed on any tree they found. Bushes and plants of all sizes, especially pink geraniums, covered the canyon floor and ran up its sides. Possums, raccoons and owls were sleeping down there somewhere, resting up for a night of foraging and hunting. A hawk soared overhead. Jessica stood, raised her arms and imagined herself floating over the canyon.

Elsa meowed at the screen door. Jessica let the cat in to sleep in the warm sun on top of the desk in the bedroom. With her foot she blocked Ishmael from following.

She decided to give the balcony a much needed cleaning. Using a rag and a scrub bucket full of warm soapy water she washed the chairs, the little glass-topped table and the railing, with Ishmael hissing and slinking away from the bucket each time she approached. She couldn't resist sprinkling him with water now and then, sending him scuttling under a chair.

The trumpet flower vine and the two jasmines in pots needed work. She pulled off dead leaves, then trimmed and watered them. To finish the job, she swept the balcony floor, lugged out another bucket of soapy water and a scrub brush, got on her hands and knees and scrubbed. She was beginning to tire, but her muscles felt alive, wonderfully responsive, probably because she'd defied Fernando and pushed herself into action whenever she could.

This was an afternoon's work to be proud of. People who'd never been disabled probably couldn't appreciate the pleasure of being able to clean their own balcony.

The next morning she awoke to the sun glowing through the peach-colored drapes behind the desktop picture of her with friends hiking in the Sierras. She could think of going there again. Maybe this summer when the proposal was finished.

After Fernando returned from eight o'clock Mass, they went outside onto the sparkling clean balcony, which Jessica made sure he admired, to read the Sunday paper and munch on bagels. Elsa crouched on part of Jessica's paper, while Ishmael lay stretched across Fernando's foot, his yellow eyes following Jessica's every movement. She reached over and stroked his fur. Not even he could spoil the happiness she felt.

"Fernando, it's only April. There's still snow in the Rockies. Why don't we go skiing?" She'd find some way to explain an absence from work. Or Rank could fire her. What did she care? Plenty of places would be glad to hire her and she'd be free of Armor and his threats.

"We'll see."

Fernando's cautiousness could be exasperating, but she had plenty of time to work on him.

When they'd finished the bagels, Jessica picked up the plates and started inside. Ishmael darted through the door as she slid it open, bumping into her. She faltered, reached the kitchen entrance, then pitched forward on her hands and knees. Dishes went flying, shattering on the linoleum floor.

Fernando stuck his head in the door. "What happened? Are you all right?"

"That damned Ishmael. He ran into me." She didn't like the way the strength was leaving her arms.

Fernando took her hand and tried to help her up, but couldn't. He had to drag her across the floor, hands clasped under her ribs, all the way to the couch.

"That damned cat has it in for me." She looked to him to confirm that her fall was Ishmael's fault.

Fernando said nothing. His expression was that of a man God had deserted.

She lay on the couch and shut her eyes as fear crept up her hands and arms, feet and legs. Don't panic. Meditate. Mind over matter. Mind over brain signals. When she opened her eyes a few minutes later, Fernando, elbows on knees, was sitting on the piano bench, studying her.

She winked at him. "Bet you thought I was having one of those attacks again. Silly you." She sat straight up, swung her feet to the floor, and stood.

Fernando put his arms around her and held her for a long time.

"Maybe it's a good thing I fell," Jessica said, clutching him tightly. "Reminds me not to take my health for granted like I used to."

After sweeping up the broken crockery, they went out on the balcony and resumed reading the paper. In the early afternoon, they decided to go to a movie starring that team of cute old reprobates, Jack Lemmon and Walter Matthau. She felt like seeing a corny, warm-hearted comedy.

But when they were standing in line in front of the theater at the pe-destrians-only outdoor mall, switches began flip-flopping in her brain. Trying to stall them off, she grabbed Fernando's arm and mumbled "Help."

He maneuvered her to a concrete bench, where she sank into a help-less heap. She couldn't bear to think about anything. The air chilled her as the sun set, causing her to shiver. It was illegal to drive a car onto the mall and she couldn't walk to the parking garage.

Fernando called over a policeman on foot patrol and explained their predicament. The officer stayed with Jessica while Fernando went for the car.

"Bet you've taken in drunks that looked better than me," she said.

"You'll be okay once you get home, miss." His voice was gentle, his face full of concern.

She didn't want his concern. "Aren't you going to search me? I could be carrying a concealed Uzi," she said in what she hoped was a teasing way.

"I'm sure I don't have to. You look like a nice lady."

He didn't understand. She needed him to help her laugh.

When Fernando drove to the curb a half block away, he honked. The officer went over and motioned him onto the mall, then helped Jessica into the passenger seat. On the way home, she flopped her head back on the headrest and watched the cars and trucks rush by. She could throw herself out the car door and into the freeway traffic. What a finale that would be to this whole stupid melodrama.

CHAPTER 16

When she awoke next morning, Fernando, swaddled in his white bathrobe, was perched beside her on the bed tugging at her hand. "Come on, Jessica, get up."

Rising up on her elbows, she squinted at the clock on top of her dresser beside the Sierra hiking picture and burst into tears.

Fernando picked up a pill and a cup of water from the nightstand. "Time for your Mestinon." He thrust the pill close to her face.

"I can't." There was no way she could swallow that thing while she was crying.

"You've got to. You should never have gone off it."

"I thought I was well again," she sobbed.

"Here." He lifted her hand and put the pill in it. "This will help." His voice was strong and commanding, not shaky like hers.

It was too much trouble to resist. She forced down the pill and a sip of water.

"Now let's get you dressed. You have an eight thirty appointment with Trumpower."

She remembered thinking last night about throwing herself out of the car onto the freeway. She should have done it.

"Come on. Let's get ready."

She pulled away and turned her back to him. She would like to just lie here until she died. The hope of being well had been nothing but a cruel hoax.

"Please don't turn away from me." He was pleading.

"Don't you understand? I'm no good for you. Or myself. I can't even do my damned job."

"You are good for me." He stood and tugged on her hand. "Shower time. Vamanos."

She didn't have the will to argue. On the way to the shower she stopped, snatched up the hiking picture and slammed it into the back of a desk drawer.

In the bathroom, Fernando turned on the faucets, adjusting them until he was satisfied with the temperature. "Look, I bought this so you won't slip and fall if you get weak." He laid a white rubber mat on the bottom of the stall. "Now get undressed."

She pulled the nightgown over her head and stepped inside onto the mat. A mat for her, who'd climbed mountains. She loathed the damn thing.

After showering, she scooped up a dirty pair of jeans from the floor and was putting them on when Fernando came into the bedroom. "You don't want to wear those."

"Yes, I do." She pulled the top of the jeans to her waist.

"You'll want to go to work after your appointment, won't you?" His voice sounded tight with irritation. She couldn't blame him for being disgusted with her.

"I told you I can't handle my job anymore. If I have to go on welfare, it might as well be now." She knew this was over the top. She should probably shut her mouth until she wasn't so depressed. But that time might never come.

"Welfare! What are you talking about? You've only been sick two months and you don't even know what's wrong."

She flopped back onto the bed. Everything was wrong.

Mouth and eyes set grimly, Fernando grabbed the cuffs of her jeans and dragged them off. "How about this?" He picked out a two-piece, fawn-colored, soft wool suit on a hanger from her closet and held it in front of her. "I've always liked this one."

She rolled over onto her stomach so she didn't have to·look at him. "I don't want to get dressed again. Ever."

He laid his hand on her shoulder. "You have to get ready." His voice was soft, pleading. Why couldn't he just leave her alone.

"You took off my jeans."

"You don't want to wear this outfit?"

"What?" She rolled onto her back again.

He waved the suit in front of her face.

"I don't need it anymore."

Fernando ran his hand over the soft skirt. "Then can I give this to my sister? With a few alterations, it'll fit her perfectly. She'll come visit you in it."

Jessica propped herself up on her elbow. "My suit?"

"Sure. You'll be sitting here in your dirty jeans, and she'll be wearing this pretty suit."

Let Fernando's sister, dressed in that suit, watch her sitting here in the dark, drinking beer, in dirty jeans? "No way. Leave my clothes alone."

"What do you care?"

Jessica snatched at the suit. "I'll need a slip and a blouse."

When they arrived at Trumpower's office, she was already wishing she hadn't come. He was just one more thing that had failed her.

Plus she was in such a foul mood she couldn't trust herself to be minimally polite.

Fernando introduced himself as they sat down.

"Good morning. You're my first patient today." Trumpower's voice was cheery, but he sank down in his seat and squinted at her.

Just what she needed—a doctor who dreaded seeing her. "I bet you wish you were starting out with some sophomore with a cold or a jock with a sprained thumb. But you're stuck with me." She heard her own voice, strangely loud and insistent.

"She had a bad day yesterday," Fernando said.

"Don't explain me to other people like I'm a child," Jessica snapped. And now she was being nasty to Fernando when what she really wanted to do was cry.

Trumpower leaned forward. "I'm trying to help you, believe me."

Jessica believed he meant it, but he wasn't and couldn't. No one could. "Pretty soon I'll be on welfare and Medi-Cal. Then you won't have to see me anymore."

Fernando waved his hand as if to erase a blackboard. "Please, let's do something constructive. Dr. Cowan recommended that Jessica see Dr. Henry Hatfield. He's the only one here at Gebauer who can give her a single-fiber EMG to determine whether she has myasthenia gravis."

Trumpower studied the top of his desk and fidgeted with a pen. "I know Hatfield by reputation. I suppose I can make the referral." He made out a slip for Jessica to see Hatfield with copies for himself,

Cowan, the insurance company, the Gebauer central files and the head of neurology.

All these people getting her personal, private information and not one of them willing or able to do a thing to help her. Their uselessness was probably in direct proportion to the amount of paper they accumulated.

"One more thing, please." Fernando raised a hand. "Jessica needs a wheelchair."

Trumpower looked at her. "You're walking just fine."

"Most days she has several hours of severe disability." Fernando's voice was calm and reasonable, but Jessica could see the muscles in his neck and jaw tighten. Too bad he cared for her when she was such a fucking waste of his time.

"You see, in order to write a prescription for a wheelchair, I have to justify it as a medical necessity." Trumpower was making the steeple with his fingers again and peering over them at Fernando.

"Probably the only way to prove it's a medical necessity is posthumously." Jessica found it difficult to tone down the sneer that had crept into her voice.

Trumpower lowered the steeple a little. "What do you mean?"

"After I'm run over by a car when I fall in a crosswalk I could easily have been wheeled across." She pictured herself bloody and mashed.

Abandoning the steeple, Trumpower reached for the prescription pad.

Jessica didn't feel much better. Picturing herself in a wheelchair was almost as awful as picturing herself mashed and bloody.

After Fernando drove Jessica home, he brought up a box from his apartment. "I got you a present three weeks ago," he announced. "When you seemed better I put it away for a special occasion."

How nice. Something to cheer her up. She'd begun to fear she'd never enjoy anything again.

"Tada!" He pulled out a thirty-inch high gray object and placed it on top of the piano. "Beethoven! After he became deaf, he didn't let it get him down, he kept on writing great music. What an inspiration!"

Scowl lines were etched between the plaster bust's ferocious eyes, its eyebrows were arched.

Jessica could easily believe Fernando had brought her the hateful head because it expressed his repressed, but true, feelings toward her.

"He doesn't like me. And neither do you."

"Don't be silly." Fernando settled her on the living room couch, facing Beethoven. "He's here to give you courage and so am I." After admonishing her to get a good rest, he went off to school.

Jessica tried to read a magazine, but Beethoven kept staring at her. She got up and turned him around, but his hunched shoulders sent an accusing message. She put him under the piano, but he peered at her from beneath it. Finally, she put a paper bag over his head.

Part of her knew her battle with Beethoven had a funny side. But depression was depriving her of the laugh she should be having.

Fuck depression.

She had to get out of the apartment. She picked up her purse and headed for the garage. Where should she go? It didn't make any sense to go to work in her condition, but that made it perfect. A perfectly senseless act to fit with the rest of her perfectly senseless life.

CHAPTER 17

The minute she walked into the proposal area, she heard Armor's loud bearish growl from the war room. Thank heavens the door was closed. She didn't want a confrontation with him. He always had to win, and she was in no mood for more losing.

The uproar subsided as she sidled past the room. Then the door was yanked open. Armor stood gripping the knob. "You're finished here!" he bellowed.

She fled to a nearby drawing board, then heard his voice again. "You promised me thirty per cent efficiency and you didn't deliver by half."

Was he talking to her? Her heart was thumping.

A man came stomping out, head down, hair hanging over his eyes. He was a lab engineer working on some design; she couldn't remember what.

"Idiots! I ask them for competent engineers and they send me idiots!" Armor shrieked. He punched the door and it banged against the wall with a loud crack. "I can't count on anyone around here."

The woebegone man scuttled out of the proposal area without looking back.

Jessica froze, staring at the shuddering door.

"I'm not normally like this." Lunatic Larry was looking right at her, nostrils flaring. "Moron engineers do this to me. They drive me crazy."

"Don't take it out on me," she squeaked. "I have enough trouble."

Armor gave her a puzzled look, as if he were having a dream and didn't know why she was in it. He backed into the war room and pulled the door shut.

Jessica looked around for a place to sit down and stop her trembling, but the only seats nearby were occupied.

Don Skipper, a white-haired, leather-skinned man she'd never seen anywhere except behind his drawing board, winked. "I'd like to get a grenade and roll it into that room."

For support, she propped an elbow on his board. "I guess that's the end of me on his project."

"Naw," Skipper said. "He's in another zone. An hour from now, he won't remember what he said, let alone what you said."

She shrugged. "Not that it would matter—whether I'm out of here today, tomorrow, what's the difference."

Skipper appeared to ignore her remark and started explaining the commotion. "I heard the transmitters in the satellite were only fifty percent as efficient as the proposal design called for. That's what he's in a snit about."

What did she care?

He went on. The transmitter problem was huge. The whole system was in trouble and it was less than two months before the proposal was due. Armor was demanding major redesigns.

Blah, blah, blah. So Armor was having another lunatic fit. What else was new?

"Armor's leading the trade-off effort himself." Skipper leaned toward her and lowered his voice in a confidential manner. "If you want to call it that. In the morning he screams 'Lower orbit,' in the afternoon, 'Bigger antennas.' Everyone's lying low until he tells us what the answer is."

"Terrific. We're stuck with the worst project in Rank." Her whole life lately consisted of being stuck with one thing after another she didn't want.

Skipper got down off his stool, taking a cane from where it leaned against the drawing board. "My eyes need a rest. Want a cup of coffee?"

Lacking the strength of will to resist, she followed him to the coffee urn near the secretary's desk. Watching his slow uneven progress, she remembered the description of her mother's grandfather. When he was eight, he'd tried to vault an iron fence, but had fallen with his leg impaled on a metal spike. It hadn't healed right. By the time he was grown, the injured leg was several inches shorter than the other so that for the rest of his life he had to use a cane for support. Mom had described how his canes were varnished hickory with carved silver handles. He had a habit, when approaching people, of poking the cane aggressively out in front of himself. It now amazed Jessica that he could behave aggressively when he had such a depressing lifelong disability.

She pushed down on the spigot and filled a Styrofoam cup. Preferring the taste and sensations of fruit juice or green tea, she usually stayed away from coffee. But what the hell. She'd have coffee. It was all she deserved.

"Need any help?" she asked, seeing Skipper balancing himself on the cane with one hand, while trying to press the spigot and hold the cup with the other.

"With what?"

"I just thought maybe—" She let her glance rest on the cane.

"I can manage just about anything. I do just fine."

"Don't you get tired of the hassle?"

"Don't think about it much anymore." He peered at her over his glasses. "I hear you've been having troubles too."

She didn't really want to talk about her troubles. "Nothing getting out of this place wouldn't cure."

"Got a better alternative?" His blue eyes were riveted on her, a worried, paternal look on his face.

"Go on welfare. Sit home all day in my wheelchair watching soaps." He could stifle his worrying. After all these years without a father, she didn't need one now.

Skipper snorted.

Jessica took the cup back to her cubicle. If she were her normal go-getter self, she'd dash out and find what she could do to help in the crisis. But she decided to sit at her desk and wait. Trouble would find her soon enough.

She took a tentative sip of coffee and stared at the rows and columns on her time card. No more sick leave or vacation left. Everything she'd once counted on was being stolen from her—her health, her work, her ability to make a living. Her very independence. It wouldn't be long before her life became as pathetic as her father's had been.

And while she was mired in this funk, she could worry about her mother too. Whether she wanted Mom to be burdened with her troubles or not, she knew Mom would take on as many of them as she could.

Or even more than she could. This illness could destroy them both.

In midafternoon Armor called an all hands meeting in the conference room. Jessica positioned herself in the last row on the end so she could sneak out the door if she needed to.

"You've all heard about our problem," Armor began. "The transmitter people have let me down. Because of their failure, we're going to have to change the design. Big time." Hair disheveled, he paced up and down, waiting for the room to fill. He looked as if he was hyperventilating.

He outlined the alternatives—higher transmitter power, more satellites in lower orbits, bigger ground and spacecraft antennas. In the end, he declared there was only way to go and laid out his decision to rework the transmitter and spacecraft antenna designs.

"Time is short. We've got to start redesigning, rewriting, recosting, rescheduling today." Armor jabbed an index finger at the audience. "We can do this. I know we can."

She wasn't involved with the power sections, but the antenna managers were bound to want new write-ups from her. She should have stayed home.

"We can do this without killing ourselves," Armor shouted.

Jessica could feel it coming—another dumb-ass slogan.

"Work smarter, not harder." Armor's glowing eyes spoke for him—he had inspired the troops and now the seemingly difficult would miraculously become easy.

Switches began flipping in Jessica's brain. Armor's mania was about to drive her into collapse.

Not wanting to fall in front of him and everyone else, she stood and shuffled through the double doors at a pace she thought she could sustain. Past the entrance to the coffee room. Out into the hall. But she'd guessed wrong. Her legs gave way and she sagged, then sprawled, the side of her face skidding along the gritty floor.

Behind her, double doors opened with a bang. She cringed, dreading the humiliation of being seen on the floor, then kicked off the job.

Heavy footsteps hurried out and clomped past. A little way down the hall, the feet stopped, then returned. Someone was standing over her in polished cordovan loafers. She could smell the expensive leather.

"What's the matter with you?" It was Armor, shouting. "What's going on?"

"I'll be okay in a minute." She'd get off this floor if it was the last thing she ever did.

People came pouring out of the conference room.

"Over here," Armor barked.

Jessica saw two more pairs of shoes.

"I don't have time for this. Take care of it," Armor ordered. "Get hold of Health and Safety. Call 911 if you have to."

She clenched her fists. That's what she was to him—a pile of "it" on the floor. She tried to roll over so he'd have to look her in the face. No luck, too weak.

"That's Jessica Shephard," a man, whose deep voice she didn't recognize, said. "She gets these spells all the time."

Armor grunted a noise that sounded like a rooting pig. "Just what I need. One more useless person on this job."

A few weeks ago he'd applauded her devotion to his project and now she was useless. "I'll be all right in a minute." She tried to lift her face from the floor so she could speak better, but was too weak.

"Get her off the floor," Armor said. "Find out what's going on. Who's her supervisor? I can't have anyone on this proposal who can't pull their own weight."

There it was—the end of her job.

Downsized.

Downloaded.

Dumped.

Jessica watched as Armor's shoes receded, then disappeared. She felt a hand gripping under each arm as two men lifted and dragged her. She recognized the man with the deep voice as one of Armor's toadies, a lean and hungry looking fellow who wore his sandy hair in the same loose and frenzied disarray as Armor's. He did everything like Armor, including rave and rant. Armor loved it. The other was a pink-faced pricer in a fancy three-piece suit he probably couldn't afford. Another toady, she'd bet. One of the worst things about being so helpless was that people you hated could drag you anywhere they wanted.

They propped her in a chair and she rested her head against its back, trying to suppress her trembling. No telling what these trogs planned to do with her. "Looks like I overdid the aerobics this morning. You know what they say—no pain, no gain. Take a lesson from me—don't listen to them."

The Armor imitator stuck his bug-eyed face within six inches of hers. "Who do you report to?"

"Look, I'll be okay if you just leave me alone."

He stood up, the bottom of his pointed chin the only part of his face visible to her. "She's not cooperating."

"I think we should take her to Health and Safety." Mister pink-face this time. "They'll know what to do with her."

Health and Safety, where such fates as long-term medical leave and unpaid leaves of absence lurked! Willing strength, she managed to stand up. Then, concentrating so hard she felt her face and brain go hot, she leaned on a wall and edged along it toward the art room several feet away. When she reached the door, she pushed it open, then turned to face her tormentors trailing behind.

"See what a fuss you made over nothing. Get her supervisor! Call Health and Safety! I told you I'd be fine in a minute." She staggered inside, let the door close, and ran, even though she knew she wouldn't get far this way. Sure enough, at Joe DiCarlo's work station her thigh and calf muscles buckled. Using a chair to ease her fall, she crumpled to the floor behind the work station.

The art room door creaked open. "No one here. She's gone." She heard a deep voice. "God! She's fast. Maybe she wasn't kidding about the aerobics." To Jessica's amusement, he sounded impressed.

The door closed.

She lay on the dirty carpet, curled up in a fetal position, breathing in the smelly acetone and other odors, conjuring up Beethoven lying here beside her, scowl lines between his ferocious eyes. Now she understood him. Life had dealt her and Beethoven the same kind of ironic blow. He was a musician who'd gone deaf and she was a comic too depressed to laugh.

CHAPTER 18

Jessica was becoming increasingly annoyed by Fernando. He could drive a person crazy. He didn't understand anything, including that she was being nasty so she could repel everyone from the useless piece of garbage she'd become. Today, to get away from him, she was almost glad to be keeping her appointment with Hatfield.

Down the hall leading from the waiting room which she'd dragged herself into, the recorded racket of a bass drum, two pianos, a chorus and a symphony orchestra blasted away, making her want to scream.

Carl Orff's *Carmina Burana*. The chorus shrieked and moaned about Fate working against them, destroying their lives. It was as though Orff had extracted his music and words from somewhere inside her. Mom and Richard kept insisting she had to fight back the same way she had before the remission and relapse. Friends were always chirping that a positive attitude could work miracles. Fernando tried to distract her with funny movies and New Age music. None of them understood what it was like when Fate dealt you a heavy blow. But Orff did.

Accompanied by clashing cymbals, the chorus howled as if in pain that Fate had set out to demean them.

She knew what it was to be demeaned—to crash flat on the floor at someone's feet. Jessica clenched her fists, trying to put a face to Fate so she could hate it more. Her father came to mind—he'd bequeathed her his bad genes, then deserted her. But it made no sense to believe he'd wanted lupus or to die young. In fact, he'd loved her. Shocking what love could pass on to a person.

She tried picturing Armor's face—he'd be easy to hate if he weren't such a caricature of a fanatic.

She thought of God. But picking out one in twenty thousand to afflict with myasthenia gravis was too vicious and calculating for any God she wanted to contemplate.

More shrieking about how all effort to achieve well-being is futile.

"Open the gates. Let the first one in," a man's voice bellowed over the music. A nurse in a crisp, white uniform, her dark curls visible under a starched cap, appeared. "Doctor will see you now."

Jessica made her way across the room, suffering only a moderate fuel limitation. It was still early—eight thirty.

"That music…" Jessica began, following the nurse down the hall.

"We call it Hatfield music. He likes it loud, but I'll turn it down a bit now that the office is open." She came to an open doorway and waved Jessica in.

"Clara says it'll drive patients away." A tall, big-boned man, probably in his late fifties, with a hank of unruly gray-blond hair falling onto his forehead, stood up from a desk chair. "But it hasn't succeeded yet. You keep coming."

Jessica felt the tightness in her chest ease its grip. "Orff knew what he was talking about."

Hatfield took a moment to consider the lyrics. "Fate can be a monster. Right. He did." He looked at her with eyes full of empathy.

Jessica wanted to hug him. By now she knew better than to hope each new doctor was going to find a cure for her, but she sensed Hatfield at least empathized.

"And just consider, my dear." He waved her into an armchair beside his desk before he sat down. "That same Fate has brought us together today."

Jessica sank into the chair, which was more comfortable than the lumpy chair in Trumpower's office or the straight-backed ones in Cowan's and McDonald's. "Let's hope Fate is on our side this time."

Across from her an oscilloscope and a pile of cables sat on a wheeled cart, beside it was a raised, padded bed covered with a paper sheet. That must be where Hatfield administered the single-fiber tests. On the wall above the bed one glassed-in case displayed a bow and two crossed arrows and another held an array of forty or fifty arrowheads. It looked as if he spent vacations in the wilderness, living and hunting more like a Neanderthal than a highly skilled, high-priced MD.

Hatfield observed her with a penetrating gaze he might use to seek out prey, sending her mind into confusion. "What did I do to deserve this?" she asked, her facial muscles becoming flaccid, jaw beginning to droop.

Hatfield scowled, the penetrating eyes almost disappearing under fleshy eyelids "We don't get what we deserve or deserve what we get. Causes have consequences. That's it. That sums it up." He snapped his mouth shut as though he'd delivered an incontrovertible pronouncement.

Then Hatfield didn't really believe Fate meddled in people's lives. She wanted to believe in Fate, a concrete Fate she could come to terms with, not some random uncontrollable force.

Still, if you substituted the word God for Fate, he thought as she did, that there was no evidence that God directed events in individual lives. God was definitely more of a generalist, more interested in the broad picture.

"What's the cause and consequence of this?" she managed to say with her head now drooping forward.

"Right. Time to quit babbling philosophy and see if we can figure you out." He opened a folder more than an inch thick with her name on it.

Over the next half hour they went over the situation at work, the cat bite, the tetanus shot, the tingling, the euphoria, the episodes of paralysis with their variations in length and depth of weakness, the allergy theory, all the negative test results, and the effect Mestinon had on her. The whole sickness-focused mess that had become her life. His interest in every detail showed he was attentive and involved, but she'd had reason for optimism in each of the doctors she'd already seen.

"With the possible exception of the Tensilon test, all this says you're a hell of a good specimen. In perfect shape." Hatfield shut the folder.

"Half the time I can't walk. My mouth hangs open like I'm an idiot. I can't hold my arms up to brush my teeth or hair. Sometimes I have a hard time talking. I'm about to lose my job. I call that a bit short of perfect." She'd felt her job was in jeopardy since Vole's secretary had called her Friday morning to set up a meeting. She wouldn't say for what, but Jessica feared that Armor had told him to get her off the proposal.

"That's a sad story. Let's take a look at you."

Hatfield ran her through the familiar push, grip, stand, stare up at the ceiling, and reflex tests. As Gebauer's guru of the neuromuscular junction, maybe he could learn more from her symptoms than other doctors had. More likely, this was a futile hope.

After the tests were over, he paced up and down before her, hands clasped behind his back, frowning.

"I have lots of myasthenia patients who have trouble walking, lifting their arms and keeping their jaws closed like you. Interesting, with most of them the head falls backward so they have to put pillows on their chair-backs. Your head hangs forward. Must be affecting a different group of neck muscles." He wrote in her folder. "Let's see you walk."

She plodded around the room, wresting each foot individually from the clutches of overzealous gravity.

"You walk funny." He rubbed his chin.

"You should see me do aerobics."

"For a myasthenic, I mean. They're slow, but they don't walk like they're just learning how."

She eased herself into the chair this time, avoiding an awkward plop.

He dropped his pen, reached to the floor and picked it up. "Oops. My myasthenia is acting up again." He winked at her.

He understood like few others in her life. Anything you can laugh at becomes less frightening, even myasthenia gravis. Still, she wanted to get on with the diagnosis, the crucial single-fiber test.

"My lady of the mysterious malady, your symptoms are weird, your antibody and EMG tests negative, your Tensilon ambiguous." He shook his head over the fat folder. "Let's keep your June sixth date for a single-fiber EMG. Maybe that'll show something definitive."

"That's more than three weeks away."

"Maybe my music will drive away a few patients. If I get any cancellations, you can come earlier. Otherwise, we'll just have to wait."

"I might be able to stand the wait if you could increase the Mestinon. I need a bigger dosage." Of course, she didn't really know if she could cope if she had more. "Otherwise I might as well give up and die. This isn't living." Her voice trembled. "I hate myself this way."

Hatfield grimaced. "How much are we talking about?"

From their reading and contact with other patients on the Internet, she and Fernando had decided what she should ask for. "I'm on thirty milligrams a day now. Do you think it would hurt to up it to sixty?"

Hatfield leaned back in his chair and put his hands behind his head.

"Sixty. Okay, let's try it for a week. Mestinon has to be treated with respect. Call me immediately if you notice any big changes—like more extreme weakness, difficulty swallowing or breathing."

Getting her dosage increased was about as positive a thing as any that had happened to her the last couple of weeks.

She had one more subject to discuss. "I've been wondering when to go to emergency."

"I always tell my patients to go to the ER when they have the slightest swallowing or breathing problem. But nobody likes being intubated and put on a respirator. ER people can be quick to do that. So some patients would rather tough it out. They seem to learn when they really need to go."

Her hands clutched each other in her lap. "They don't make any big mistakes while they're learning?"

"You should get one of these." Hatfield held up a Medical Alert bracelet, then began writing a requisition.

This doctor didn't dish out definitive answers, leaving a lot for her to think about and decide. Kind of scary—she didn't know much of anything. But she couldn't help liking his implied respect for her.

As he wrote, she studied the bows and arrows. The arrows were flaked flint and the bows were made of light-colored wood tightly wound with coarse fibers. "Impressive collection."

"Those were made by Eskimos—Aleuts. Every year I go to the Iditarod thousand-mile dogsled race to look after the drivers. Donate my valuable time. They get a damned good doctor for free."

"That must be special for you."

"Man over nature. Like man over myasthenia. I'm a warrior, a conqueror." He struck his chest with his fist. "How about you?"

Jessica gathered what little mental and physical energy she had and struck her own chest once, lightly, with a half-closed fist.

Outside, she gazed across the two hundred-foot wide medical plaza at the pharmacy. She could request a wheelchair. Or she could try for the other side on her own.

Edging along the perimeter of the plaza step by step, she leaned her body against the semicircular building for support. As she scraped along the rough stones, she cleared her mind of all emotion, focusing on each step forward. When gravity overwhelmed her, she slid down the wall to a squat. Passersby stared at her. Some offered to help, but she turned them down. She wished they wouldn't even look her way. For one thing, although her skirt came below her knees, she didn't know if her panties were showing. She rested a while, then slid back up using the building for support. In twenty minutes, she stumbled into the pharmacy and knocked over a display of antihistamines.

The pharmacist hurried from behind his counter with a folding chair, nervously settled her into it and set the display upright. While she waited for him to fill the Mestinon prescription, which he read with a grave demeanor, her gaze fell on a gleaming gold Medical Alert bracelet on display. She remembered stories about her great-grandfather's silver-tipped cane poking out ahead of him as he walked.

She looked at the price tag. Five hundred dollars! "Do you have a diamond-studded model?" she asked the pharmacist.

He peered at her over half glasses. "No, ma'am."

"Too bad. I just don't know what I'll do for formal occasions."

A smile appeared on the man's lips, the muscles around his mouth relaxed and crow's feet crinkled at the sides of his eyes. She smiled back at him as she put in an order for a gold bracelet engraved with her name, the Medical Alert number and the words "Myasthenia Gravis" Hatfield had written on the prescription. Even if it meant more credit card debt, she had to have this bracelet. "Let me know when the diamond-studded ones come in." She winked at the pharmacist as she left him chuckling.

"Five hundred dollars for a bracelet!" Fernando yelled when Jessica unwrapped the UPS package a few days later. "Are you out of your mind?"

It was so obnoxious of him to belittle the expense she'd meant as a bold statement, treating her as though she'd done something rash and stupid. "I wanted it to say 'I'm a person of worth, and a five hundred dollar gold bracelet is not too good for me.'"

"Give it to me. I'll wrap it up and send it back." Fernando reached out his hand and snapped his fingers. "I can get a cheaper one at the hospital."

"What right do you have to tell me what I can and can't do? It's my money, not yours. Why don't you mind your own business for a change?" Jessica fingered the smooth gold. She wondered if anyone had sneered at her great-grandfather's silver-tipped cane. "If you want to do something for me, throw this away." She tossed the paper the package had come wrapped in at Fernando.

He caught it, left-handed. "You ought to listen to me. You're not thinking straight these days."

She glared at him and put the bracelet on. "You listen. I'm telling you I have to keep it. I'm going to keep it. With or without your support."

His grim face told her it would be without.

CHAPTER 19

"Super strategy," Stone said. "I think it'll work. Now you keep your spirits up, young lady."

"Thanks, Jim. I had no idea what I should do." Jessica believed that the purpose of the meeting Vole had called this afternoon was likely to be her removal from Armor's proposal team.

Stone waggled a finger at her. "Your boss doesn't know it yet, but he's going to play right into your hands."

Jessica nodded. Even though she was far from sure her job wouldn't be gone by the end of the day, she was strengthened by Stone's confidence in the scheme they'd just hatched. He could be a slave driver, but that little Texas town must have loved him, the way he stood up for people in distress.

She balled up the wrapper for her cheese sandwich, which the new Mestinon dose had helped her chew and swallow without difficulty, and stuffed it into an empty Styrofoam cup. Then she gathered up Stone's lunch debris. If he had asked she would gladly have scrubbed his floor and polished his desk. Part of her reason for wanting to keep this job was so she wouldn't let him down.

When Vole and the woman from Human Relations showed up, Jessica was waiting. It couldn't be coincidental that they were meeting in Armor's office.

Jessica was weak and nervous, but able to stand and shake hands when Vole introduced her to Shirley Skowron. She hoped Skowron and Vole noticed her gold bracelet, gleaming under the overhead lights.

Dressed in a tweed skirt and jacket and sensible brown pumps, Skowron was fortyish and trim, with smooth, shoulder-length brown hair and darting brown eyes. Her glasses hung from her neck on a beige cord and she carried a thick notebook in a blue imitation leather binder embossed with a red RANK logo.

Vole settled into Armor's chair, the seat of power, behind a desk that could probably hold her entire cubicle, while Jessica and Skowron took curved-backed, leather-upholstered chairs that were not only smaller, but had lower seats, chosen no doubt to make Armor's visitors feel like children facing an adult, their chins barely above the desktop.

Vole cleared his throat. "It's good Shirley can join us today."

Skowron put on her glasses, opened the notebook on her lap and wrote something brief.

"Yes," Jessica agreed, hoping she was successful in hiding her inner trembling. Stone had told her an HR rep would be here as a witness, in case she later tried to claim Vole had abused or lied to her. They had everything lined up against her. Both of them looked as of they'd already reached a decision.

Vole pressed his fingertips together. "Larry Armor called me. He's rather upset. He believes your problems are preventing you from performing on his proposal."

"I think I'm doing a pretty good job."

"He doesn't. He wants me to replace you."

There it was, just as she feared, total rejection. No thanks for her hard work. Just get out.

"Proposal work is so stressful." Skowron spoke with worry on her face and in her voice as if she were actually concerned about Jessica. "Under the circumstances we think it would be best for you to take a less demanding assignment."

These weenies had to know how hard it would be to find another assignment if she was thrown off this one. Jessica tried to control her fear and rage and focus on what she needed to do. "Hard work isn't a problem for me."

Vole cleared his throat again and ventured a glance in her direction. "I understand that at a recent meeting you collapsed on the floor."

"That's true. But I was okay in a few minutes."

Skowron scribbled furiously in the notebook. "That must have been very distressing for you," she said, looking up from her notes. "Exactly what do you have, Jessica?" Skowron's voice was quiet, meant to placate, Jessica would bet.

"Myasthenia gravis, or something a whole lot like it." Jessica tried to speak just as calmly and quietly. She'd do her own placating.

"Could you tell us a little bit about that?" Skowron asked, writing all the while. Jessica, doing her best to keep her cool, explained that MG was an autoimmune illness, not contagious. It wasn't curable, but was treatable.

"You're very sick," Vole said. "For your own good, you shouldn't be on this job." Jessica could sense his growing relief, as he began believing it would be easy to get rid of her.

Maybe it would be easy for him. She'd heard he'd dumped a lot of employees over the years. But she'd decided, at Stone's urging, that her best hope was to go all out to protect her job. She was going to make things as tough for him as she could. She took a deep breath. "I'm not sick in the sense that I'd get better if I stayed home in bed or get worse if I came to work." She felt a rush of adrenaline. Here came the magic word. "I'm more what you'd call disabled."

Skowron stopped writing. Her body tensed.

Vole blundered on, not yet realizing what was coming. "Armor thinks you can't pull your own weight."

Jessica leaned forward, her arms and hands resting on the huge desk, chin clearing it by only a few inches. "Rank is an Equal Opportunity employer. It's against the law for them to discriminate against a disabled person. Isn't that true, Shirley?"

Skowron sat back and removed her glasses, letting them dangle from the cord. "The law's very clear on that, Fred. The Americans with Disabilities Act."

The federal law that Stone had downloaded for them to study. Stone had told her Skowron would know all about it. Jessica felt encouraged that at least one of his predictions had come true.

Vole crossed his arms over his chest and frowned.

Jessica pressed on. "I have a right to this job."

Skowron fiddled with her glasses. "Under some circumstances."

Vole turned a pleading gaze on the HR lady.

"Like my circumstance," Jessica said. "I have a disability, but I can work. I can prove it. Just ask Jim Stone."

Skowron cleared her throat and returned Vole's gaze. "Actually, as long as the work is here and Jessica can do it, Armor *may not* remove her from her position. He can't replace her." Her soft voice now had an edge of authority.

Jessica could have cheered. Just as Stone had predicted, the HR lady had been obliged to come to her defense. She was actually beginning to feel she had a chance to win this battle.

Vole's white-knuckled fingers clutched the edge of the desk. "Armor says she can't handle her job."

Jessica was ready to give this twit a big, fat, richly deserved headache. "I can. Go ahead. Ask Jim Stone. Ask the antenna engineers and the ground station designers." This was almost fun. "If I'm provided with the proper means as a disabled person, as the law requires, I can do my job. I'll need an office large enough to accommodate a wheelchair, wheelchair access to my office, and a handicapped parking spot. Right, Shirley?"

"It's the law," Skowron replied. "And I will talk to Mr. Stone, if you don't mind."

Vole's eyes bugged out. He looked as if his face would crumble. "I don't know what Armor's going to say about this."

"It's illegal to disregard a disabled person's rights." Skowron threw out her chin. "Armor could get the company in trouble if he disregards the law. It's my job to see that he doesn't."

Jessica was amazed. She would have bet Skowron didn't have it in her to face down a manager.

Skowron turned to Jessica. "Can a wheelchair fit into your cubicle, dear?"

Jessica shook her head. "None I've seen will fit into the passageway, let alone in the cubicle itself." Even folded up, her wheelchair was too big and awkward for her to maneuver and cram into the car trunk if she was the least bit weak. She'd been considering the possibility of trading in the Honda for a station wagon.

"I know we can make your life easier, Jessica." Skowron put her glasses back on and wrote in her notebook. "We'll just have to find a more appropriate office for her, Fred."

Jessica didn't try to hide her happiness that her job was saved. She smiled, she grinned, she hugged herself. "Thank you so much." She touched Skowron's arm.

Vole gaped at Skowron.

"Do you have suitable handicapped parking?" Skowron asked.

"Actually, no. There's one place and it's supposed to be closest to the entrance, but it's several spaces away. If I had the spot by the front door, when the weather's bad, I'd only have to roll my chair a few feet in the rain." Armor's space was the one right by the front door.

Skowron wrote in the notebook. "That will have to be changed." She glanced up at Vole, who seemed to have slipped into a trance.

On the way out Skowron told Jessica that helping people like her was one of the satisfactions she got from her job. Jessica pressed her hand in gratitude.

As soon as she could, Jessica stuck her head into Jim Stone's office. He had two engineers with him, so she simply made a thumbs-up sign. He winked in reply.

Only when she was back in her cubicle, did an uneasy feeling about what she'd just done begin to creep over her. She'd declared herself a disabled person.

She remembered the hush around disabled people she'd encountered, the avoidance of contact. Perhaps the disabled reminded others of a frightening side of life, one they didn't want to think about. No one wanted to be held back in doing a job or enjoying themselves by a handicapped person's problems.

A TV news anchor had been given a horrible time a year or so ago because of a disabling deformity, mostly because she'd already had one child who'd inherited it and was soon to have another with a fifty percent chance of getting it. She'd received a load of nasty mail, her ratings had dropped, and eventually she'd felt forced to resign from her position. The worst problem with her condition was people's disparaging perception of it. Jessica feared other people's perceptions could become as intractable a problem as the illness she was facing.

CHAPTER 20

Sitting in the wheelchair and sweating in the hot sun, Jessica could hear nothing over the machine gun-like rattle of wheels clattering and screams from the Matterhorn. She was learning what it was like to be disabled and in a wheelchair.

Early this morning, Fernando had driven her, Whitney and Whitney's husband, Dave, to Disneyland in the six-year-old Subaru wagon she'd traded in the Honda for. Even though she'd felt up to it, with no sign of the dreaded switches or overzealous gravity, she'd let him drive so the others wouldn't be nervous. The wagon, a lustrous silver, had two rows of seats and a rear area that easily accommodated a collapsed wheelchair laid on its side.

This was the first Saturday in a long time that she and Whitney hadn't gone in to work. Even though she'd have to put in a few extra make-up hours tomorrow and Monday, Jessica had been looking forward to today and caring about nothing beyond having a good time in "The Happiest Place on Earth."

A disturbing thought crept into her mind. She couldn't remember seeing any disabled employees here, much less disabled cartoon characters—Disneyland is perfect and the disabled aren't.

Best to keep thoughts like that to herself. They all wanted to have a good time, and Whitney was worried about Dave as well as Jessica. A muscular ex-football player, Dave seemed always to be tense and intense. Mostly, he couldn't let go of work where he was an associate in servitude, as Whitney put it, in a downtown law firm. It might be that every adult here without a child in tow was trying to escape or forget something.

Jessica felt so good after they'd parked in a disabled spot right next to the front gate that she left the wheelchair behind and dashed off to the ticket booth.

They started with the monorail because you could see all of Disneyland from it. Jessica easily got herself up the broad stairs to the loading platform.

Next came the submarine ride. On board, Jessica felt only a slight elevator effect as they slowly submerged. As they drifted past deep sea divers and under the polar ice cap, the underwater motion was smooth.

Dave led them to the Star Tours ride.

"What's this?" Jessica asked.

"It's new," Whitney said. "Everyone says it's great—like being on a space ship."

The Star Tours line snaked between iron railings, then up a ramp. Jessica looked at Fernando and pointed to an overhead sign that warned not to ride if you had a heart or other condition that might be aggravated by motion. "Relax. I'll hold on to you," he assured her. "Not to worry," Whitney added. "Everything here is super-safe."

After they'd clambered onto adjoining seats in a waiting Star Speeder, a voice ordered them to fasten their seat belts across their chests and laps and prepare to travel to the faraway Moon of Endor.

Jessica sucked in her breath. "Endor—Biblical home of the prophetess of death and defeat."

Fernando shook his head disdainfully. "Pure hype." He fastened her seat belt, then his. "There are no wheels on this thing. We're not going anywhere."

She supposed she should relax. She was getting too twitchy. She fingered the seat belt and leaned back.

A woman's soothing voice announced the launch, not preparing Jessica for the Star Speeder's lurch when it jerked forward to simulate the acceleration of a rocket launch. The seat belt caught her and flung her backward. Her head snapped back, then forward, flipping switches throughout her brain; her mouth flew open; her legs wouldn't move. All she could do was grip the bar in front of her seat.

A giant gleaming ice crystal zoomed onto the screen in front of them and the seats careened violently sideways as if to dodge it.

"Are you all right?" Fernando shouted.

She wasn't, but couldn't answer.

She peeked through slits between drooped eyelids. Oh no! A space fighter, blasting missiles at them. The seat made a swooping evasive maneuver. Flaccid, except for her gripping fingers, Jessica clung to the bar, terrified.

Whitney put a hand on her arm and said something, but Jessica couldn't look up, couldn't answer.

"Stop the ride!" Whitney screamed.

On they went, dodging fighters and missiles, whizzing down narrow chasms, careening around sharp corners. This was like being inside a tornado.

When the ride lurched to an abrupt stop, Jessica couldn't stand or raise her head. Dave and Fernando loosened the grip of her fingers on the bar and each lifted under one of her arms, carrying her off the Star Speeder to a concrete bench near the exit.

"I'm so sorry." Fernando looked anxious. "I don't know what came over me, talking you into how safe that ride was."

Head on her chest, Jessica maneuvered to peer up into her friends' anxious faces. Now she'd really done it. Spoiled a perfect day for everyone. All they'd remember about this trip was what a drag it was to bring her along when they went to Disneyland.

After fifteen minutes she'd recovered enough to talk, but still couldn't get up.

"Maybe we should go home," Whitney said.

"Don't even think it," Jessica answered. Whitney looked so woebegone. She'd make it up to her somehow. No more risky rides for one thing. "We're all going to stay and have a good time. Why don't you get my wheelchair?" She handed Fernando the keys to the wagon.

Only the desire not to dampen her friends' good time drove Jessica to ask for the chair. She'd never been in public with it before, never taken it to work.

That was half an hour ago. Now she was sitting in the sun, sweating, in front of the snow-capped Matterhorn while the others were careening down its slopes in a bobsled. She could hear screams of happy terror from above. Happy because the ride would soon be over with no harm done. Not like the terror of being in a wheelchair the rest of your life.

Of all those waiting in line, buying popcorn or pretzels at a barn-red cart, hurrying to the next amusement, only the eyes of children and other people in wheelchairs were down here. She wished the kids wouldn't stare.

When she'd arrived this morning things were different—she was standing and people in familiar up-here land had looked at her and talked to her. Now no one noticed her except gawking children and a few people in wheelchairs. The down-heres saw each other, but the up-theres were oblivious. Two worlds alien to each other—the up-here/down-there world of the standers and the wheelchair-bounds' down-here/up-there. Worlds the Disney planners never imagined.

Jessica watched the butts of up-theres passing by. A trim young couple in skin-tight jeans flaunted their asses. An obese woman's cheeks seemed to rotate independently of each other.

But most of all she watched the smooth, effortless motion of young people hurrying between pleasures. Legs swinging from hips, feet moving in fussy little steps or long strides and faces carefree, they needed to put little conscious thought into going where they wanted.

By midafternoon, Whitney, Dave and Fernando were worn out enough to leave Tomorrowland. "Where do you want to go next?" Dave asked Jessica.

"Pirates of the Caribbean!" Speech almost back to normal, she wanted to show she was feeling more vigorous, more adventurous. "And let's eat in the Pirates' restaurant afterward." After parking the wheelchair at the ride booth, an attendant led Jessica and the others to the head of the line and helped her into a twenty-seat boat next to Fernando. The lapping of the water around her, the smell and feel of the wetness were invigorating.

The boat whooshed down a small incline—not nearly as debilitating for Jessica as an elevator ride. Bouncy, quirky music wafted toward them. They floated past a burning city being ransacked by pirates gaudily dressed in seamen's jackets, striped socks and pirate hats. Buildings flamed into a dark sky, sweaty pirate faces gleamed by lantern light, pirate hands ran through pilfered gold and jewels, prisoners in cages and shackles pleaded for release, drunken pirates sprawled in a plaza and dangled from an overhead bridge while others chased screaming, bosomy women from a tavern. All to fiendish, jumping, jivey, electronically created music.

Jessica thought about whom to identify with. The rampaging pirates were the only ones having a good time, the townspeople their sorry victims. She began to picture pirates in wheelchairs, drinking and carousing, collecting lucre and loving every minute of it.

She was saddened when the last pirate leaned over the water and leered at her. She wished the ride would go on and on.

They floated into a narrow, rocky passageway. With a stomach-grabbing plunge, the boat plummeted down to the unloading platform and splashed to a halt. Jessica flopped sideways onto Fernando's lap. She'd forgotten how this ride ended. When she'd been well, that final plunge had been fun.

Again, Dave and Fernando had to carry her through a gawking crowd. An attendant brought her a plastic chair to wait in until Fernando got the wheelchair. He, like all the other Disneyland employees, was very attentive to people with disabilities. But when she looked up at him and said, "Thanks," she saw the young man's eyes dart away from her.

Fernando wheeled her around the corner to the outdoor restaurant where tables were arranged on a subterranean waterside plaza lit only by tiny, twinkling firefly lights strung between posts. A waitress made room for the wheelchair by removing one of four chairs at a table by a dark lagoon. Boats full of \riders were bobbing past, toward the burning, pillaged, pirate-infested town ahead. It was as though she had a seat at night beside an enchanting bayou in eighteenth-century New Orleans, with the added advantage that her slumping, wheelchair-bound figure would be hard for others to see and stare at in the near darkness.

The menu was mostly seafood, but Jessica had been here several times and knew how to handle that. She found a pasta with vegetables and seafood, which in past visits she'd requested be prepared with sautéed vegetables only. The others chose crab cakes and a bottle of chardonnay. Not for her. Patients on Mestinon were warned not to drink alcohol and she certainly didn't want to get any worse than she already was. They'd have to carry her out on a stretcher.

A young waitress in a ponytail and a black-and-white uniform came to the table. She took Whitney's order first. Then she turned to Fernando next to Jessica. "And what will the other lady have?"

Jessica was stunned. She wasn't a child—she could give her own order. Then she pictured herself as the waitress must see her—slumped in a wheelchair, arms flopped to her sides, head drooping, mouth hanging open. The woman was probably drawing all kinds of wrong inferences about her mental state.

"She wants..." Fernando began.

"I want the seafood pasta with vegetables, but leave out the seafood. Just the vegetables." Jessica thought her voice was clear, even though she couldn't hold her head up.

"Does she want the seafood pasta?" the waitress asked Fernando.

"Yes, but leave out the seafood," Jessica answered.

The waitress's eyes remained on Fernando's face. "She wants the seafood pasta, hold the seafood?"

"Yes," Fernando said.

"Should I serve the seafood on the side, sir?"

Jessica tried hard to sit up straight and hold her head up, but failed. "No seafood. I'm a vegetarian."

The waitress, smiling steadfastly, held her pen over the order pad.

Fernando put his hand on Jessica's. "That's all right. I don't mind taking care of this." He turned to the waitress. "No seafood."

"Anything to drink?"

"Orange juice for the lady," Fernando said, without asking Jessica. Orange juice was high in potassium, which Fernando believed was good for the neuromuscular system. "And a bottle of your house chardonnay and three glasses."

"Fernando, you're not helping when you speak for me," Jessica said.

She felt like letting the waitress know how disabled people wanted to be treated. But Whitney's face was glowing, Dave looked relaxed and Fernando pleased. She, Jessica, was the only one with a problem and it wasn't going to make anyone's day if she had a snit.

When the waitress came for the dessert orders, they all wanted Pirate ice cream sundaes. Again she asked Fernando for Jessica's order. To keep the party happy, Jessica held her tongue.

CHAPTER 21

She'd leave the wheelchair in the station wagon. Just because she'd hauled it to Rank didn't mean she had to take it inside.

Pulling into the lot, Jessica caught sight of a shiny new blue sign with a white wheelchair on it by the parking spot nearest the door. The totem of the disabled—her tribe.

Turning off the ignition, she tried to calm her pounding heart and looked around. No one nearby. Still, she hesitated to get out of the car. If she brought the wheelchair inside, worse yet if she actually had to sit in it, everyone's attitude toward her could change in a minute. At Disneyland last weekend she'd been treated as hard of hearing, feeble-minded, a down-there of no consequence.

But falling while trying to do without the chair would be worse.

She stepped out and went to the rear of the wagon. Luckily, she was strong enough this morning to pull out the wheelchair from where it lay on its side in the trunk, its shiny, lightweight, tubular frame compactly collapsed. It wasn't ugly; it was useful. She shouldn't hate it as she did.

After dragging it carefully over the bumper, she landed it, wheels down, still folded, and propped it against the wagon so she could pull it open using the bumper for support. The squeal of brakes made her turn and look behind her. There sat Larry Armor glaring at the "Disabled" sign from the window of a big, black BMW, eyes aflame as if lit from an internal volcano. His gaze raked across the station wagon and down to the wheelchair without glancing at her. She watched him drive slowly down the aisle and pull into a space several cars away.

As she rolled the chair toward the door, she recalled once walking into a Rank building behind him and another executive. The other man had pointed to a large bird perched directly over the entrance on the roof of the two-story building. "Peregrine falcon. They're territorial. Look at him strut up there like he owns this place."

"If I had a rifle, I'd shoot the son-of-a-bitch," Armor had snarled.

Jessica just knew he'd like to shoot her too. She'd grabbed off his parking place, a piece of his territory. She was defying his order to be gone from his proposal. She tried to squelch the rising fear, wishing she'd been satisfied with the former, more distant, disabled spot. Now she had another problem with Armor she didn't need, and she'd brought it on herself.

At the entrance, she turned around to open the swinging glass door by pushing with her back. She'd learned this was a lot easier than trying to enter forward while reaching over the wheelchair, struggling to keep the door open with one hand and rolling the chair with the other.

Armor strode up and waited, face averted, until she got inside the lobby. While she was fishing in her purse for her badge to show the guard, he flashed his and darted past.

As Jessica entered the main proposal room, she drew a deep breath. Several of the designers looked up from their computer terminals. A couple of them said hello, one looked quickly away when she caught his eye and another gawked openly. Nothing terrible. But they hadn't yet seen her *in* the wheelchair, slumped, slack-jawed, open-mouthed.

She headed for the art room, intending to park the chair there since it wouldn't fit in the narrow passageway to her cubicle.

The minute Joe DiCarlo spotted her, he jumped up and hurried toward her, eyes and mouth tense. She braced herself for profuse expressions of pity and suffocating offers of help.

"I can't make out your writing. What do you want on the mod/demod diagram?"

She tried to gather her confused mind together. "Mod/demod?"

"The one you brought me Friday, you twit." He grinned.

"Oh, that. Sorry. I guess I'm so concerned about my first day coming to work with a wheelchair, I can't think of anything else."

Joe nodded. "Looks comfortable. Now about the diagram…"

She pushed the wheelchair to his work station and sat happily beside him. He didn't seem to care what she was sitting in.

Only a little weak and droopy, she worked until late morning when Shirley Skowron showed up with a man in a facility services uniform. "I've found you a suitable office," Skowron announced with a smile. She appeared to enjoy standing up to the bureaucracy rather than knuckling under to it.

The man loaded Jessica's books, papers, laptop and printer onto a metal cart. Its rickety wheels screeched and squealed, attracting people's eyes as the three of them crossed the design room. Her fellow employees' curiosity was so palpable Jessica knew it wouldn't be long before everyone found out about her new office and why she had it.

They entered a carpeted hallway with three doors—the first to Armor's office, the second to a smaller one for his secretary. Skowron pushed open the third, normally reserved for Armor's business staffers, who mostly tried to stay in their plush quarters in the executive building.

"It's beautiful. I love it," Jessica exclaimed.

Chestnut brown paneled walls scented with polishing oil glowed on all sides. A waist-high wooden bookcase stretched the length of the back wall. A wooden desk three or four times the size of her cubicle desk faced the door, the only object on its polished surface a phone with a large bank of buttons. Behind it crouched a tawny, leonine upholstered executive chair with wooden arms carved like paws. In the corner was a round, wooden parquet table with four swivel chairs. No windows. But the whole building was like that to prevent industrial espionage.

When Skowron and the man left, Jessica gently closed the door, enjoying the solid click of an expensive latch. She eased into the chair and snuggled back into the soft cushion. How nice. The chair fit as though it had been made to conform to her body.

One of the phone buttons lit up red. She punched it and picked up the line.

"I did tell her she had to leave," she heard Vole saying. "But Skowron contradicted me. Jessica has her convinced she's disabled. So Skowron says she can't be forced to leave."

"The girl's situation is very unfortunate." Armor was keeping his voice low. "I'm sympathetic, of course, but she can't handle her assignments. She's dead weight. And I can't afford dead weight. You've got to get her out of here."

"Shirley insists we can't. There are laws."

"Then you and Skowron—better yet, get a staff lawyer—read the damned law and find the loophole, Vole. She's moved into one of my offices, for Chrissake. And some asshole gave her my parking spot." Jessica could almost see his jaws clenching and his rabid dog's eyes flashing the way they did whenever he flew into a rage.

She pressed her finger gently on the receiver cradle before Armor could hang up and see that the phone button was still red.

Now she'd done it. With Armor already looking for an excuse to dump her, she'd taken not only one of his offices, but his precious parking space.

She got up and headed for Jim Stone's office.

"Are you sure you want to stay on this proposal?" Stone squinted at Jessica after she told him about the phone call.

"Yeah, I want to stay. I need the paycheck and the insurance. Besides, if I don't want to fear for my job for the rest of my life, I'll have to figure out how to deal with people like Armor."

"My advice is to keep a low profile and study the Disabilities Act until you know every word of it."

As she left Stone's office, she spotted Kyle Bumpers slithering out of Armor's office and down the hall toward her.

"Morning, babe." He winked and gave her a what-a-good-boy-I-am smile.

She looked away, refusing to acknowledge his presence. It wasn't fair. Bumpers probably wasn't doing anything legitimate while she was working her tail off. Yet he enjoyed Armor's favor and she was in fear of losing her job.

CHAPTER 22

Keeping up with her job was tough. Keeping up while pursuing a diagnosis was tougher. Today's test was going to take hours and she'd be away from work half a day.

Hatfield's waiting room was filled with the recorded sound of Bach's poignant *Fugue in A Minor*. Jessica wondered who the pianist was. Maybe Alicia deLarrocha; like Mom, she kept to Baroque music rules. Certainly not Glen Gould; he'd played Bach any old way that pleased him at the moment.

"I see what you mean by 'Hatfield music,'" Fernando said. "Very unprofessional, if you ask me. Loud music is as out of place in a doctor's office as dancing and drinking."

She hadn't asked him. "I like it." Some days Fernando got on the wrong side of her from the start and stayed there all day.

A nurse stuck her head into the room. "Doctor is ready to see you."

Head drooping, so that all she could see were her own too-heavy feet, she leaned heavily on Fernando's arm as they made their slow way down the hall. She was very weak because Hatfield had wanted her off Mestinon this afternoon for the single-fiber EMG test.

In a white coat, forelock of hair hanging down on a forehead glistening with perspiration, Hatfield was plugging cables into an oscilloscope and adjusting knobs.

He glanced up. "You look pretty bad."

"No Mestinon. And I rode the elevator up to your floor."

Hatfield bent over the scope, adjusting knobs and watching wriggly green lines cross the screen.

"Want to come and see me when I ride down and back up?" Jessica suggested. Surely such a startling effect would reveal something about her condition.

"Hell, I don't know what's going on there."

"Did I tell you I think laughing makes me weak too?"

"Laughing?" Hatfield looked up.

"When laughter gets a grip on me, I'm wasted. I totally lose it."

"She gets so carried away laughing she pushes herself over the edge when she's about to have an attack," Fernando said a bit disdainfully.

"Who's this?" Hatfield looked at Fernando.

"Sorry. My friend—Fernando Munoz. He's a doctor too."

Fernando informed Hatfield he was an oncology Fellow at Gebauer. "Expect to finish soon. I'm acing my courses," he added.

Jessica suppressed a smile. Evidently Fernando couldn't resist trying to impress the renowned Dr. Hatfield. This morning he was even wearing the suit, shirt and tie he usually reserved for going to Mass.

"You're here to keep me honest, huh?" Hatfield snorted. "Here, young man, you and Jessica look this over while I finish getting ready." Hatfield tossed a pamphlet at Fernando and pulled a tall stool up to the oscilloscope.

Jessica bet Fernando wasn't thrilled at being called young man.

The pamphlet was a reprint of an article Hatfield had written on the single-fiber EMG test. It described how a tiny probe is inserted into a single muscle fiber in a patient's arm. The patient then makes a tight fist. A Polaroid shot of a normal muscle fiber response on the oscilloscope showed two closely spaced electrical pulses, with the pair repeated at very regular time intervals. All the pulses were the same size and duration. Shots of several MG patients' responses showed smaller, or even absent pulses, and pulses that looked like they'd struggled to rise, then petered out.

Fernando nodded. "Direct measurement of the success or failure of neurotransmission, fiber by fiber. This will nail it."

Jessica trembled. Nailed to the myasthenia gravis cross. Crucified. Mestinon her only hope for resurrection. Centuries of accused persons about to hear the verdict "guilty" or "not guilty" must have felt this fear.

Hatfield asked her to get up onto the padded, bed-like platform near the oscilloscope. Jessica took off her cardigan and shoes and lay down on it. To her left stood Dr. Hatfield and the oscilloscope, above her on the wall the bow with crossed arrows and arrowhead display. Weapons. Not much good against MG.

"Come here." Hatfield motioned to Fernando. "Watch this with me."

Fernando jumped to his feet and joined him. Jessica sensed his pride was recovering at being asked to observe at Hatfield's side.

Hatfield approached Jessica with a thin wire attached by a cable to the oscilloscope. She cringed. His hands looked too big and rough to manipulate the tiny needle. She braced herself, tensing arm and leg muscles. But when the probe was inserted, she felt only a tiny prick. What a relief. She clenched her fist and felt no pain. This wasn't going to be half as miserable as the EMG she'd had in Cowan's lab.

Hatfield and Fernando bent over the scope. "No abnormality," Hatfield muttered.

"That's the way I see it, too," Fernando said.

"No abnormality," Jessica echoed, trying not to worry this early that nothing conclusive would come of this test.

Hatfield snapped a Polaroid of the screen. Then he lumbered over to her, pulled out the probe and moved it to another spot on her forearm.

Jessica clenched her fist.

"Success!" Fernando's voice was orgiastic. "Look at this." He pointed to the scope, his dark eyes gleaming triumphantly.

"Success?" Jessica cried. What did he mean success?

"Look at that!" Hatfield shouted. "Textbook deformation."

These two arcade junkies thought her test was some kind of electronic game and they'd get a prize for a perfect set of deformed pulses.

Fernando gripped the top of the scope with both hands. "Second pulse in every single pair never quite makes it. Takes too long to rise, then gives up and dies out."

Jessica lost control over the circuits of her mind and went limp. She had it for sure. And there stood Fernando almost hugging the scope.

Fernando rocked back on his heels. "However, the pulse pairs, poor as they are, repeat rather regularly."

Hatfield studied the screen. "Some randomness over here." He pointed to the right.

"How do you know whether you've got normal aberrations or an abnormal condition?" Fernando asked.

"Purely subjective."

"Subjective?" The word came out of Fernando like a breathy belch. "But surely you've studied enough normals and abnormals to distinguish the differences."

Hatfield put his hand on Fernando's shoulder. "I hate to be the one to break the news to you, son. You seem to be taking this rather hard. But medicine has a subjective component—part science, part art."

"But surely—surely," Fernando sputtered. "The range of irregularities in pulse timing for a normal patient is always much smaller than for an MG patient."

"You wish." Hatfield's voice was soft and low. "I wish."

"*I* wish," Jessica called out. She was the important person here.

Hatfield came over and, with deft fingers, moved the probe to another spot on her arm.

This time Fernando thought the pulses looked pretty normal.

Hatfield snapped a picture and probed another spot.

"That's more like it," Fernando said. "Lots of missing pulses. About a third of them."

"I have MG, don't I?" Jessica thought it was time for Hatfield to commit.

He gazed at the arrowheads in the case above her. "Possibly."

"You're saying I have it?" She knew she had it. He had to know she had it. The evidence was right there. Why else would so many of her pulses be missing? Was he going to prescribe the medication she needed, or wasn't he?

"We just saw enough defective cases to convince me." Fernando's voice was authoritative.

She shot Fernando a glance of gratitude.

"Now listen, young man." Hatfield stood over Fernando, glowering at him. "I'm almost sure she has MG. She probably has MG. That's the best I can do. If that dirties up your nice clean world of certainties, then so be it."

Jessica tried to sit up, but had to lie still and mumble. "What I want to know is how I'm going to get through the rest of my life."

Hatfield's face softened. "None of us knows that."

Jessica smacked the bed with her fist in frustration. "Is there anything you can do to help me?"

"MG's highly probable. I'm willing to go with it for now. Let's try upping your Mestinon to eighty milligrams a day and see what happens.

That's two pills each dose, no two doses any closer than four hours apart. Closer is too risky."

More Mestinon would be an improvement, but she longed for certainty. Hatfield wasn't quite sure she had MG. Probably she had it— probably the probability was high. She felt like she was walking a tightrope above a net full of holes.

CHAPTER 23

Jessica was doing better on eighty milligrams and the new office gave her a lift she hadn't anticipated. It wasn't just the beauty of the polished paneling and furniture. Or the thick carpet, nubbier than home carpeting but not as coarse as indoor/outdoor, that gave under her feet. Or the comfort of the lush, soft desk chair. The office was isolated and quiet enough for her to think without interruption. No bickering engineers, conversations meant to be private, unanswered phones ringing. In an office like this you could begin to believe you were a valued employee. She owed all this to Shirley Skowron.

She glanced at her appointments calendar. Skowron was due at three. Probably to see how the new office was working out.

With a few minutes left before the meeting, she continued to whip out Jim Stone's frequency multiplexing write-up. Although she was fairly stable this afternoon, her daily fuel supply was getting lower on average. Where she used to worry about how far she could walk, now she had to carefully ration her energy and medication just to keep her hands above the keyboard for the better part of the day. She didn't like to brood on how much weaker she might get. She was on the maximum dose of Mestinon.

There was a light knock at the door. That must be Skowron. Whitney or Joe would have barged in, and Stone would have banged on the door.

"Come in," she sang out.

The door eased open to reveal the smiling HR lady, clutching a Rank notebook to her chest. She sat down across from Jessica, smoothed her skirt underneath her, pulled a ball point pen from her purse, clicked the pen point in and out several times and opened the notebook. "How are you, my dear?"

"I'm doing just fine." Jessica was glad to see the smiling Skowron. She was very grateful for her help in keeping her job and getting this office.

"I wonder…" Skowron's smile remained stiffly in place. "If you could show me what you do to perform your job."

"What I do? I sit behind a word processor most of the day." She pointed to the laptop on the desk.

"You're able to lift your arms to the keyboard?"

"I set the chair up high enough so that my arms come down on the keyboard." Jessica put her hands on the keys.

Skowron scribbled in the notebook. "And you can work that way for five minutes, a half hour—how long?"

"Look." Jessica gestured at a thirty-page pile of paper. "I turned that out this afternoon."

Skowron squirmed in her chair and fingered the loop of cord hanging from her glasses. "You're able to meet your deadlines?"

Jessica realized Skowron was after more than seeing if the new accommodations were suitable. "Haven't missed one yet. Had to pull a couple of all-nighters, but I got it all in on time." MG or not, no one got out more work than she did.

Skowron reared back in her seat. "Surely you don't try to work all night."

"When I have to." Jessica tried to sound nonchalant, but she was getting nervous. "I don't get any worse when I do." Until lately.

Shaking her head, Skowron wrote in the notebook in a rapid, scratchy scrawl.

Then she leaned forward, toward Jessica. "Are you really happy on this job?" The woman's voice was low, almost whispered, as if she and Jessica were about to share a secret.

Happy with the job? More like happy to have a job. "I like the work. I like being self-supporting."

Wake up, Jessica. This woman's curiosity gland is pumping on high. And she's writing everything down like she's compiling a dossier. What was Skowron planning to do with her notes?

"If you want to see what I can do, come around here." Jessica motioned to her side of the desk.

Skowron bustled over, laid the notebook beside Jessica's laptop and leaned over her shoulder.

"This is a table of frequencies to be used by satellites and ground stations. Watch me fill it up." Jessica zipped through the entries using tab stops, straight type and italics. She added a title at the top, an asterisk and footnote at the bottom. "There you go. Bet that didn't take two minutes." She laid her hands in her lap to hide their droop.

"I'm impressed." Skowron stood straight and nodded.

That had to make for a good report in Skowron's notebook. Jessica went on to explain that the skill of which she was most proud, and which was never impacted by her illness, was her ability to size up poorly written technical material and rewrite it clearly. Head drooping, her glance fell on a stapled document peeking up from Skowron's open notebook. "The Americans with Disabilities Act—Title I Employment." Armor had told Vole to get someone to find the loopholes in the law protecting the handicapped. And here was Skowron with what looked like a copy of that law.

Try to remember what the law said. Switches flip-flopping in her head, she fumbled to maintain her concentration as her jaw and tongue weakened and her breathing became difficult and labored. She hoped Skowron was too wrapped up in getting information to notice the changes in her condition.

Skowron snatched up the notebook and went back to her seat. "Do you have many meetings, Jessica?"

"Sure. Never miss them." Well, hardly ever. But this wasn't the time for telling the truth, the whole truth and nothing but the truth. This had turned into a cat and mouse game and the mouse was in danger of running out of breath and energy. She did her best to distance herself from all emotions and focus on holding off the switches in her brain.

"And how do you get around when you do this?"

Jessica had to come out of her trance and respond. "This." She patted the wheelchair beside her desk. "It has really smooth bearings. When I'm weak, I get in and roll it. Hardly takes any effort." Damn! Her jaw was hanging open like an oven door.

"What's wrong?"

"My mouth. Sometimes I can't quite close it." Her breathing was getting shorter by the minute. Because myasthenia gravis could cause the diaphragm to fail, Hatfield had told her to get to an emergency room if her respiration became shallow and exceeded thirty breaths per minute.

"Then you don't need help from others?"

Stay cool. Don't panic. "Rarely. Once in a while to get to the parking lot and put the wheelchair in my car."

"You're still driving?"

"Oh, yes." Actually, driving was becoming more of a concern. She was having to rely more and more on Mom or Fernando to get home. And that meant she needed a ride back to Rank the next morning since her car was still there. Her coworkers must have noticed that her car was sometimes in the disabled spot all night. Maybe one of them had told Skowron.

"Well!" Skowron closed her notebook with a snap. "I'm delighted you're doing so well. I'd like to think I had a little something to do with improving your situation." She looked pleased with herself.

Jessica relaxed and her breath began to flow deeper and more easily. She'd survived another crisis. But how many more would there be?

Armor must have sent Skowron. Would he be satisfied when the HR lady reported Jessica was able to do her work? Or would he continue his campaign to get rid of her?

It was five o'clock before Jessica got a chance to take a look at her copy of the Americans with Disabilities Act. It said an employer could hold an employee with a disability to the same standards of production and performance as other similarly situated employees without disability as long as reasonable accommodation for the disability was provided. The employer may not exclude any individual with a disability who is satisfactorily performing a job's essential functions.

Just as Jessica had figured. Skowron had tried, at Armor's insistence no doubt, to find evidence that Jessica could not perform as well as the other tech writers. Couldn't meet schedules, couldn't type long enough or fast enough, couldn't go to meetings. Or maybe she was trying to prove to Armor that Jessica could do all these things.

A puzzling woman. Skowron did Armor's bidding, but seemed to enjoy herself most when she was helping Jessica. On the other hand, it could be Skowron's pleasure was highest when her power, deriving from the Disabilities Act, trumped Armor's. Maybe she and Armor were engaged in the company's most passionately played sport—the corporate power contest. She'd like to know what Skowron's motives were. But either way, she was grateful for her help.

CHAPTER 24

Jessica felt her job was safe for the time being, but tenuous. So the next day when she noticed how junky the gray metal, two-level in/out box she'd brought from her cubicle looked on the new desk and began to think of replacing it, she stifled herself. Wood would look good, but only executives were entitled to wood. Rank executives were so notoriously sensitive about their status symbols that someone—Armor came to mind—was sure to give her trouble if she bought one and put it on her desk. It was best not to provoke him any more than she already had. "Keep a low profile," Stone had advised. She would listen to him. He was adept at keeping out from under the bureaucratic elephants' large feet.

But maybe she could play with the rules just a little bit, bending without exactly breaking them. What if she took the metal receptacle home and pasted wood veneer on it? What if she brought a wooden one and covered it with plastic to disguise it? Or with feathers? She mused over fanciful mailbox decors while she got ready for a meeting with the antenna engineers.

Following the meeting, Jessica pushed the wheelchair slowly back to her office to avoid depleting her limited fuel supply. It was the second day of her period and she invariably got sicker and weaker the first day or two. Another mystery neither she nor Fernando could explain.

As she entered the hallway to her office, a roll of carpeting the same color as hers was blocking her way. There was no way around it, so she'd just have to force her way over it, difficult as that would be. She dragged the chair backward over the two-foot thick roll, pausing each time she felt the weakness getting deeper.

At the door she saw half her office floor was bare and two workmen in T-shirts and jeans were busy pulling carpet and black spongy padding off the other half.

Suddenly drained of strength, Jessica drooped into the wheelchair. "Stop! What are you doing?"

The men halted and looked up.

"That's my office. What are you doing?"

One man, sweating from his work, stood up and brushed a hank of dark hair from his forehead. He pulled a folded, wrinkled piece of paper from his back pocket. "Here's the work order. This the right office?" He pointed to a number on the form.

"That's my number. But there's been a mistake. I don't want this carpet removed. Please call your supervisor."

After phoning, the workman hung up with a disgusted look on his face. "We're taking this carpet out because you can't have it. It's executive stuff." He stared at the floor and the wall, anywhere but at Jessica. "Sorry lady. I don't want to take no carpet from a crippled lady."

Jessica trembled. She knew only executives were entitled to carpeting. But who would authorize spending the money to rip out and destroy a perfectly good carpet just because the occupant wasn't entitled to it? And why?

She looked around the room. The large wooden desk and parquet table were gone. A small gray metal desk like the one she'd had in her cubicle stood on the bare linoleum floor which was soiled by remnants of sticky carpet adhesive.

"May I see that order?"

The workman handed it to her. It was signed "Larry Armor."

Only yesterday Skowron had blocked his edict to get rid of her.

Switches flipped all over Jessica's brain and she lost the mental strength she needed to fight off collapse. Armor not only had the power and will to make her life miserable, he could throw her out of the company.

Jessica feared it wouldn't be long before she became a pile of mush if she sat here witnessing more of the ravaging of her office and suffering alternate spasms of fear and hatred. She needed to get to her car and go home.

Kyle Bumpers was sauntering down the hall toward her.

"What a mess!" He leaned into her office and looked around.

"That mess is my office." Jessica wheezed out the words. "I'm not an executive so they're ripping out everything I'm not entitled to, no matter how much it costs."

"Don't take it personally. It's the good old Rank caste system at work."

"Will you wheel me to my car? I need to get out of here." She wished he were anybody but Bumpers, but she was getting so weak she had no choice.

Bumpers looked startled. "Me?"

It wasn't surprising he was startled. People didn't often go to a guy like Bumpers when they were vulnerable. He wasn't used to it.

"I need help." She told him how to handle the chair and how to go through doors backward. Following her directions, he pushed her to the parking lot.

"I've never touched a wheelchair before." He shook his head in disbelief.

"It won't hurt you and I'm not contagious." Jessica stood, gave him the car key and asked him to load the chair. He folded it and lifted it into the rear of the station wagon with an ease she envied.

"You don't look like you should be driving," he said as he helped her into the driver's seat.

"It'd be a lot harder to walk home."

He hung onto the door, apparently uncomfortable with her answer, but unable to figure out what to say. When she started the engine, he shut the door. She drove slowly through the parking lot, getting dizzier by the moment, but she had to keep going.

Drive home.

Take freeway on-ramp.

Getting weaker.

Breath coming short. MG dangerous, bad for breathing.

Should never have gotten on the freeway. Breathing too shallow and rapid. Don't feel right. Head fuzzy.

Rivers of cars whooshed by in both directions. Rivers have beginnings and ends. But the freeways were all interconnected so that traffic gushed off one onto the other and re-entered somewhere else.

No beginning, no end. Just flowing round and round. She was trapped in an unending stream of traffic going from no place to nowhere. No way to escape this rushing river.

This isn't a river, Jessica. It's a freeway. Look at the signs. Take the Bathgate exit. Go to the ER. Don't pass out.

Was she gasping more than thirty times a minute? Hatfield had said that was dangerous. She gripped the wheel. Don't think about how hard it is to breathe. Just drive.

High into the sky went the freeway. Water flowing uphill. Water cascading downhill. What if she got washed over the side? Her head was spinning as if she were already in free fall.

That's no waterfall. That's the Bathgate off-ramp. Get off.

Jessica summoned her last bit of energy to shuffle in from the ER parking lot. At the check-in window, she leaned heavily against the counter.

"Identification!" the clerk behind a glass partition demanded.

Jessica couldn't reach into the purse that hung by a strap from her shoulder, couldn't say a word. But she managed to thrust the hand with the Medical Alert bracelet through the opening in the partition.

When the clerk put her face down close to the bracelet to read it, Jessica could feel the woman's breath, steady and even on her wrist, unlike her own fast, shallow sucking. A second woman appeared, asking questions Jessica couldn't move her tongue or mouth to answer. This must be the triage nurse. Fernando had said there was a new requirement that the ER triage patients medically before triaging their wallets.

A gurney appeared. Help was here. She wasn't going to have to wait by the security desk as she had the first time she was here.

Two men in white laid her gently on it and strapped her in. They headed down the corridor past the examination rooms. Fluorescent lights in the ceiling were so bright they hurt her eyes.

They were wheeling her a long way, to the double doors at the end of the hall. The place where she'd previously seen paramedics wheeling a man gushing blood. The place where you went when your life was in danger.

Don't panic. Breathing will get worse.

The doors opened, the gurney was pushed against a wall, and rubber curtains hooked to ceiling tracks were yanked partway around to make a private alcove.

She couldn't see who stepped inside, but he lifted her arm, looked at her bracelet and read: "Myasthenia Gravis."

"Call the number on the bracelet. With MG, respiratory failure's a risk." A woman's husky voice. "I'll try to reach her doctor."

Her life was in the hands of people she couldn't even see from where she lay flat on her back.

"Respirator!" the first voice called out. "Prepare to intubate."

"No." Jessica managed to wheeze a word out. "Pen. Pa—per."

A rubber-gloved hand held a clipboard with paper on it in front of her, put a pen in her hand and wrapped her fingers around it. Her hand was so weak it took a minute or two to scrawl out "Not yet."

"Let us decide that," a man's voice with a New England twang said from above her. "Just relax." This wasn't Dr. Chapman. She wished it were.

She tapped a finger on the words "Not yet." She didn't want a respirator unless it was absolutely necessary. On the Internet she'd talked to patients who'd been on respirators. No one knew exactly when it was safe to take them off, particularly if they were on medication, so they sometimes lay motionless for days or weeks with a tube down the windpipe, a mask clamped over the face and a machine pumping every breath. Lying helpless for a long time would be almost as dreadful as death.

Almost, not quite. She had to stay alert, stay in charge of her situation.

Someone felt her arm. "Here's a good vein," a woman's voice said. Then there was a prick. Funny—they took her blood when her problem was that she couldn't breathe. She had to hope they knew what they were doing.

The face of a bespectacled, tight-lipped young man appeared above her. He introduced himself as a respiratory technician and unwrapped a cellophane-covered plastic device. "This is a spirometer." He waggled the white plastic mouthpiece of the device in front of her face. "I want you to breathe into this as hard as you can as long as you can."

He quickly realized he had to hold her mouth closed around the mouthpiece. She had little strength for blowing, but tried, hoping the effort wouldn't make her worse.

"Three point two liters," the technician said. "We like it to be at least three point eight. But three point two's no disaster."

He looked at his watch and put his ear to her nose. Then he stood up and looked at the watch again.

"What's the rep rate?" the New England man's voice said.

"Thirty-five."

Jessica trembled. Five over the danger level.

"Three point two and thirty-five. Blood work back yet? If possible, I want the blood oxygen levels before we put her on a respirator," the voice said.

The technician stood by with the spirometer.

Jessica needed someone on her side to speak for her. Still clutching the pen she'd been given, she wrote her mother's phone number on her hand and the word "Mom."

Mom just had to be home to answer.

"Breathe into this again." The technician held out the mouthpiece. "Hard as you can."

This time it was a little worse—three point one liters. He counted her breathing rate. It was holding at thirty-five.

A deep, authoritarian voice: "I got hold of Hatfield and he says try six migs of Tensilon if she's no worse than thirty-five. She had a big improvement during a test on eight migs."

The chest-thumping Hatfield. Her hero.

Another man she couldn't see. "The blood work's not back yet, but we're going to put her on the respirator if she goes a point over thirty-five. Can't risk waiting."

She hated not knowing who was in the room or who was making the decisions. "No." Her voice was so soft and breathless she feared no one heard.

The technician put the mouthpiece to her mouth. She suspected if she breathed as hard as she could into it, her breathing rate would go up and get more shallow. So she held back when she blew.

"Down to three point zero," the technician said, putting his ear to her nose.

He soon announced she was down to thirty-three breaths per minute.

"Go to the nurses' station. Get six—no, make that eight—migs of Tensilon," someone said.

The technician disappeared.

Suddenly she was alone, seeing no one, nothing but the curtain where it hooked to the ceiling track and another like it a few feet away. If she was without oxygen for as little as four minutes she'd be brain dead.

No one around to help. Where had they all gone? Try to sit up. Get more air. Can't.

Panic. No. Breathing would get worse. Chill out.

She heard a man's voice, not clearly, but she thought he said, "I've got the Tensilon."

"Check her again." Another man.

The respiratory technician leaned down to her nostrils. "Thirty-three."

The face of a man who looked like he hadn't slept or shaved for a few days floated above her. "Blood work's back. Arterial oxygen is low, among other things. I don't want to give the Tensilon."

Over the next fifteen minutes the technician took two more spirometer readings.

Mom, in grimy sweatpants and sweatshirt, face contorted with concern, was suddenly standing beside her bed. "What happened?"

Jessica saw a white-coated arm extend toward Mom. "Dr. Davenport, Mrs. Clement. We're going to take good care of your daughter."

Jessica gathered her breath. "Ten—si—lon," she whispered.

"My daughter said 'Tensilon,'" Mom said.

"If that's what she needs, that's what she'll get."

"Would you call Dr. Henry Hatfield, please? He's been treating Jessica."

"I spoke to him a few minutes ago," Davenport answered.

"Did he advise you to give my daughter Tensilon?"

"Yes, but that could be risky."

"Why is that?"

Jessica could have hugged Mom for the tone of authority in her voice.

Davenport reappeared within Jessica's view, his face almost in Mom's. "We know we can count on the respirator, but Tensilon can be tricky. I don't know if I want to risk using it."

"I—do." Jessica spent precious breath forcing out the words. She hoped she'd have some influence on him. These days so little of her life was under her control.

In a few minutes, she was connected to a bag of warm saline solution through an IV needle. She watched as Dr. Davenport inserted the head of a vial into the IV plug and squeezed it.

She lost control of her eyeballs and they jerked around in her head independently. The room and faces broke apart into kaleidoscopic pieces. She gasped for air, more desperate than she'd been all afternoon.

Tensilon!

She sucked through her gaping mouth for breath. Then the air came. It filled her lungs. The kaleidoscope reassembled into an ER cubicle. Gravity returned to normal. She lifted her arms toward the ceiling. "Look at me. I'm ready to fly."

Mom laughed.

Jessica unbuckled the restraints and cautiously sat up. She was alive. When she gave Mom a hug, she herself was shaking, but not too much to notice how feeble the return embrace was. Mom seemed suddenly to have been drained of energy.

"Mom, are you okay?"

"I'm fine. Don't worry about me."

Jessica took a good hard look at Mom's tense face, red eyes and shaking hands.

Breathing crises became almost the only subject of conversation between Jessica and Fernando. In the future, he wanted to be called if she had the slightest sign of one. He pleaded with her take a leave of absence from work. But the prospect of not being able to work, of losing her independence, was so frightening she didn't want to discuss it with him or anyone else. She'd find some way to cope.

Cruising the Internet, she learned that myasthenics who used orally inhaled albuterol when they had difficulty breathing were remarkably successful in avoiding visits to the ER. When she called Hatfield, he said he didn't understand why albuterol helped as some patients claimed—it didn't affect any basic neuromuscular function. But since it couldn't hurt if taken in moderation, he was willing to prescribe it.

Jessica made a point of telling him how grateful she was that he listened to her. Many MG sufferers complained their doctors discounted anything they had to say about their symptoms or medication. She was doubly pleased when he replied that his patients were his most important source of information.

She made a second lucky discovery during one of her visits to Hatfield. A man entered the waiting room with unusual crutches.

Instead of jutting into his underarms, they had sturdy leather sleeves that supported the length of his forearms. There was no underarm abrasion as with ordinary crutches. "They're called platform crutches. You ought to try them." He showed how he could lean into the sleeves, transferring his upper body weight to the crutch legs, and stand indefinitely. She saw that he could speak to people face-to-face as one of the up-theres. That was for her.

CHAPTER 25

Jessica sat back and enjoyed the view of sparkling sunlit water while Fernando struggled to hold back the wheelchair on a hill that plunged past Chinatown down to the wharf area. A warm July sun took the biting edge off the chilly, wet, salty air that swept in off the bay. A rickshaw-like ride in a wheelchair was a great way to tour San Francisco. Fernando uncomplainingly took her up and down hills far too steep for platform crutches.

Mom and Richard had been aghast when they'd learned she and Fernando were planning to make this trip after the proposal Jessica was working on was over. She'd chosen San Francisco because it was a place within driving distance where, with Fernando's help, she could be a tourist. Mom had protested. "What if you fall or have trouble breathing when you're way up there?" Jessica reminded her that she'd had a lot of success with albuterol and had to call the paramedics only once in the last month. Even then the ER hadn't put her on a respirator. Besides, Fernando knew an intern at the University Medical Center where there was one of the best ER's in the state. "Fernando will be with me every minute."

Mom would be pleased to see how Fernando had taken complete charge of her well-being on this trip. Jessica guessed she owed him a lot for his solicitude. Today she was breathing well, but her legs were weak.

"Let me know if you want me to put on the brakes so you can rest," she said. "This hill's like an Olympic ski jump."

"No way. I'm getting the best workout I've had since I started med school."

He enjoyed being a workhorse. Hers was a guilt-free ride.

"Let's stop here for a minute." Jessica pointed to a store window in the corner of a large wood and stucco shopping complex. "Don't you love that blue coat?" It was probably microfiber, hanging softly like suede from a mannequin's shoulders. The window was full of sharp-looking coats and jackets. There was a brown leather one she liked too.

Fernando laughed. "Anything for the rich lady."

Not exactly rich. She, like many others on the proposal, had earned a lot of overtime pay—twenty-five hundred dollars—for all the extra hours she'd put in. Now, for two weeks, she intended to deny herself nothing, a bit reckless considering she wasn't sure what her position would be when she returned from vacation, what Armor might attempt to do to her next. But she simply couldn't resist abandoning herself to pleasures still accessible to her.

Fernando wheeled her to the bottom of a flight of steps leading up to store level. No ramp. That was a problem they'd read about in a San Francisco newspaper—the city was just beginning to recognize the needs of the disabled. Only last week, wheelchair riders had demonstrated downtown against the scarcity of beveled curbs and chair lifts for buses that often would not stop for a lone person in a wheelchair. She would have liked to have been here to demonstrate with them. She'd welcome a chance to be active on behalf of others, not just wallowing in her own misery all the time.

Jessica stood and made her way up, planting both feet on each step before tackling the next. Fernando folded the chair into a pancake and carried it.

Inside, she felt like standing on her own. Walking up and down the hills was tough, but in the store she could certainly use her legs.

Fernando unfolded the wheelchair and rolled it next to her. "Here."

"I want to walk," she said as sweetly as possible. She wanted him to know she appreciated his kindness, but right now she needed to move on her own.

His dour look and head shake said she might as well be taking up cocaine or hang gliding.

"Use it or lose it," she reminded him firmly. Dr. Hatfield himself had approved of her determination to stay on her feet as much as she could. Too much inactivity and her muscles would atrophy.

She headed for the microfiber coats, trailed by Fernando pushing the wheelchair. She slipped into a narrow space between two racks where he couldn't bring it.

He peered at her from the other side through a gap in a long row of coats. "You should be in your wheelchair."

"Peekaboo!" she squealed.

He pushed the coats that framed his taut face farther apart. "You've been better on this trip because I haven't let you overexert yourself."

That was Fernando—sweet and helpful, but he could certainly be tiresome. She yanked a blue-gray coat—like the one she'd admired in the window—from the rack and held it up in front of her. "Jessica's hiding from Fernando. Naughty Jessica."

"Come on, Jessica," he hissed. "Quit playing around."

"You started it," she giggled. "With your head sticking between those coats. You look silly."

"A beautiful coat." A sales woman about Jessica's age, dressed in a smashing sweater and skirt outfit, came up. "Why not try it on in front of that mirror over there?"

As Jessica made her way to the full-length mirror, Fernando hurried to intercept her with the wheelchair. He seized the coat and held it for her. She slid an arm, then her body and other arm into the coat, feeling the silky lining. She stroked the supple, feather-light material. This was luxurious.

"Very becoming," the sales woman said. "Fits you perfectly across here." She patted Jessica's shoulders. "And the length is right too."

"I love it." In the mirror Jessica admired the elegant coat falling gracefully from her shoulders to mid-calf.

"Too long," Fernando said. "Not practical for Southern California. And too awkward to manage in a wheelchair."

The woman shot him an irritated glance.

"Who needs a wheelchair? Not me." Jessica prodded a finger into her own chest. "You must be thinking of someone else." Why did Fernando have to bring up the wheelchair in front of someone so chic, someone her own age?

"This material's amazing," the woman said. "You can compress it tightly for packing, then wear it wrinkle-free straight from the suitcase."

"You'd get more use out of a shorter, lighter jacket," Fernando said. "It'd be easier to manage in the wheelchair."

The sales woman pursed her lips and frowned, as though she'd like to tell him to butt out.

Jessica smirked, baring her teeth at Fernando. "You're a barrel of fun today." She turned her back on him and faced the woman. "How is it for stains?"

"You'd never guess to look at this coat. But you can take almost anything out in a washing machine."

"In a washing machine?" This was a miracle coat. "How much?"

"Your lucky day. On sale for only one ninety-four."

"I've got to have it." She tried not to think about the cost, which under normal circumstances was affordable on her salary, especially with her overtime stash. The problem was her future didn't guarantee any income.

Back in the street, Jessica hugged the red-ribboned silver box where the coat nestled in tissue paper. She began plodding down the steep hill toward the wharf area.

"Jessica!" Fernando called. She felt the full force of his doctor-in-charge persona. He was rolling the wheelchair right beside her.

"I told you I don't need that thing." The hill was very steep. Feeling her thighs starting to give way, she turned sideways to its slope and began to sidestep down, the way cross-country skiers did when they climbed steep inclines. "I'm through with wheelchairs."

"You're being foolish."

"And you're no fun." It was frustrating, not being able to kid him out of his bad attitude.

She kept on sidestepping.

"Do you want to fall on this goddamn hill and break your neck?"

Jessica fought the heavy gravity she'd gotten to know so well, but lost the battle and sank slowly onto the sidewalk, dropping the coat box. There was no way she could struggle down this precipitous sidewalk on foot. She'd have to crawl. That's what she would do. She began creeping along the cold, rough cement on her hands and knees, dragging the box, which scraped along beside her.

Fernando put his arms under her armpits.

"Let go of me," she cried, trying to wriggle from his grasp.

"I will not." He clasped his hands under her rib cage, dragged her over to the wheelchair and sat her down forcefully.

"It's my choice whether I want the wheelchair or not." She sobbed. "It should be."

He plunked the coat box onto her lap. Gripping the handles, he held the chair to a slow roll until they reached the bottom of the hill in silence.

She hated him for doing this to her.

He waited for the light, then began pushing her across the street toward the wharf. Seagulls flew overhead and perched on rooftops and streetlights, calling to each other in ringing voices like crows that had learned to sing. Chilled air laden with sea foam and the heady aroma of chocolate from Ghirardelli's down the street whipped her clothing.

Jessica drew a deep breath. Today was too good to waste. If Fernando kept up his overbearing solicitude, she wouldn't argue or let it get to her, she'd endure him in silence. Until they got back home.

"Let's go out on the wharf, take in the shops, have dinner some-where overlooking the bay," she said.

Fernando pushed her to the bottom of a short flight of bleached wooden steps heading to the wharf. Placing the coat box on the wheel-chair seat, Jessica climbed the steps with the help of a railing while Fernando pulled the chair up backward, expertly tipping it toward him-self so the box wouldn't fall off.

On the wharf she was able to walk energetically enough to hear the kerplunks of her feet on the wooden boards. Fernando's heavier footsteps thudded after her, accompanied by the rhythmic squeak of the wheelchair. She had an urge to dash down the walkway before the squeak caught up with her.

Impossible. But at least she could walk a little faster. Stepping up the pace, she laughed to herself at how she must look, like a rolling, listing sailor just returned from months at sea.

A deep, sternum-shaking boat horn blasted a departure warning. Jessica paused to lean against a rail and watched last-minute passengers hurry aboard a triple-decked red and white tour boat moored at the next wharf.

Fernando leaned beside her, the wheelchair shoved against the rail on his other side.

"Is it too late to take a boat ride today?" Jessica asked. "The bay looks lovely, and I think the tour only takes an hour."

"The water's too choppy. You'd get weak every time the boat rises or falls."

"Goddammit, Fernando!" Jessica gripped the rail until her fingers hurt.

"What? What's the matter?"

She bit her lip. She wouldn't even try to kid him out of his mood. Once he may have thought she was the funniest woman he'd ever met and laughed with her, but now he was too preoccupied with taking over her life. She clearly saw that, left in Fernando's hands, she would become a permanent, perpetual cripple. A shut-in. That would suit him just fine. He'd be happy if she was in her apartment all day, every day, where no harm could come to her.

She forced her attention further down the wharf to where a large ferry boat was tied up. Beyond that, across an expanse of water, loomed the dark lump of Alcatraz Island.

She turned away and tottered down the wooden walkway, Fernando trailing in her wake. Soon they came to a shop painted bright red. "Sea shells. Let's go in," she said.

The store had shells in every size and shade of cream, pink, orange and pearl gray. One glass case displayed perfect specimens of large conches. After looking at all of them, she settled on one with a brilliant medley of fleshlike pinks and oranges blending into a deep rose throat. It would look stunning in her living room displayed against the dark wood of the bookcase.

She tried to resist when Fernando wanted to buy it for her—she had extra cash now—but he was so insistent it would have meant a fight if she didn't give in. He supervised the wrapping of the shell, demanding it be packed in several layers of tissue paper. He didn't ask how she wanted it packed.

They made their way along the wharf to a candy shop and then a beachwear store, the sun and wind scouring their faces, not buying anything, just passing by the bright displays, until they came to a restaurant near the end of the wharf. It was only six o'clock and the restaurant was half empty.

Inside, windows on three sides afforded a view of the bay from any of the sturdy wooden tables, each set with paper place mats printed with tourist maps of San Francisco, squeeze bottles of ketchup and mustard, a paper napkin dispenser, a small vase of carnations and a candle in a wide-mouthed glass. Jessica liked the place right away. Anyone could have a good time here—from families whose parents wouldn't have to worry about the kids' messiness to couples looking for a romantic view.

Jessica insisted the wheelchair remain at the hostess desk. She didn't want to look at the thing during dinner.

When Fernando asked to be seated where Jessica could look westward toward the sunset, only an hour or so away, the maitre d' obliged with a table for two by a window. She laid the bag with the conch on the table, leaned the coat box against the legs of her chair and sat down to a view of Alcatraz over Fernando's shoulder.

Their ponytailed waitress took Jessica's steamed vegetable plate order before Fernando's sea bass and half carafe of house chardonnay. Waitresses responded to her when she could hold her head up.

She thought Fernando had to be tired from pushing her up and down the steep hills, but he looked robust and healthy, cheeks glowing from exposure to the invigorating air. That his eyes were bright and eager she attributed to the thrill he got from being caretaker to his helpless Jessica.

He was sweet with her. If only he'd get off her back, just for this vacation. If they could only laugh again like they used to. She clutched and twisted the paper napkin in her lap.

"You look good," he said. "Being outdoors is good for you."

"Tell that to my parents when we get back. They're worried sick about my traveling."

The waitress brought sides of coleslaw and the wine. Shiny drops condensed appealingly on the outside of the goblet. Jessica usually didn't mind giving up alcohol for Mestinon, but now she wished she could have a drink.

Fernando frowned. "Your parents should realize that I'm perfectly capable of caring for you."

Jessica tried to force a smile of appreciation. "They really should. The way you hover over me, you seem more like their son than I seem like their daughter."

She watched his Adam's apple bob as he swallowed a mouthful of wine. Then he set the goblet down, without loosening his grip on the stem. "I don't know how to take that."

"You know I love my parents, even when their attitude isn't perfect." It should be easy for her to say she loved him too, but it wasn't.

Fernando's eyebrows turned down at the ends, in a way Jessica knew meant he was hurt. "I do everything I can to help you."

She twisted hard on her napkin. "I know and I appreciate it. But don't you realize I'm the one who should decide when I need help and when I don't?"

He composed his face and leaned back in his chair. "I'm a doctor."

"I thought you were my boyfriend."

Fernando began explaining how it was his duty, maybe even his moral obligation, to use his medical skills when they were needed. Scarcely hearing a word, Jessica gazed out over the bay. A large red sun hung only inches above Alcatraz and would soon set.

The waitress set down their hot, heavy dinner plates, then lit their candle. Since she'd twisted her napkin into a tight rope, Jessica yanked another from the dispenser. It fanned the candle which flamed very close to the carnations. She tried not to listen to Fernando going on about how privileged she was, in her condition, to have a doctor close at hand. A few carnation petals turned black, singed by the flame. As she watched, a flower began to smolder. A petal from another blossom caught from the first. Embers of petals floated onto the table and settled beside the paper bag containing the conch Fernando had bought her. Soon the top of the bag blackened, and began to curl. Inside the bag the shell was tightly wrapped in the layers of tissue Fernando had ordered. She had time to douse the fire with a glass of water. If she wanted to.

"I have a huge advantage over Dr. Hatfield, seeing you every day," Fernando went on, dissecting his fish with a sharp knife and fork. "He only has your word about how you're doing."

Only her word?

She watched as hot red spots began glowing against black ash over much of the bag. The tissue paper inside must be ignited by now. Small flames were licking up from every carnation in the vase.

The bag began to smoke. Fernando sniffed the air. "What's that?"

With a bang and a pop, the conch exploded.

Fernando jumped to his feet. "My God!"

Jessica got to her feet too. The water glass on her place mat was winking at her in the firelight, inviting her to pour it onto the fire. She wondered how many pieces the conch had broken into.

Fernando splashed his glass of wine on the bag. A man from the next table ran over and emptied a full bottle of Heineken's on the burning paper, splattering Fernando. A child screamed. An older couple seated nearby got up and hurried to the door. The bartender dashed up with an ice bucket full of water and dumped it on the vase with the smoldering carnations.

Jessica watched the embers die on the charred bag. The dancing, flickering flames were gone.

CHAPTER 26

In the month since her return from San Francisco Jessica had rarely driven. Occasionally she crept around the corner from her apartment and down the street a few blocks to a grocery store and pharmacy. But she had become afraid of freeways and traffic-clogged streets. Today, in the backseat of Mom's car, being trundled to a Myasthenia Gravis Organization meeting, she mourned the loss of mobility and independence.

These losses were causing all kinds of problems. Needing a ride was her primary excuse for not distancing herself from Fernando. He often drove her to and from work, to the doctor's, anywhere she needed to go. He cooked, did her laundry, bought the groceries, even fed the cats, leaving no opportunity when she could guiltlessly tell him she didn't want him around, and making her increasingly fearful of what she couldn't do if he weren't around. She often asked herself if she loved Fernando, whether she had ever loved him. It was hard to remember when she was confronted with so many problems, and he was determined to take over all of them, which was like taking over her whole life.

Last weekend she'd made up her mind to tell him he was smothering her and she needed to see less of him. But he'd offered, the very day she planned to speak to him, to take her to an MG outing at Dodger Stadium. She didn't care about baseball, but she'd wanted to go to meet other MG patients. So she'd put off telling him again.

The trip had been an eye-opener. In the section donated to the MG organization she'd met several patients—like Max, sitting with his wife and two young children. Max was having trouble with drooping eyelids and a slack jaw, but otherwise seemed fine. She'd watched a thirtyish couple come down the steps and find their seats, the woman leaning on the man's arm, apparently needing only a little help. An older woman sitting nearby introduced Jessica to her husband. "Frank's just retired and hates it when he gets too weak for golf," the woman said. "After waiting all these years, he wants to play whenever he feels like it." Jessica sympathized, even though she doubted she could stumble through even one hole.

"Me, I hate falling down when I laugh hard," Jessica said. "Does that ever bother your husband?"

The woman gave her a puzzled look. "When you laugh?" She hadn't heard of anyone who got weak when they laughed.

To her further astonishment, Jessica saw no crutches or wheelchairs, no one slumped in their seat. When she asked about this, Frank's wife again looked puzzled and said most patients stayed home when they were really sick. Jessica was shocked. "Why wouldn't they come in a wheelchair if that's the only way they could get here?"

"I suppose it's hard to deal with the world when you're very weak," the woman replied.

"No one here's as sick as I am," Jessica told Fernando.

"You wouldn't be here yourself if I hadn't brought you."

"What's your point, Fernando? That nobody as sick as I am has someone to look after them as capable and devoted as you?" It was just like him to rub it in that she was so dependent on him.

She had a sudden urge for comfort food. After downing nachos and a Coke, she asked for pizza. "You don't want to have a carbohydrate crash, do you?" he scolded. He had it wrong. What she didn't want was any of his nagging. "So I'll slump a bit. So what?" Twenty minutes after she ate the pizza she slumped. "What did I tell you? Are you happy now?" Fernando sounded so snippy.

The more he got on her case about eating junk food, the more of it she consumed. When Frank's wife said she was going for a frozen malt, Jessica asked if they'd bring her one too. By the time the game was over, she'd managed also to get her hands on a bag of peanuts, a cup of beer, ice cream on a stick and a candy bar. She became so weak it took both Fernando and another man to help her out to the parking lot. But she was happy. It was a thrill to be childish and defeat the over-the-top adult Fernando.

He'd been furious all the way home. She'd lost the opportunity to tell him to go fly a kite because she'd been preoccupied with trying not to throw up.

Fernando was clueless when it came to the tension between them. Being sure he was always right seemed to immunize him against awareness of interpersonal stress. Like nagging. And like their sex life. She couldn't get over his attitude toward their nonexistent sex life. As far as she could tell, he wasn't bothered a bit. An obvious explanation was that he didn't want to push her. But her instincts told her taking charge of her medical case had a bigger grip on him than sex ever had.

He got no complaints from her in the sex department. She had no libido at all these days. Zip, none, nada.

At today's meeting Jessica wanted to show support for the MG organization and its research fund drive. And very important to her, this was advertised as a self-help group. She could hardly wait to hear about self-help and see it in action firsthand.

Imbued with the spirit of independence and lightly leaning on Mom's and Richard's arms, she walked with as much dignity as she could muster from the parking lot to the meeting center. Just inside, patients, families and friends were milling about in the lobby, standing in line to order MG Christmas cards and T-shirts and buy raffle tickets.

Her heaviness eased perceptibly at the sight of people greeting each other warmly and enjoying themselves. They were all dressed up for this special occasion. Here was proof you could have MG and have a good time.

But as she looked closely, her enthusiasm dimmed. Just as at the ball game, no one here was on crutches or in a wheelchair, no one had fallen on the floor. Nobody in a lobby armchair was slumping. Only a few, maybe not more than in any busy crowd, looked tired or droopy.

She ran into a couple she'd met at the ball game; he was the retired golfer. It turned out they were regulars at MG events, as were several others she'd seen at the stadium. Not one was on crutches or in a wheelchair. Quite a few were actively walking or engaged in lively conversation.

As she and Mom and Richard drifted past the sales booths, Jessica eyed the crowd, studying the variety and depth of symptoms, searching for coping techniques, looking for clues to functioning independently. She soon came to the conclusion that no one she saw needed help—they were all functioning independently. Could they be taking more Mestinon than she was? Hatfield had said she was on the maximum dose.

She bought a couple of boxes of Christmas cards to support MG research, as did Mom and Richard. There was no outward sign that anyone selling or buying them had MG.

Mom carried the boxes and Richard held onto Jessica's elbow as they entered the main auditorium where Dr. Hatfield was to lecture on treatments and research. She was eager to see how the three hundred or so people in the audience would react to him.

Once they'd found seats near the front, Mom twisted and turned to scan the crowd, many of whom were still finding seats. "No one here looks as disabled as you."

Trying not to let her jaw hang open, Jessica couldn't help drooping forward until her head almost touched the shoulder of a woman in front of her. She could guess where the sicker ones were—at home, the worst in bed or in the hospital.

After a series of acknowledgments by organization office holders and thank-yous to the many people who'd worked hard to bring the meeting about, Hatfield was introduced. High up on the stage, he looked out of character in a dark gray suit, ordinary striped tie and the forelock of hair that usually flopped onto his forehead slicked back. Nothing of his unique personality was in evidence. That ended right away, when he showed the first slide—West Africans force-feeding an accused person a serving of the ordeal bean. According to Hatfield, if the accused died from eating the bean, he was adjudged guilty of a crime. If he survived, even if barely, he was innocent. The chemical in these beans, physostigmine, which put the accused through the ordeal, became the basis for Mestinon.

Jessica's body grew heavier. That her medication was as perverse as her illness was depressing news.

Hatfield extolled the revolution in treating myasthenics brought about by Mestinon. When Mestinon wasn't enough, he said thymectomy, the removal of the thymus gland, was becoming the most effective treatment. There was evidence that the gland was responsible for producing immune system elements that caused MG. Because the surgery was so traumatic—the breast bone was broken and the defective gland beneath it cut out—only the most severely affected patients were subjected to it. Its big advantage was that it usually helped, sometimes totally ridding the patient of MG.

Hatfield had never mentioned thymectomy to her, which Jessica assumed meant he thought she didn't need it. But he hadn't seen her for over a month.

He went on to describe immune system suppression techniques used in very drastic cases—administration of the medication prednisone and the flushing out and exchange of the patient's plasma. Prednisone often left patients puffy, exhausted and even psychotic. Plasma exchange required hospitalization and could result in systemic infection. Jessica realized that any of these procedures, no matter how terrible, could be one she'd someday need, even welcome, as a last resort.

When it was time to leave, she did her best to walk out on her own, smiling and introducing herself to others. But in the middle of the lobby outside the auditorium she lost her place in the universe of normal speed and viscosity and fell into her own slow, sticky one—shuffling along with head drooping, mouth hanging open like a panting dog's. She got Mom to support her on one arm and Richard on the other. No one else in the lobby was anywhere near as spectacular a mess as she was.

"How about I get the wheelchair out of the car?" Richard offered.

"No!" Jessica whispered. "I can go a bit farther." She didn't want to be the only one here being wheeled around.

"Look how you have to struggle to move your feet at every step. I'm exhausted just watching you," Mom said. "It would be so much easier if you took the wheelchair."

"Then get me a Groucho Marx nose, mustache and a pair of glasses. So no one will see it's me."

Mom laughed. "Jessica!"

"Wouldn't that be a sight!" Richard said, as they crept across the lobby.

She'd won a reprieve from their efforts to stuff her into the wheelchair, but she wished they'd understand. More than anything she wished they would tell her they admired her when she tried so hard to stand on her own feet.

But Mom had never understood Daddy's need to do what he could. How could Jessica hope for more for herself?

On the way home Jessica thought over her deteriorating condition. In the eight months she'd had MG she'd become sicker than any patient she'd seen in public. She'd already had four trips to the ER with breathing crises, each time narrowly escaping being put on a respirator. Work and driving were becoming major problems. Who knew how far downhill she might go if something drastic wasn't done. A thymectomy seemed to offer more hope than anything else she'd heard of.

CHAPTER 27

If only she'd get a chance to deal with one problem at a time. Daily mental and physical struggles had left her exhausted. Too exhausted to deal with her nearly unbearable relationship with Fernando. The only progress she'd made was to persuade him to move back into his own apartment so he could study and she could lie wherever she'd collapsed and feel free to turn on the TV or CD player using the disabled person's saving grace, the remote control. She slept on the floor or the couch as often as she slept in bed.

Now she had to face moving to a new building at work.

This was the first time she'd worked on a major proposal. She soon learned the interim between proposal submittal and contract award might take months and was even harder to endure than the proposal effort. If a full crew of fifteen hundred or so was brought on before contract start, salaries plus the bill for facilities, labs, assembly line and test chambers could run into the millions. But if project managers didn't stake out buildings and bring some people on board, they could end up with no one and no space when the company won the contract, leading to a slow startup and costly schedule delays. Striking a balance between holding onto enough staff and building space and spending devastating amounts of money was nerve-wracking. Trickle-down edginess from upper management permeated the atmosphere. People worried that Rank might lose the contract and be forced to make massive layoffs. Rumors infested every level and every corner of the company—Rank had won, Rank had lost, another company had gotten its hands on Rank's secret design, Rank's president had sold out to the competition and on and on. Jessica was terrified of losing her job and with it her medical insurance at a time when she might need major surgery.

The skeleton crew Jessica was on was newly installed in a building housing both offices and spacecraft manufacturing facilities. Her office was on the third and top floor, reached by way of a steep stairway. Sometimes she got up the stairs by leaning against the wall, sometimes by using crutches or even by creeping on all fours. As for the wheelchair, no one was strong enough to go up and down stairs with her in it—when she needed it a janitor with a key to the freight elevator had to be called.

At least she had an office. Her first thought when she'd heard about the move was that Armor would see to it she had no place to go. But, thanks to Stone, she had an office of her own, much smaller than his and not windowed, but a regular four-walled office where she could work in peace and quiet and hide how weak she'd become. And Skowron had seen to it that she had a handicapped parking place by the front door. She owed a lot to Stone and Skowron.

Her office, Stone's and three others were located off a large bay with supply cabinets, a small refrigerator, a secretary's desk and a table cluttered with coffee paraphernalia in the center, an arrangement designed to give a family feel. To Jessica's dismay, Enid, Stone's new secretary, began to make the bay a no-man's-land as soon as she arrived, filling it with her deep, rasping cigarette-smoker's voice, sticking her large nose into everyone's business. When Stone had brought her in, he'd told Jessica to get used to her. She was fast, efficient and knew the company inside out.

Across the hall and only two doors down was Armor's suite. Jessica sometimes heard his shouting and the plaintive, defensive voice of his secretary. She'd not seen him since he'd had the carpet and furniture removed from her old office and hoped that keeping out of sight and off his mind wouldn't be impossible with his office so close.

Kyle Bumpers' office was next to Armor's, but he was never around. Rumor was he was recovering from an accident that happened while he was landing in a small plane on a clandestine mission.

Like everyone else waiting for the contract, Jessica was not nearly as busy as she'd been during the proposal. Spending her days sitting in her office, not totally idle, but laying out formats for a few contractual reports, she could hide how weak she was. After the contract came in, her workload would increase rapidly beyond what she was now able to handle. She would have to come out of her office more and people would see how sick she was. She began to pin her hopes on a thymectomy.

With little to do, time passed slowly. Sometimes she escaped the tedium and her tendency to brood when alone and idle by going to the third floor balcony of the empty, giant integration and test chamber. The proportions of the chamber were a breathtaking distraction in themselves: a balcony on each floor offered a view of the steel-beamed walls and ceiling towering twenty feet above the third floor level. The chamber, she'd been told, was where newly assembled satellites, typically weighing several tons and as big as a school bus, were checked out.

From the balcony, she sometimes watched Stone, who wasn't busy either. At one end of the chamber he'd set up a washtub as a target for practicing fly-casting. Watching someone fly-cast, she decided, was about as boring as her current job.

Now she had time to read up on thymectomies, download information from the Web, and scour medical journals to understand the benefits and risks. One paper said that eighty percent of myasthenics improved after surgery, fifteen percent experienced no improvement, and five percent got worse. Not very good odds considering the risk and pain involved in having your sternum cracked open and thymus gouged out. She felt her breast bone and pictured a doctor in a white coat like Fernando's, hammer raised high above her supine body, ready to smash a chisel through it. Terrible as the operation was, there seemed to be no alternative because she feared no amount of Mestinon could deal with her worsening condition.

Recovery took six to eight weeks. That meant if she were to be on her feet when the contract was awarded in early January, the operation had to be no later than mid-November, only a month away. She'd have to schedule it soon. Then there'd be the ordeal of telling Fernando, Mom, Richard and Jim Stone, dealing with their anxieties as well as her own.

She particularly dreaded telling Fernando. Sometimes she couldn't believe how antagonistic her feelings had become. She felt guilty being ungrateful for all he'd done and was doing, but she needed her independence—more than the average person, she supposed. He didn't recognize this need and never would, an obtuseness that was hard to understand in such an intelligent person. Perhaps his Catholicism, with its ingrained authoritarianism, had influenced him. Or his parents' control in steering his life—from the assignment of childhood chores that had left him with little idle time, to his choice of career. Whatever the cause, he always tried to control his world, and she knew that in her weakened condition, from his point of view, she looked particularly in need of control. She was determined to avoid becoming helpless in his hands, as her father had been in Mom's.

At least she'd get two of the recovery weeks off on paid Thanksgiving, Christmas and New Year's holidays. The rest would have to be leave of absence, when she'd receive only long-term disability payments at seventy percent of her salary rate. Her biggest problem might be finding someone to look after her after the operation. It might have to be Mom. She didn't know if either she or her mother could survive that arrangement.

Jessica looked at her watch. Whitney would soon be in the down-stairs lobby to pick her up for lunch, the highlight of Jessica's week. She eyed the platform crutches propped in the corner and the wheelchair on the other side of the table. She liked the idea that the visitor chair was the wheelchair because it made normal people think about what it would be like to be confined to one.

Today she was doing better than usual—only a few after-breakfast droops, no brain switch activity. And she'd be with Whitney. Take a chance and leave the crutches behind.

At the door leading into the corridor, she peered across to Armor's office, prepared to duck back inside if he appeared. Seeing the coast was clear, she hurried down the spooky corridor, about fifteen feet high and wide as a small street, paved with rugged industrial tile to accommodate the movement of heavy racks of electronic instruments. Without the bustle of people and equipment, the corridor was a silent mausoleum where even her soft footsteps echoed.

The stairs to the first floor were long and steep and she negotiated them slowly, leaning on the railing at each step. At the bottom, she needed all her remaining strength to shove open the heavy metal door to the lobby. She was sure she was getting weaker, even during her best moments, probably a result of muscle wasting from inactivity on top of the MG.

Whitney was waiting just outside the glass-enclosed lobby, her blond hair blowing in the blustery wind. Jessica waved and was halfway to the door before she noticed him. On the far side of the lobby, a man was propped up in a wheelchair. Kyle Bumpers.

He tried to look up at her as she walked by, but his head was flopped to one side. His inert body was smartly dressed in fine wool slacks, hand-tailored shirt and an exquisite cashmere jacket. A lopsided version of his old what-a-good-boy-I-am smile flashed across his face above the neatly trimmed goatee. Jessica walked by with a small nod in his direction.

Outside, she pointed him out to Whitney. "That's Kyle Bumpers. In a wheelchair."

"My God, look at him. He's not going to be up to his old tricks for a while."

Jessica saw him slump and stare blankly at the floor.

During lunch, she only half listened to Whitney's complaints about her new job assignment, which she described as Mickey Mouse work. She was preoccupied with thoughts of Bumpers. Bumpers in the down-there world of the wheelchair-bound. Bumpers unable to swagger in the hallway. Bumpers unable to press up close to young women and leer at them. Bumpers with nothing left of him but a cockeyed little boy's smile.

Jessica managed to rouse herself to urge Whitney to nose around, find a job within her department that appealed to her, and let management know she wanted it. Whitney said it should already be plain to them she wasn't happy and they weren't doing anything about it. She was going to look for a job outside the company.

And what then? Jessica could easily see Whitney falling into the same pattern of not speaking up for herself at any job she took. Wherever she went there were bound to be people eager to order someone like Whitney around. Somehow she had to persuade her to go for what she wanted. Whitney was too good to be wasted. And life would be very lonely at Rank without Whitney.

After lunch, Jessica had a post-food fade and needed to hold onto Whitney's arm in order to drag her leaden feet up the two flights of stairs to her office. Clinging to each other in the corridor after the effort, they swayed, teetered, staggered and then began to giggle.

The switches in Jessica's brain went into action. Before she'd started giggling she'd already been weak. Now laughter was putting her over the edge. She went completely limp and, when Whitney lost her grip, slid to the floor.

The floor was gritty with who knew what grime and smelled of sulfurous, industrial nastiness. She was thinking she'd better get up before anyone saw her when she heard the unmistakable clicks of wheelchair bearings.

Whitney's blond head appeared a few inches above Jessica's. "Look what's coming this way," she whispered. "Kyle Bumpers."

Twenty feet away, the wheelchair crossed Jessica's line of sight, veering across the corridor and into the wall. She could see Bumpers struggling to back up using his right hand on a wheel. The left lay limp in his lap.

"Give me your hands," Jessica said, slurring the words badly. When she and Whitney had gotten hold of each other, she said, "Pull." In a minute, Jessica was not very steady, but on her feet.

She toddled over and took hold of the black plastic grips on the back of Bumpers' wheelchair. "Thanks," she said to Whitney. "See ya."

A look of doubt clouded Whitney's gray eyes as she left.

"Where to?" Jessica's words to Bumpers seemed to take forever to form. When she managed to close her mouth for a second, her jaw soon hung open again. She hated that—it made her look so stupid.

"Damn—wheel—chair." Bumpers' words were just as halting as Jessica's, but broken up and unsteady in pitch, whereas Jessica's were soft and slurry.

"Your office or mine?"

"Mine." He gave her a lopsided grin.

Gripping the handles as firmly as she could with only a fraction of her normal strength available, she pulled the chair away from the wall. Good thing wheelchair bearings were smooth—Bumpers was heavy.

She'd nearly reached his door when she stopped. "Better to go in backward." She wanted to warn she was about to turn him around because when she was being pushed by someone, she always found it disorienting and disconcerting to be barreling along facing one way and then spun without warning in the opposite direction.

She backed carefully through the door. "You can't handle a wheelchair with one hand. You need two to steer."

His office was bigger than Jim Stone's. She shoved him past a glass-topped coffee table, two armchairs and a rust-colored sofa to a hulking walnut desk.

"Guess I'll have to hire a wheelchair chauffeur." Bumpers raised one hand and spoke with half a mouth, revealing he was paralyzed on one side and apparently okay on the other.

"What you need is an electric wheelchair. Don't become any more dependent on other people than you have to. Does your neck hurt?" She saw his head was tilted awkwardly to the side.

"I'm okay."

She could see pain in his eyes.

She went around the desk and maneuvered the wheelchair until he was nestled into the intersection of two walls. Gently, with two hands, she moved his head until it was resting upright in the corner. "There. That's what I do when I have the droops." His smooth-shaven cheeks, even on the paralyzed side, felt surprisingly warm. Without knowing why, she'd supposed the paralyzed side would be cold, like dead.

Bumpers looked startled and tried to pull away from her. "Leave me alone." His eyes were full of misery.

Jessica was appalled. His eyes had once been full of lots of things—lechery, evasiveness, egotism—but never misery. It was as though his pilot light had gone out.

"No one likes to have a disability."

"I'm not disabled," he croaked.

"Right. You and I will go out dancing tonight."

"Therapy and time, I'll be as good as ever."

Jessica plopped onto the sofa. It was uncomfortable, too hard and the upholstery was coarse. "I hope so, Kyle."

"You don't have to stay with me. I'm fine."

From the way he was straining the left side of his face, Jessica supposed he was trying to be as emphatic as he could without being able to raise his voice. "I know how you feel, Kyle. It's hard to admit you're not like you used to be, that you need help."

"Don't need help."

Jessica thought his cockeyed face might have a sneer on it. "You helped me once."

"You needed it."

"You do too."

His face turned red. "There's nothing for you to do here."

"You're hard to understand because you're mushing your words. You should learn how to make hand signals."

"I can say go to hell. That clear enough?"

"Why should I go anywhere when I enjoy tormenting you so much?" She let a big Cheshire cat grin spread across her face. "I like it when you sweat and squirm. I think I'll try shoving paper clips under your finger nails next."

"I bet you would!" He couldn't help himself, couldn't stifle a little smile.

She had won.

The smile floated in and out of her mind for the next several days as she sat in her office tediously formatting documents. Today it was the channel electronics specification tree, where requirements were shown for each little amplifier, filter, mixer, all the electronic parts. There were thousands.

If the contract came in, her job would be to go to the engineers and gather up their inputs to documents, such as this tree, and insert them where they belonged. She wouldn't be writing much of anything. There'd be nothing of her in the work, not like the technical writing she'd done on the proposal. But even this routine drudgery would be too challenging if she didn't get the thymus operation, or some medication more effective than Mestinon.

Outside her closed door she heard a machine humming smoothly and clicking almost inaudibly. It stopped. Jessica waited a minute before taking the two small steps needed to get from her chair to the door, which she opened cautiously.

She didn't know which sight was more startling—Kyle Bumpers or the electric wheelchair. The right side of his face was beaming or leering or sneering, she couldn't tell which, while being dragged down by an uncooperative left side. Whether he was here to share with her the joy of new-found mobility or to one-up her simple, hand-propelled wheelchair, she could only guess.

"Watch." He pushed one of several small levers under his right hand. The black chair glided backward, silent except for a purring motor mounted beneath the seat. As he operated the levers, the chair performed figure eights, smooth turns, starts and stops at a speed Jessica could hardly believe. The chair had a thick, padded seat and back, armrests and a molded headrest. This had to be the Ferrari of wheelchairs, costing she could not guess what.

"Forty-five thousand bucks." Bumpers, still struggling with speech, croaked the words out. "The best money can buy."

He had to know she couldn't afford such a chair. He'd come to lord it over her.

She wouldn't give in to pettiness. "It's stunning, Kyle. Fast, smooth, turns on a dime, smashingly elegant." She touched an armrest and felt the softness of kid leather. "And luxurious. You'll be the envy of every disabled person around here, especially me."

He arched his right eyebrow and gazed lopsidedly at her. "Thought you'd appressshhate—"

"You thought I'd eat my heart out. That's what you thought," she said with mock sweetness.

"You're such a smart ass."

"You're complaining?" she said as if daring him to.

"No, acsshhly like it." She could swear one eye had an affectionate look in it.

She stepped away from him. She didn't want affection from the likes of Kyle Bumpers. She might feel sorry for him, empathize with him a bit, want to help him as she would anyone in his condition. But share affection with him?

Head cocked to one side and cushioned by the headrest, he stared into the coffee pot. Enid had brewed some before she'd left for the company stationery store.

The silence was too stressful for Jessica. "Want some coffee?" Why was she asking Bumpers that? She could just imagine how shocked Whitney would be if she were here.

"Yess. Thankss." He was having trouble letting go his *s*'s. He was also being very polite.

She sat next to him, wheelchair beside wheelchair, she nursing a cup of tea, he the coffee with sugar and cream she'd brought him. She fumbled for something to say.

"Your job has always seemed so exciting, Kyle." Whatever his job was. Maybe he'd reveal something she'd enjoy telling Whitney about. "Think you'll find it boring if you have to slow down now?"

He raised his eyes to meet hers. "Don't worry 'bout me. Look what I can do." He stretched out the fingers of his left hand, then relaxed them again.

"You're improving," she said admiringly. Now she really did envy him.

"And you?" It was hard to tell, but there might have been a tinge of genuine concern in his voice.

"Not good. Worse every day. I'm going to see my doctor this afternoon about the possibility of a serious operation." She described the thymectomy, which she hadn't even told her mother or Fernando or Stone she was thinking of having, and the odds of success.

After confiding in him, she became nervous. No one confided in Kyle Bumpers. He was, after all, a reputed company spy, blackmailer and womanizer. "I'm going downhill fast. If I don't have this surgery, I don't know where I'll end up." She just couldn't seem to stop blathering to him about herself.

"I'm rooting for you."

"I actually understand, Kyle. We've never been friendly—maybe someday I'll tell you my reasons—but since the other day, when I saw you sitting in the lobby then running into the wall up here in the hall, I couldn't stop thinking about you."

She must be out of her mind, telling him her reasons for anything. A close relationship with a reprobate like him was not what she needed when her every day was a struggle.

He asked how she planned to get herself to the doctor's. When she said she'd call a cab, he offered to arrange for a company car to take her and bring her back. She was too astounded and grateful to refuse.

CHAPTER 28

The limousine driver had to help Jessica out in front of the medical building and get her arms into the crutch sleeves. She was grateful to him for enabling her to keep her appointment with some independence and dignity.

The automatic doors of the building sucked open, and she crutched slowly across the lobby to the elevators. On the way to the fourth floor her brain circuits went wild. By the time the door opened, despite support from the crutches, she was barely able to hold herself upright. Even if the thymectomy totally rid her of myasthenia gravis forever, she wanted to find out someday what the elevator effect was all about.

Jessica entered Hatfield's waiting room, which was resonating with a soprano's aria, and eased onto one of the cushioned chairs. Grand opera. She seldom went because the seats were expensive and the plots pathetic, but she did like some arias. Like this one from *La Forza del Destino*, where the gypsy tells everyone's fortune, predicting victories in upcoming battles. She pictured a dark-eyed gypsy, bracelets jangling, cards spread out on the waiting room table where tattered magazines were scattered. "Your thymectomy will be a great success." The woman breathed out each word to convey its truth. "And utterly painless."

"Jessica Shephard." The nurse had to shout to be heard above the music.

When Jessica got to Hatfield's office he took her crutches, propped them against a wall and then seated her at the side of his desk not far from him. Hatfield never dominated patients from across a big desk.

"You're looking well, my dear." He sat back in his swivel chair and gave her a fleeting smile.

"I always do. I'm the biggest example of 'looks can be deceiving' you'll ever see."

He flipped open a folder on his desk. "How do you feel?"

She sighed. "I'm getting worse." She told him how much sicker she was than any MG patient she'd seen at either the Dodger game or the MG meeting.

Hatfield picked up an arrowhead and began running his thumb over its sharp point. He used it to point to the crutches. "I've noticed you're not very mobile these days. And your head droops all the way to your chest."

"I heard you lecture about thymectomies at last week's meeting. I want to talk about having one before I go downhill any further."

He opened his mouth and some words came out.

"What?" She hadn't understood him at all.

He leaned toward her until his face was only a foot away. "I said I can't recommend that. I don't think you have myasthenia gravis." He was making an attempt to soften his normally gruff voice.

"That can't be!" She could barely squeak out the words. She was counting on this surgery. Without it, she had *no hope* of stopping her decline.

"I've been thinking about this a lot. When I saw you staggering around the meeting, starting to fall and grabbing your mother's arm, I became sure of it. Myasthenics are never stricken so abruptly as you. They don't recover and walk abruptly either. Their heads droop backward, not forward like yours. And I've never known one to fall after an elevator ride."

"Then what do I have? What am I going to do?" Jessica heard her own voice as if it were coming from far away over a poor quality phone line.

Hatfield scowled and pressed the arrowhead hard into his thumb. "I don't know."

Jessica's glance fell on the silly oscilloscope that had registered her single fibers twanging and felt laughter burbling in her throat. Surveying the ridiculous array of Eskimo weapons in the case above the bed, she began to giggle uncontrollably. And, finally, at the sight of Hatfield's broad, well-thumped chest she shrieked with convulsive laughter. He gawked as she slid onto the floor.

"A patient who goes down laughing." He lifted her under the arms and deposited her gently back in the chair. "That's a first for me. Someday I'm going to write a book about you."

When she was settled back in the limousine, behind a built-in TV and compartments containing who knew what luxuries, she tried to relax and calm down.

But how could she be calm when her world had gone crazy? If she didn't have MG, what did she have? Something so bizarre it was unknown to the medical world? Something triggered by acceleration and stress. Eating started attacks, exercise weakened her, her period made whole days worse.

And laughing. In Hatfield's office she hadn't been particularly weak until she'd laughed. Only after the situation had struck her as ridiculous had the switches flipped. Could it be that her preoccupation with the comic side of life had weakened some neural pathways so they were defective and vulnerable? What sense did that make?

"Stop!" she yelled to the driver.

He pulled into a mini-mall parking lot and she went into a drugstore and bought the largest bottle of vitamin B-12 they had. Lack of B-12 produces neurological problems, so taking the stuff might help if you were already in neurological trouble.

She rode back to work clutching the bottle. Treating herself, she couldn't do any worse than the doctors she'd seen.

CHAPTER 29

One by one Jessica told the important people in her life she didn't have myasthenia gravis. She also told Kyle Bumpers.

"Have some." Jessica stretched across his desk and plunked the giant bottle of B-12 capsules down in front of him. "Your driver was very nice. He stopped at a drugstore so I could buy these."

Bumpers blinked at her as though he'd been dozing, then picked up the bottle and read the label. "Doctor prescribe this?" He was still croaking his words out.

She eased into one of his leather chairs. "Hah! What do they know? I prescribed it for myself. Good for the nervous system." Right now she felt fairly strong, her symptoms continuing to fluctuate as though she had MG, but more rapidly. Much more rapidly, Hatfield had said.

"Are you nuts? What makes you think it'll help you or me?" He was almost breathless from the effort of pushing out so many words.

"Tell me something that's better. Go ahead, tell me."

"That operation?"

"It's off. I don't have MG. No MG, no operation."

He raised his good eyebrow.

"The world renowned expert Dr. Hatfield doesn't know what I have. I'll have to figure out what to do for myself."

"So you came here to tell Daddy Bumpers all about it." The eye on his good side winked at her. "Nothing exciting going on in here 'til you walked in, babe. You made my day."

"Nothing exciting! You looked like you were asleep when I came in." She flicked her fingers as if to dismiss him. "I have to work hard to keep my job."

"You seem to have time to hang out with me." The good side of his face grinned. Or smiled. Or leered.

She turned her head. She didn't even want to look at him. "I'm wasting my time in here."

"You play the joker, I play the playboy. No difference, sweetie." He continued to smirk.

"No difference? Come on, Kyle. I get people to laugh. You act the letch."

"Right. I act the letch."

"You're trying to say that's just an act? Then why do it?"

"I control my audience, same as you when you kid around."

Jessica gasped as though she'd just taken a punch in the gut.

Kyle's gaze held hers for a moment. "We're a lot alike, Jessica."

Jessica felt her face flush. "You couldn't be more wrong." She got up and rushed out of his office, risking using up her fuel allotment before she could reach her office, a big risk since she never knew when Armor might appear.

No one would agree with Kyle—she was nothing like him. He was a womanizer, a sleaze. Who knew how and where he got his money. She, on the other hand, kept her friends' spirits up and entertained them. She made their lives a little better. She had integrity. Kyle might be right about himself, but he was dead wrong about her. She never tried to make people laugh to control them.

True, a long time ago, when she was a small child, she'd acted silly to distract and amuse her mother so she could quit practicing the piano. And she'd eaten that ridiculous amount of junk food at the baseball game to counter Fernando's nagging. But these were rare exceptions.

Jessica flopped onto one of the chaises on the patio overlooking the garden. What she saw looked more like a giant overgrown vegetable than a mother. In oversized plastic garden sabots, a dirt-streaked blue sweatsuit, green kneepads Velcro-strapped on top of the pants, and long, leather-palmed gloves reaching almost to her elbows, Mom stood up from her work. She'd just finished ripping out the last of the summer vegetables, dumping the stringy skeletal remains into a wheelbarrow. The garden was barren.

Mom stretched and rubbed her lower back. "How are you feeling?"

"A little weak. But I'm okay to drive. Fernando's with his study group." Her mother's eyes lit up momentarily at the mention of Fernando. Someday she'd have to let Mom know Fernando was not going to be her life partner. Not right now, though. There was a lot to talk about. "I saw Dr. Hatfield the other day."

Mom slip-slogged over to the patio, sabots dragging over a wood-chip-covered pathway. "You owe so much to that man."

Jessica grimaced, then sighed. "I can't count on him anymore."

Mom sat on one end of the chaise. "Myasthenia gravis is so hard to live with."

Jessica leaned forward and held tight to her mother, head buried on Mom's shoulder. "I don't have MG, Mom," she sobbed. "He doesn't know what I have. I don't know what to do." She hated burdening her mother with still more of her troubles, but for all her life Mom had been the one to help her through hard times.

Mom held Jessica and patted her back. "What makes him think you don't?"

Jessica pulled away so she could look into Mom's face and reported what Hatfield had said—her symptoms were different from any MG patients he'd ever seen and her tests had been inconclusive. "He says he can't recommend me for a thymectomy or prednisone or anything he normally prescribes. He's even thinking of weaning me off Mestinon."

"Maybe you should see someone else. Get a second opinion."

"I'm sick of doctors."

"It's not like you to give up." Mom laid her hand on Jessica's. "We'll just have to figure out something. We can, I know we can."

Jessica looked out over the barren garden. Mom would fix it up by next spring. When she was a little girl, she'd believed Mom could fix anything.

Jessica sat across from Whitney in a nubby, upholstered booth in the Parkview Café, its pale blue walls and white linen-covered tables awash in sunlight from the front windows and skylight. In the sun's rays, Whitney's golden hair had turned into a halo. Perfect restaurant. Perfect Whitney. In contrast, Jessica couldn't hold her head up or keep her mouth closed. She glanced around at the other tables to see if anyone was staring at her.

"Would you mind ordering for me, Whit?"

"Having trouble speaking?"

"No. No appetite. And I need to eat. So order something I used to like and I'll eat it."

Whitney ordered blue corn pancakes stuffed with vegetables in a delicate cream sauce for both of them. Jessica popped a Mestinon and a couple of B-12's. Hatfield had decided she should taper off Mestinon slowly and see if it made a difference. He didn't think B-12 would hurt, but doubted it would help. By the time the pancakes arrived, she was able to sit up straight and close her mouth.

"I've been thinking," Whitney said. "About getting out of engineering and going into marketing. If I can't do it here, then someplace else. At an aerospace company, of course. Where I'd know something about the business already."

"You can't be serious," Jessica gasped. "Why would someone who went to all the trouble of getting an engineering degree go into marketing? If you want more of an intellectual challenge, that isn't it, Whit. It would be a bad move."

"I'm serious. I know I'll never get anywhere in engineering. I'll always be frustrated and unhappy—no lectures about assertiveness, please—and I think I'd be great at marketing. I'd have way more technical background than anyone else in sales. And men like talking to me." She grinned in mock lasciviousness. "I could make use of that for a change."

Jessica had to bring Whitney to her senses fast. "You're selling yourself short just to avoid a fight with your management over getting a better assignment."

"I'm trying to get out of a stressful situation. Engineering hasn't worked out for me."

"You think you're stressed out now. I can just see you, your hair just like it is now, in that gorgeous outfit you have on. Guys hitting on you all the time—marketeers, managers, customers hanging from the chandeliers to get your attention."

Whitney's eyes glistened as though she was about to cry. "Don't make fun of me, Jessica. I'm serious about this."

Jessica realized she'd shot off her mouth. Someone, Kyle for instance, might even think she was trying to control Whitney by getting a laugh, or maybe even laughing at her. What was she thinking of, criticizing

Whitney for wanting to get out from under those who were ignoring her potential when that was exactly what she'd always urged her to do? Even if it wasn't the career move she would have picked for her. "I'm sorry, Whit. It's going to take me a while to get used to you as a marketeer, but I will. Go for it!"

"I'm so glad you said that." Whitney exhaled as if she'd been holding her breath.

Jessica saw that Whitney was really happy to get her support, happier than she'd ever been with getting advice. This was a disappointing development. "I'm on your side, Whit, even if I don't sound like it sometimes." Or even if she didn't feel like agreeing with her.

"I know."

"Are you going to need some courses in business or sales?"

"Maybe. I'm hoping I can slide into a good spot here at Rank."

"You've got to stay. How else can I see you wowing customers, bringing in the big bucks, traveling around the world." That is, she would if she was able to keep her own job. "Most of this company's okay. Armor and his henchmen are evil anomalies."

"This is what I need to do. I know it." Whitney's chin was set.

"To Whitney's marvelous adventure." Jessica raised her water glass in salute. "And to mine. You'll have a new job. You know where you're going. I'm looking for a new disease and I don't."

Whitney lowered her glass. "What do you mean?"

Jessica leaned back on a dilapidated sofa pirated from a closed lobby in another building, its stuffing protruding from tears in the cracked leather.

"The trick is to keep the wrist firm and not rush the back-cast," Stone was saying as he prepared to cast toward a tub fifty feet away in the test chamber. To combat his nerves and those of others as the date for the contract announcement got closer, he was teaching anyone who'd listen how to fly-fish, or at least how to make basic casts. She couldn't decide whether Stone, who'd so far been her stalwart defender, would be more likely to want her on his staff if he knew she didn't have MG, or less likely because she had no diagnosis and no treatment in sight. There had to be a limit to what he would put up with.

She heard a whoosh and a hiss as the line uncoiled smoothly from a tight back-cast loop. He expertly deposited a small fly in the tub, and Jessica applauded, as she knew he wanted her to. After retrieving the line, he turned to her. "Your turn."

"There's no way out of this?" Hands and feet tingling as if electric currents were passing through them, she stood up.

He held out the rod and reminded her how to position her fingers on the cork butt. "You're doing pretty well these days," he remarked.

It was a relief to hear he thought that. "I have my good days." She hid the bad days.

She moved closer to the tub than Stone had been and focused on its center. This time she was going to hit the target. Spending so much time on casting lessons, she might as well try to accomplish something, and it wouldn't be a bad idea to show Stone some competence. She pulled out a length of line, slowly raised the rod, cocked her wrist for the back-cast. But as she cast forward the fly flipped into her hair. She stomped her foot and screamed.

Stone laughed, a little giggle at first, then a snort he tried to cut short. "Sorry, Jessica. Didn't mean to laugh. Maybe MG's bad for coordination."

This was her opportunity to tell him she didn't have MG. "I don't need to be sick to be rotten at fly-fishing."

He picked the fly out of her hair and took the rod from her. "Then you don't want me to take back my laugh?"

She giggled. "How could I possibly object to someone getting a laugh from me?" She'd rather laugh with him than share her fear of this unknown disease that was doing who knew what to her.

He wound the line onto the reel. "Something I admire in you. You've got gumption. You hang in there," he said. "Now this time, stop the tip at twelve o'clock." He demonstrated the movement of the rod with a locked reel. "Like this. Gin clear?"

"What?"

"Gin clear. Some streams are so clear you can see fish all the way to the bottom way over on the other side of the stream. Fly fishermen call that gin clear."

"Gin clear." She reached for the rod. It was a sad state of affairs when fly-fishing was the feature of her life she was clearest about.

Jessica could scarcely hear her own voice, let alone anyone else's, in the large dining room reverberating with chatter, celebratory toasts, clattering dishes and music from the small combo that had been hired to play at her cousin's wedding reception. She was sandwiched between Fernando and a young man, one of six at their table, who worked with the bride at the medical school. Across the room, she glimpsed Mom on the move, circulating among the twenty-five or thirty tables, gathering family news and gossip.

Fernando was explaining, as best he could over the racket, what he was studying in medical school. He had the same fire in his eye that had first ignited Jessica's interest. With his intensity and dark handsomeness, she could see how people might think he was a good catch. She guessed he would be a good catch—for someone else.

She'd always wanted marriage and children, and now, even as she knew for sure she had to break up with him, she worried that no one except Fernando would want her as a wife. Worse yet, between the illness and the medication, her libido was so low these days that she hardly cared about attracting him or anyone else.

Circuits began flipping wildly in her brain and she closed her eyes, concentrating on holding them off. It worked for a couple of minutes, but soon she had to plant both elbows firmly on the table to keep her face out of her plate. The carbohydrate slump again. It had never fit with the myasthenia gravis diagnosis.

"Don't worry. She's not drunk or falling asleep," Fernando explained. "She's suffering from an uncommon neurological disorder—myasthenia gravis. She'll be all right in a few minutes."

People eyed Jessica warily, then resumed their conversations. As gravity returned to normal, she sat up and closed her mouth. "I don't have myasthenia gravis." She shivered as she said the words. Every time she said them her blood got icy.

Fernando laid his hand on hers. "How nice it would be if you could decide, just like that, not to."

She turned to look into his condescension-filled face. "I don't have myasthenia gravis. Dr. Hatfield says I don't."

A tablemate's grin remained frozen in place as he glanced back and forth between her and Fernando.

Before Jessica could elaborate, Fernando jumped in. "You never said anything to me about this." His curled lip and raised eyebrow said he didn't believe her.

"I went in to see Hatfield about a thymectomy and he said no, because I don't have MG." Jessica felt her throat going dry with guilt. Instead of dragging her feet because she couldn't face the ordeal of confronting Fernando, she should have told him days ago—in private.

Fernando's face reddened. "I should have come along when you went to see Hatfield. What does he think you have?"

"He doesn't know. I'm treating myself with Vitamin B-12." Until now she'd deliberately hidden her B-12 habit from him. He didn't need to know everything about her anymore. "And I'm not getting worse—I may be getting better."

"Not that I've noticed."

She leaned toward him so she could whisper in his ear. "There's a lot you haven't noticed lately."

CHAPTER 30

Burrowed into a corner of the backseat of her mother's car, Jessica had plenty of time to think in silence as they drove home from the reception. She stared at the back of Richard's white-haired head, not even peeking over to see how far Fernando had retreated into his corner. She didn't need to look to feel the wheels in his head turning. He'd lost his grip on her case, and the minute Mom dropped them off, she knew he'd try to regain control.

She wouldn't let him. Hadn't she lectured Whitney about taking control of her life? And hadn't Whitney done just that? How could she do less? Tonight she would inform him of the decision she'd really made months ago in San Francisco.

The problem was she didn't feel up to a row tonight. She never felt up to a row, and that was one of her excuses for letting the situation drag on so long. Too many ordeals were already loading her down. Just being around the overbearing Fernando was a daily stress in itself.

Of course, if he weren't around, there'd be no pasta dinners waiting for her. No one to go downstairs to get the laundry or to the grocery store if she couldn't manage. Getting back and forth from work would become a lot harder.

She'd have to come up with a way to get the shopping done and stockpile essentials when she got the chance. And there had to be other ways to get to work in emergencies, even if it had to be cabs. She'd find ways to manage. If she didn't get too sick.

Leaning her head back, she let the freeway lights strobe across her field of vision, mile after mile after mile.

Mom and Richard had barely pulled away from the curb at the apartment building when Fernando started in.

He held the courtyard door open for her. "Let me see those vitamins."

Jessica sank onto a bench near the rows of mailboxes and leaned back against the stucco wall, eyes closed against the glare of entryway lights, purse clutched to her body. "Let me be."

The purse began to slip from her grasp. Damned if he wasn't pulling on it. She snatched it back and clutched it more tightly than before.

"I need to know what you're taking." His voice was a harsh whisper, no doubt meant to intimidate her without attracting the attention of the neighbors.

"No, you don't. You're not assigned to my case anymore." She was too tired to feel the emotion she should have at breaking the news to him. All she knew was she couldn't stand one more day of fighting off his attempts to run her life. Struggling with him took more strength than she had left.

"What the hell does that mean?" His voice was louder and hoarser.

"We were okay when you were my boyfriend and I was your girl-friend. But now you're Doctor Munoz, I'm your favorite disease and you think you have the right to take over my life."

"Stop talking nonsense."

She forced herself to stand up and started shuffling across the court-yard between the rows of lighted palm trees that had once seemed so romantic. "Fernando, I'm too tired for this."

He easily kept pace with her. "I'll call Hatfield in the morning and work out a next step for you."

"Don't you dare!"

Fernando stopped.

"Fernando, just leave me alone. I want to lead my own life and you won't let me." She felt calm, or maybe dead was a better word for her condition. "I tried to tell you that in San Francisco. I've been trying to tell you for a long time."

He leapt in front of her. "You can't do without me. You need me and you know it." She caught the glint of tears in his eyes. He needed her.

"Look, I appreciate all you've done for me."

He put an arm around her waist and pressed himself so close to her that she stiffened all over. "Let's go to bed. I'll make you feel better."

Jessica groaned, pulled away and plodded toward the bottom of the stairs to her apartment. "Don't. I'm sick and I don't feel like it. I haven't for a long time."

He gaped, completely stunned. "You've had it rough and I've been busy. We just need some time together. To get back to normal, as you once put it."

She was guilty of never clueing him in about her vanished libido. Another cruelty, in addition to rejection, she was heaping on him. "You need another kind of woman. Even if I were well, we wouldn't be right for each other." She felt guilty for the pain she was causing him because she hadn't told him decently, in private, what she'd needed to say; because she couldn't stay with him in spite of all the help he'd given her; because she didn't know what she had and whether she'd ever be able to work and live her life like a normal person; and because her brain, on overload, had shut down and was no good for dealing with anything.

"I'll call you in the morning. You'll feel better then," he said.

"Fernando, don't. I'm sorry, I really am, but it's over." Without looking back, she trudged up the pebbled steps.

There it was. He was gone and she didn't know how she'd manage without him. She'd dumped him when she didn't know what illness she had or what ordeals it would put her through, when she was in danger of losing her job.

A half flight above, she saw a raccoon, waddling up with much the same gait as hers, probably looking for scraps not cleaned up after a meal on a balcony. Every day the raccoon must wake up in the canyon below and start wondering where to get the next meal, how to escape the dogs and coyotes. She felt like inviting it inside for a drink.

CHAPTER 31

"You can't break up with him," Mom said, rapidly adjusting stop tabs and pistons. She had only an hour to rehearse before a Christmas program with the choir. "You simply can't."

Jessica had hoped for her mother's emotional support, to be told she'd done the right thing. Now, here in the organ loft, she was dealing with a mother who looked as disapproving as the dour saints below. "It's my life. I know what I need."

"I can't believe you're doing this."

"He's too overbearing."

"You need him to take care of you, if nothing else."

Jessica clutched her hands in her lap. "I'm not doing so bad. I'm here, aren't I?" This morning, she'd been capable of trudging very slowly to the garage and cautiously driving the few blocks to the church on surface streets.

"You land one who cares about you, a doctor, sick as you are, and that's not good enough?" Mom fumbled with the knobs on the bench, finally managing to crank it low enough. She flexed her thumbs and fingers ten times, rotated each ankle ten times and began playing.

Jessica reached across with her left hand and turned the page. "He was stressing me out. I can't deal with him and being sick at the same time."

Mom kept her eyes on the music. "He must think you're the most ungrateful person in the world after the way he's taken care of you."

"He tried to run my life."

"You need someone to run your life."

This was hopeless. To Mom she might as well be five years old. "I can't tell you how much I wish you'd understand." She should have known better than to wish for something so unattainable.

Mom gave the music a gentle crescendo. "I guess I'll have to give up the dance studio job and my organ music and take care of you myself. Someone has to do all the things Fernando used to."

"You will not." Jessica felt her chest tighten. She hadn't thought Mom would take this news as a personal burden.

"I didn't mean I'll have to. I'll be glad to." Mom seemed to swallow her words as she shifted to the second of the three upper keyboards. "You can move back in with us. Into your old bedroom."

Jessica could feel the tug of her mother's devotion, the lure of shelter at Mom's house, the siren call that had been her father's undoing. "All I want is for you to accept my decision and let me lead my own life." Turning the page with a snap, she saw her mother's mouth working, preparing more arguments she feared hearing.

She reached for a stop knob and yanked. Organ music thundered through the church. Mom slammed the knob back in. But as her hand returned to the keyboard, Jessica yanked the knob out again, then reached for a tab labeled "Flute Principal." It tootled high notes. She pulled on "Celeste" and it tinkled like glass breaking.

She looked over at Mom, whose lips were pursed as if stuck in midword, then added "Drums" that thumped and "Oboes" that moaned a lugubrious accompaniment. She giggled and pulled out "Cymbals" that clang-crashed, adding the final touch to a reverberating carnival version of the Bach fugue.

"Have you gone crazy?" Mom frantically pushed knobs and tabs, choosing right ones and wrong ones in her haste.

Jessica pulled out each one Mom pushed in and added a sassy, brassy "Trumpet."

"This isn't funny, Jessica," Mom cried out over the racket.

Jessica leaned on the railing where she looked down into the face of a woebegone, humorless saint. She had half a mind to sneak downstairs and give it a big lipstick smile and maybe a bright red clown's nose.

CHAPTER 32

The morning after New Year's Jessica felt no stronger despite the week-long holiday. The problem was she'd not had a real, refreshing, recuperative rest. Most of her time was spent agonizing over one life crisis or another.

First there were the aftershocks from the organ loft incident, a misguided climax to all the Mom-inspired rebellions in her life. They'd started when she was little. She'd act up during piano lessons or practices that went on too long by hooking her feet underneath the keyboard and hanging upside down from the piano bench, or by tackling an assigned piece from the bottom of the page to the top, playing each measure backward. If she got Mom to laugh, which she sometimes did, the lesson or practice would be over. The biggest crisis had come when she'd turned her back on a career in music. Her mother believed anyone with talent like hers had a duty to use it.

She knew that some people, like her mother, thought laughter was frivolous and silly. But humor was as much a talent as music, a talent she'd worked hard to develop, one for which she was known. It was the kind of person she was, it was her identity. She believed humor helped people face distress and danger and was every bit as beneficial to humanity as music.

The problem was she'd misused her talent to abuse Mom's music. Mom's identity and self-worth were as much entangled in her music as Jessica's was in her humor. The organ loft incident was not just a rebellion—it was a stab in the heart. Directly, openly and deliberately she'd messed up Mom's music, made it laughable. This wasn't like when she'd hung from the piano bench or played music backward and made herself the object of laughter. She'd stopped Mom's harangue about Fernando by making her sacred music ridiculous.

When Kyle had accused her of using humor to control others, she'd denied it. She was no controller, she'd said.

For days, Jessica worried Mom would never forgive her. What if her own mother stayed angry with her because of a stupid joke? It was time to realize that she had a comic power and that power, like any other, could be used well or misused.

In penitence, she'd choked down the entire fruitcake Mom had made her for Christmas. The sticky, heavy, saliva-absorbing, penitential fruitcake.

When Mom asked her to be a page turner at one of her Christmas programs, Jessica lectured herself on self-restraint. Predictably, Mom launched right in as soon as they got to the organ loft. "I want your hands off the organ today." Her demeanor was grave. "No clowning around. Is that a promise?" Jessica had desperately fought down her mind's attempts to come up with a joke involving a clown's organs. "I promise." She forced herself to sound meek.

Now both the rebellion and her self-imposed humor restrictions were eating at her. Laughing was too important to abandon lightly. It was a highly honed skill she'd used to deflect trouble all her life, especially with her mother. She could set free a whole room full of people with it; she could relieve awkward situations. Once she got someone to laugh, they became happier, but weaker, and she became stronger.

But if she laughed when she was having an attack, she became disastrously weak. For everyone's sake it would be a good idea to set limits on her use of humor.

During the holidays, when she wasn't worrying about Mom or the illness, she'd been alternately pining for and fending off Fernando, while repeatedly berating herself for not finding a better way to break up with him. Couldn't she do anything right?

The night she'd broken up with him, she'd been exuberant over her new freedom; the next morning she was apprehensive about a future without him; by nighttime she was despondent that their relationship had failed. The next day when she let him collect his things that were scattered around her apartment, she'd been excited, almost happy, to see him. He'd been so kind to her, so good-looking, so smart, so loyal and dependable. She felt like hugging him and saying, "Let's start over."

Until he started in on her. He said he didn't hold her "little temper tantrum" against her. She was sick and couldn't help herself. He wouldn't give up on her, and he'd get her a better doctor who wouldn't give up on her either; he'd take her to the Mayo Clinic; he'd read up on more rare diseases they could look into. And he'd get them back on track with their sex life. He was so caught up in his ideas that he was shocked when she pushed him away as he tried to kiss her. "Don't," was the only word she managed to choke out without crying. Then she helped him gather up his things and put them into two cartons he'd brought.

She'd argued about only one item he wanted to take—the Beethoven bust. "He's mine. You gave him to me and I want him," she'd said.

After Fernando had given back her key and left with the cartons, he hadn't given up on her. She'd grown sick of the whiny pleadings he left on her message machine, making promises she knew he couldn't keep.

Most depressing of all was the e-mail about how he'd been praying for her. "Haven't you ever noticed," she'd e-mailed back, "that when a plane crashes, everyone—the prayers and the blasphemers—go down together? Whatever God is busying Himself with, it isn't answering people's prayers for intervention in their favor." It seemed evident to her that God started the world going, maybe at the Big Bang, and let it choose among the infinite possibilities He'd provided. He'd even supplied a variety of religions for people to choose among, each with its own embodiment of Him. People should pray for wisdom in their choices because freedom of choice is what He'd given them, not control over their own lives or anyone else's.

She was struggling with her thoughts and doing her lift-one-foot-at-a-time baby toddle down the corridor when Armor burst from his office.

Jessica was the first person he encountered.

"I did it," he said, face radiant with joy. "I got it."

Jessica started shaking, afraid of what coming face-to-face with him could cause. "You mean the contract?" she finally stammered, trying desperately to calm the hysterical switches in her brain.

He didn't seem to notice her confusion. "I mean the contract!" He put a hand on each of her shoulders and looked as if he might hug her. "A billion dollars over six years." His gruff voice cracked with emotion.

He called across the hall to two technicians. "It's in! I got the contract for you."

Knees bent like a football player's, he charged down the hall to Jessica's bay, stuck his head in and yelled. "I won. The job's coming here."

As she watched Armor cavort down the hall, she recovered from the encounter. This was the best possible news. Everyone's hard work had paid off. They'd all have jobs. She'd still be insured. At least she hoped she'd have a job. Hadn't Armor almost hugged her a minute ago? With a big win like this, a lot could be forgiven and forgotten.

She hurried to Kyle's office. If anyone needed good news on the job front, it was the two of them.

Kyle looked up from the *LA Times* comics, coffee and a Danish at his right hand, *The Wall Street Journal* by his left.

"We won." To Jessica's surprise she was nearly breathless. "One billion dollars. Can you imagine? Armor's running up and down the hall telling everybody."

"My God." Kyle's right eyebrow shot up. "I'd begun to think it was all a fantasy." He still had trouble with his voice cracking, but his speech was greatly improved. Jessica hadn't seen him since before the holidays.

"You're talking much better."

"And look." He raised his left arm, wiggled his fingers, and almost managed to clench them into a fist.

"That's great, Kyle." On a day like today she could be happy for anyone.

"I almost called over the holidays to tell you. What would you have said?"

"I'd have said, 'That's great, Kyle. Merry Christmas and a Happy New Year.' What else would a polite, socially correct person like me say?" Actually, she would have been delighted if he had called and they'd exchanged witty sarcasms. Anything would have been a relief from stewing over the situation with her mother and dealing with the loneliness, sorrow and anger caused by the breakup with Fernando.

"Think you'll get a good position when the award comes in?" She settled on his sofa and put her feet up on the coffee table to exhibit a confidence and lack of vulnerability she didn't feel.

He seemed amused when he glanced at her feet. "I wish I was as solid with my boss as you are with yours. You know his stuff inside out. He'd have to start over again with someone new."

"I'm not real worried." She wondered if something in her attitude was cueing him about her nervousness and pulled her feet off the table.

"Good. Because I can guarantee you Stone's not worried."

Seeing her situation more objectively than she could, Kyle must have a better perspective. Jessica felt suddenly grateful to him. "What about you, Kyle? How are your prospects?"

Kyle shook his head. "If I'd completely recovered by now, I'd feel better about them."

"Maybe there are some things you used to do." She wanted to probe the cloak-and-dagger life he'd been rumored to lead. "Things that would be dangerous for you to attempt now?"

"Like taking airline flights with dangerous stewardesses? My plane accident, as everyone calls it, happened when I fell asleep in my seat, my head slipped off the cushion into the aisle and this babe rammed me with a service cart."

"Then those rumors you were hurt smuggling aren't true?"

Kyle shook his head. "I guess I might have encouraged those rumors. People want to talk about cops and robbers, heroes and villains. What fun is a guy run over by a cart with his dinner on it?"

She wanted to believe him, but she wouldn't get carried away. He'd been the subject of a lot of gossip, not just this accident. It would be a stretch to believe all of it was baseless. "Want to hear my idea for you?" She had an inspiration, a way to help him back onto his feet, so to speak, and on the straight and narrow.

"Do I have a choice?" As he grinned, his eyes seemed to warm with anticipation.

"A little birdie told me something a while ago. Armor's thinking of offering this guy John Gerald the job of new business manager when the contract comes in." She wasn't going to tell him that she'd eavesdropped on Armor from the phone line she'd shared with him in the other building. When dealing with Kyle, she wanted a moral edge. "You know, developing new product lines related to our satellite system, learning what the customer wants in a follow-on contract. That kind of thing. With your experience, you're better qualified for that job. And you've got the Americans with Disabilities Act behind you."

Kyle drew the fingers of his left hand into a half-clench. "That's exactly the job I want. But here's how it is." His face was glum. "I can handle phone calls, meetings and deskwork. But how am I going to travel, give presentations, work the hospitality suites? Who'll pay attention to a guy in a wheelchair? Put yourself in Armor's shoes and compare me with Gerald."

A memory of herself in the down-here wheelchair world at Disneyland being ignored by the up-theres flashed into her mind. "It's not going to be easy, but speak up. Get noticed."

"I don't like getting noticed when I'm like this."

"Do you want to sit here in your office and wait until you're completely well? How long's that going to take?"

For once he was silent.

"You can travel. You can make plans and get with customers by phone and e-mail, give PowerPoint presentations from your wheelchair. Use your imagination. Let Armor know what you can do. And tell him you're getting better every day." Jessica made a speech about how Kyle knew the ropes and had all the right contacts. He could eventually become manager of all new satellite business.

By the time she left, she felt better. If he listened to her, he could get a real career boost. She'd never noticed before how good she was at solving other people's problems. Her own didn't seem so terrible now. Preoccupied, she nearly collided with a jaunty Shirley Skowron.

"It's been a wonderful day." Shirley beamed, abandoning herself to celebration. "Aren't we lucky to work here?"

Jessica would count herself lucky to keep working anywhere.

She invited Skowron into her office, indicating the wheelchair as the only place for her to sit. Skowron stared at the chair before easing tentatively into it as if she feared it might infect her. She laid her arms gingerly on the arm supports.

Pausing to watch Skowron's reaction, Jessica confided how concerned she was that Armor might not want her on the contract. She didn't mention she now knew she didn't have MG. After all, she was still a mess, even if she didn't know why.

Skowron sat up straight. "He must keep you on. It's the law and Rank has to obey it. I'll explain it to him again. Very clearly."

Jessica was admiring the aggressive look on Skowron's face when an idea came to her. She told Skowron of Kyle Bumpers' desire to apply for the new business manager's position and his fear that, because of his disabled condition, he wouldn't be considered. She included the story of how John Gerald, a competitor for the job, had tried, encouraged by Armor, to get her off the proposal because she was disabled. Gerald was bound to be an obstacle to Kyle.

Then still another brainstorm. She told her Whitney wanted to go into marketing and could serve as Kyle's assistant, barely hesitating over the thought that she should really talk to Whitney before discussing this. There might not be time. Good positions on the project were going to be snapped up fast. She talked up Whitney's capabilities, her brains and attractiveness.

"I don't have to warn you to watch over Whitney Barron's career path—you already know Armor's attitude toward women professionals."

Skowron nodded several times, took copious notes in her notebook and then clapped it shut. "I'll go up the hall and get on Armor's calendar right now. It's best to get things settled fast before he's had a chance to make too many commitments." She swept off her glasses and twirled them in large, sweeping circles on the end of their cord. Her smile no longer looked preprogrammed for display—it was exuberant.

Jessica felt really good about what she was doing except for one thing. She knew Whitney didn't want to work for Armor or Bumpers. Still, she'd given Whitney a chance for a position she might never have considered before it was too late. "Maybe he'll be easy. He's having such a good time."

Skowron pursed her lips and furrowed her thinly penciled brows. "He'd better cooperate. There's a lot of money at stake on this contract. We can't afford to be cancelled because of equal employment opportunity violations. Armor has to learn he can't disregard Human Relations. At Rank we represent the law."

Jessica had been right in her hunch. The power struggle was on. She wished she were in a position to fight for a career upgrade for herself. That was one of her reasons for joining the proposal team. She wanted to be rewarded in recognition of her hard work and accomplishments. But now she'd be lucky if she could get a job of any kind, however dull and unsatisfying.

She popped another couple of B-12's into her mouth. Hatfield said he had no idea why or if the vitamins were helping, and exhaustive research on the Web hadn't yielded any information on B-12 helping with episodic paralysis. But it was known for preventing some neurological problems. As long as it seemed to help her be strong, even for short times, she intended to keep on taking it.

And today she'd experienced a modest triumph. However uncertain her future and health, and she felt like a ship heading into a dense fog as likely to be hiding a rocky reef as a safe harbor, she could still help Kyle and Whitney. In fact, the worse her own situation became, the better it felt to help other people solve their problems. It occurred to her that, when she couldn't stop lupus from destroying Daddy, Mom may have felt this way about guiding her daughter's life.

At the Parkview Café on Monday, Jessica saw immediately that Whitney was all revved up. Like everyone else at Rank, they were excited about the award. "Of course, I'm glad we won," Whitney said. "But wait till you hear my other news. Kyle Bumpers called me and I went to that big office of his. And do you know what he wanted?" Whitney's face was flushed, her eyes agleam with excitement. "He's going to be new business manager and he offered me a job as his marketing assistant. Can you believe it? I only told my boss I wanted to do marketing two days ago." Whitney's smile was Christmas-morning bright.

Jessica raised both thumbs to show how great she thought this development was. "Whatever else he is, Kyle's not dumb. You're exactly right for the job. Congratulations, Whit." Much as she wanted Whitney to know her part in getting the offer, she bit her tongue and kept silent. This was Whitney's happy day, and to say, "You only have this because of me," would be deflating.

"Wait. I haven't told you everything. He thinks I'd get a ten thousand dollar increase. There's just one little hitch."

"No job's a hundred percent perfect, like no romance."

"I'd be reporting to him, and he reports to Armor."

"So Kyle will be a buffer between you and Armor. You won't have to deal with him face-to-face." Jessica paused a minute. "Besides, I think Kyle has changed."

"Because of the accident?"

"Partly." Jessica wanted to take credit for helping a different Kyle emerge. But she shouldn't fool herself. He might be playing a new game. "He's smart. You could learn a lot from him."

"Like how to seduce secretaries and bribe engineers?"

"How do we know he really did those things? If it turns out you can't stand him, just quit. Anyone can leave a bad relationship if they've had enough. Meanwhile you'll pick up valuable experience and find out whether you should go back to engineering." Staying with Rank, Jessica felt, would be a much better career move for Whitney than running off to some company where she didn't know the ropes. "If you stay here, you'll keep the vacation and sick leave you've accumulated. Not to mention retirement."

With a flourish, a waiter in black trousers, white shirt and black bow tie laid menus in front of them.

"Wow. Such service," Jessica commented. "You'd think we were men." Lots of Rank executives lunched at Parkview where they were known and catered to.

"Maybe it's my new aura." Whitney sat erect and grinned.

"Just wait till you've been fawned over at restaurants coast to coast."

"I get the feeling you really think I should take this job."

"Isn't it what you wanted?"

"If I stay, one of my reasons, maybe not the strongest, would be so I could be here when you need me."

"Thanks, Whit. That means a lot to me." Jessica felt her face burn and had trouble choking back tears, but she pulled herself together. She had something else to say. "I have news too. I'm not seeing Fernando anymore, so I'll need your support more than ever."

"Oh, Jessica!" Whitney sagged into her seat. "How will you manage without him?"

"Will you help me now and then if I need it?"

"You know I will. But Jessica—"

"Listen, Whit, it was absolutely necessary. I've figured it out."

"Figured out what?"

"Fernando is a totally controlling person. Before I got sick, it bugged me once in a while, but I just didn't pay much attention. Then, when I was down and out and needed help he saw a chance to take over my life and went for it. If I didn't break up with him, I was afraid I'd eventually cave in and let him."

Whitney sat back. "Cave in? Sometimes it's a good idea to let other people help you and figure out what's best for you."

"Whit, that's not for me. I saw my father become completely help-less when he was sick, and my mother took over his life."

"Do you have to do this now? When you're sick?"

"Especially when I'm sick and it's tempting to let someone else take over. Take that job, Whit, and we'll both be starting new lives."

CHAPTER 33

Hatfield absolutely refused to give Jessica what he called unfounded opinions. He said it could be the B-12 was helping. Could be she was having a partial remission. Could be she had an autonomic disorder. Could be this, could be that. Never decisive about anything.

He'd appealed for help at a multidisciplinary panel of specialists that met weekly, but got no offers. With everyone swamped by hordes of HMO and Medicare patients, time was too precious to spend on cases that weren't yours. He didn't want to get her hopes up.

"You have to realize the only condition we know how to cure for certain is good health," he'd cracked.

She'd laugh at almost anything, but his attempt at humor did not strike her as funny. "I need a diagnosis. You know that."

He frowned, then sighed as though he was about to give up. "You know, in diagnosis you have to ask the right question to get the right answer. If you don't wonder if a patient has a lung disease, you never take a chest X-ray and discover lung cancer. Trouble is I've run out of good questions."

"I can't just give up."

"I know." He sighed again. "Some people collapse and recover rather rapidly because of autonomic disorders. They're normally not as debilitated as you, but we could test for neurally mediated hypotension. We might take a look at that."

Hatfield picked Dr. Kiratani, an elderly Chinese-American cardiologist who kept a dead-pan face as she read aloud the steps of the test for neurally mediated hypotension. Strapped to a swiveling metal table,

Jessica was to lie horizontal for twelve minutes, tilt at a seventy degree angle for forty minutes, then be lowered for fifteen more supine minutes, all the time wired up for pulse oximetry, cardiac rhythm and blood pressure measurements. Then an EKG.

After Jessica endured the test, snarled in wires, struggling to keep her mouth closed and her head aligned with her body, the verdict was delivered in a monotone: no neurally mediated hypotension symptoms.

"Well, now what am I going to do?" Jessica said aloud, half intending the question for the doctor, half for herself.

The woman peered over half-glasses. "If I were you, I'd get busy and find out what you have. Time's getting short."

"What do you mean?"

"You need to deal with your illness soon."

Jessica's hands began to shake. "What are you saying?"

"I'm saying you need to do something soon."

"Soon?"

Doleful as one of the saints in Mom's church, the woman hung her head. "I can't be exact, but five years. Maybe."

Five years? Did she mean five years to live? "What makes you think I have only five years left?"

"An educated guess. You've weakened tremendously in the months you've been sick. If you get worse, any little thing could be a big problem for you—a bad fall, respiratory failure, the flu, choking on something when you can't swallow properly. I hope you find treatment soon."

The automatic doors of the medical building swooshed open and Jessica, platform crutches and all, plunged into a mid-January, rain-sopped wind. A devilish eddy of wind toyed with her umbrella, trying to jerk it inside out. Hampered by weakness as well as by having to reach through the crutch sleeves, she lost the fight to get the umbrella fully open. By the time she got to the car she was soaked and her shoes were waterlogged.

Cold, wet and shivering, she sat in the car, banging her head against the steering wheel, sobbing convulsively. All the evils in the universe were aligned against her. No matter how hard she fought back she was losing and she would only die in the end. Maybe it would be easier just to cut the torment short. Sit here, cold and wet, until she got pneumonia and died. Once she got past the aches and fevers, death would come easily, like drifting off to sleep.

The scientist side of her had a problem with this and began to speak up. With pneumonia, she'd probably slowly suffocate, which didn't sound like an easy death. And if she didn't die, she'd get sick and have a runny-nosed cold and an achy fever on top of all her other miseries. She'd be more of a burden for Mom.

Bad as things were now, they could get worse.

She should go home and get some dry clothes, but was too weak to risk driving. She could call a cab, but didn't have enough money.

Think, Jessica, think.

She finally came up with an idea. She'd call a cab on her cell phone and have the driver take her to an ATM.

CHAPTER 34

A nother day, another set of problems.

Today the macaroni and cheese casserole Mom had brought her was in the refrigerator and Jessica had fallen facedown in the living room, far from the crutches in the bedroom. The short distance over the dirty carpet and crud-covered kitchen floor to the refrigerator might as well be a mile. Wresting her head to one side so her cheek, rather than her nose, was pressed to the floor, she thought she caught a whiff of urine from the carpet under the piano. Probably a political statement from the cats about the filthy condition of the litter box.

If she ever got to the macaroni and cheese, she'd heat it in the microwave and eat it right out of the pot. All the dishes she owned were stacked in and around the kitchen sink, covered with food in various stages of hardness and decay. And the kitchen wasn't the only disaster. She hadn't changed the bed sheets or bath towels since before the neurally mediated hypotension test, and that was two weeks ago. Her only accomplishment was doing the laundry, her top priority since she couldn't bear the humiliation of going to work in dirty, smelly, wrinkled clothes. It had taken most of the weekend to get up and down the stairs a few times to do that. Vitamin B-12 was now effective for only a few short intervals each day.

Unable to lift her head, she could only glimpse the top of Beethoven's head and his ferocious scowl. "We're having a bad day, Ludwig," she told him. Once she'd understood that he scowled because he was miserable and not because he was angry with her or hated her, she'd taken the bag off his head and kept him on top of the piano where she could see and talk to him. They'd become buddies.

Elsa's tawny paws moved toward her. The cat squatted and began washing Jessica's face with her warm, sandpaper tongue. Jessica grimaced, but endured the washing. Elsa cared about her.

Elsa needed food. So did Ishmael.

"Well, I'm not dead yet, Ludwig. I can still feed these guys." She realized instantly she'd made a *faux pas*, bragging to Beethoven that she was still alive when he wasn't. "Sorry, I'm a bit uptight today. I need to relax. I get better faster when I stay calm and concentrate." After waiting a few minutes, she managed to get her knees down, butt raised and upper body supported on arms and elbows so she was able to scoot and shuffle toward the kitchen, trying to avoid dragging her face through the darkest of the carpet stains.

The step stool, piled high with dirty bed sheets, was blocking the kitchen entrance. On all fours, she placed her hands on the lowest step, got to her knees and pushed it in front of her into the kitchen.

Reaching between the stool steps, she pulled open the cabinet under the sink and took out a cat food can with a flip top. Easy to open if you had any strength at all—a snap for Fernando. "Well, Fernando isn't here and I'll just have to do it myself," she called out to Beethoven. "You're no help. You haven't got any hands." There she went, being totally careless of his feelings again. But surely he understood. She got a fingernail under the pull-tab, but couldn't budge it. What was needed was something to pry with.

Feeling blindly around the sink above, she located a table knife which she stuck into the tab's finger hole and pried. The lid peeled halfway back and stuck. More groping by the sink produced a dirty saucer and a spoon, which she used to empty the can onto the saucer. Together Elsa and Ishmael gobbled, with none of their usual fuss about having to share a dish.

Now for the macaroni. She rested against the stool a few minutes before reaching with one hand to open the refrigerator. No problem locating the casserole—it, a bunch of rotting grapes and several single-serving cans of tomato juice were all there was.

Risking letting go of the stool, she edged toward the refrigerator, still on her knees. One hand grasped the casserole, but couldn't hold onto it. It hit the floor and she slumped beside it. She hoped she wouldn't get a cold, lying in front of the open refrigerator.

She still missed Fernando, who had moved away, breaking his lease, not even saying good-bye. It was hard not to miss his attempts to keep her spirits up, his doing everything for her.

By the time she was strong enough to move again, her right side was cold from the hips down. But she was able to reach up a hand to push the refrigerator door closed, get to her feet, pick up the casserole and put it into the microwave. In a few minutes she lifted it out with oven mitts and set it on a place mat on the table. Back at the sink she rinsed out one of the cruddy spoons.

How hungry she was. She dug in. What good macaroni and cheese Mom made, adding a bit of Roquefort for a piquant taste. She shoveled it down, wincing when the hot cheese burned her tongue. Can't stop. Have to finish eating before the droops hit and it becomes impossible to chew or swallow.

She wished she'd started to eat in front of the TV. From where she sat, there was nothing to look at and nothing to think about but her troubles. Glancing up from the table, she saw grocery bags stuffed with trash. She hated this chaos.

And getting to and from work had become an ordeal. Even if she managed to drive in the morning, which wasn't often, she couldn't drive home anymore. Mom had gotten her a few times, disrupting her teaching schedule, each time pushing for her to move back home. Whitney might help out in a pinch, but she lived miles out of the way. She'd heard Pasadena had a bus service for the disabled, but couldn't count on getting downstairs and out front to wait for it or on being able to sit stably on a bus seat. Cabs were about all that was left and they were expensive.

And, when she got to work, she had to face hordes of new people brought on for the project and her fears of how they might react to her. There were six new engineers in the bay she and Stone and Enid had had to themselves before the award. The project was getting organized and she'd soon have a heavy workload and a demanding schedule. Meetings were harder than ever to get to in the huge new building. Sometimes she was forced to delay or cancel those in the more distant offices.

Unless she found a diagnosis and treatment soon, she was heading downhill toward poverty and death. How soon would be soon enough? Five years like that cardiologist had said?

She looked at the wall clock. Twenty minutes since she'd started eating. Better clean up the dishes and get to bed. She picked up the casserole pan and stumbled to the kitchen. Switches flipped in her head, gravity grew stronger. She went into a trance, using extreme mental effort to blank out all emotions, and was able to buy enough time to squat on the linoleum and let her shoulder come down gently, easing the way for her head.

In the middle of the night, she woke up stiff and sore. She could hear a steady drizzle outside on the canyon foliage. Vague shapes she knew were cabinets and the refrigerator loomed in the darkness above her. "Hey, Ludwig!" she called out in the dark. "We got through another day, didn't we?"

CHAPTER 35

The cab Jessica called the next morning squeaked and rattled as all its parts clamored at the demands being put on them in their old age. The ride in this old crate to see Hatfield was going to cost at least six dollars plus tip. That was affordable. So was seventeen dollars to get from her apartment to work if it was just two or three times a month. But not every day, week after week. Just thinking about the mounting cost made her weak.

In the elevator on the way up to Hatfield's office, she leaned into the sleeves of the platform crutches, bracing herself against the acceleration and deceleration. When the door opened she swung herself outside and waited, concentrating on calming the switches in her brain.

Einstein wasn't the only one who understood gravity. He'd based general relativity on the equivalence of gravity and acceleration, which she'd now felt firsthand. And she'd discovered another equivalence with vigorous exercise, surprise and laughter. Levity and gravity correlates? A nice oxymoron.

When she sat beside Hatfield's desk, she spotted a newly hung photograph on the wall next to the arrowhead collection, a ruddy-faced young woman in a bright pink parka radiating health and joy. Across the bottom was scrawled "Susan Butcher."

"Susan won the Iditarod seven times," Hatfield said. "Tiny gal. She was the first to figure out that sled dogs can pull a light weight faster and longer than a heavy one. That's one reason she's a champ, but not the only one."

"Like you." Jessica thumped her chest in imitation of him.

Hatfield winced. "I feel more like a sled with no runners. The only news I have for you today is that your last blood tests show you don't have polymyositis."

"You feel like you've lost your runners? Let me tell you what my life is like. I can hardly ever drive, so I'm having an awful time getting to and from work. I spend most evenings alone in a filthy apartment I don't have the strength to clean. Even getting something to eat is hard because I can't get to the store by myself."

He blinked and then looked down. "I'm ashamed of how little help I've been to you."

"Kiratani, the cardiologist who tested me for neurally mediated hypotension, said I'm going downhill fast. Thinks I have five years at best."

Hatfield let out a low whistle. "Based on what? Sounds presumptuous."

"Then you don't agree? Can you tell me I'm not going to die within five years?"

"You're asking me to play God when I sometimes doubt I'm up to being a good doc."

"The only thing you never doubt is the value of doubting." She was near the limits of her frustration.

"Well put!" He slapped his hand on the desk. "You certainly have a way with words, Jessica."

She glared at him. This visit didn't look like it was going to be worth the cab fare.

Maybe she should just get used to the thought of dying.

"We once talked about mitochondrial myopathies," Hatfield said.

Another guess. There was nothing better to pin her hopes on than another wild guess. She'd read about mitochondrial myopathies. There were dozens, all rare and caused by genetic flaws, some mild, some catastrophic.

"Let's pursue those next. I'll schedule you for a stress test. Look at your metabolic products before, during and after pedaling a bicycle. If you do have a mitochondrial myopathy, the byproducts in your blood will show it."

"Pedal a bike! Are you kidding?"

"You'll start out easy."

"You're not thinking of me. You're thinking of someone like her." Jessica stabbed a finger in the direction of the photograph.

"Want to hang it up? Go home and pull the covers over your head?"

"Of course not." Accusing her of being a quitter wasn't fair. Not after all she'd been through.

"Another thing," Hatfield went on. "This is the *Medical School Alumni Magazine*." He tapped a finger on its cover. "I want you to do me a favor and write an article for it."

"First a bicycle and now an article!" Jessica couldn't believe this lunacy. "Do you advise your paraplegic patients to go rollerblading?"

"Our graduates could use a primer on what it's like being disabled and having to live in an able world, maybe gain some human understanding of the people they're treating. I'd write the article myself, but my time is measured in human lives and yours isn't." He gave her a sly look.

"It's my meek and humble opinion that you have no idea what it's like." She'd bet he could scarcely imagine the distress of last night's macaroni dinner.

"Will you do it?" Hatfield allowed a flicker of a smile to cross his face.

"On one condition."

"What?"

"Take that superwoman's picture off your wall." She pointed to the Susan Butcher photograph. "And hang a picture of a disabled person, preferably in a wheelchair or on crutches, in its place. One of your patients. Show some pride in us."

Hatfield jumped up, lifted the photograph off its hook and set it on the floor facing the wall. He reached into a desk drawer, pulled out a camera and took a photo of Jessica leaning on her crutches.

CHAPTER 36

The cab ride from Hatfield's office cost another eleven dollars. Now she was out almost twenty and at the end of the workday she'd still have to get home.

As she entered the bay, Enid peered at her over half-glasses. The scowl line between her eyes didn't soften as she grunted "Hi" in her husky voice. Jessica was relieved when she'd crutched across the bay, past Enid's taloned stare and into her office.

She tucked the magazine Hatfield had given her into a drawer and unfurled a three-foot long sheet of vellum covered with squares, spreading the tiresome thing across her desk. "Antenna Specification Tree—Sheet Number One, Gain." Gain, Stone had explained, was the power or strength of an antenna. Her assignment was to lay out a tiered configuration of squares where the top square, total gain, connected to a thickly branched tree of smaller squares setting specs on so many lower level contributors she hadn't the courage to count them.

The spec tree might be interesting if she were involved in the antenna design. But she wasn't. She was meeting with engineer after engineer who'd tell her what squares to put on the tree. Eventually, they'd tell her what number to put in each square. She was like a shoe clerk whose only function was stuffing shoes into boxes, never designing, making or even selling them.

Dull, dull, dull. But she had to get every detail right. If she made mistakes and Armor learned of it, he'd be able to say she couldn't perform her job and she'd be out, out, out.

First she'd take a peek at the magazine—just enough to see what kinds of articles were there.

The cover had a picture of the building where Hatfield had his office. Inside were technical articles on treatments for dwarfism and breast cancer. There was only one non-technical article, written by a patient chronicling her rehabilitation after a stroke. Nothing was more than ten pages long, most only four or five. It wouldn't be hard to write such a short piece.

She turned to the stroke article. There was the author in a full-page color photo, walking across the medical plaza using only a cane. The caption was "Pride in Progress." In six pages, she'd described the stroke onset and aftermath and her progress toward recovery in collaboration with physicians and therapists.

Jessica now had a feel for the type of material the magazine published. She could write a lot about being disabled, but it wouldn't do to just ramble. She'd need a message, a point of view like "Pride in Progress."

Arms weakening, she put the magazine back into the drawer. Better take the spec tree around and get some more squares filled in while she could.

By midafternoon, she'd managed to meet with three engineers before grinding to a stop. The final, total collapse struck when she was in her own office, had closed the door, but hadn't quite made it to the wheelchair. She landed facedown on the floor beside it.

A light rap startled her. What if that was Enid and she saw her like this? She turned her head to the side to see the door opening. It was Whitney. Her office was just up the hall now that she was working for Kyle.

"You in here? Thought I heard something." Whitney stuck her head inside.

"Close the door." Jessica didn't want Enid to see or hear them.

Whitney clicked it shut. "Are you okay?"

"See if you can help me up." Jessica could barely form the mushy sounding words. Whitney had to grab her under the armpits, drag her into alignment with the wheelchair and, with a lot of grunting, lift her high enough so that Jessica could maneuver into the seat. Little by little Jessica described her predicament. She couldn't get to any more meetings today and didn't know how she was going to get home. Maybe Whitney could call a cab and help her downstairs when it came. Never mind the fare. She had to get home whatever the cost.

Whitney leaned back in the desk chair. "Did you know Kyle lives just north of you above Foothill Boulevard? He could drive right past your place if he doesn't already. No problem for him—he's hired a driver."

"Me, hitch a ride with Kyle Bumpers?"

"What's he going to do? Grope you? He's not that crude."

"I don't like owing him anything."

"Want me to ask him?"

"Never thought I'd be hitching a ride with Kyle Bumpers."

"Is that a yes?"

"What choice do I have?"

In a few minutes, the ride was arranged.

"How can he afford a driver?" Jessica asked, the words still coming out slowly and indistinctly.

"He's making a mint on tech stocks. At least that's what he says."

The trip home was boring. She and Kyle were buckled up in their seat belts at opposite corners of the backseat of his Lincoln Towne Car. While he jabbered on, obviously trying to impress her with what he knew about hot tech stocks, she inspected the spotless interior—the seats were plush and the backs of the front seats had more buttons and switches than she knew uses for.

"Pick you up at 7:30 tomorrow," he said when they reached her building. "The least I can do after you goosed me into going for this job."

She was exhilarated. He appreciated that she'd made his life better. About to gush with gratitude over his offer of a ride, she stopped herself. It wouldn't be wise to get all mushy with Kyle Bumpers. "Thanks" was enough and risked nothing.

After the driver unloaded her wheelchair and lugged it up to her apartment, she waited for him to reach the bottom of the stairs before opening the door. She didn't want him to see the disorder inside, didn't want to face it herself.

The usual trash and dirt and smells of decay greeted her.

Knowing better than to look in the empty refrigerator for dinner, she got down a box of toasted oatmeal squares and a box of powdered milk. The last time someone had taken her to the store she'd gotten smart about buying things that kept a long time. Basic coping required an unrelenting, exhausting effort to plan and think ahead.

She put the cereal on the table beside the laptop, which she plugged in, opened and booted up. Maybe an idea for the article would come to her and distract her from this misery. What message from the disabled would she like to communicate to doctors?

Her mind drifted back to the day at Disneyland. People had noticed and paid attention to her when she'd been upright, but once she was wheelchair bound, she'd been ignored. A waitress had even insisted on taking her order from Fernando. She remembered another time when she'd tried to get into a crosswalk in her wheelchair before the light changed and people in front of her had stood talking, then dashed across in the last second. They'd never noticed she was there, let alone realized she couldn't run like they could. In the wheelchair, she'd had to yell at department store clerks to whom she seemed invisible. That was why she used crutches as often as possible. But some disabled people didn't have that option.

She had a theme. Look at us, we want to be seen, we want to be part of your world. She thought of a title and laughed. "Look to Me Only with Thine Eyes." Corny, but it might get attention and that's what she wanted.

She held off eating so she could write a while before the post-carb slump hit. "Look at me. I'm Jessica, I spend a lot of time in a wheelchair and I'm eager to talk to you. Yes, me down here. Don't think of me as a dropout from humanity. Think of me as short, not very mobile, but otherwise like you."

When she finished, she liked what she'd written. But it had taken several pages to describe just one tiny aspect of her illness—getting noticed. There were so many difficulties and miseries. In the future, would she want to write about them all? What could she tell someone else about handling the grief she experienced watching normal people hurrying about their lives, unhampered by crutches or a wheelchair? Or the frustration of not being able to keep a home decently neat and clean?

There were bigger, longer term heartaches: choosing a career, even having a career, might no longer be an option; she might never find someone to love and be loved by; she might never have a child. Was it possible to give hope to others as hers was dwindling?

CHAPTER 37

In the morning she woke up in bed, where she'd stumbled in the middle of the night. Her gaze fell on the empty spot on top of the dresser. Hiding that damned picture of her hiking hadn't made it vanish. Like an afterimage when you look into the sun, it still appeared to her.

At least today was Saturday, safe Saturday, and there was still safe Sunday. Two days when she didn't have to drag herself around at work, hiding in her office as much as possible where the severity of her weakness wouldn't be seen.

Today she'd concentrate on the challenging housekeeping tasks—laundry, buying groceries, cleaning the apartment. Straightening out this mess wouldn't be the same as straightening out the mess that was her life, but for a little while it might feel that good.

She phoned a home cleaning agency. It wouldn't be cheap, but what else could she spend money on these days besides rent, groceries, medical care and taxis? Everything else was out—dinners in restaurants, movies, shopping trips. Her hair hadn't been cut in weeks and was getting alley cat shaggy.

By midafternoon the apartment was clean and orderly—kitchen and bathroom scoured, trash thrown out, carpet vacuumed and smelly spots scrubbed off, laundry piled neatly on the bed which now had clean sheets. Things were back under control.

She e-mailed Hatfield the draft article she'd finished last night. What an intense experience that had been. The words had erupted from her. Being cut off from both writing and piano playing for such a long time had built up a pressure inside she was happy to release.

Maybe she'd take Kyle a copy of the article. He might find it helpful. Or he might sneer at her efforts. Better not take the chance.

When her mother made her daily phone call, trolling for an opportunity to help, Jessica accepted. She'd heard about companies that delivered groceries to people's houses, but the only one she'd found near her had gone out of business. Without a food infusion she and the cats would have to get by on cereal, powdered milk and canned tomato juice.

Today there'd be no reason for harangues about her lack of ability to look after herself. When her mother got here and saw a clean, orderly apartment—she'd be sure to inspect everything as inconspicuously as she could manage—she'd see her daughter was getting on pretty well.

Jessica settled herself on the couch to watch the Health Discovery channel, hoping, as always, for a medical revelation. When she heard a knock, she stood slowly and moved slowly to the door, saving what energy she could.

Mom looked her up and down. "You're feeling all right?"

"Pretty good. Not perfect, but pretty good."

Richard came in behind Mom and the two of them scrutinized the living room and kitchen before peering down the hall to the bedroom and bathroom.

Jessica kept silent. To say anything about how clean she'd gotten the place might give away the rarity of the condition.

"Your apartment looks beautiful," Mom said. "You're keeping it very nice."

Mom's eye was still roving over the living room carpet, the furniture, the kitchen floor and counter. "You never kept your place this neat and clean before."

Jessica tensed up. Mom's instincts were kicking in.

"When you don't get out much, what else is there to do besides read, watch TV and clean house?"

They were in luck. There was a handicapped parking spot right in front of the market. For Jessica such a place sometimes made the difference between getting to a store or not. Even the effort of walking a short distance on crutches could sap her energy.

When they entered the gleaming food palace, its air heady with bakery and delicatessen fragrances, Jessica realized with a pang that cooking aromas had lately gone missing from her life.

"I'd love something fresh—a couple of bags of baby lettuce, some grapes, strawberries, bananas." Jessica leaned into her crutches, conserving energy, while Richard and Mom scurried around loading the things she called for into a cart. When they'd finished with produce, she asked for ice cream—two big quarts of rich chocolate—and frozen vegetarian dinners. No more starving. For a while she could feast on whatever she pleased.

They neared the magazine racks. "I need something to read." She had a lot of sedentary time on her hands these days. "Could you pick up a case of canned cat food and something from that bakery—a loaf of sourdough and some of those really fudgy brownies?"

Mom and Richard took off.

Jessica put all her weight into the crutch sleeves and scanned the magazines. There was never anything written especially for the disabled, a big omission and a big business opportunity overlooked.

A man thumbing through a paperback stared at her. She wished people wouldn't gawk when she was on crutches.

"Funny." The man smiled, returned the book to the shelf, gave her a bemused look and hurried away.

Funny? She reached for it through the crutch sleeve just as she spotted Mom and Richard coming down the aisle behind a cart now heaped above its top.

The book was a collection of schoolchildren's homework papers. Her glance fell on an essay written by a fourth grader. "The sultan was a very rich man. He lived in a palace with fifty wives and two hundred porcupines."

She visualized fifty women and two hundred sweet little porcupines, living together in opulent splendor, wearing tantalizing gold-fringed skimpy costumes, feasting at sumptuous banquets, exciting the carnal appetites of the sultan. Brain switches flipped. She lost all control, her mind was hijacked. Giggling from gut to diaphragm to esophagus to fast-weakening jaw, she dropped the crutches and clutched at the nearest rack to slow her fall onto a wide bottom shelf.

Mom and Richard came rushing up.

Jessica weakly waved the book she was still clutching. "Shouldn't have looked at this. Too funny."

Mom began to sputter and tap her foot. "Humor in a grocery store. Of all places." She turned to Richard.

"You were doing so well until now," he said reprovingly.

Mom kept on foot-tapping. "She knows laughing can push her over the edge when she gets weak."

But Jessica was certain that this time laughter hadn't merely been the last straw. She'd been only slightly weak before she'd read the essay. As she'd reacted with laughter, she'd distinctly felt switches grabbing her mind, then her body being consumed by weakness. Whether it made sense or not, collapsing when she laughed was a symptom of this crazy illness. Her obsession with humor may have worn rutted pathways in her brain over the years, leaving it vulnerable.

That was horrible to contemplate. She was a humorist, a comedienne. If she had to always avoid laughter to keep from collapsing, who would she be? Could such an individual exist—a humorist who must never laugh?

There was no way she could carry the groceries up to her apartment, especially since she had to go up the stairs on her hands and knees. On all fours, she recited the porcupine joke for Mom's benefit.

"Sometimes you drive me crazy," Mom said, her voice partly muffled by an armful of grocery bags.

Inside, Jessica lay down on the couch while Mom and Richard put away the groceries. "I made an important discovery today," she announced. "I fell because I laughed. I'm certain of it. Just like I do from elevator rides or after meals or when I try to walk fast."

"That's just you," Mom said. "You fell down when you laughed when you were little."

"Maybe I've had a mild case of this for a long time."

Her mother looked insulted. "You were healthy. I took very good care of you." She headed for the kitchen with another bag of groceries. "You have hardly anything in the refrigerator," she called out. "I can't believe you let yourself get so low on food. How do you expect to get well without eating?"

"I needed a few things." Jessica resisted the impulse to lash back at her mother's criticism.

Richard set a case of cat food on the living room floor. "Where does this go?"

"Bottom of the pantry. I'm sure I'm collapsing because of what happens when I hear something funny."

"Don't you think that's unlikely?" Richard lugged the case to the kitchen.

"Yes, it's unlikely," Jessica called out. "I know it's unlikely. Everything about my illness is unlikely."

"I say it's a good thing we took you to the market," Mom said. "I'm putting the soup cans in the cupboard over the microwave."

"Next time don't let yourself get so low," Richard said from the kitchen. "Give us a call."

Jessica sighed. "I will. If I need help, I'll call."

When Mom reached down and hugged her good-bye, Jessica felt her linger as if to sense from Jessica's body tone just what her condition really was.

"Thanks a lot." She would have liked to say more, to tell Mom how much this shopping trip meant to her, but she was afraid to reveal how desperate her situation had become.

"Careful, you're tickling me," she said instead of talking about what was on her mind. "If I laugh, I'll be a basket case again."

By six o'clock it was dark and she turned on the lights. The place looked elegant when it was clean—dark wood bookcases; couch in stormy-day blue; the rich reds, purples and brown of the rug draped over the piano; and the table with floral patterns woodburned into the corners, her own personal touch. The stainless steel kitchen sink and tile counter gleamed. Only the stacks of books and articles on episodic paralysis were still piled on the furniture and piano; there was no more room on any of the bookshelves. At least the piles were neat now.

Not one thing she'd read in any of this stuff had mentioned collapsing with laughter as a symptom of any type of episodic paralysis. A reader of this heap could easily conclude there was no such illness. But now she was convinced she was suffering from just such an ailment. She was a comedienne who couldn't laugh without paying the price of paralysis.

CHAPTER 38

Sunday. Jessica lay in bed, thinking of the Sundays she used to spend with Mom in the organ loft. Although she welcomed not having to deal with immobility and job stress, she knew she now spent too many evenings and weekends alone.

She tried to cheer up by treating herself to a breakfast of cantaloupe, scrambled eggs, toast and orange juice she'd bought yesterday. Accustomed to gobbling so as to finish her meals before the twenty-minute post-food slump, she instead lingered over every bite. She could afford to collapse, she wasn't going anywhere today. Her plan was to grind through the sections on mitochondrial myopathies in two hefty books she'd bought in the med school bookstore.

She eyed them topping one of the stacks of books and papers spread over the piano. Photocopied articles, as well as books she'd bought, represented an investment of hundreds of dollars and hundreds of hours of her time. And nothing to show for it. The mitochondrial myopathies Hatfield wanted to test her for might well be another dead end.

Hoping for a reply from Hatfield, she checked her e-mail. "Received your article. Excellent first try. Sent it in with a touch of my editing. What do you want to write about next? Scheduled your exercise test for March 3—HH."

He liked the article. He had to like it. She'd poured her heart into it. But what nerve to ask for another! Yet how flattering. She had more topics in mind, but he couldn't know that. Like how the media portrayed the disabled. Her kind was rarely shown with charisma, sex appeal or any other gifts. Only music—she was proud of musicians—seemed to accept the talented, whether blind or unusually short or paraplegic.

What a message the other arts usually sent to the disabled! You don't count among the contributors to society; you have the sex appeal of a corpse. Out of sight and out of mind is the best place for you.

She could hardly wait to begin writing again.

But first she had to pursue a diagnosis. What she managed to distill from intensive reading that lasted into the late afternoon was that about seventy percent of the energy requirement of resting muscles is met by the oxidation of fatty acids in mitochondria, the tiny energy factories in the body's cells, and exercise is even more demanding. Before the body can use them, the fatty acids must be broken down into energy-giving chemicals. Failures in mitochondrial fat metabolism can cause severe loss of strength and energy, perhaps like what she experienced as limited fuel supply. Who would have suspected fats of having a hand in her illness?

Fatty acids are transported to the mitochondria and prepared for oxidation by enzymes. Depending on the particular enzyme, a genetic flaw could be benign, produce mild disability, severe disability or even death. Some flaws are easily treated, some harder, some incurable.

She read on. Some enzymes incorporate carnitine, and about seventy-five percent of adult human carnitine is provided by red meat. What if her vegetarian diet had caused a carnitine deficiency so her body wasn't processing fats?

She tensed with dread as she read on. The body normally makes its own carnitine if it's not in its diet. Only when there is a genetic mistake is there a problem. So vegetarianism alone couldn't have created the problem, but might have made it worse. The book did offer the consoling revelation that doses of L-carnitine sometimes miraculously turned the disease around. As soon as possible, she'd get some. There was no mention of enzymes incorporating Vitamin B-12.

She came across material on diagnostic methods, learning that before-and-after exercise tests, such as Hatfield wanted her to take, are commonly used to measure enzyme and oxidation product levels.

Another tool is the biopsy. A slice of muscle, usually from the thigh, is removed and examined under a microscope for abnormal cell configurations and unusual fatty deposits rarely present in normal tissue. Biopsies are done under local anesthetic, but damaged or even severed nerves can cause pain for several months afterward.

Suddenly the exercycle test seemed more appealing.

In a chapter on clinical observations, she read about SCAD, one of the few mitochondrial myopathies with sudden adult onset, where fats cannot be broken down properly. So much metabolic debris accumulates in the mitochondria that the body can't produce enough carnitine-based enzymes to get rid of it. Overflowing with trash, the energy factory bogs down and the muscles lose their energy supply. Loss of energy—that sounded like her. Again, carnitine was involved.

She tried comparing her symptoms to those of SCAD patients. They experienced fluctuating muscle weakness. But how fast were the fluctuations? The speed of onset of her symptoms varied widely. She got worse during the first few days of her period, within a few minutes after beginning to exercise, within seconds after an elevator ride, twenty or thirty minutes after she began eating, and seconds after she started laughing. Recovery could take a minute or hours. None of the articles said anything about the rate of mitochondrial myopathy fluctuation.

Because SCAD patients can't produce energy efficiently or get rid of waste byproducts they get weaker after exercise. That fit her. She felt like she ran out of fuel every time she walked fast.

A physiology book revealed it takes twenty minutes or so after eating before fats begin to be absorbed into the blood and sent on their way to the mitochondria. Twenty minutes after eating, just like her postprandial droops, which she'd perhaps mistakenly labeled carbohydrate slumps. A better term might be fat flops. A couple of her symptoms—collapsing from elevator rides and laughing—didn't fit anything she'd read about SCAD.

Her reading put her back in the same frame of mind she'd been in when she'd begun to think she had myasthenia gravis—hope she might finally be diagnosed and fear of the disease she might have. But this time she wouldn't allow her emotions to go on such a rampage.

She e-mailed her thoughts to Dr. Hatfield. To compensate for inundating him with a five-page, single-spaced technical treatise, she agreed to write another article for the alumni magazine. Wanting him to feel she was offering to make an arduous self-sacrifice, she didn't mention she was looking forward to more writing. But she was.

The next day, sitting in her office and slurping down chop suey and noodles Whitney had brought from the mall, Jessica checked her e-mail. Hatfield had already replied.

"Jessica—

Well done. Wish more of my students had your ability to synthesize a diagnosis by comparing symptoms with textbook information. SCAD appears plausible. Let's try a two-pronged approach. (1) I've asked Dr. Kavalier to see you. He specializes in pediatric genetic pathology, mitochondrial and other. Maybe he'll have some insights. (2) Take the exercise cycle test I scheduled for March third.

Will give you a one-month rest in March before your next article is due in April. See, I do have a heart—HH."

Simultaneous with a sharp rap on her door, Enid yanked it open. "How you doin', hon? Haven't heard a sound from in here for a while." Enid's smoker's voice was raspy.

Actually, gravity sucked today, sucked Jessica's chin to her chest, pressed her body firmly into the wheelchair. "Good."

"See you've got something for lunch. Some nice person must have gotten it for you," Enid said.

Facedown, staring into the computer keyboard, she could almost feel Enid's finger on her pulse, eyes scrutinizing her body. "It's from the mall."

"You couldn't have gone there yourself."

"You'd be surprised what I can do, Enid."

"You can't do much when you're like this, poor thing. Constance— you know, Armor's secretary—wanted to see you a while ago. But I told her to try again tomorrow. I told her you were so bad this morning you could hardly get to the john and back and I knew you didn't want to be bothered."

A chill shot through Jessica. By now Armor had probably heard she was too weak to meet with Constance. "Of course I could have seen her. In the future please, Enid, let people into my office unless I say otherwise."

"You're so brave. I don't know how you do it." Jessica heard Enid's pumps clomp across the bay, but not the click of her door closing. Now anyone in the bay, especially Enid, would be able to look in and see her.

Hyperalert, Jessica recognized Stone's footsteps returning to the bay. She listened as Enid told him first about his phone calls, then how weak Jessica was. "I admire you so much, Jim. Taking a chance with someone like her. That takes real courage."

Enid was going to be a major problem, Jessica just knew it.

A few days later, Jessica sat slumped in her wheelchair in the med school cafeteria where Josie from the MG organization had brought her. Josie was recovering from a thymectomy, the surgery Jessica had once hoped for, and was feeling pretty good now. She lived near Gebauer and had volunteered to pick Jessica up and bring her here. Jessica vowed she'd never forget the kindness that sick people like Josie often showed each other.

A tall man with thinning black hair and a Gebauer picture badge on a neck chain stood just inside the entrance surveying the people in the cafeteria. If this was Dr. Kavalier, he'd know to come over in spite of the fact she couldn't wave or call out. People slumped in wheelchairs with their mouths hanging open stood out, even here.

Without hesitation he crossed the room and slipped into a chair across from her. "You must be Jessica." He shook her weak, floppy hand. "Glad you could meet me here, only free time I've got this week."

Hatfield had already briefed him, but she went over her symptoms anyway, adding that she wanted him to see how quickly B-12 helped her.

"I can't imagine B-12 having any affect on mitochondria," he said, fiddling with the badge chain.

"I'll show you what it does for me." Jessica hadn't taken any this morning so he could see what her symptoms were like. As she popped a couple of pills into her mouth, he explained that he'd never had an adult patient and was not under contract to treat them at Gebauer.

Within five minutes, Jessica was able to sit erect, hold her head up and talk normally. Kavalier was amazed.

"It used to work for me all day, but not any more. I'm getting worse. Maybe because of the B-12."

Kavalier shook his head. "Not likely. People can easily tolerate very large doses."

"Will it do me any harm?"

He shrugged. "Can't hurt."

When he went to get something to eat, Jessica unwrapped her sandwich and chewed it slowly, careful not to expend unnecessary energy. She hoped Kavalier would open up, be more informative.

After half an hour of lunch and conversation, she was weaker than before—arms flaccid on the table, head down, jaw open and tongue immobile.

"Your condition changes so fast I don't know what to think." Kavalier's nose twitched like a nervous rabbit's.

"I'm deteriorating." Jessica drawled out the words. "Can you help me?"

"I'd like to refer you to someone in San Diego who sees adult patients."

"San Diego's so far. Can't you help me?"

"I don't know what to make of you." He turned his head to look at the wall TV blaring news of terrorist bombings in Jerusalem.

"You know I need help and soon."

"You have time. You're not going to die tomorrow."

"How long do you think I have? A month? A year?"

He kept his eye on the TV showing a bombed-out street and stores. "At least."

At least. At least one year. The words rang in Jessica's brain. If he thought she had only a year or so, why didn't he show any sense of the urgency she felt? She was right here, not in Jerusalem, and she needed help now. "Can't you do something to help me?" She hated wheedling and struggled not to cry.

"Wish I could." Kavalier meticulously folded his paper napkin before he put it on a food tray with the remains of his lunch and stood to go.

Back in her apartment Jessica studied herself in the full-length mirror, half expecting to find she now looked like one of those women in Picasso's paintings—shattered into a million pieces no one would ever be able to put together again.

She didn't look like that and she didn't look as though she'd die soon. Smooth healthy skin. Clear eyes. Full head of glossy brown hair with what she'd always felt were attractive glints of auburn. There were a few small hints of what she'd look like in old age—wrinkles beginning at the corners of the eyes and mouth, a touch of fullness below the jaw, gray hairs here and there. Body still trim, though. Maybe she'd never get flabby, if she ever got back to running.

She wanted time to be around for the classic stages of a woman's life—marriage and children. At least enough time to see if she could make better choices in men than in the past. She'd steer clear of controllers like Fernando, for sure. She wanted to live long enough to love someone and be loved in return.

Could she think about a world without her?

She preferred not to think. Her mother and Richard would be devastated and Whitney would be sad. She wondered if Kyle would miss her if she disappeared.

Not that she was going to disappear, just because a crotchety old woman and a bored man had carelessly, off-handedly semi-predicted it.

She'd like to do something about her career, change its direction. But she didn't really know what she wanted to do—something relevant to at least a small part of the world. It would be great if she could use what she'd learned about science and medicine to write about fighting illness and disability. She liked the idea that after her death, whenever that was, people might remember her with gratitude. Even if she was severely disabled, she could write.

She looked into the part of her the mirror couldn't see. The place, deep inside, where fear lay coiled like a snake ready to strike at any time. Fear of disability, fear of loss of independence, fear of leaving the earth without either a child or an accomplishment to mark her passage as significant. She could never make a pet of this snake, but if she was going to live a good life, whatever was left of it, she'd have to keep it confined to its dark place.

CHAPTER 39

Jessica awoke in a small bed, not her own, and looked out the window at a familiar garden. What was she doing at Mom's house? Her eyes—was it really her eyes, or her demented mind—were playing tricks on her. Flowers and winter lettuce were dancing and shimmying in the sunlight.

She tried to clear her aching head. Yesterday—it must have been yesterday—she'd been taking the exercycle test, pedaling and pedaling. Faster, longer, she'd been urged. She'd obeyed until she started shaking and shivering uncontrollably. She remembered being in the ER leaning against someone, trying not to fly apart, her breathing short and labored. Then blank until this morning. What had gone wrong?

Mom was standing in the doorway. "Ready for some breakfast?"

"Breakfast?"

"The last time you ate must have been sometime yesterday."

Jessica aggravated the headache by trying to sit up, but she was too weak. "My head hurts. I can hardly think."

"They kept you going too hard and too long. If I'd been there that wouldn't have happened."

"You weren't there? But I got here somehow."

"They called after you collapsed. They almost put you on a respirator."

Jessica recalled gasping for breath. For minutes? Hours? "The tests? Do they know anything yet?"

"You said it would take two weeks to process all the blood samples."

Jessica nodded, remembering nothing of that. And she couldn't remember how she'd gotten out of her clothes and into one of her mother's flower-printed nightgowns.

Mom propped her up on a pillow in bed and spoon fed her orange juice—she was too weak to sip from a glass or suck on a straw—and a little oatmeal which she had trouble swallowing. She had to allow each teaspoonful to slide to the back of her mouth and down her throat. She saw her gratitude for being well cared for reflected in Mom's warm, hazel eyes.

She woke in a panic. The blinds were drawn, the bedroom was dark. What time was it? How long had she been asleep? She called out "Mom! Mom!"

The door opened and Mom, dressed in a piano-lesson pantsuit, stuck her head inside the room.

"What time is it?"

"After two thirty. My first lesson's due in a few minutes."

"I have to call work. Where's my purse? I need my cell phone."

Mom crossed the room and brought her black, oversized purse. "Anything else?"

She could sit back and let Mom take care of her, lie here day after day, like Daddy, listening to Mom teach piano, waiting for attention after the lessons were over. "Thanks, I'm okay. Go take care of your student." She had to get back to managing for herself.

Mom continued to stand over her. "First let's see if you can get up."

"In a minute. I need to call work first. You go ahead." As Jessica punched Stone's number, she stared at Mom in a plea for privacy.

Mom took her time leaving and didn't shut the door. Just like Enid.

She could hear Stone's number ringing. What was she going to tell him? He'd known about yesterday's test.

She reached his voicemail. "Hello, Jim. Jessica. Sorry I didn't call earlier, but I have to go in for more tests. I'll be in tomorrow for sure." She hated lying, but didn't want anyone at work to know how sick she'd become. She could just imagine Stone telling Enid she was at home recovering after a trip to the ER and Enid telling everyone in the building.

As soon as Jessica ended the call, Mom popped in again. "I don't think you should go to work tomorrow. Stay here a few days."

Had Mom been hovering outside? "I have to go in. No sick leave left."

"If you have to, I'll drive you." Mom put a lot of stress on "have to."

Kyle and Whitney were away on business and it would be hard to arrange another ride except a taxi. "Thanks. We'll see." Her mouth went dry with fear—fear of not being able to go to work, fear of once more becoming a child in her mother's house.

The doorbell rang. "My first student."

Jessica wondered what extremity Mom would have to be in before she'd cancel a lesson.

Very extreme—Mom would always hang on to her career and the order it brought to her life.

In a few minutes, she heard scales played one note at a time, then in major chords, finally in octaves. From the speed and strength of the sound, she guessed this was an intermediate or advanced student.

Jessica slid to the edge of the bed and sat up. She was stronger than she'd been this morning, but had nothing to wear except the sweatpants and shirt she'd worn for the exercycle test. She needed clothes, needed to feed the cats. Richard should be home by five thirty. Maybe he'd be willing to drive her to the apartment. Until then she'd rest.

Sometime later, she half roused from a stupor to hear voices.

"I'm exhausted." Mom's voice from somewhere in the living room.

"Get some rest. Let me help you," Richard answered.

"I don't know who I am or what I'm supposed to be doing anymore. She needs help and she's my daughter. Trouble is, the whole situation puts us both back to when I was the person who took care of her, who nursed her back to health when she was sick, who made her decisions. I suppose it's natural for her to resent that."

"You're on an identity seesaw," Richard said. "Child's mother, adult's mother, child's, adult's, child's, adult's."

"She's probably going through the same thing, only in mirror image."

Their voices faded as they went to the other side of the house. Jessica lay awake, pondering whether Mom was right. As with Daddy, Mom's instincts to treat her as a child had sprung strongest in times of distress, just when Jessica, and probably Daddy too, had needed her help the most. In both their cases illness had forced itself into their life and stomped all over their relationship with Mom.

When she and Richard returned from the apartment that evening, Jessica smelled enchiladas baking. Spinach, sour cream and cheddar cheese enchiladas. Her favorite. Somehow Mom had found time to prepare them.

Richard lugged in two paper bags with her clothes, shoes and pajamas, while Jessica carried only a drugstore bag containing the carnitine she'd just bought. Tonight she'd eat Mom's enchiladas, but tomorrow she'd start on a low fat diet. If she did have the type of mitochondrial myopathy that clogged her cells with half-processed fats and debris, getting rid of fats should help.

Mom bustled around, setting out the enchiladas and homemade coleslaw. She seemed almost cheerful.

Richard dragged his TV tray near Jessica's. "She's happy to have you back home where she can look after you."

Jessica sighed.

"Listen, Jessica." Richard lowered his voice and leaned toward her. "Your mother's a wonderful person. She loves you and wants to take care of you. You're very lucky."

"I know. It's just that she wants to feed and clothe me and put me to bed like I'm a little girl again."

Richard smiled and winked at her. "You're twenty-six now. She can't make you into a baby again unless you let her. That's up to you."

Jessica hung her head, feigning weakness, to avoid his gaze. Her father had lacked the strength to resist Mom's domination. She'd always feared she had Daddy's propensity for dependency.

When her mother dropped her off at work the next morning, Jessica climbed the steps with little difficulty, dragging the crutches behind her. There was no disputing the fact that when Mom made breakfast, helped her to the car and drove her to the front door she saved energy. Every bit saved early in the day would allow her to work a little longer. Her mother's help made a difference.

Head high, body as erect as she could manage, she strutted across the bay past Enid's desk. Enid squinted at her over the top of her word processor and said an unsmiling "hi," probably disappointed that Jessica's vigor gave her nothing new to gossip about.

Jessica called the office of the San Diego doctor Kavalier had recommended and got an appointment two weeks away. His office wanted her to send them a copy of her medical records and bring the results of the exercycle test. Wait until they saw the two-inch sheaf of paperwork laying out all the tests showing what she didn't have.

Now there was a workday to face. She pulled a roll of spec trees from her file, stuffed them into a crutch sleeve and headed for the thermal/mechanical department on the other side of the building. She didn't dare leave the crutches behind.

It was nearly noon before she returned to the bay after spending hours toiling with a group of engineers over the one hundred twenty squares they were responsible for. After they'd told her the specs for one set of equipment, she'd been able to infer others so accurately that the task went more easily than expected. Whenever she managed to do a task especially well, she celebrated.

At her bay door she stopped. Should she try to cross in front of Enid, carrying the crutches under her arm, or take the safe way and use them? A few weeks ago the choice would have been automatic—go for it. But now she had to worry what Enid would see and might do if she collapsed. And who knew what the new engineers in the bay thought and were saying about her? She tried to be friendly, but hid in her office with the door shut whenever she was having an attack.

Jessica slouched to her office on crutches and closed the door.

Enid's pumps clomped across the bay and out, no doubt to lunch. Jessica had no lunch and there was no one to get one for her. She laid her head on her desk to save energy and let her mind float free. Disconnect all circuits. No stray thoughts or feelings.

Sometime later Jessica felt the shock of a loud rap on the door ricochet through her body, setting off SPAM. She'd begun to think of her brain switch disturbances as disruptive SPAM. Her brain tried to resist, but to no avail. She couldn't raise up from her desk. The door opened.

"Are you sleeping?" Enid stuck her oversized nose into the office.

"No. You startled me." It was hard for Jessica to talk with her face pressed to the desk.

"A nap would be good for you."

"I'm not napping."

"Mr. Stone wants to see you, but I'll tell him he'll have to wait."

Jessica pushed partway up from the desk. "No such thing. Tell him I'll be right there."

Enid stood there, twisting the door knob.

"Go! Tell him." If Enid left, Jessica thought she could collect herself.

Enid turned away, as usual leaving the door open. Now Jessica had to figure out how to get herself thirty feet across the bay and into Stone's office. The crutches were propped against the desk within reach. She managed to raise herself up, laid one over the space between the desk and table, and used it as a handrail to grope her way around the table and into the wheelchair.

As she tried to get rolling, her arms failed her. Head hanging, she could see Enid out of the corner of her eye. She made another effort, but couldn't budge. There was only one way to get to Stone's office.

"Enid," she called.

Enid came right over.

"Could you push me? Please?"

"You can't even manage in a wheelchair, poor thing." Enid rolled her out the door. "And it's so easy to make it go. You poor thing."

"It's all your fault, Enid. You're not making the coffee strong enough."

"What do you mean?" Enid, as usual, manifested no sense of humor.

"My day is measured by your coffee scoop. Six scoops in the urn and I can sit up, seven and I can speak up, eight and I can roll the wheelchair. Today feels like a five-scooper."

"I don't count scoops. I don't have to after all these years."

Enid knocked on Stone's door, opened it and pushed Jessica inside. "Here's our brave little girl. She's not well at all today."

Jessica imagined that by the end of the afternoon everyone in the building would know she'd been too weak to roll her own wheelchair a few feet over a level floor.

CHAPTER 40

M om got to the driver's side of the station wagon at the same time as Jessica and reached out her hand.

Jessica clutched the key to her chest. "I'll drive." With no brain SPAM she knew she could drive, at least for a while. "You just relax and enjoy the ride."

"Are you sure you're up to it?" Mom eyed the key and for a moment Jessica feared they were going to wrestle for it.

"Would I say I'm driving if I wasn't?"

"I hope you know what you're doing." Mom rolled her eyes, waved her hands toward heaven and then plodded around to the passenger side. A martyr's resignation.

Jessica ground her teeth. *I hope you know what you're doing.* Plod, plod, plod. Such a vote of confidence. Couldn't Mom say, just once, she'd be delighted if Jessica drove and she could relax.

As they set out for San Diego and Dr. Frist, Jessica thought of the many times she'd driven, ridden or walked up Mom's quiet, tree-lined street with its orderly row of houses and broad, well-kept lawns. It was the kind of neighborhood where she'd had the feeling since childhood that nothing could go wrong.

But she could hardly credit the neighborhood itself for this sense of security. And it wasn't Daddy. He'd been too sick to work or do much to help raise her. Mom had provided the security—Mom with her determination to make a living for them all, with her steadfast devotion to her husband and daughter. Mom had been their Rock of Ages. She glanced over at her mother, wishing it were not so difficult, so risky, to express these thoughts out loud.

She turned into a busy avenue. Cars rushed in both directions and a motorcycle roared by. Pedestrians were crossing, drivers honking. Too much confusion when she needed to concentrate on driving and holding the SPAM at bay. Switches in her head began to chatter. She tried to focus, but with the grip on her mind slipping, turned down a small side street and parked.

"I'm not quite ready to drive."

"That's okay. I'll do it."

"I'll just be a minute," Jessica said, realizing how ridiculous her reply was since she had no idea when she'd be better. Could be a minute, could be an hour, could be half a day.

"Why are you being so stubborn?"

Jessica stopped herself before she could make her usual smart-ass quip. She was not going to zap her mother at times like this anymore.

The problem was that, with joking out, she wasn't in control. She didn't know how to handle the situation. "I'm harder for you to deal with than Daddy was, aren't I?"

Mom stopped, hand on the door handle. "What do you mean?"

"What I mean is he let you do everything for him while he lay on his back and never argued." Jessica felt an elephant had moved into her chest, crowding her breathing, the pain of it making her gasp for breath. Now she feared a breathing crisis.

Maybe she'd made the decision against wisecracks too hastily. One little quip couldn't be so bad. She'd get relief if she could blurt it out and derail this wretched conversation. "You want to do everything for me and I won't let you. I can't." She slapped her hands on the steering wheel with all her remaining strength.

Mom gulped and appeared to be seriously struggling with her emotions. "I helped him whenever he needed me. I want to help you too."

"I know you helped him and I've always loved you for that. But too much help isn't good for a person, no matter how much you love them." Jessica always wished she'd tried to stop Mom from making Daddy so helpless, but hadn't thought she could. Mom was always so formidable, so in control of everything. Still she wished she'd tried. "You always go too far. You make the person you're trying to help helpless."

"I refused to let our problems destroy us—you, me, our family. I carried on. I did what had to be done then and I can do it now for you."

Jessica could hear so much pain in the tightness of Mom's voice that she couldn't bear to look at her. She couldn't bear for the elephant in her chest to get bigger either. "I don't want you to take over my life. I'm afraid I won't be able to stop you." Jessica felt her breath coming short and fast.

"Do you have any idea how bad this makes me feel?" Mom's voice was getting unsteady.

"You have to back off, let me live my own life as much as I can. Do you understand?"

"I've tried my best to help you." Mom's face was flaming red. "You don't know how hard I've tried." She was choking back sobs.

"I know and I appreciate it. But just let me decide what I need. Okay?" Jessica heard her voice rise in pitch. "Will you do that for me?"

Mom's mouth worked silently. She stared out the window, looked back at Jessica and sighed. "If that's the only way to get some peace around here."

"I think we've said enough. I think the elephant is leaving." Jessica tried to disconnect her brain to calm her breathing.

"Elephant," Mom mumbled. "I won't even ask what that's about."

"I need you to drive." Jessica handed Mom the car keys. "Please?"

They traveled a long time down the freeway in silence. Mom's short stature forced her up against the steering wheel at the closest, highest seat position where Jessica could see the taut muscles in her reddened face. For Jessica, her mother's face was like a neon sign flashing: "My Hard-Hearted Daughter Did This to Me."

Shameful, self-centered, uncaring daughter.

But a daughter who had had to get through to her mother sometime about not babying her, not trying to take away her independence. Now might not have been a good time—if there even was a "good" time—but that's the way it had happened and she'd done it without a single joke.

Maybe it was a good thing Mom was angry. If her mother were a joker like she was, nothing would ever get resolved.

Having read up on mitochondrial diseases, she should have been better prepared for what she saw in Dr. Frist's waiting room. The room was sunny and decorated with pictures of children and toys. Shiny mobiles hung from the ceiling. On a large, circular table was a board with colored rings on pegs and a stack of picture books. A little wagon and a plastic truck with pedals, large enough to be sat on, stood near the table.

Most of the children here could only look. Like the girl across the room, who Jessica overheard was twelve, strapped into a wheelchair, head separately strapped to a support pad, fluid dripping from a bag into her arm. The girl's mother, talking to another mother of a similarly afflicted child in a wheelchair, described how her daughter had to be fed by IV because she couldn't swallow. Yet when the woman said "She just loves coming here, it's a pretty drive," Jessica heard the daughter grunt a reply of agreement and caught sight of an unmistakable, though only partly formed, smile.

Two giggling little boys chased each other around the table, frequently falling to the floor. One father said to the other, "My son's four. How old's yours?" "Four also." Jessica was stunned—they looked no older than two. She heard the men comparing the boys' progress. One could say a few words, the other none. Both had difficulty keeping their balance and staying on their feet. But they looked happy.

Perhaps these children would stay happy as long as they were protected and isolated from healthier children. The attitudes of others, she'd come to realize, had a lot to do with the self-respect and happiness of the disabled. The problem was that able people didn't want to be slowed down or held back by those who were not able to keep up, which often led to demonizing or belittling the disabled to prevent feeling guilty about ignoring or neglecting them. She wondered if anyone had thought of ways to deal with this problem.

As far as she could tell she was the only adult patient here, the least disabled, and the only one who'd brought crutches. "I don't remotely resemble any of these kids," Jessica whispered.

Uncharacteristically silent, Mom seemed transfixed by the grave disabilities around her.

When the nurse called Jessica into Dr. Frist's office, Jessica needed her crutches. The children stared as she went by.

In less than fifteen minutes Jessica stumped out of Frist's office as fast as she could move on crutches. "Let's go," she said.

"What happened? What did he say?"

"Let's just go." Not waiting for Mom to get to her feet, Jessica crutch-thumped to the exit. She waited for her mother outside on the windswept plaza. "I shouldn't have been surprised. Kavalier said my symptoms fluctuated too fast for mitochondrial myopathy. Frist said my exercycle test results didn't show any toxic levels of metabolic products. And I don't look like anyone in that waiting room."

"You seem upset," Mom said.

"That's putting it mildly. Frist said I don't have anything he's ever seen. 'Your symptoms come and go so fast they must have a psychological cause. I hope you'll find yourself a good therapist.'" She imitated his preachy voice, then burst into tears.

Mom wrung her hands, twisted her pianist's fingers almost into knots. "Well, I'm glad you don't have this mitochondrial thing. You should be glad too."

"Every time I've gone through reading, testing, going to doctors' offices and hoping, it's ended dreadfully. Seeing this string of doctors is the most depressing thing I've ever done. I'm never going to see another one in my life. I'm never going to take another test."

Mom gasped. "You can't mean that. You've got to keep trying."

"I don't want to hear one more word about what I have to do." She gnashed her teeth. There she went taking her frustrations out on Mom again. "Sorry, Mom. I don't know how you're managing to put up with me."

After they got home, Richard brought a Marie Callender's dinner, which they ate while watching a health channel. Jessica was happy not to have to talk. She only wanted to disconnect her mind, go brain dead.

But the segment they'd tuned to on narcolepsy was interesting. A man was shown falling asleep in the middle of a conversation, then a woman sleeping soundly at a dinner table with her family around her. The scene shifted to a golf driving range, where a stocky middle-aged man was teeing up. "Many narcoleptics are also afflicted with cataplexy," the on-site announcer said. "Watch this." The man lined himself up, club in hand, wound up, and drove a golf ball into the distance. With a smile of success he turned toward the camera. Then his knees buckled and he collapsed on the ground.

Jessica was instantly alert.

"He's totally out cold," the announcer was saying.

Jessica leaned closer to the TV. "Maybe not."

"He fell just like you do," Mom said.

The man began to stir and was helped to his feet by the announcer. "I wasn't out. I could hear everything you said."

"You didn't move. You didn't say anything," the announcer said.

"I have narcolepsy, a sleep disorder. Sometimes I can't sleep when I want to, sometimes I sleep when I don't want to. Sometimes my brain thinks I'm asleep and dreaming when I'm not and tells me not to move and act out my dreams. Like your mind does when you're asleep and dreaming. Then I get weak. I often fall like I just did. That's cataplexy."

They watched and learned that most narcoleptics have cataplexy, which can be brought on by sudden emotion or exertion.

"Sounds like you, but you obviously don't have narcolepsy," Richard said.

"You should see what Dr. Hatfield thinks," Mom said. "Just a suggestion. Not an effort to run your life."

Jessica shook her head. "I don't have narcolepsy like these people. And I usually don't get right up again like that golfer. So I probably don't have cataplexy any more than I have chemical allergies or myasthenia gravis or neurally mediated hypotension or a mitochondrial myopathy."

"Cataplexy seems worth looking into." Mom was trying to sound casual, not forceful.

"I can hardly stand the thought of a new disease. I told you I've had enough tests and I'm sick of doctors."

"How about I look this up on the Web?" Richard offered.

Jessica shrugged. "If you want to." She wondered how the scenario would go if she died undiagnosed. As in some mitochondrial myopathies, would her heart muscle fail? As in myasthenia gravis, would her diaphragm stop and with it her breathing? Would she be unconscious or witness her own death, know what was happening or not? Unconscious was too out of control, too lacking in good-byes.

CHAPTER 41

Jessica couldn't recall what she'd just said, but Jack Murray was replying. "Of course we need specs for the test models. Why didn't I think of that? The thermal model for the antenna feed needn't contain the actual electronics, but it should include something that behaves like them thermally. Good catch, Jessica."

Good catch? How had she managed that? Morbid thoughts and battles with brain SPAM had so fatigued her she could scarcely concentrate. She'd almost wanted to have a mitochondrial myopathy, wanted her enemy identified so there'd be something concrete to fight against. Now she was back to square one—no diagnosis, no treatment, no hope for a cure.

Murray drummed his fingers on the desk. "We'll need more squares on the spec tree for test models—thermal, electrical, mechanical, deployment." He squinted at her, the way people often did these days, as though evaluating her. No one had confidence in her anymore.

She tried to lean forward to put the new squares on the spec tree, but her weakened arms dragged to a halt on his desk. "I'll put a line from each antenna feed to a square with the heading 'Test Models.'" She looked to him for agreement, wondering whether he could even think about what she was saying while her jaw drooped so far that her mouth hung open. He was clearly trying to avoid staring at her.

"Jessica, I don't know how to say this. But maybe you shouldn't keep working when you're not feeling good."

She began to tremble. "Even if my body goes out to lunch now and then my mind's still here." Would he try to get her off the project? Fear could make her collapse right in front of him.

He didn't answer, but his worried eyes and tight lips told her that working with her was a strain, a problem. She wished he saw her as brave and determined, rather than incapacitated.

When they were through, he had to wheel her back down the long corridor. Once she called out: "We're really burning rubber. Watch out for speed bumps."

She got no laugh from her old joking buddy, hadn't in months.

She'd barely been deposited in her oppressively confining office, a match for her oppressively confining apartment, when Whitney phoned. "Kyle and I want to take you to lunch."

"Thanks, but I'm a basket case today." They'd regret eating with her—she'd be dead weight on their hands

"I'm coming over." A few minutes later Whitney barged in without knocking. "Having a bad day?"

She was having a bad life, but why spread the gloom. "Tomorrow'll be better." She could barely form the words.

"We'll take you anywhere you want to go. How about the Parkview Café?"

"Whit, I just can't hack it. Kyle wouldn't want me there anyway." He was still improving, could now use his hand almost normally and was able to walk short distances with the help of a cane. She, on the other hand, was going downhill fast and had no idea what to do to stop it.

"Of course he wants you to come. He likes you a lot. He repeats your jokes, even the dumb ones. He asks about your cats. He says he worries half the night when he drops you off after work that you'll fall and hurt yourself and no one will be there. By the way, I worry about that too."

"His driver always brings my wheelchair up and if I can't walk he helps me to the couch. Can't fall far from a couch, can I?" That is, she let him bring her inside when the apartment was halfway clean. Otherwise, she propped herself in the doorway and waited until he was downstairs before she pushed the door open and fell in.

Whitney laid a hand on Jessica's head and stroked her hair. "You're avoiding my message."

"About Kyle?"

Whitney nodded. "He wants to help you. He told me he just doesn't know how to make an offer you won't refuse."

"He's tougher than that. I bet you talked him into asking me to lunch."

"You're not seeing things straight."

"Are you telling me I'm wrong about you talking Kyle into lunch with me?"

"You're wrong about Kyle. Now knock off the persecuted Saint Jessica bit and come to lunch with us."

Only a week after the lunch, where Kyle and Whitney had insisted on planning a picnic, Jessica was struggling to dress herself in cut-offs and T-shirt. She was happy to be going someplace, rather than spending the long Memorial Day weekend alone or visiting Mom's where the mood would be tense and the air thick with unasked-for advice. Kyle and his driver were going to bring a picnic lunch and take her to Will Rogers State Park over on the west side of LA to meet Whitney and Dave.

Will Rogers, who said everything is funny as long as it's happening to someone else, would probably have gotten a lot of laughs out of her pratfalls. Delving into his old columns in the Gebauer library while she was in college, she'd learned to love not only his humor, but also to admire his devotion to the afflicted. He'd raised money for victims of drought in Arkansas, floods in Mississippi, earthquakes in Nicaragua and the unemployed during the Great Depression. She bet he'd have loved helping victims of a disease that made them fall down laughing.

When Kyle's immaculately shiny car arrived, Jessica hoped her neighbors would see her being helped into it. She'd like them to think of her as something besides that sick girl in number 236.

"Got a great picnic basket." Kyle was beaming, his smile appearing especially full-lipped since he'd trimmed his goatee shorter and away from his mouth. "Stuffed portabellas, roasted pepper and feta cheese on focaccia, arugula and pine nut salad, fresh bing cherries, and chocolate-orange biscotti. All vegetarian, all first class. Oh, and two bottles of pinot grigio." His eyes seemed to search hers for a sign he'd pleased her.

"My dream picnic. And you're getting better all the time." Without planning it, she reached over and laid her hand on his now lithe, limber one, lacing her fingers with his. She liked the feel of new life in his fingers.

He leaned so close she felt the heat of his body and said, "I like doing things for you."

What was she thinking? She slid her hand away and didn't look to see his reaction. He was such a mysterious mixture—the smiling, generous Kyle sitting next to her and the Kyle of corporate spying, womanizing and large amounts of unexplained spending money. Getting close to him was inviting trouble. "Oh my goodness, oh my soul. There goes Jessica down the hole," she muttered, paraphrasing a bit of childhood doggerel.

"What?"

"Nothing." This outing was just for a good time and she had to keep it that way.

Inside the park, the driver deposited them near the picnic area, where Whitney waited in a thin-strapped little blue and yellow sundress that billowed in the breeze. Jessica half wished she could run home and change. Compared to Whitney she must look like an adolescent in her cutoffs and T-shirt.

She gazed up at the rolling hills, rising through the remnants of a morning fog to merge with the chaparral-covered Santa Monica Mountains. Once out of the parking lot, she'd have to cope with grassy inclines, dirt hiking paths and rutted gravel-covered fire roads. No place for a wheelchair, but crutches might help on the smoother, easier grades.

Leaving the picnic basket for Dave, who looked strong enough to carry anything, Kyle started up the hill, leaning heavily on a cane made of dark wood, silver-handled and silver-tipped like her great-grandfather's was said to have been.

Jessica crutched along beside him, trailing Whitney. Breathless and unable to talk because of the effort, she let her gaze wander over a wide, freshly mown lawn to the bougainvillea-covered ranch house where Will Rogers had once lived. The thinning fog let through sunbeams that grazed the housetop and lit the bougainvillea like Christmas lights.

In a few minutes, they were laying out Kyle's gourmet spread, complete with a blue and white plastic table cloth, extra-thick paper napkins and stainless cutlery. Jessica put out the stuffed mushrooms, using the table to support herself as she moved around it. She moved slowly, partly to save energy, partly because she was in a fret over the seating arrangement. Should she sit next to Kyle or across from him? Next seemed provocative, across cold. Why hadn't she thought this out beforehand? Then she realized there was only one possibility—she had to sit next to Kyle because Whitney would want to sit next to Dave. Two couples. That's what they'd look like. Kyle didn't even glance her way when she slid onto the bench beside him. But she sensed that every inch of him knew she was there just as every inch of her knew he was there.

Today it had seemed an easy step to go from riding home from work in Kyle's car to riding to a picnic in Kyle's car. But she was unprepared for how this arrangement had evolved: she, of all people, appeared to be on a date with the infamous Kyle Bumpers.

When they'd heaped the food onto plastic plates, Jessica, driven by a hunger she didn't feel in her alimentary tract, immediately attacked her sandwich as though she were starved. Even her thoughts were in anatomical and medical jargon these days.

"Like that sandwich?" Kyle asked with one of those looks that Jessica could never tell was smiling or smirking. "I hoped you would."

"Oink, oink," she said, using a snorting sound that would be very unattractive on a date.

"Slurp, slurp." He sidled close and nudged her gently with his elbow.

"Gobble, gobble," Whitney warbled.

"Rooty-toot, toot," added Dave.

"Rooty-toot, toot!" Jessica said. "That doesn't fit. You have to make a sound, a piggish one."

"You mean crunch, slurp. Like a hungry hyena with a fresh corpse." Dave did his best on a chocolate-orange biscotti that crunched better than it slurped.

"I think he's got it." Kyle laughed.

The conversation meandered from one bit of silliness to another, just as Jessica had wanted. She even tried two fingers of pinot grigio in the bottom of a plastic glass. It went down well and she remained upright.

She stood and, without crutches, carried some trash to a nearby can. "I feel good. Let's walk over to the ranch house."

Kyle got up and leaned lightly on his cane. "Lead on."

They stowed the picnic items and crutches in Dave's car, then headed up stone steps into the shade of a wide veranda, embowered by bougainvillea and bordered with yellow daisies and thick spiny cactus. They peered through the windows and glass-paned doors at faded western furniture and elk and buffalo heads on the walls. A balcony railing, draped with ropes and lariats, overlooked the living room and dining area, where the ceiling rose to fourteen feet so Rogers could practice roping indoors. Jessica pointed out his favorite target, a stuffed calf that could be set rolling on its casters. "Rogers was so into roping he was called the 'Poet Lariat,'" she said. Where the veranda ended, steps led down to a pathway that skirted a spacious lawn, crossed a wooden foot bridge and joined a rutted, uphill gravel road. Two years ago it had been easy for her to jog the mile up that road to Inspiration Point.

"This far enough?" Dave asked. He and Whitney, holding hands, were swinging them up and down with each step. They seemed so free and easy these days, dating, Jessica thought, from the time Whitney changed jobs. She was secretly proud of the hand she'd had in that change. But even here Whitney was being led. Whitney never took charge.

"I'm still okay." Jessica looked up at Kyle before starting across the arched bridge. "Coming?"

He poked the silver-tipped cane forward, attempted to get his left side up first, listed, dropped the cane and had to grab the wooden rail to keep from falling. "Damn!

Jessica picked up the cane from the dirt path and handed it to him.

He sighed. "Go ahead. I'll wait here." He headed for a redwood bench beneath a weather-beaten wooden sign.

"'Warning: rattlesnakes, mountain lions and bears,'" Jessica read aloud. "I'll stock up for my canyon—all we have is a few old possums and a fat coon."

Kyle grinned mischievously. "I wish I could go ahead and warn those critters who they're up against."

Jessica laughed. Kyle was getting better every day and probably wasn't particularly upset over sitting out a hike. "I want to go a bit further. Who knows when the next time will come when I'll be able to."

She skipped over the bridge to join Dave and Whitney. She hadn't skipped in over a year. They crunched along the gravel road, passing out of the shade of eucalyptus trees, then climbing through wispy remnants of wind-driven fog.

"It's work from here on," Dave said as the road steepened and the scrub brush, now seldom higher than Jessica's waist, grew thinner. "You okay?"

"Fine." Her limbs were free, gravity felt normal, the switches in her head barely nattering. "Only thing is my hands and feet are tingling like mad."

"You used to say that when you first got sick," Whitney said. "Maybe you're backing out of your illness the same way you went in."

"Hah! I've been through too many ups and downs to pin my hopes on that." Hatfield didn't think the tingling was a good sign, but, as usual, had no firm opinion about it.

Lots of other hikers were out on the road—men with sinewy legs protruding from khaki shorts, tanned women in faded cutoffs and sandals, scampering children. People smiled and exchanged hellos. Hikers were friendly like that.

They passed chamise shrubs beginning to show spears of white blossoms, small bush lupine sprinkled with deep blue flowers, and an occasional splash of red Indian paintbrush. On the mountainside above them, dark green manzanita, ceanothus and sage clung to barren rock and gravel.

"Halfway there." Dave stopped a minute, breathing heavily, after they'd rounded a large boulder.

Jessica's legs were slightly tired. "I can make it," she said, blaming the tiredness on lack of vigorous exercise for over a year, rather than on the usual weakness.

They climbed on past increasingly rocky, arid terrain, finally arriving at the broad, flat hilltop where the "Inspiration Point" sign was posted. She'd done it, hiked more than a mile uphill. With twenty or thirty others the three of them stood and looked out over the Pacific Ocean and Santa Monica taking shape as the fog lifted.

"I feel so good," Dave said. "I could have pushed your wheelchair right up here to the top if I had to."

Just when she was beginning to feel upbeat, he had to say such a thing. "Do I look like I need a wheelchair?" She turned and started back at a fast jog. Let him try to keep up with this pace!

They'd hardly gone halfway down, Whitney light-footedly keeping up, Dave panting along behind, when Jessica heard a whir she hadn't heard in years, but recognized immediately. She held out her hand to caution the others as a diamondback, trailing its rattles, slithered across the path and into the brush.

How close death could be. A chance step here or there could determine whether it was avoided or stumbled into.

"Some people say Will Rogers used to rope rattlers, but I read he only claimed to be 'death on dead calves,'" Jessica said, wishing she'd known the man.

As they worked their way downhill, Dave recited Boy Scout instructions he'd learned years ago on how to treat snake bite. Whitney was nodding appreciatively; Jessica was wishing he'd shut up.

When the lawn and ranch house came into view far below, they stopped to look for Kyle. At first they couldn't spot him.

"There he is." Whitney pointed to a figure on the wooden bridge, groping his way slowly along.

"He's practicing," Jessica said, almost proud. "Let's hurry and catch up with him." She began to lope incautiously down the hill.

They reached Kyle as, cane tucked under one arm, he let go the rail with both hands to step off the bridge.

Whitney got to him first. "Let me help you." She tried to hold her hand and arm under his arm and elbow as she did when she helped Jessica.

Kyle pulled away. "Thanks, but I need to do this by myself." He glanced past Whitney at Jessica.

He wanted her approval. Jessica could see that. If she recognized his appeal, she'd have to show she'd read his silent message, implying a certain degree of intimacy. What should have been a trivial decision had suddenly become important.

But didn't she know what she needed to do? His act of independence was supremely important. "Good for you, Kyle." She turned her head away just after she'd caught his look of gratitude.

Down the path they went, Dave and Whitney hand in hand in front, Kyle hobbling along beside Jessica. Two by two.

Which maybe was not so bad. Kyle had been a sweetheart all day.

When the driver parked in front of her building, he went to the back of the car to get her crutches from the trunk.

"It was a nice day," Jessica said. She didn't like the intense tingling that had developed in her hands and feet.

Kyle leaned over and took her hand. "Let's do it again sometime. Soon. Or maybe you'd like to go to a movie."

Jessica didn't know what to think of the burning pain emerging in her hands, feet and face. "I'd like that."

"I'll pick you up tomorrow at 7:30." Kyle was still holding her hand, pulling her gently toward him. Even that gentle pressure burned. She put her arms around his neck and he held her for a minute. It was so nice to be held by a man, this man, but the light pressure of the embrace hurt her face and hands.

She pulled back. "I have to go."

The light in his eyes faded. She was sorry to be so abrupt, but she was in pain.

CHAPTER 42

The second she stepped out of the car the bottoms of her feet began hurting like a bad sunburn. She tiptoed gingerly across the lobby flagstone. "Ow. Must be something in my shoes."

While the driver waited with the crutches and a bag of picnic leftovers, she sat on a stone bench and took off her shoes and socks. Nothing. She brushed off the bottoms of her feet. It felt like she was pulling skin off. "I think I have a couple of blisters." She hadn't seen any, but sometimes they took a while to swell. After a painful attempt to put on a sock, she decided to remain barefoot.

Carrying her shoes and socks, tiptoeing to minimize contact with the pavement that hurt her feet, she took what felt like forever to get from the street entrance to the canyon end of the courtyard. The warm stones of the stairs up to her apartment burned like hot coals.

At her door she forced herself to smile as she said good night to the driver. She could smile through anything if she knew it would last only a few seconds.

Once the man left and she was in the stuffy, hot apartment, she picked her way gingerly across the soft carpet to the air conditioner control and started soothing, cool air flowing. She held her hands up in front of the outlet and wished she could put her feet there too. At first her hands felt better, then the cold began to make them hurt.

What was wrong with her? Was this related to the tingling of the past few months? An allergic reaction to something in the park? She'd been to Will Rogers dozens of times and nothing like this had ever happened.

In the bathroom, she switched on the ceiling light and examined her palms. No rash. Not even redness. And yet there was this burning pain. She got down on the floor and pulled one foot up to examine the sole. No redness, not the slightest sign of blisters.

It had to be that damned tingling, somehow turned into pain. Her whole screaming, miswired nervous system was screwed up. Not only was she dying, she was going to be painfully tormented on the way out. She wanted to cry, but couldn't.

Elsa climbed onto her lap and gently, delicately, kneaded her bare leg. Ishmael stood in the doorway and meowed in complaint. Dinner time. No matter how bad things got it was always someone's dinnertime—hers or the cats'.

On her knees she rummaged in a drawer and found some Tylenol. She swallowed two and, to spare herself more pain, crawled on knees and elbows, fighting the nattering of her brain switches and an ever stronger pull of gravity. As if things weren't bad enough, the damned weakness was coming back.

Barely able to send dry food pellets clattering into their dish before collapsing onto the kitchen floor, she lay listening to the cats crunching and gulping food.

At least she could still feed the cats. She fed them well and sheltered them from cold, rain and predators. But would they be better off, in some ways, running wild? After all, she'd named them Born Free Elsa and Banished Ishmael. Truth was, she controlled their lives, no matter what she named them. Maybe controlling their lives was what she liked best about having cats.

What she liked best about cats was certainly not their sense of humor. "Now would be the perfect time for a joke," she said. "Take my mind off this pain and misery."

They were engrossed in licking their paws and washing up after dinner. For all she could tell, she was talking to herself.

Even if they could, they probably wouldn't laugh anyway. No one had laughed when she fell that first time in the waiting room. Jack Murray hadn't laughed when she fell in his office.

"I believe I've earned the right to a little humor around here," she said. Neither cat paused in its after-dinner grooming. "In Egypt you were considered sacred. So how about getting my prayers answered—I need something really funny."

Ishmael lay down on the kitchen floor, his front paws tucked under his chest, his expression smug. Elsa sat in profile, chin raised, as if to say "I'm clean, well-fed and gorgeous. Admire me."

She might control them in every other way, but not in the humor department. Her feline friends seemed perfectly happy that she was down here on the floor, prostrate before them. They were the top cats, she the underdog. They were the cat's meow, she was what the cat had dragged in. Like Ozymandias, they looked down on her as if to say, "Look on me, you who were once so high and mighty, and despair."

She laughed at her cat hyperboles. But she didn't weaken more. It seemed that humor had to come as a surprise to trigger collapse in her.

The next morning, in the backseat of the car with Kyle, their arms and thighs brushed casually as they chatted and tentatively agreed to a movie date Friday night. She was feeling pretty good. Washed out, as though she'd been through an ordeal, but free of pain with little weakness. She told him she was sorry she'd left abruptly the day before, but she'd had some sort of bad skin irritation. She thought he looked relieved to get her apology.

At the office, she e-mailed Hatfield about the pain attack, then pulled a few rolled-up spec trees from a safe and stuffed them into a crutch sleeve. The engineers she met with must have had a good weekend too—they were in a happy mood, humming, smiling and relaxed as they sat around a small table and worked their way down a very long list of equipment. Jessica's head drooped a bit, but her speech remained clear and her hands and feet felt normal.

Until midmorning. This time there was only about a minute of tingling before the burning started in her hands, feet and face. At first it felt like a mild sunburn and she was able to shove it to the back of her mind. Then it became more severe each time she picked up a pen or paper or allowed her feet to touch the floor. Without saying anything, she took two Tylenols from her purse and popped them into her mouth.

As the pain ratcheted up to that of burning candles held to her hands and feet and cheeks all the way up to the scalp, she did her best to show nothing in her voice or attitude. She forced herself to participate in a discussion about specs, nearly freaking out at the sight of the oblivious, smiling faces around her.

By the time she was ready to leave, the Tylenol had kicked in, but only enough to moderate the pain to the sunburn regime. And it, or maybe the mental struggle required to keep working, had exhausted her. She tucked the rolls of specs into a crutch sleeve and clomped slowly back to her office. The crutches provided some relief, allowing her hands to protrude without touching the sleeves, and permitting one foot to be off the floor at all times. She thought she looked like everything was under control as she underwent Enid's scrutiny. But she didn't know how she'd be able to keep working today if this pain kept on.

She slumped into her chair, then checked to see if Hatfield had responded to her pain e-mail. He had and was suggesting she try Aleve.

Now how was she going to get that? A cab? She'd have to go downstairs to meet it. Pure agony.

But here she was, the self-appointed First Lady of Independence again, who'd almost literally rather die than ask for help. And why? Because she feared becoming dependent on other people? This sounded more like a phobia than a fear. She phoned Whitney and in half an hour had a bottle of Aleve. Out of gratitude, she gave Whitney her last box of the fine-tipped felt pens they both treasured. The Aleve made her so much better, she was able to work all afternoon.

By Friday, she'd fought through the week, although the burning was worsening again despite increasing amounts of Aleve. And she was growing more feeble every time she took some.

But luck was with her in one way. All she had to do today was sit in her office and write a status report—which of her spec trees were complete, which needed last bits of information, when she expected to finish the ones she hadn't started. And there was the evening to look forward to. Kyle called and said he'd come by her office in the afternoon and they'd pick a movie. It had been months since she'd been to a movie.

As the morning went by, she got weaker and the pain became excruciating—like a flame was burning each of her hands and feet. Her strength of will totally depleted by the struggle to work through her agony and weakness, she screamed. She tried to stifle herself by pressing a hand across her mouth, but screamed again.

Enid came running in. "What's wrong?"

Jessica was powerless to speak through convulsive sobs.

"Tell me what's wrong. I don't know what to do." Enid's face was so close Jessica could smell tobacco on her breath, a stench that made her weaker.

"I'll be okay." Jessica forced the words out and groped in her purse for more pills. "I just need to take my pills."

"You're under too much strain. That's what I've said all along."

Jessica managed to set the Aleve bottle on the table.

"I'll get something to wash this down." Enid clomped out into the bay, returning with a Styrofoam cup of gritty coffee. By now three or four engineers were standing in the bay peering into Jessica's office. "She's in terrible shape," Enid told them.

Jessica was grateful for anything that helped get the two tablets down. More than she was supposed to take in one morning on top of the two she'd already had, but she couldn't stand the pain anymore. Even handling the cup made her cry out again.

She looked up to see Constance, Armor's secretary, standing in the doorway, her thin face showing more than its usual anxiety.

"She's hysterical," Enid said. "Didn't I say this was going to happen?"

Constance let out a little squeak and turned her face away.

"We ought to tell someone," Enid said.

"Yes, we ought to," Constance said.

"Mr. Stone isn't in. You'd better get Mr. Armor."

"No!" Jessica had only one mode of speech left—screaming. The pain was so terrible she looked at her hand, half expecting to see it smoking like flesh roasting on a spit.

Constance looked frightened, then vanished.

"Hold on as best you can, dear. Mr. Armor will be here in a minute," Enid said.

Jessica moaned. "I don't want him around."

But in a few minutes there he was, standing in the doorway, glowering. "What's the problem?"

"There's no problem." Jessica managed not to scream this time, but felt switches begin to flip in her head. She put her whole mind to stopping them, but little by little her control slipped away. In slow motion she wilted until her face was pressed cheek down on the table.

"She's so sick," Enid said. "I don't know what to do."

"You need a doctor," Armor said in a commanding voice.

"No," Jessica sobbed, unable to see anything but his belt and gesturing hands.

"You don't want to see a doctor?"

"I have a doctor. I see him all the time." She could barely mush out the words.

"Maybe you should go to an emergency room."

Jessica heard a belligerent edge on his voice. "No," she said.

"No, no, no! That's nonsense. I don't think you're mentally or emotionally capable of making decisions."

"No one can know what I'm capable of but me."

Armor turned to face into the bay. "Constance, get me HR on the phone. In my office."

Where he could say things out of everyone's earshot, Jessica surmised.

"What's going on?" Jim Stone's voice came from behind Armor.

"Shephard's sick, but refuses medical attention." Armor lowered his voice to a hoarse whisper Jessica could hear clearly. "She's getting to be a real problem."

As Armor stomped off, Stone eased into the wheelchair across from Jessica. "What's the trouble, Jess?"

"Pain. Worst I ever felt."

"Got anything for it?"

"Aleve."

"When did you take it?"

"Ten minutes ago. Maybe it'll kick in soon."

"Jessica, you know what?" Stone's face looked as though he too were in pain. "I think you should consider taking a medical leave of absence. Just concentrate on getting better."

"All I need is more pain killer." She choked back her sobs so he wouldn't hear them. If only the Aleve would take effect so all these people wouldn't see how sick she was. If only they'd go away and give her a chance to get better.

"This time it's going to be a lot harder to fight Armor. He can say you can't do the job and you're disruptive. If you go on leave of absence right away, you'll prevent his doing something extreme."

Fear elbowed its way into Jessica' consciousness. "I don't want to go on leave of absence."

"I know how he thinks. In his mind, you're a recurrent problem.

You're soaking up money and he gets nothing for it. If he manages to terminate you, he not only gets rid of your salary, but your overhead—medical coverage and sick leave, for instance. Better to leave on your own terms and keep your benefits."

"Won't the Americans with Disabilities Act protect me?"

Stone sighed. "It's getting harder to say you can still do the work and that you're not keeping others from doing theirs."

Jessica heard tightness in Stone's voice. It was so hard to decide. The ebb and flow of pain led her out of good thinking and back in, out and back. "Do I have to decide right now?"

"It would be a good idea." Stone's voice was soft and gentle.

"Okay," she whispered. She couldn't get her face off the table.

Things began to happen fast. Stone went to HR and got the leave of absence forms. Within an hour, Jessica had filled them out, as well as an application for Long Term Disability insurance so she could receive seventy percent of her current pay for up to a year. At Stone's direction, Enid packed Jessica's personal belongings and a company phone directory in a cardboard box. Skowron came up to oversee her departure after calling Vole, who made no objection to Jessica's leaving. Jessica could picture the relief on his face when he realized he no longer had to deal with the Jessica problem.

She had a last talk with Stone. "Thanks so much, Jim. I know I'll never have as fine a boss as you again in my whole life."

"Keep in touch, kid." He grinned, but his eyes were shiny.

Whitney, after a call from Jessica, accompanied her and Skowron on a slow crutch-supported walk down the dimly lit, shadowless corridor and stairs. When they passed other employees, Jessica insisted they laugh and pretend she was barely able to stand because of some great joke they were sharing.

CHAPTER 43

Minutes became hours, hours became days. Time piled up like the drifts of dust and grime coating the furniture. Confined to her apartment for the two weeks since she'd left Rank, Jessica had seen no day different from any other. Get up, feel pretty good, put a robe on over pajamas, eat breakfast. Pain starts. Take Aleve. Play VCR movies—no funny ones, afraid to laugh. Get weak and dopey. Sleep. Wake up in pain. Take more Aleve. Microwave dinner. Rinse fork, put in dishwasher. Watch TV. More pain, more Aleve. Fall asleep on couch. Wake up and go to bed in the middle of the night. No shower again, still wearing the same pajamas as last week.

The sounds she heard were those of the rhythm of the lives of others in the building. In the morning, doors opened and shut, women's heels clicked on the walkway outside her door and men's shoes thud-shuffled. Cars started in the garage and drove away, then stay-at-homes headed down the steps near Jessica's place to the laundry room. Women chatted on neighboring balconies. The afternoons were mostly silent until people came home. Once or twice a week, in the evening, the woman next door would knock to see if Jessica needed anything. Jessica always thanked her profusely—she knew the woman had a high-pressure job that left her with little spare time—and only occasionally asked her to pick up a few groceries.

Lack of joy was permeating every part of her being. Her unwashed hair itched and stuck to her scalp, it hurt when she tried to clean under her fingernails, everything she ate caused either pain or weakness, warm water burned her skin, air conditioning made her hurt from cold. Nothing felt good or even pleasant.

Kyle called. He'd heard about her leave of absence from Whitney. How was she and when could he come and see her? What could she tell him? That he should forget her? That she was in pain and dying?

The piano was no comfort. Her fingers hurt when she touched the keys, her feet burned when she touched the pedals.

She e-mailed Hatfield that Aleve wasn't cutting it. His nurse phoned in a prescription to a nearby drugstore for Tegratol, which she took a cab to pick up. Tegratol proved better at dulling the pain, but not much. Toss out the useless nostrums—carnitine, B-12, Mestinon.

Stone phoned twice, Skowron once, and Whitney almost every day. Checking up on her. What could she say? She was weak all over, had no job, no place to go, nothing to do, and she still hurt. She had no idea how fast she was going to deteriorate.

She phoned Mom almost every evening, but never told her she was on leave of absence, essentially unemployed.

Only the cats were happy, basking in her constant companionship. They took turns cuddling in her lap when she was lying on the couch. Sometimes she slept the day away with them on the balcony above the wild tangles of the canyon, taking Beethoven along to sit on the glass-topped table for the view and some fresh air. His face seemed more relaxed when he was outdoors.

She didn't begrudge the cats and the canyon creatures their vitality and freedom, even though she'd almost given up on hers. They weren't going to live forever either.

Why couldn't she even get a diagnosis? She tried to rouse her mind from its Tegratol haze to think. She hardly knew where or how to begin. The ways her sickness presented itself, to use medical jargon, had become familiar but not revealing or enlightening: she got weak immediately from elevator or Disneyland rides, twenty minutes after eating, with sudden stress, and when she caught a strong whiff of cigarette smoke. Symptoms were worse and lasted longer when she was having her period. Physical effort could bring on an attack or make one worse. The more vigorous the exercise the more severe the attack. All these stimuli must cause something vital to her neuromuscular system to be disconnected.

And then there was the laughter. Commonly, people were said to fall down laughing, but no one actually did it but her.

Her illness had left its footprints all over Jessica, but not one doctor could read a thing from them. And now there was the pain. What was the common thread to all this?

By Saturday she'd been home almost three weeks. More awake than usual, she decided she had to talk to her mother. Putting it off any longer would make it awkward and embarrassing when she finally found out.

"I hate to tell you this, Mom, but you know that tingling? It's turned into pain. Started in my hands and feet, now it's up my arms and legs and in my face."

"Oh, my God."

"It's kind of laid me low. I thought you'd want to know." Jessica was glad she couldn't see Mom's face right now.

"Of course I would. Have you talked to Dr. Hatfield?"

"Yes. He keeps upping my pain medication. It helps a little, but I think it's making me weaker. I'm so doped up I can't tell for sure. Like I'm floating somewhere off the edge of the world."

"How are you managing to go to work?"

"I'm not. I took a leave of absence."

"I think you're wise."

Jessica was not so dulled by medication that she couldn't tell "I think you're wise" from "Finally you did something smart" or "I thought all along you should stay home."

"Do you have any time today to do a few things for me?" Jessica's voice was tight. Even though she could scarcely survive without help, these were hard words to say.

"I'll be there in half an hour."

After hanging up, Jessica looked around the apartment. It was a mess. Trying not to think about the pain, she cleaned dishes off the sink, dusted and picked up the strewn laundry, books and papers. She didn't want Mom to take on housecleaning on top of running errands.

When she arrived, Mom pulled a stack of cataplexy articles Richard had downloaded out of a shopping bag and handed them to Jessica. Tossing them on the piano bench—the piano top was stacked to overflowing—Jessica muttered, "Thanks." She'd look at them when she felt up to it.

"I need a lot of stuff, Mom. I hope you don't mind." There it was, a request for help right out front. She half expected the world to collapse.

A short time later her mother was out the door with a grocery list, Jessica's last pay checks to deposit, and the dirty underwear and putrid pajamas she'd worn the past week to stick in the downstairs laundry. Jessica had put on a cotton skirt and short-sleeved top, neither of which came anywhere near touching her hands, feet or face.

It was a couple of hours before Mom returned with two bags of groceries. "I'll get the rest after I put the wash in the drier," she said and was out the door again.

Jessica unpacked frozen foods—juices, vegetarian dinners, ice cream. If she had to, she could live off this for a couple of weeks.

Mom soon hustled up from the garage with two more bags. Dropping them heavily onto the dining table, she exhaled with a huff.

"Thanks so much. You're a wonderful mom." Jessica risked some pain to embrace her mother and felt her hug back.

"I try," Mom said, plopping down in a chair as hard as Jessica sometimes did.

Jessica studied her mother. Her breath was coming in fast gulps. Carrying all the laundry and groceries would be an effort for any woman of sixty, let alone a small one like Mom. She had asked her mother to do too much.

As, side by side, they unloaded the groceries, Jessica saw and loved the synchronism in their movements, the simultaneity with which they looked up and smiled at each other. They lined up cans and jars, cereal boxes and soy milk cartons in rows as straight on the shelves as they'd always been at her mother's house.

"Sometimes I forget to tell you how much you mean to me, Mom."

Her mother smiled. "When you were a child, you used to write me little love notes."

"Before Daddy got sick."

Mom nodded. "Before all that."

When they finished, Jessica sat on the couch while Mom raised the keyboard cover and began playing a Chopin etude, giving it a military, marching cadence. Her mother always brought a mood, an attitude, to her music that drew the listener's attention.

Jessica realized she was hungry. "I think I'll have some of those chocolate chip cookies you brought." She grabbed her crutches.

Mom looked up. "Want me to get them?"

Jessica hesitated. Part of her wanted to sit back down and let her mother bring the cookies.

She stumped to the kitchen, trying to keep her burning hands from touching the crutch sleeves and letting only one foot at a time rest gingerly on the carpet.

She saw Mom's body twisting, head turning as she played while tracking Jessica's progress.

Sunday morning Jessica thought again about the organ loft. She had to keep believing that eventually she'd be back turning pages, eventually she'd hike in Will Rogers Park again, eventually she'd be back at work. At Rank? There were some things she liked about the company and her job. She'd made some good friends. But the company existed to enhance the wealth of its stockholders. Fine for the stockholders, but there had to be more worthwhile aspects of humanity to enhance than their bank accounts.

She'd thought lately about making her living writing about sick people maintaining their independence and about how the disabled wanted to be treated. The problem was that wasn't likely to generate an income she could live on. Perversely, an enhanced bank account was just what she needed. Fate was playing a joke on her again.

Monday morning the pain was excruciating despite a double dose of Tegratol and Aleve. Another e-mail exchange with Hatfield resulted in his prescribing a small dose of clonazepam, a powerful drug that had to be eased into gradually. It could impact emotions and short-term memory, even induce coma if too much was ingested. As she was working up the courage to call a cab for what was bound to be a pain-ridden ride to the drugstore, the phone rang.

"Kyle here. How you doing?"

"Not too good."

"How so?"

She brought him up to date on the pain and the medication waiting for her at the drugstore, speaking slowly and breathing in short gasps. She tried not to panic. No breathing troubles needed today.

"Want me to pick it up and bring it after work?"

"Would I!" She'd welcome the Devil himself if he brought something to relieve the pain.

"Pizza too?"

She didn't have to say the topping should be meatless. He suggested it.

Now she had to wait. It was three o'clock. How soon would he get here? When they rode home together, they usually left work about five thirty or six. If he left at five thirty, he might get to the drugstore by six. There'd be a line by then. So figure another half hour. Then half an hour for the pizza, unless he thought to phone the order in. He wouldn't get to her apartment before six thirty, maybe as late as seven or seven thirty. The wait was going to be long and terrible.

She went to the bedroom, closed the door, pulled the curtains and lay on top of the bedspread with nothing touching her hands or feet.

Kyle would come with the clonazepam and her dinner. Laughing, joking Kyle. Kind Kyle. He'd been so sweet on the picnic. And sensitive. Maybe he'd even flirt a bit. He'd know she wasn't up to anything really physical. But he'd hint at it. She smiled.

If she stayed absolutely still and let her mind drift, she felt much less pain and the weakness wasn't a problem. But how long could she lie here? What did she look like? Hair not shampooed for over a week, in rumpled pajamas and dirty robe, nails untrimmed, a freak. She couldn't let him see her like this.

She could call and tell him not to come. For a long time she lay on her back staring at the ceiling light, a square of featureless white glass, until she became reconciled to the inevitable. She couldn't do without the medication. She'd have to get up and make herself presentable, or at least not grotesque.

Hair first. Gingerly, she rolled over and sat up on the side of the bed where she could reach the crutches. In the bathroom she removed her pajamas and took the shampoo and conditioner bottles into the shower stall. Cross-legged on the tile, she turned on the water, washed herself, shampooed her hair and applied conditioner. While her body luxuriated in the warm soapy water, her hands, feet and face felt as if flaming gasoline was being poured on them. With no one to hear, she drowned out the pain by screaming.

When she got out of the shower and onto the soft bathroom rug, the pain was less extreme. Lying on her back, she filed and trimmed claws unrecognizable as her pianist nails, always trimmed shorter than the finger pads for good keyboard contact.

She tried to remember if Kyle had ever complimented her on any of her outfits, but all she could think of was the blue wool dress she sometimes wore to work. Too elaborate. Jeans rubbing on her legs would be excruciating. She thought through her wardrobe and remembered a denim skirt and a bright pink, almost fuchsia, short-sleeved knit shirt. She had lipstick that matched it exactly. Perfect. She took her time getting up and putting on the clothes. The only concession to pain was soft terrycloth slippers for her burning feet.

By the time the doorbell rang, the struggle with pain and weakness had nearly exhausted her, but she'd gotten dressed and combed her hair. Although the new medication was what she most wanted, she really was looking forward to seeing Kyle, the only person besides the cleaning lady, the next door neighbor and Richard and Mom she'd seen in two weeks.

A smile of anticipation on her lips, she opened the door wide. For a fleeting second Kyle seemed to take joy in the sight of her, just before his mouth turned down and his shoulders slumped. With one hand he was leaning on his cane and gripping a small paper bag. The other was balancing a cardboard pizza box. "The only parking spot I could find was three blocks away."

Jessica stood aside to let him in. "Why didn't your driver help?" She took the bag from him and opened it to find the little orange vial she was looking for.

"I drove myself." He tossed the pizza box onto her dining table and sat down. "You didn't tell me there's no place to park."

"They only let us have one space in the garage."

"Damn! I wish I'd kept that driver one more day."

"Sorry. But isn't it wonderful you're driving? Aren't you happy?" Jessica checked the vial to make sure the label said "clonazepam" and took it into the kitchen. She gulped down a pill.

He frowned. "At least I started the day out happy."

So he was going to blame his misery on her.

She didn't know if she could stand to wait the twenty or thirty minutes Hatfield had said were needed for the medication to take effect. "How much do I owe you for the pills? And for my half of the pizza."

"Your insurance covered the medicine and the always gallant Kyle is springing for the pizza."

She got the picture—he was selflessly noble, she was a lot of trouble. "Let's see what we can do to cheer you up. How about a little pinot noir? From Napa, no less." She hoped it was still drinkable after lying in a drawer for a year and a half, since just before she'd gotten sick.

"Pinot noir? Beats paint thinner."

"I serve only the best paint thinner, you creep." She endured some pain to open a drawer and pull out the bottle and a fancy corkscrew. "See if you can handle this." Depending on how well the clonazepam worked, she might try a little wine herself.

Kyle extracted the cork with a professional flourish. "A couple of months ago I couldn't do that." He was staring at the Steinway. A class M grand, it took up two thirds of the living room. "You play that?"

"Since I was a kid. My mom teaches piano."

"How about playing something? Cheer me up."

"Maybe later." If the clonazepam worked.

He poured wine into each glass and then gulped his. "I should never have taken that damned job with Armor."

The job she'd egged him into going for. She guessed he was laying the blame for that on her too. She used a cutter to slice the pizza into wedges and served him and herself. "What do you mean you shouldn't have taken it? Everyone's counting on you to keep business coming in to Rank."

"Who the hell told you that?" He finished his wine, but the pizza sat untouched on his plate.

"You, for one."

"I thought you never took me seriously." He didn't wink, as he usually did after such a remark.

She contemplated her pizza slice. Would picking it up with her fingers or pressing down to cut it with her fork be worse on her hands? She took the cutter and pressed lightly, gingerly slicing it into slivers.

Kyle glared angrily at his pizza. "That egomaniac Armor has no understanding of what I'm trying to do."

This definitely was not going to be a night when Kyle told funny stories, winked and smiled. "He's always mad," she said. "Hasn't he ever given you a hard time before? 'You have just been struck by lightning.'" She pointed an accusing Armor-like finger at Kyle. "Didn't he ever hit you with that?"

"No."

"You must be the only one. You must have gotten special treatment. Maybe he felt he owed you something?" She'd never thought about it before, but Kyle's black hair and pointy goatee, attractive and even suave at a casual glance, were revealed up close to harbor unmanaged tangles under their surfaces.

"Special treatment! That nutcase thinks I should have reeled in a big customer by now, that I'm slow because I'm being a pissy perfectionist. 'Better is the enemy of good enough.' He's the pointy-haired boss straight out of Dilbert." Kyle deftly poured himself a refill without trickling a drop down the side of the goblet or bottle.

Jessica eyed her wine. Although the pain was a little better, she decided not to risk a sip yet. But she wanted one.

"Yell, yell, yell! Four months and no action. That was his reaction to my progress report. No appreciation at all for the damned good job I'm doing—and Whitney too, by the way—working our three biggest customers. If even one of them works out, it'll mean another contract the size of the one we just got."

"I hear the only way you can stop him is with a stake through the heart."

Evidently in no humor to laugh, Kyle sneered. "Enough about him. How about some nice piano music."

"Later maybe. I'm feeling a little better now, but I was pretty sick today."

"It's hard to think of you as sick."

"It's hard to think of me as sick?"

"I mean look at you. You're a babe. You look like you were never sick in your life." He picked up a pizza slice and wolfed it down.

"Well, I am," she said in as even a tone as she could manage. "And you know it." Annoyed at his insinuation that she might be malingering, at the same time she was flattered hearing he thought of her as a babe. "I overheard Armor say he suspected I was only trying to get attention. But I never heard anyone else say they didn't believe I was sick. Did you?"

Kyle fingered the stem of his empty goblet in silence.

Jessica held his gaze

He shrugged. "People talk. You know how it is."

"And what did you say?"

"What could I say?"

She had the creepy feeling he'd agreed with them, at least tacitly. "Think I'm not sick? Watch this."

She raised her glass and downed almost half her wine, then set the glass down and waited for the swoon that inevitably followed when she drank alcohol. But she felt only slightly lightheaded. There was only one thing to do. Fake it. She sprawled face down on the table, being careful to avoid the pizza.

She felt him lean close to her. "You drank that on purpose to fall over. All you want is sympathy."

"I deserve some sympathy." Jessica slowly sat up again. "I feel bad when people doubt me, like I'm crazy or malingering." What craziness to fake a fall to convince him she wasn't malingering. She felt like she was on an emotional jag she had no control over. But the pain was decreasing and she hadn't really crashed. Had the clonazepam worked? Was it relieving her pain and her weakness?

Kyle poured the last of the wine for himself. "Women are usually mesmerized by my savoir-faire. Guess tonight's not my night."

He was apparently totally oblivious to the relief and hope surging through her. "I didn't say you were faking it or crazy when you couldn't use anything on your left side." She gave him a serious "Hah! So there!" look.

"That's different. I was paralyzed."

"I'll bet you went into paralysis every time you thought of facing Armor. That's called conversion disorder."

"What'd I do to deserve this? I brought your medicine and I had to walk a mile to get here."

Jessica turned away from him and rubbed her face with her napkin, hoping to hide the tears she couldn't entirely stifle. "It makes me feel awful when people think I'm mentally unbalanced or faking it." At the same time she was feeling better, apparently because of the clonazepam, than she had in weeks. She shook her head in amazement at herself.

"You worry too much about what other people think."

"God, you're smug. You have the luxury of saying that because you're not that sick anymore."

He hung his head. "How'd we get into this pushing and shoving contest?" The knuckles of his big hands writhing, he wadded his napkin into a tight ball. "Is my job more rotten than your illness or does your disease trump my job? What a pair we are."

"Speak for yourself. I'm not pushing and shoving you."

He raised his eyebrows and leaned forward. "No? You try to control just about every conversation by going for sarcasm or a laugh."

"Did I tonight?" Tonight, at first anyway, she'd actually tried to deal with him seriously and compassionately. What a useless effort.

"How about the paint thinner bit?" he sneered.

"You've got to be joking. You started that." To her consternation, the dimple in her cheek deepened as Mom always said it did when she was about to laugh. "That's a laugh." She giggled in little spasms, growing weaker with each one.

"Now what's so funny."

"Laughing is a very complicated thing."

"Come on. You have to get serious sometime." He sounded like he was pleading.

"I'll die if I laugh and I'll die if I don't. So I might as well enjoy myself."

Kyle picked up his cane and leaned on it. "I'd better go. If I get too tired, I'm no good at getting down steps or driving."

She hadn't meant to drive him away. "Wait. I haven't played the piano for you."

"I'll take a rain check." He limped toward the door.

After he left, she started to cry. As she sobbed, she ate the remaining slices of pizza, so cold the tomato sauce was slime. She picked up the crumbs in the pizza box and ate them. She drained both wine glasses and wiped out the dregs with her finger, which she licked off.

It had all been Kyle's fault. He'd been a pill. Not like on the picnic when he'd been so sweet. Tonight, he'd insinuated she wasn't really sick. He was pushing her away at the same time he claimed she was pushing him. So what could she do but kid around. It was the only way to deal with him.

He was impossible to understand. She didn't even know what she didn't know about him. In a way, he was like her illness.

She cleaned up, rinsing the dishes and stacking them in the dishwasher. So few friends were left in her world and now there was one less.

CHAPTER 44

The clonazepam was working. After each of her daily allotment of two doses both the pain and the paralysis disappeared. Unlike the other painkillers she'd taken, which had made her weaker, clonazepam miraculously restored her to near normal strength. When it wore off, the pain and paralysis returned. During the few available hours of pill-induced respite she packed in all the activities she could—showering, doing the laundry, walking unassisted downstairs to the mailbox and back.

By the start of the second week on clonazepam she'd more or less caught up on personal hygiene and house chores and began to miss the constant activity of her job. No good to sit here feeling unemployed and useless. It was time to resume writing for the alumni magazine. The theme of her next article was an easy choice: Why people think that if you don't look sick you aren't, and the harm in such thinking. And why doctors often think what they can't discover by testing exists only in the patient's mind.

To get started she had to remove the cataplexy papers Richard had given her from where they were piled in a heap covering the laptop. She really should take time to read them. Even though clonazepam was as good at wiping out anxiety as it was at relieving pain and paralysis—it was sometimes prescribed for depression—she couldn't avoid the reality that her disease was still undiagnosed and severe disability, even death, still lurked. She had to keep searching.

As soon as she finished this article.

Wanting real anecdotes, she went to computer chat rooms where people afflicted with rare and hard to diagnose diseases—myasthenia gravis, periodic paralysis, lupus, multiple sclerosis, dystonia, narcolepsy, mitochondrial diseases and more—exchange information and compare symptoms. It was heartwarming how sharing an illness brought people together. Differences in age, education, race, wealth, religion and politics were forgotten as patients fought a common enemy. She loved the patients and could think of nothing better to do with her life than to try to improve theirs.

She began writing, starting with the story of a very sick woman she'd met on the Web.

"If there is a God, I hate to think he only laughs at my cries for help. But I've evidence he's never touched by my pleas to watch over me in doctors' offices. Doctors with failings they can't face, who malign my sanity to save their pride."

These are the outcries of a vital woman, aged twenty-five, college-educated, who pays her rent, reads novels and has a boyfriend. But she is sometimes so debilitated that crossing a doctor's office is a struggle.

During her first disabling episodes, she tried to ignore thoughts of creeping sickness. At work, she would wait out the faint spells at her desk. If she was driving her car, she would always pull over. One day when she fell on the kitchen floor and lay there all afternoon, she was forced to admit her problem was possibly serious.

She began a frantic race to doctors who came up with anemia, mononucleosis and sick thyroid tests—always negative. No evidence of a physical problem, each successive doctor shouted louder than the one before.

"I am convinced by lack of physical evidence you lack a physical problem. Must be in your head. Might be willful. See a psychiatrist or a psychologist. You're sick in your psyche, not in your body."

"You are depressed, your self-esteem bottomed out," the psychologist said emphatically. "Take public speaking, build your strength at a gym. Do something daring, climb a mountain. You'll soon see how strong you can be." So she built up her pecs, her abs and her glutes, whenever she wasn't exhausted. But no improvement. "Time to go for it," said the doctor of minds. "Sign up for an expedition."

She chose a Guatemalan jungle adventure (it was cheaper than Nepal), first trekking, then mountain climbing. The trek was a bear, the climb caused a collapse. Airlifted to a hospital and put on a respirator, she was examined by a neurologist who took a blood sample. Three days later he said she had antibodies symptomatic of myasthenia gravis, of which she'd never heard. He described it: episodic failure of neuromuscular receptors, causing weakness, or even paralysis, of the limbs, face, neck, jaw and eyelid or eye muscles. And sometimes of the diaphragm, resulting in severe breathing difficulties. Exercise makes myasthenia gravis worse, he said. She should never have done anything so strenuous as mountain climbing, particularly at high altitude. She could have died.

The premise that lack of physical evidence is evidence for lack of a physical problem almost killed this woman. None of her American doctors had tested for MG because they hadn't been savvy enough. In their case, lack of physical evidence was evidence for their lack of knowledge. That goes double for the psychologist.

Jessica went on to write about three more cases where patients were declared to be psychologically disturbed or malingering until they were diagnosed—a young woman with chronic fatigue syndrome who was trying to distract herself from misery by writing about the racehorse Seabiscuit, an actor struggling to keep his career going while combating myasthenia gravis, and a high school athlete with narcolepsy.

Then she got to her conclusions.

Where did the thinking underlying all these misdiagnoses come from? Possibly the oldest, deepest roots lie in our human history of ascribing maladies we can't understand to gods and devils purported to have infested the sufferers. The ancient cures were nasty—trepanning, exorcism, scourging, burning at the stake.

In the sixteenth century, a reaction against this way of thinking swept over Europe. Descartes insisted on tangible proof, not ideas of vaporous spirits, gods and devils, as a foundation of science. He divided the world into the rational and the irrational, the provable and the unprovable. Scientists had to come up with well-defined properties they could measure. It was only a matter of time, in some quarters, before this reaction to primitive thinking went too far, as most human reactions tend to. In medicine, the idea evolved to 'If you can't see or measure it, it does not exist.'

Mix this background with physicians' very human pride that gets in the way of admitting when they neither know nor understand what's going on, with their desire to rid themselves of intractable problems, with the time/money pressures of modern medical practice and you have a perfect brew of ingredients for predisposition to "It must be in your head" misjudgments.

I implore medical practitioners to rise above forming opinions in this manner. Rigorous thinking is a must in clinical practice, just as in science. Consider the practical, as well as theoretical, implications.

Carol comes to mind. A single mother of an eleven-year-old girl, she sometimes could not get out of bed to go to work, often fell asleep when she got there. Threatened with loss of her job, she began an odyssey through doctors' offices. Some concluded she was a malingerer, some she was mentally unsound. None diagnosed a physical illness. She lost her job. Too sick to work, she could not collect Medicare or Social Security disability money because her only diagnoses were maladjustment or malingering. On meeting her, narcolepsy patients recognized she had symptoms like theirs and was certainly narcoleptic. Her doctor didn't agree. Suspecting her problem was all in her mind, he didn't refer her to a sleep center for months. When she was finally tested, it was unfortunately on one of her better days and the results were judged inconclusive. The sleep doctor said this tended to corroborate that her illness was mental. He did not identify this mental illness or its cause. His conclusion was an offhand remark.

Now she is terrified. She has herself and a daughter to support and no job. Without a diagnosis, she cannot collect supplemental Social Security or Medicaid or Medicare for her disability. No doctor is trying to help her. Her parents are dead; she has no close relatives.

A doctor who makes an "it's all in your head" diagnosis pronounces a heavy sentence on his patient. No further exploration of the illness is likely to be pursued and no useful treatment provided. Other clinicians reading the opinion will not take the patient seriously, and he or she will not be able to collect any medical or financial support the government offers for the sick and disabled. A downhill spiral of illness, poverty, feelings of abandonment, depression and despair is inevitable for those who cannot get financial help from their families. Even for the affluent life will be tough.

What, then, do I advocate? First of all, I would like for the medical profession to eradicate the assumption that lack of evidence of a physical problem is evidence for lack of a physical problem. Mental or emotional origins should not be diagnosed except by a qualified psychiatrist after appropriate testing—testing as demanding as is required for diagnosing physical illnesses. If a doctor cannot figure out what's wrong, he should say so and write in the patient's records that the illness is of undetermined origin. And, I would say to him, please keep trying to discover what's wrong with your patient by whatever means are at your disposal. Abandonment is scary.

When doctors glibly attribute lack of physical evidence to lack of a physical problem, they also do social harm. Society, with its back history of gods and demons and spirits, is ripe for scorning an ill person who doesn't look sick. The poverty-stricken, desperate patient becomes an object of anger and disgust for not pulling his or her own load. A social pariah.

Isn't it time to cast off the medieval way of treating difficult to diagnose patients? Isn't it time to help each one have a life? A patient wants and needs financial security, social dignity, employment and the best health care possible. Financially, socially and morally it is too costly to consign sick people to oblivion with "it's all in your head" rip-off diagnoses.

CHAPTER 45

Jessica printed out the article, read and reread it. She had the same good feeling she'd gotten when she'd participated in sit-ins for better housing for the poor or in demonstrations to help the Kurdish people who'd been savaged by Saddam Hussein in Iraq. And she was pleased with the musical rhythm of her writing, even though the rhythm faltered and petered out toward the end.

But after e-mailing the draft to Hatfield, she was left with facing another day when no one was expecting her to come to see them or was coming to see her. No one would give her an opinion on any subject and no one would ask hers. She would meet no one at a movie or in a restaurant. Life was going on without her.

And she worried constantly about money. Her long-term disability pay barely covered rent, utilities, food and her credit card debt. One financial emergency and she'd be in big trouble.

With all this pressure and with time on her hands she had to get back to pursuing a diagnosis. But she needed people.

She phoned Whitney.

"I'm traveling a lot now." Whitney sounded breathless, as if she couldn't get the words out fast enough. "Dave came with me last week to Washington and the three of us went on to New York. Kyle got us tickets to all the best shows—*Candide*, *Chicago*, and something called *Titanic*, of all things. I'd never been to a Broadway show before. It was great."

"I can just imagine." Jessica had never gone to a Broadway show.

"And guess what? We bought a new car."

"What did you get?" Jessica hadn't been able to drive her station wagon for weeks. Every few days she went down to the garage and ran the engine to keep the battery charged. As her finances worsened, it was getting hard to justify keeping the wagon. If she could get back the ten thousand she'd bought it for six months ago, she wouldn't have to worry for a while.

"A Jaguar. Used—but still, can you imagine?"

"I'm trying to."

"It was more Dave's idea than mine. He says driving it will relieve his job stress. But I love it too. You just step on the gas and it goes as fast as you want without effort."

Nothing Jessica did was without effort. "Who replaced me at work? What's Jim Stone up to?"

"Oh, he got a tech writer that works for your old boss, Vole. Don't know much about him."

"When did he start?"

"A few days after you left."

Then he'd been there for three weeks. "He never called to ask me anything." Stone hadn't told the new guy to call? He didn't need her advice? Didn't want it?

"You doing okay with Kyle, Whit?"

"You'd be amazed how well. He's super-ambitious, works really hard. He's never tried to hit on me, always sees to it I'm comfortable with what we're doing. I think he wants to get along with people, but he doesn't want anyone to see his soft, vulnerable spots. That's why he goes out of his way to sound like the man about town—his great tech investments, his gossip about who's doing what to whom, all that big macho-guy talk."

"That's a really smart assessment, Whit." What a terrific insight! If Whitney was right, Kyle's being uptight when he'd come to her apartment might only have been the result of being yelled at by Armor and his exhaustion after walking so far from where he'd had to park. His feelings of vulnerability must have been pretty intense.

"How are you doing, Jess? Better? Is staying home helping?"

"I think so. I've got a new medication and so far it's working." Hatfield had allowed her to increase the clonazepam dosage a little.

"We're going to the PlanetFest in Pasadena on the Fourth of July. The Mars Lander's going to touch down and it'll be on big screen TV. Want to come with us?"

That was less than two weeks away. "I'd love to get out of this apartment for a while. I haven't been out once since I quit work. I'm not driving, you know."

"Dave and I can pick you up."

After talking to Whitney, Jessica felt better. The Fourth was something to look forward to. Thinking and planning what she'd wear and how she'd peak her clonazepam for best effect, she savored her anticipation. But her good mood soon dissipated with the caw of a lone crow in the distance and the sighing breath of sleeping cats—the sounds of silence.

What about Kyle? He hadn't called, and she hadn't tried to call him, since their dismal evening together. If she called now, would she seem uncaring for taking so long? Or overeager in view of his silence? Since she hadn't phoned him, did he think she was pissed at him? Was he pissed at her? Did he even care?

She had to think of an excuse to call. Like she needed him to pick up some more clonazepam.

"Hi, Kyle," she said.

"Jessica?"

Listening carefully, she thought she heard a trace of warmth in his voice. "It's me."

"Well, hi."

"Guess what?"

Long pause. "What?"

"I'm almost out of medication." She tingled with anxiety and anticipation and wished she could see his face. Was he looking angry or pleased?

"Let me guess. You want me to pick it up."

She strained her ears to hear if he was being sarcastic. "Could you?"

"Sure."

He certainly wasn't bubbling over with enthusiasm at hearing from her. But he wasn't hanging up on her either.

She told him how he could park on a strip of pavement between the sidewalk and the lobby door for a few minutes to avoid a long walk. "Visitors and people moving in do that all the time. Okay?"

"Sure."

"I don't know how to thank you." Or what to make of his monosyllabic responses.

"That's okay."

At least he was going to help her.

After hanging up, she felt like playing something to give her strength, something militant and aggressive—a Chopin polonaise or a Prokofiev piece. But before she could sit down on the piano bench, she had to clear off the junk, which was mostly cataplexy research. As she gathered the papers up she realized they'd been there a month, unread. She could scarcely stir up any enthusiasm for another disease investigation. But how did she ever expect to get a diagnosis if she didn't keep pursuing leads? Best to get cataplexy out of the way, then get on with the next candidate. No more procrastinating.

CHAPTER 46

She would read one article before she started to play. No need to sit down. One article wouldn't take long.

The first sentence of the first page of the top paper said: "Most narcoleptics suffer from cataplexy, as in the case of a fifty-six year old woman who experienced attacks of weakness and collapse, usually when she laughed or was startled."

When she laughed! Here was a disease that caused people to collapse when they laughed! Her symptoms existed in other people.

"During attacks, which typically lasted about a minute, she was conscious but could not move. Sometimes she could remain standing by leaning on something, head drooping forward, jaw hanging open."

In shock, Jessica flopped into a chair at the kitchen table. Her head drooped forward, her jaw hung open. Except for the facts that the collapses lasted only a minute and accompanied narcolepsy, this article could have been about her.

But hold on. She knew better than to let herself be quickly seduced by yet another disease, even one where the victim fell down laughing. Hadn't she been certain in the past about myasthenia gravis and mitochondrial myopathy? Not to mention allergies and neurally mediated hypotension.

Taking only enough time to gulp a second clonazepam, Jessica dove into the pile of papers. Attacks could be precipitated by emotional or physical stress. The patient is not unconscious, but a heap of toneless muscles.

That was exactly how she always felt.

Recovery is prompt, with the body no worse off after an attack.

Cataplectics often are able to delay the onset of an attack long enough to slide down a wall to the floor or get to a nearby chair. Sagging jaw, drooping head and shoulders, buckling of knees, slurring speech, irregular breathing were among the symptoms listed by various authors.

Right on. These symptoms were right on.

Most attacks last from a minute or less to as long as twenty. In a few rare cases patients experienced cataplexy without narcolepsy.

Rare. That was certainly the right adjective for her illness. Still it was prudent to keep in mind that her collapses often lasted much longer than a minute and that cataplexy almost always occurs with narcolepsy, which she obviously didn't have.

Precipitating emotions include anger, surprise, physical activities with emotional content—such as smashing a tennis ball, orgasm and performing in public.

Orgasm? Who could have orgasms during attacks like she had? She'd almost forgotten what an orgasm felt like.

Laughter and tickling inevitably cause attacks in over ninety percent of cataplectics.

Like her. Maybe all her life. When she was a little girl, if someone tickled her or told a joke, she fell. That could have been a precursor to her present condition.

She found little information on the physiology or neurology of cataplexy. It was simplistically described as a mistake, in conjunction with narcolepsy, where the brain believes it's asleep and dreaming and, just as in normal dreaming, inhibits the body's ability to move. She read that narcolepsy and cataplexy are thought, but as yet not proven, to be autoimmune or autoinflammatory. Nothing was mentioned about sensations of switches flipping in the brain. Or about collapses after acceleration or deceleration.

There was a knock on the door. Could that be Kyle? Already? She looked at the living room clock. She'd been reading for almost five hours. She hobbled to the door and opened it.

Paper bag in hand, Kyle was pacing up and down, raking his cane across the wrought iron railing bordering the walkway to her door. On the move, on the prowl, like the wild animals in the canyon, that was Kyle now that he was mobile again.

"Hi." He handed her the bag. "Someone let me into your lobby."

"Come on in."

He jerked his thumb toward the front of the building. "My car's definitely illegal. It's crammed into that space between the lobby and the sidewalk."

He was uptight. If she didn't treat him gently, he could become difficult. "Come in for a minute, I'll play the piano for you."

"And leave my car to be towed away? I'm not that crazy."

"For just a minute." She deliberately let her dimple show.

"You witch."

Jessica asked him to wait on the couch. In the kitchen, she got the orange vial of clonazepam and the pharmacist's instructions from the bag. She'd been in too big a hurry to read them the first time, but she looked at them now. Take four times a day. Used to treat convulsions, epilepsy, severe pain and depression. No mention of episodic paralysis. Side effects include short-term memory loss, poor judgment and drowsiness. Addictive in large doses.

Well, she had no adverse side effects. She took one of the tablets. How could so much relief be packed into such a tiny thing, smaller than an aspirin?

She waltzed over to the piano.

Before she could sit down, Kyle gestured at the papers heaped and scattered on the table, beside him on the couch, and a few that had slipped to the carpet. "What happened here? Avalanche?"

"This mess? Medical articles about a disease called cataplexy. I've been reading all afternoon." She scooped up the first article she'd read. "Here. Look at the first couple of paragraphs. See what you think." Tense with anticipation, she perched across from him on the piano bench. He probably wouldn't want to spend time reading a dry medical article, particularly since his car was illegally parked out front, but she was eager to hear what he thought.

He read the entire article. So she gave him another describing patients' symptoms, both rare and common.

"Falling. Head drooping. Mouth that won't close. Just like you. Amazing. You're going to look into this, aren't you?"

"I'll see what Dr. Hatfield says."

"Why don't you find yourself an expert? Look through the bibliographies of these papers and see who gets quoted the most. Then call him. Or her."

"What a great idea!"

"Do you collapse when you laugh? I've never seen you."

"All the time. I guess you've never made me laugh."

"I'll try to think of a joke. Maybe next time I see you. When will that be?"

"Would you like to come with Whitney and Dave and me to the PlanetFest on the Fourth?" she asked impulsively. She was hoping she'd be able to go; she wanted to go. "We're going to have brunch in Pasadena first."

"Perfect. I'd planned to work the crowd there with Whitney anyhow. You could help me—listen in on what the competition is saying."

"You want *me* to spy for Rank?" The rumors about his industrial espionage moved into her thoughts like a dark cloud.

"I'll bring a fedora, a mustache and a big fake nose for you. My favorite disguise," he said and waited, watching her.

"A mustache? Yuck." Not a switch nattered in her head, she felt strong.

"You're right. No mustache and fake nose for you. I'll go as 007 and you'll be my sexy female partner."

"You're incurable. You're worse than me." To her consternation her dimple began to show and a hint of a giggle began to bubble up in her throat.

"Wear something slinky and revealing so my oversexed competitors won't be able to think straight."

"I'll rub up against them and purr like a pussy cat, all the time concealing my secret weapon." She grabbed a butter knife and stuck it down the front of her T-shirt, its handle protruding at her neckline.

He grinned evilly. "They'll have their minds on you for sure, and I can close in and steal everything, all their secrets. What a team we'll make!"

"Us?" Jessica felt giddy with silliness, but she wasn't falling. "Us a team?"

"Could be."

She thought he looked half serious. The idea of teaming up with him didn't seem half bad.

CHAPTER 47

Jessica's legs made her happy. Thanks to clonazepam she could hurry along the sidewalk to the Pasadena Civic Center, where the PlanetFest was being held, with the rest of the Fourth of July crowd. All gussied up in a three-piece suit and wingtips, silver-tipped cane thrust aggressively ahead, Kyle labored to keep up with her and Whitney and Dave on a walkway packed with families, casually dressed professors and aerospace engineers, and executives from NASA and the Jet Propulsion Laboratory in suits and ties. In her most slimming summer dress, which she felt was easily as attractive as Whitney's, Jessica radiated optimism.

An optimism she hoped was based upon more than the clonazepam-induced euphoria she'd begun to experience. The stuff was, after all, used to treat depression and lately she thought of dying no more than once or twice a day.

An optimism for which Kyle deserved a lot of credit. It had been his idea to plow through cataplexy articles looking for heavy-hitter authors. Las Flores University easily stood out—it had more published articles and was cited far more often in bibliographies than any other place. At first the Las Flores Sleep Clinic had refused to see her—she had no symptoms of narcolepsy. But after she cited a reference article about rare cases of cataplexy that had appeared without narcolepsy, a physician reluctantly scheduled her for three days of testing in August, warning her not to get her hopes up for a diagnosis.

She hadn't forgotten past disappointments, never let herself forget them. But she was optimistic enough to take on the financial risk of going to Las Flores. Hatfield had been of enormous help in this area. Convinced there was at least a twenty percent chance she had cataplexy, he'd argued her HMO into letting him refer her there. Not at the usual eighty per cent coverage level—Las Flores was outside their network—but at fifty percent. That meant for two days and one night of tests costing eighteen to twenty thousand, she'd owe nine or ten, and the Sleep Center wanted half that up front. She still had a little over a thousand of her proposal overtime bonus left, but couldn't save anything now that she was on seventy percent disability pay. She owned only two things worth ten thousand or more—her car and her piano—and was putting off having to decide which one to sell in the hope that somehow the money would turn up.

For now she could enjoy the PlanetFest—it was free. Swept into a vast exhibition hall dominated by an enormous video screen, she joined the crowd watching telemetered colored pictures of the rock-strewn, dusty red Mars terrain. The Lander, like any eager tourist, was snapping pictures left and right. As each new view filled the screen, the crowd applauded and cheered. She'd thought this would be a low-key way to spend the Fourth, but Mars was rivaling a fireworks display for excitement.

A male voice described the little vehicle's bumpy, bouncy landing, cushioned by airbags, and the deployment of its antennas and cameras. When a computer-generated image of the Lander was shown on the screen, Jessica was proud she could pick out the data transmission and command receiver antennas, the camera and a robotic instrumentation arm. She was awed by the control engineers here on earth had over a robocar in a harsh world millions of miles away.

After they'd had their fill of Mars pictures, Kyle pointed his cane down the hall. "NASA has a VIP room over there. I have a pass that'll get me and Whitney in." During brunch, he'd laid out his master plan to pitch a satellite system to NASA for two-way communication with remote sensors in inaccessible spots—mountain tops, deserts, canyons—measuring temperature, rain acidity, carbon dioxide, methane gas levels and other environmental data. When Jessica had praised him, said he should be proud of his part in such beneficial missions, she was surprised to see him become flustered and stammer.

They wove in and out of the random streams of visitors, occasionally bumping or jostling someone. Loud, attention-getting noises came from one exhibit. None of the chaos caused Jessica's switches to natter or her fuel gauge to drop low.

This was pure joy. Before clonazepam, she would have long been sprawled on the floor.

After Kyle and Whitney went into the NASA room, Jessica and Dave opted for an auditorium next door where a NASA executive was making an emotional pitch for a manned mission to Mars to look for signs of life. He was showing slides of little squiggles in rocks found in Antarctica believed to have originated on Mars, claiming they showed evidence of primitive life. Some members of the audience applauded in support.

"That's bullshit." Jessica elbowed Dave. "A physicist at work showed us pictures of six rocks with squiggles like that. You were supposed to pick the ones created by life forms. Turned out not one of them was. Everyone at Rank thinks this is just the grossest kind of hype to get funding for a big Mars program."

This man was presenting as truth what served his own self-interest and NASA's. He wasn't stupid; he made his pitch easy to understand and appealing for the audience to believe. Ease of understanding bolsters the listener's self-esteem, difficulty diminishes it. She wondered if this was the reason some patients accepted their doctor's verdict that lack of evidence of a physical problem is evidence for lack of a physical problem. The words are easy to understand, even though the message is false.

"I thought today was supposed to celebrate science and engineering achievements," Dave said. "If NASA engages in hype like this, who'll trust them?"

"Exactly." Jessica hoped at least some of the people here—some of them had to be experienced scientists and engineers—wouldn't accept the life on Mars claim without critical examination. She had less hope for the general public.

A former astronaut got up and predicted commercial travel to Mars would someday be available to people sitting in this very room. He gave the impression he'd be opening a ticket agency any day.

Jessica nudged Dave. "More pie in the sky."

They got up and left.

Kyle and Whitney were in the hallway talking animatedly. "NASA is definitely interested." Whitney's face was aglow.

Jessica had never seen Whitney so pleased about her job.

"Let's keep up our momentum." Kyle pointed toward the other end of the building with a flourish of his cane. Jessica could easily imagine him keeping the cane after it was no longer needed, just for flash and dash.

Hurrying along behind him, past exhibits of fanciful, brilliantly colored, acrylic paintings of planets and moons, she could hear Kyle giving Whitney instructions on whom to approach and what to say. He did all the talking. Again, it struck Jessica how much Whitney was enjoying what she was doing. Not only was she smiling more, her every movement was infused with energy, her face alive with eagerness. Whitney liked having someone exciting to follow; she enjoyed pleasing others. Jessica was through lecturing her on being assertive and taking control.

Someone nearby said, "Isn't that Lander cute? I bet it's having a good time."

Kyle stopped to look back at Jessica. "You could sell any space program to this crowd. They eat this stuff up. They anthropomorphize planetary probes, identify with them. Can you believe it?"

"Of course they shouldn't anthropomorphize the Lander." Whitney made a face. "It won't like that."

Jessica began to laugh. "Whit, that's funny." Brain switches flipping, she leaned against a wall covered with a soft-textured material and slid down it, slumping sideways until she lay in fetal position on the carpet.

Well, there it was. Clonazepam could not overcome her sensitivity to humor. The medication had overpowered her reactions to loud noises, crowds and vigorous exercise, but not to laughing. Whitney's joke, with its internal contradiction, was, for her, overwhelmingly funny.

"You okay? Want help?" Kyle bent over the top of his cane, his bad leg too weak to allow him to kneel or squat beside her.

"I need for everyone to be calm, let me be. I do better when there's no big fuss." She hated to think how many strangers were gawking at her.

"You were doing so well."

"I'm okay. If everyone stays cool, I'll be up in a minute." One good thing about the laughing collapses was they seldom lasted long.

By now Kyle, Whitney and Dave had formed a buffer ring around her and were telling people everything was under control. It took a few minutes before she could get to her feet and lean on Kyle's arm. "I think I've had enough running around for a while."

"Want to sit down and rest?" Whitney asked.

"I see just the place," Kyle said with an eagerness Jessica found puzzling. "See those three guys under that spacecraft photo? There's an empty chair near them."

"Looks good." Jessica pulled on his arm.

"Dave, would you take her over there while Whitney and I talk to some people?" Kyle asked. "They don't know either of you like they know me and they happen to work for our worst competitor. So, Jessica, you might hear something interesting." He gave her elbow a squeeze.

"I thought you were kidding about spying."

"You don't have to do or say anything. Just listen."

"I didn't bring my slinky, revealing dress or my secret weapon." She couldn't hear herself saying spying isn't nice.

"You won't be doing anything dishonest. You won't have to do anything at all, as a matter of fact."

"We're a team?"

He winked.

Dave assisted her down the hallway, eased her into the chair and left to prowl the exhibits.

She opened a PlanetFest brochure in her lap and let her droopy head hang over it. She didn't know whether to hope she'd overhear something significant or not.

"We've done about all we can." She couldn't see who was speaking. "Let's go pretty soon."

"Look, there's Kyle Bumpers over at the GE booth," someone else said.

Jessica was all ears. It had never occurred to her that they might talk about Kyle.

"I heard he was in a plane accident and couldn't work anymore. Looks like he wasn't hurt that bad."

"Knowing him, it was probably some kind of scam. I bet the cane's just a prop."

Jessica kept pretending to read.

"Look at that babe he's got with him."

"Always does."

"He's the shadiest marketeer in the business, but nothing's ever been proved against him."

"He's too slippery."

"Big spender, always bragging about the money he's making in the market."

"When he talks about anything a lot, you can bet it's a cover for something else."

"Even the women?"

"Well…"

They all laughed.

A soft drink can clanged into a receptacle. "We've done our bit, haven't we?"

"I thought my pitch on the new antennas and three-axis stabilizer went pretty good."

"Apparently nobody's wise that when our antennas slew, our spacecraft goes unstable."

"Let's hope the guys at the plant get that fixed before anyone hears about it."

"You up for dinner?"

"Some place with a well-stocked bar."

Jessica forced herself to not look up as they left. She was so excited she could hardly breathe. The competition's spacecraft became unstable when its antennas moved, which they had to do in order to perform missions. And, deserved or not, Kyle's reputation was as bad outside Rank as it was inside.

She was faced with a dilemma. What should she do with this intelligence? Tell Kyle? Or say nothing?

Looking up from the brochure, she saw her friends walking toward her. Her loyalties—where did they lie? Officially, she was a Rank employee on leave of absence. Whitney, Kyle, Jim Stone and Shirley Skowron worked there. She owed them all for supporting her.

But what she'd just learned was sensitive info proprietary to another company. Not that she'd stolen anything or sneaked into someone's office and ransacked their files. She'd simply overheard a bit of careless conversation.

While attempting to spy.

Halfheartedly.

The guys she'd overheard were dead wrong about two things—Kyle's claiming to have had an accident wasn't a scam and the cane wasn't a prop. They'd assumed that since Kyle was running around at PlanetFest he couldn't have been badly injured. If he didn't look sick, he probably wasn't.

Those jerks had no basis for their opinions. Anger totally swamped her thoughts.

Whitney arrived, flushed with pleasure. "It was great," she exulted. "Everyone crowded around and wanted to hear what I had to say."

Kyle winked at Jessica.

She knew he appreciated Whitney's ability to draw attention.

"And they listened to me. When I was in engineering, no one listened."

Jessica stood up, feeling better. "Maybe it's because your jokes have improved. That one about the Lander had me on the floor."

"Oh, Jessica." Whitney scowled and giggled at the same time. "Will I ever be anything but a straight man for you?"

"You're my very favorite straight man." Jessica squeezed Whitney's hand.

They met Dave at the main entrance and plunged outside into the torrid afternoon sun. Jessica stopped to put on sunglasses.

"You seem okay now," Kyle said.

"I am. Guess what I heard?"

Kyle raised an eyebrow, his gaze sharp.

"Those guys you wanted me to sit next to think your accident was probably fake and your cane just a prop."

Kyle grinned. "I'll be damned."

"Of course I couldn't defend you. I was spying." She smirked at him.

"They say anything else about me?"

"Yes, but the main thing wasn't about you." She was surprised how exciting it was to be reporting on her spy mission. "I heard them say their spacecraft goes unstable whenever an antenna slews. They're hoping to get it fixed before anyone finds out."

Kyle let out a long, low whistle. "That's major. Terrific. We can emphasize all the antenna motions our spacecraft can sustain without destabilizing and contrast it with theirs. It'll be devastating."

"It was so easy. I just sat there with my nose in a magazine and they kept on jabbering." Once again she pondered how little she knew about Kyle's reputed exploits with women and espionage and how much of his apparent affluence derived from investments. Sticking to what she knew personally, the worst she could accuse him of was chatting up women and eavesdropping on competitors. He'd gotten her to do his bidding, but she certainly hadn't needed coaxing. And she'd felt protective when those guys had said he must be faking being sick because he didn't look sick.

A lasting relationship had to be built on more than protectiveness and an exciting spy caper. She doubted she would ever love him, but she felt free to be herself around Kyle. Maybe too free for her own good.

On the way home, she was silent as Kyle and Whitney talked over what they'd seen and heard. Whitney's career was in high gear and she was happy. Kyle evidently felt the day had been a great success.

In contrast, today had been the only stimulating one among a succession of lonely, dull days for her. Spying was the highlight of her week. She envied Kyle and Whitney their satisfaction—the contrast to her own empty life was hard to endure.

CHAPTER 48

For the two weeks preceding her trip to Las Flores, Jessica had to do without clonazepam so her symptoms would be fully evinced. She spent her days collecting dust alongside everything else in her apartment.

At the start of the second week, she was sitting on the balcony listening to the faint sounds of creatures below scurrying through the tangle of bushes, vines, geraniums and nasturtiums. A blue jay landed on the railing and cocked an eye, first at her, then at Elsa dozing in a pot where flowers had died. Bird droppings festooned the table and balcony floor, grasshoppers kerplopped busily in and out of plants she had given up tending and the bougainvillea was trying to make its escape into a nearby tree branch. Neglected by its unmedicated, dysfunctional owner, her place was being swallowed up by the surrounding wilderness.

A grasshopper landed on her thigh. No wonder. As inert as she was, it had probably mistaken her for a tree.

Late last night she'd tottered up the steps from the laundry room after waiting hours to gain enough strength to walk down and back up. Dragging her laundry in a canvas bag, she'd suddenly looked straight into the red eyes of a creature in a tree beside the stairs. It opened a mouth full of jagged teeth and hissed. The horror of being slashed to pieces went through her mind before she realized it was only a possum eating the sour green tropical fruit that grew in the tree. The shock flipped circuits in her brain, but what really laid her low was when she began laughing. She'd barely made it up the last steps before collapsing onto her doormat.

The number and severity of her crashes were evidence clonazepam had been masking the fact that she was getting worse. Since discontinuing the medication, she'd been ranging from barely able to shuffle around the apartment to spending hours on end totally inert. And she was having frequent difficulty with breathing and swallowing. She was never symptom-free.

Only a week ago, when Kyle had taken her to see *Laughter on the Twenty-Third Floor*, she'd been able to time one of her last clonazepams to peak during the show. The Sid Caesar character and his crew of gag writers had come up with hilarious skit after skit, ad-libbing as comedically as they wrote. Kyle had kissed her afterward and she remembered how good that felt and at the same time scary. The two of them were like anxious first timers, afraid of where their relationship might lead them. But her libido was definitely back.

If she went to that play or kissed him now, she'd end up a helpless puddle of flesh on the floor. Nothing was much fun, all a struggle made worthwhile only by the hope of diagnosis and treatment. Every morning, she took an hour to get dressed, feed the cats and eat a bowl of cold cereal. And she never knew when she could begin doing these simple things—she might lie flaccid in bed until nine, ten or even noon before she could get up. Then she would usually try to accomplish something essential—like struggling up and down the stairs to the laundry room, dragging herself to the mailbox in the lobby, or sitting in the bottom of the shower to wash her hair. She didn't always succeed. The other day in the garage, where she'd gone to run her car's engine so its battery wouldn't run down, she'd smelled marijuana smoke and had to prop herself against someone's car to keep from falling. The sharp odor had precipitated a sudden collapse with scarcely any warning SPAM, just like the elevator effect.

The pain came and went at the level of a mild sunburn. She was constantly afraid it would become unbearable without medication.

She hoped this suffering wouldn't be for nothing, but a cataplexy diagnosis wasn't a certainty. It rarely occurred without narcolepsy, she didn't have narcolepsy and her collapses lasted much longer than any case she'd read about. Her symptoms had always differed in small ways from those of every disease she and Hatfield had tried to fit her to.

Maybe she could come up with a physiological reason for her symptoms. Cryptopathologist Jessica Shephard would track down their genesis.

Take laughter. She'd heard it described in many ways—the flip side of sorrow, a cover for embarrassment, a means of conquering fear. But this affliction of hers was revealing laughter to be a poorly understood cousin of surprise to the mind and body. Surprises like the sudden appearance of a possum at night, a whiff of marijuana or the acceleration of an elevator. These reactions must all involve the same brain circuits, yanked willy-nilly from going about their ordinary business. That could account for the sensation that circuits in her brain were being flipped just before every attack and why she could stall them off with mental effort and why she sometimes couldn't exert as much mental effort as was needed.

Apparently she couldn't afford to have her circuits yanked away. Maybe she'd lost some to autoimmune attacks. Her father, after all, had died with an autoimmune illness. Her searches in the medical literature had revealed that, even in normal people, many brain circuits are disconnected during the low estrogen part of a woman's cycle and during the insulin shock of carbohydrates after eating. Vigorous exercise requires the attention of a large number of neural pathways. Maybe she became weaker longer at that part of her period and after eating carbohydrates or exercising because of abnormal circuit losses on top of the normal ones.

How many connections could she lose and still carry on? How far would this thing go? If all her circuits were eventually destroyed, wouldn't she die?

This was a problem with being alone so much. Sooner or later she began thinking depressing thoughts.

She opened a book Whitney had brought her. One offhand comment that she'd like to write about the controversy over manned versus robotic planetary exploration and the so-called evidence of life on Mars, and Whitney had deluged her with how-to-get-published information. She missed Whitney in her daily life.

She turned to a section on requirements magazines place on authors hoping to be published. She could start writing about Mars. But why not pick the low-hanging fruit first? She'd already produced three articles for the *Medical School Alumni Magazine*. Why not try to get them republished in a place that paid?

The book listed a small number of publications aimed at medical practitioners, wanting submissions on a handicapped person's private and business life with emphasis on how to overcome difficulties. Perfect. She'd submit the first article she'd written, on speaking up and getting noticed when you're in a wheelchair. Of the three pieces she'd done, her favorite was the one imploring physicians not to attribute illnesses they couldn't diagnose to mental problems or malingering. There appeared to be a small market for that type of submission.

None of the magazines paid more than a thousand dollars, some as little as twenty-five, for an article. She'd have to become a writing machine if she hoped to earn a living this way. But if she were only trying to pay the nine or ten thousand she'd end up owing Las Flores, she might hope to do it within a year if she managed to get one or two articles a month in the right publications. Meanwhile, she didn't want to ask Mom for a loan—Richard was about to retire and they needed to be careful with their money until the last two years of their mortgage was paid. So unless she wanted to carry ten thousand on her credit card, when she'd always been nervous about even a few hundred, she'd have to decide what to sell—the car or the piano. If she got effective treatment at Las Flores, she might be able to go to work soon and she'd need the car. She was probably going to have to sell the piano.

Elsa, who occasionally opened an eye during her naps, suddenly leaped at a grasshopper. Good for her. They were all mouth, chewing up the few tomato plants that still survived. The grasshoppers vanished into the plant thicket at one end of the balcony. Elsa squatted, watched and blinked her eyes, hoping for their return.

Jessica went inside to play the piano. One of her favorite pieces, maybe a Beethoven sonata.

CHAPTER 49

Mom drove the airport rental car between massive, sandy brown towers of stone that could have been hewn from the nearby sun-bleached hills shimmering in the August heat. Imposingly tall palm trees, their fronds motionless in the still air, flanked the roadway on both sides. Bark-covered fingers on shorter, gnarled trees drooped almost to the ground. Everything was rooted in dry dust. The University of Scorched Earth—Jessica's first impression of Las Flores. It was hard to imagine any *flores* growing around here.

"This place is not exactly inviting," Mom said.

A grasshopper thudded onto the hood of the car and instantly flew off to keep from frying.

Jessica sighed. "Everything looks like it's dead or dying." There was nobody outdoors.

Rounding a corner, they saw a sign for the Sleep Center. Mom pulled into a disabled person's parking space in front of a sprawling, three-story, tile-roofed building.

Jessica's heart beat faster. She could scarcely stand the agony of anticipation and fear of frustration. Hatfield, guru of probabilities, gave her only a twenty percent chance of being diagnosed with cataplexy.

"Crutches or wheelchair?" Mom asked. They'd crammed the wheelchair into the trunk, along with the luggage, and laid the platform crutches across the backseat.

"Neither." She was walking fairly well this morning. Despite the dry hot air assaulting her as she stepped outside the air-conditioned car—this was typical central California in August—she easily crossed the parking lot to enter a brilliantly windowed and mirrored lobby. Mom trailed, carrying the crutches under one arm.

Jessica jabbed the elevator up button. When they got to the second floor where the clinic was, her SPAM level was rising but her legs had scarcely weakened. "I'd hate to be so asymptomatic that my tests are inconclusive." She pushed "1." Back at the ground floor she could barely stand. She pushed "2." This time she lurched forward as the elevator door opened. Mom dropped the crutches, grabbed her hand and arm and managed to steer her to a gentle landing on a sofa in the waiting room.

"I'm so happy you're falling again," Mom exclaimed.

Jessica laughed. "A mother's prayer." Sinking into fluffy cushions, she looked around. Morning sunlight let in by large windows made the room's soft purple furniture, ecru carpeting and pale peach walls an eyeful of happiness. A sign scrawled across a sheet of white paper on an easel read "No noise in this section! Sleep tests in progress." There was no noise—no people either. Except for a receptionist sitting behind the admissions counter, they were alone.

"Where is everybody?" Mom asked. "This is supposed to be a world-famous clinic."

The receptionist, pearl earrings peeking through her close-cropped gray hair, turned on a friendly, but institutional, smile. "To work around our clients' sleep problems, we don't schedule appointments before ten thirty. Are you Jessica Shephard?"

Jessica toddled up to the counter, wresting one foot at a time from the clutches of elevator-induced gravity. "That's me. I guess I'm early. I've been waiting a year and a half for a diagnosis and I'm a little eager." A bevy of butterflies tore through her brain, disrupting switches. Her knees buckled and she dropped to the floor on thick, spongy carpet.

The receptionist came over and knelt by her.

"I'm okay," Jessica hurried to explain. "Don't worry."

"We're used to patients falling." The receptionist told her the Sleep Center catered to patients by providing soft furniture and carpets. "Lots of people have slept right where you are now."

Jessica felt as if she'd come to a haven designed specially for narcoleptics and cataplectics. She was still comfortably lolling on the floor when the pad-pad of rubber soles approached. "Hello, I'm Rudy Maddox. You must be Jessica Shephard."

Dr. Rudy Maddox—the man who'd written all those journal articles, the wizard of sleep worshipped by narcolepsy and cataplexy sufferers everywhere. She couldn't see anything but white shoes and trouser cuffs.

"Yes, that's me." Jessica's voice was too slurred to show the excitement she felt. And the embarrassment. It was humiliating to be on the floor, even though this man must understand very well why she was here.

"I'm her mother," Mom said. "I'll need help getting her up."

It took the two of them to get Jessica up and support her between them, each holding an arm. Maddox's grip was reassuringly strong.

"I brought her crutches," Mom said.

Maddox replied that he wanted to see how Jessica did without them.

As they crept down a silent corridor where another sign warned of sleep tests in progress, she observed Maddox as closely as she could with her head drooping. He was only a bit taller than she, mid-forties, with gold-framed glasses and studious-looking furrows across his brow. His skin had an outdoor ruddiness that showed through its basic deep black. She liked studious, outdoor people. They tended to be thoughtful and understanding.

"Let's see how you do on your own." He gingerly let go of her, Mom following his lead. Jessica's thigh muscles were useless, her knees buckled instantly.

Maddox grabbed one forearm, Mom the other. "Classic cataplexy presentation," he said.

"What does that mean?" Jessica was now so limp all over that she hung like wet laundry between them.

"It means you look like someone who has cataplexy."

"If it looks like a duck and it waddles like a duck..." Mom began.

"It could be a duck impersonator," Maddox finished.

After gently lowering her into one of four soft purple chairs in his office, the doctor picked up a folder from his desk and sat down beside her. "I've read everything in your file, but I want to hear your version. Starting with the laughing collapses when you were small."

It took Jessica more than half an hour to cover her childhood laugh-and-fall spells, her allergies, the cat bite, the tetanus shot, the early paralytic attacks, the drifting of symptoms from afternoon to any time of day, the many attempts at diagnosis, the dreadful onset of pain, and the surprising success she'd had with clonazepam in countering both pain and weakness. Tense and hurried, she rattled on about her cataplexy triggers—eating, exercising, elevator rides, laughing. She made sure to include laughing. Mom sat silently through the whole narrative.

"And you never had any symptoms of narcolepsy?" he asked. "No unusual daytime sleepiness? No nodding off at the dinner table?"

Jessica shook her head. "No. Not once."

"I would have noticed if she had," Mom said.

"Falling down laughing since you were a child," he said. "For many years the disease may have lain low in your central nervous system. Then something, maybe the tetanus shot, triggered an attack."

"Tetanus?" Jessica slurred the word.

"We don't know why it happens, but tetanus is a not uncommon precipitator of narcolepsy, and with it cataplexy. Not a cause, but a precipitator."

"When I went in after the cat bite, the nurse said it didn't matter that I'd had one or two tetanus shots in less than five years before."

"The protocol is no more often than every five years and there's a reason for it."

"You mean that one mistake could have caused me all this misery?" Jessica watched a single tear run down Mom's cheek.

Maddox looked at his watch. "You've been weak for nearly an hour. Let's try something." He walked over to a shelf and picked up a tiny hammer. "I want to check your reflexes." He tapped beneath her right kneecap several times. "Nothing here." He tapped under the left kneecap. "Not here either."

"Try again. I usually jump when someone taps me there."

"Cataplectics have no knee jerk reflex during attacks."

With a start, Jessica remembered that the first resident to test her in the ER had gotten no reflex, but the second had and she'd thought the first one was incompetent. Another cataplexy symptom! "How many people have you seen like me?"

"Like you? Patients with both narcolepsy and cataplexy come to this clinic in droves. But in over twenty years I've seen only two with isolated cataplexy who, as far as I know, never came down with narcolepsy." Maddox eyed her over his half glasses. "If this is indeed cataplexy, yours is the most severe case I've ever seen, with or without narcolepsy."

"Do you believe I have cataplexy?" She closed her eyes, held her breath and waited for him to reply.

"We'll run more tests tonight, but your lack of reflexes when you're weak and your reactions to being startled are typical. Furthermore, clonazepam is one of the drugs used to treat cataplexy and you've responded well to it."

"It was blind luck I began taking it for pain."

"Laughter is your most convincing symptom," Maddox continued. "Clinically speaking, experiencing sudden muscle weakness when you laugh has a ninety-five percent sensitivity and a ninety-nine percent specificity for cataplexy. It provides a quick clinical tool for diagnosis."

"You need to get the word out. You're the first doctor who's paid any attention when I said laughing caused me to be temporarily paralyzed." Jessica felt light-headed, giddy with happiness she hoped wasn't premature. Could she really believe she had a diagnosis this time?

"The problem is the medical profession is always looking for measurables—blood component levels, nerve conduction figures, pulse irregularities. Sometimes the obvious is discounted. Laughing sickness is the common name for cataplexy." Maddox grinned.

"Common name? You have to be kidding. Nothing about cataplexy is common. No one I've met has even heard of it."

"Most people, doctors included, think laughter is good for them. There's a lot of reluctance to think of falling down laughing as a symptom of disease."

"Let me tell you my idea about laughter." As she told him of her reactions to the possum in the tree, marijuana smoke, the joke about the sultan's porcupines, the elevator rides, she described how switches in her brain always flipped, warning she was about to collapse. With a lot of mental effort she could hold them off for a short time. She told him her idea that autoimmune attacks had destroyed some of her brain circuits so that when surprises, like laughing, yanked away circuits, there weren't enough brain to muscle connections left and she got weak. "I am probably one of the few people in the world who can describe firsthand how it feels when laughter disrupts brain function, which is not all bad, by the way. Some circuits, as I'm sure you know, activate the stress syndrome, which causes damage to the immune system, even shortens cell life. So laughter disrupts body stress and helps sick people recover faster." She had to pause for breath. "Except in cataplexy."

"That's quite a conjecture, not to mention a lecture," Maddox said. "How are you feeling now?"

"Gravity's letting up a bit. Norman Cousins had it partly figured out, that laughter helps the sick get well. Do you think I have the rest figured out?"

"It's worth considering. Anyway, you're in luck. Nowadays we have a wide range of medications to treat cataplexy. Fluoxetine, the clonazepam you've been taking, desipramine, others coming along in the pipeline. It's good we have this arsenal because they all have drawbacks—like becoming less effective with time, causing addiction, turning patients into zombies. Response varies from patient to patient and from time to time with the same patient."

"All I need is clonazepam. For weak spells and pain."

"I don't know what to make of your neuropathy. Your tests show no sign of peripheral nerve damage." Maddox sat back and stared out the window. "Following on the heels of the cataplexy and treatable with the same medication, it's likely they're related disorders. You may have already come to the same conclusion."

"My pain and burning sensations usually get switched on at the same time as the cataplexy. The same brain switches must be involved, even though I feel it in my hands and feet and face."

"Peripheral burning can be induced by the central nervous system. There are mechanisms."

"That might explain why clonazepam works for both." She was so ecstatic she could scarcely focus her thoughts. It was hard to know which to be happier about—the diagnosis, the availability of treatments or the respect with which he was treating her. How satisfying and self-affirming it was not to be told the paralysis and pain were all in her head. Even though in a literal sense they probably were. But she still had one big worry. "Will I have to go around being careful not to laugh for the rest of my life?"

His mouth contorted into a shape that managed to look like both a smile and a grimace at the same time. "Pick your place and time. I wouldn't listen to a joke at the top of a stairway if I were you."

"If you put that joker's attitude on ice, I wouldn't mind a bit," Mom said.

Maddox squirmed and cleared his throat. "Let's get back to business here. I'd like to show you off."

He phoned the receptionist and asked her to round up as many of the students and staff as she could and schedule the largest room available for a noon meeting. He said he wanted everyone to see the most extraordinary case of cataplexy he'd ever come across.

"I'm the queen of cataplexy." Jessica put her hand to her breast.

"Don't you feel honored to be in my presence?"

Maddox glanced at Mom, as if to get a quick reading on whether Jessica's sense of humor was a disease symptom or a personality quirk. Jessica got the distinct impression that she was flustering him and fleetingly relished her moment of power.

The phone rang and Maddox answered. "We should go," he said. "The room's getting full."

"How many will there be?" Jessica wondered if she should tell him strange people crowding around always made her weak.

"At least thirty," he said. "That should be enough to arouse your symptoms, don't you think?" He smiled as he opened the door for her.

So he knew. "You've been hanging out with cataplectics," she said. "Does your mother know about this?"

At the front of the room was a padded table covered with a white paper sheet. Rows of the ubiquitous soft purple chairs, occupied mostly by people in lab coats, filled the available space. A few stood in back where a man behind a video camera mounted on a tall tripod aimed it at the table.

They'd all come to see her. No one here was trying to usher her out the door while wishing her better luck elsewhere.

The thought of so many people focused on her threatened to deprive her of the little muscle tone she had left. She leaned first on one chair for support, then another, until she made it to the table, where she slouched precariously on its edge.

"This is Jessica Shephard," Maddox began. "I suspect Jessica has isolated cataplexy and burning paresthesias. Otherwise she's a twenty-six-year-old woman in good health."

"Isolated?" A long-haired young man spoke up.

"Yes. She apparently has no narcolepsy, although we're going to investigate that further. She has cataplectic attacks that last as little as a minute or as long as hours."

A murmur arose. Jessica heard the faint whir of the camera and saw spectators exchange glances. The duration of her attacks was causing a stir, even here.

Maddox related her case history and listed precipitators of her attacks, including crowds, elevators and laughter. "She falls when she laughs or someone tickles her," he said. "I know of only one consistent cause for that—cataplexy."

"That's kind of sad," a male voice in the audience said.

"It's not fair, is it?" Jessica wished she could raise her head to see who was empathizing with her. Empathy was so much nicer than the incredulity with which she'd sometimes been received.

"Notice the drooping neck, the mouth hanging open," Maddox went on. "She can scarcely sit erect." He tapped her knees with a little hammer. "No reflex here."

People in the front leaned forward, those in the back craned their necks. Jessica fell on her side on the crinkly sheet.

When a woman from the audience helped Maddox sit Jessica up again, her head was hanging and her arms and legs were flaccid.

"Are you actually awake?" a male voice asked. "You look so out of it. I could almost believe you have narcolepsy."

"*Please,*" she protested. "No narcolepsy. Cataplexy is enough." These people really were interested in her symptoms. They cared and were trying to understand. Maybe seeing her would give them new insights.

"You seem to be hyperventilating." It was the voice of a blond guy, one of the few in the audience she, with her head hanging down, could see since he was in the front row. "Is that a symptom?"

"Yes, I'm having a little trouble breathing."

"Only the intercostal muscles are involved in cataplexy," Maddox said. "Not the danger of a diaphragm failure, as in myasthenia gravis."

Jessica had a hard time believing she had enough muscle between her ribs to cause shortness of breath when they failed. "Would you go to emergency if your breathing went over thirty times a minute?" As hers had many times.

Maddox hesitated before replying. "When it comes to breathing, don't pay too much attention to anyone's rule. Your case is more severe and possibly more debilitating than any I've seen. If I were you, I'd go to an ER and let them worry about what muscles are affected."

"I'm timing you. Start counting your breaths please," a woman said. "Begin."

At "Stop," Jessica reported twenty-eight. "That's not too bad. I'm not ready for—the—res—pir—ator—yet." It was getting harder and harder to talk.

"Why don't we let you rest a minute," Maddox said.

The room grew silent except for the whir of the camera. Jessica let herself space out, allowing her mind to go blank, turning off all switches connected to the outside world. She closed her mouth and swallowed. A few minutes later she sat up erect and opened her eyes.

The silent spectators who were staring at her began to smile or sigh as she returned to normal. First one, then a few more, finally everyone began to clap.

Maddox tapped her knees with his hammer and her legs obligingly jerked. The audience oohed and aahed. "Everyone here knows what the reappearance of this reflex means," Maddox said. "Cataplexy."

"Cataplexy, cataplexy." She said the word over and over. She had cataplexy, was diagnosed with cataplexy, could be treated for cataplexy. People didn't die from cataplexy. She felt as if she didn't need to walk anymore—she could just waft through the air on happiness.

"You people have given me so much hope," she said. "Because of your interest and your work, I may someday be free of all these symptoms. I could hug you all."

The show ended with a question and answer session about her symptoms, especially laughing. Everyone here knew to connect laughing collapses and cataplexy. For Jessica, the question was: why then didn't the rest of the medical profession know about this?

The room emptied except for the blond-haired guy from the front row who Maddox introduced as George Elion, a post doc doing research on canine narcolepsy and cataplexy.

"I'd love to see your dogs," Jessica said. "I've never seen any living thing with the same disease as mine."

Soon it was decided that Maddox and Mom would take care of the arrangements and paperwork for the next day's narcolepsy sleep test, while Jessica would go with Elion to his lab.

CHAPTER 50

"Are you okay to walk?" Elion asked when they were outside. "I could get a wheelchair."

"I'd like to walk. But I'll be slow. Okay?"

He held out his arm and she leaned on it.

Under the brilliant midafternoon sun, they headed down a pebbled walkway that wound between earth-toned buildings and past the charming palms and interesting shrubs with shiny, succulent-like leaves and gnarly limbs.

She loved the heat of the sun, the hot dry air blanketing her body, the warmth of the sun-baked walkway seeping through the soles of her shoes. "I always want to live in California," she said. "I thrive on this kind of weather."

"I've learned to like it," Elion answered. "But that's probably because I enjoy my research. People generally like surroundings they're happy in."

"Nobody could be happier than I am today. I've been waiting eighteen months for a diagnosis and now I have one and it's not fatal."

"You've never met anyone else with cataplexy?"

"No. But I'd like to. If I saw someone like me, someone I could identify with, maybe I'd feel less freaky."

"Wait until you see my dogs."

"A dog I can identify with. Why have I been spending my life with cats?"

They'd walked about five minutes, which at her speed wasn't far, when they came to a four-story glass and concrete building that looked recently built. "We just moved in," Elion said, opening the door for her.

"The labs and dog facility were built specially for us."

"You must be well funded." She loved it that narcolepsy and cataplexy were taken so seriously here.

"We got some really good grants. Why don't you have a seat." He indicated a worn leather couch. Six doors opened off the lobby, each with a coded lock. "I can't take you where the dogs are kenneled. No one who isn't working on a project is allowed down there. I'll have to bring one up."

She wondered why all the security—this place was locked up like a Rank facility.

"There are organizations that try to raid labs and free animals because they think we torture them," he explained. He told her how at Las Flores they pampered their dogs—partly for the sake of scientific control and partly because they had become attached to the dogs—playing with them, holding them in their laps, feeding each by hand. The dogs never left their kennels and fenced-in yards, trusted everyone and had no fear of cars. If they were set loose, their lives would be in danger.

Jessica was drawn to Elion by the emotional intensity in his face. He cared so much for his canine charges. They were his pets, his friends, his children.

"If the dogs being treated for narcolepsy and cataplexy were suddenly taken off their medications they'd suffer, maybe die. We have to keep out people we don't know," he finished.

"Like me."

"You don't have a clearance."

"But I'm crazy to see your dogs."

He smiled. "I won't keep you waiting much longer. I'll get Froggy right now."

She watched him punch a code into a security lock and go inside, letting the windowless steel door fall shut with a mechanical clunk, followed by an electronic click.

She stared at the door. Any minute now a fellow cataplectic was going to come through it. She wondered if the dog shared any of her triggers—something resembling laughter in dogs, physical or emotional stress. She'd like to take it on an elevator ride.

The door opened and a red-haired Irish setter, straining at a leash, tongue hanging out, rushed into the lobby. Elion was pulled along, hanging on to the leash with one hand, carrying a flat-bottomed metal bowl in the other.

She could see why someone would name the dog Froggy—for a setter, he had a strange, wide-mouthed grin and a round belly.

Tail wagging, Froggy led Elion over to Jessica. The dog's moist, dark nose sniffed her shoes, then her bare ankles. She ran her fingers through the silky hair on his back.

"He hasn't eaten yet," Elion explained. "So I thought I'd feed him where you could see what happens." He set the bowl down, continuing to hold onto the leash.

Froggy's tail kept wagging and his body wriggling as he stuck his face into the food-filled bowl, a healthy, happy dog if Jessica ever saw one. He gulped a bite. Within seconds his tail stopped wagging and drooped. He backed away from the food, chewed a couple of times, swallowed and hung his head down.

Jessica looked up at Elion. "He feels an attack coming on."

Elion nodded.

Froggy's forelegs began to fold at the elbow. Soon his chin was on the floor. Rear end sticking up, he struggled to push himself back up onto his front paws.

"He's fighting it," Jessica said. "When I fight attacks, the best I've been able to do is delay them a few seconds.

Froggy flopped on the floor on his side, eyes closed. He exhaled and went limp.

"Poor Froggy," Jessica cried out. "I know how it is." She got down on her hands and knees beside him and stroked him, feeling a solid form under his long, silky hair. "I know how it is." She curled up beside the dog and flung one arm over the his limp, warm body. She rubbed the back of his neck. He remained inert, but she knew he could hear and feel her caressing him.

After a couple of minutes the dog squirmed.

"I think he's ready to get up," Elion said.

Jessica slid aside as Froggy crawled forward to the bowl, tail occasionally flipping in what looked like an attempt to wag. He staggered to his feet and began smacking his lips, splattering meaty broth into the air as he ate, all the while swaying on unsteady legs.

Jessica sat up, cross-legged, and watched for symptoms she could identify with. Certainly loss of muscle tone in the front and back legs. Possibly speech—his bark had become a mere yip. Oddly, his tail seemed most affected. She wondered if dogs wagged their tails as a substitute for laughing.

"Is he narcoleptic too?"

"Yes. Sleep can come over him quite suddenly. But his cataplexy is really profound."

Froggy finished eating and made straight for Jessica. Jessica laughed as the dog squeezed as much of himself onto her lap as he could, laying his large head on her shoulder. She wondered if he sensed she was a fellow cataplectic. "Do you know why he has cataplexy and narcolepsy?"

Elion let go the leash. "He's bred for it. Every dog we have here had both a narcoleptic mother and father. That guarantees the offspring will be narcoleptic, and probably cataplectic too. The symptoms are hard to see in newborns, but at eight weeks it gets strong. Right after their parvovirus shots."

Jessica stopped scratching Froggy's back. "How soon after?"

"About seventy-two hours."

"I had my first attack seventy-two hours after a tetanus shot." She rubbed Froggy behind the ears and got a sloppy kiss in return.

"Maybe that's not as odd as it sounds. We use dogs in our studies because their narcolepsy and cataplexy are so similar to humans'. Inoculations can excite autoimmune processes in both people and dogs."

"Do you know some doctors think cataplexy is psychological?"

Elion laughed. "That's a good one. I wonder what they'd make of dogs with cataplexy."

Jessica held Froggy's face between her hands. "You crazy dog. Are you just trying to get attention? Trying to avoid the blame for something bad you've done by behaving like this? Are your doggie screws loose?"

Elion's eyes seemed to glow with empathy as he watched Jessica and the dog. "I have something to tell you, or hint at is more like it. There's good news coming out of our lab next month. We're going to make a major announcement about the cause of cataplexy at the International Narcolepsy Conference."

"Narcolepsy conference?"

"The biggest, annual narcolepsy event there is. We'll get a lot of good exposure."

He returned Froggy to his quarters behind the steel door and came back to Jessica. "Let's see if you can walk on your own now."

She heard his footsteps behind her as she toddled toward the door.

"No offense, but you kind of waddle like our dogs." He pushed the door open for her and they went out into the heat.

She doubted her waddle looked very attractive from his view and would rather lean on his arm again than have him follow behind. "I can hardly wait to get back on clonazepam."

"You heard Maddox. He'll probably cut down on your dose and add other meds."

"I like clonazepam."

He caught up with her and held out his arm. "You want to get better over the long run, don't you? Don't push it with one drug. Addiction's no fun."

What did he know? She was taking the stuff, not him. It was great and she wasn't addicted.

She leaned on his arm. "Where's this conference? Could I go?"

"Near Santa Barbara. At a resort called the Miramar. And yes you could. It's for patients and their families as well as clinicians and researchers."

"The Miramar! I love that place."

CHAPTER 51

The minute Jessica stepped out of the car into the humid coastal air she felt at home. The Miramar hadn't changed. Clusters of blue-roofed cottages and two-story units were secluded among palms, giant birds of paradise and oleander bushes. The roses she loved still climbed the walls and fences, and the bougainvillea crept over rooftops in jeweled ruby strands. She caught glimpses of a sparkling swimming pool and tennis courts and knew that more pools, a shuffleboard court and ping pong tables were tucked here and there throughout the resort, out of sight from where she stood. Not swanky, this place invited kids to walk through it wet from a pool or sandy from the beach. She could almost feel the cool grass, the hot asphalt of the roads and paths, the gritty beach sand on the bottoms of her feet.

She waited for Richard to get her luggage from the trunk.

"I'm so glad the conference is here." She sniffed the air, soaked in sea spray. The gentle lapping of the nearby surf was always hypnotically easy to fall asleep to, punctuated by the horns of railroad trains that ran in back of the beach cottages. The trains were part of the happy ambience and had sung to Miramar sleepers since the late eighteen hundreds.

With Richard pulling her wheeled suitcase, to which he'd bungee-tied her crutches, they headed for the office to check her in. Inside the lobby a black signboard with large white letters announced "Welcome! The Miramar is proud to host the 1999 Narcolepsy Conference."

Jessica scanned the lobby, the wicker chairs and sofas, and peered into the little gift shop. Where were they? The narcoleptics and cataplectics, sinking into chairs, nodding off on sofas. An alert-looking white-haired man in an armchair was reading a newspaper. A couple with a little boy headed toward the restaurant. If any of them was narcoleptic, she couldn't tell.

After registering, she turned down Richard's offer to help her to her room and hugged him good-bye. She could tell he was reluctant to leave her here alone, but it was nearly noon and he had to get back to LA in time to be Mom's page turner at the organ recital that evening. Days before this trip, Mom had announced her decision to stay home and rehearse, making it clear she was doing this to give Jessica a chance to be on her own.

Independence! Jessica was giddy with it. She'd even paid for the conference registration and hotel herself by dipping into the six thousand left from selling her piano after she'd paid off Las Flores. Mom had been heartbroken about the piano, which Jessica sorely missed. But now she wouldn't have to fear her monthly credit card statement.

As Richard drove away, she watched the car all the way down the side road until it turned onto the freeway on-ramp.

She pulled the suitcase along one of the narrow asphalt paths she used to scamper along, remembering her young self on the run all day—building sand castles at the beach, bodysurfing in the ocean, stuffing down hot dogs and fries at the snack bar, playing shuffleboard, cannonballing off a diving board into one of the pools. But all that didn't have to be relegated to the past. On clonazepam she could often get around without either crutches or wheelchair, and there was no reason not to at least try the pool and shuffleboard. That's why she'd packed a bathing suit.

Inside her ground floor room, the furnishings were comfortably familiar. A pair of double beds with plain white spreads, a wicker chair with plump flowered cushions, a round wooden table, a TV concealed in an armoire, a desk and a glass door that led to a poolside patio.

There was a large spray of red roses on the table. Jessica sniffed them. They were fresh and sweet. The card said "Here's to you babe." She smiled. Done in true Kyle style.

Too bad he wasn't here. But now she had a chance to get better acquainted with George Elion. Both evenings at Las Flores he'd come to dinner with her and Mom, and she'd spent part of an afternoon with him looking at Maddox's sleep data from when she'd been wired up for all-night tests. She'd been relieved when Maddox had declared that even though she had sleep disturbances that contributed to her cataplexy, she appeared to be free of narcolepsy. At least for now.

George had seen her in every stage of cataplexy, apparently without being put off. In fact, he'd seemed fascinated—she couldn't avoid the thought—like Fernando had been.

She put away her clothes and changed into a bright yellow sundress and white short-sleeved jacket, one of a carefully selected wardrobe she'd packed for the occasion. There were bound to be narcoleptics and cataplectics having lunch in the restaurant by now, and she was eager to meet them.

Entering the dining room, she saw families, couples and a few singles at the forty or so tables. Then she spotted what she'd come for. By a window a lone woman with tight, honey blond curls was hunched, head drooping, arms barely holding her torso off the table.

A surge of excitement made Jessica so weak she had to grab onto the "Please Wait to be Seated" sign to keep from falling.

A hostess in a flowered cotton shift and shell necklace ambled up to her. "Where would you like to sit?"

"With her, please." Jessica pointed to the slumping woman.

"I'm Jessica Shephard," she blurted when she got to the table. "I'm a cataplectic."

"Oh, my God. A cataplectic! I've never seen another one." Chin against her chest, the woman turned her head sideways and peered up at Jessica.

Jessica knew what that felt like, but she'd never seen it in another person. As she sat down, she couldn't help gawking in what she realized was the rude way some people stared at people with disabilities.

"My name's Corky Johnson."

Jessica looked into intense blue eyes. Corky was young, maybe younger than herself, her face tanned as though she spent a lot of time outdoors.

"Happy Halloween," Corky said.

"Halloween?"

Corky grinned. "I'm getting my floppy scarecrow imitation ready for Halloween. It's only next week."

"Then we haven't got much time to practice." Jessica let her head hang like Corky's.

Corky laughed. "If that's the best you can do, I'm going to win the freak prize for sure."

Jessica knew this woman was about to become a great new friend. "Do you have narcolepsy? I have isolated cataplexy. No narcolepsy at all. I fall a lot."

"I have both."

"The full monty," Jessica said and they laughed.

They spent the next hour indulging their curiosity about each other. Jessica couldn't remember prying into someone else's business on such short acquaintance since the uninhibited days of kindergarten.

Corky lived in a small town in Northern California, where she knew no other narcoleptics and no doctors who treated narcolepsy. She'd had to go to San Francisco to get diagnosed. She lived with her boyfriend and went to a nearby college where she had part-time work analyzing data for the geology department. Before she came down with narcolepsy she'd often gone rock hunting and rock climbing with the geology students.

Outside the window a teenage boy dashed past with a surfboard. "I remember what it was like to run like that," Corky said.

"Our lives aren't over, Corky. While we're here, let's be kids again. As long as my medication's working, I'm going to walk on the beach and play shuffleboard. Maybe even go swimming. How about you?"

Corky appeared pensive and didn't reply.

After lunch, they headed for the meeting rooms in the Miramar conference center, first stopping at a registration desk where a line had already formed.

"Everyone here looks so normal," Corky whispered, as she stuck a name tag on the front of her blouse.

Jessica finished filling out the form and got her tag and conference notebook. "So do you. So do I."

They eyed the crowd. A few people were gathered by a table with large coffee urns, Styrofoam cups and baskets of donuts and sweet rolls.

Jessica nodded toward the sugar-laden table. "That's the place to watch."

A stocky man with horn-rimmed glasses, a frosted donut in one hand, face animated, was talking to two other men. His face suddenly went blank. Turning to his left, then right, he headed unsteadily for the nearest wall.

"Watch him," Jessica said to Corky. "I don't know how many times I've done this. The carbohydrate crash."

Corky raised an eyebrow. "Carbohydrate crash?"

"You don't have them?"

The man backed up to the wall, then slid slowly to the floor, head drooping.

"He's an expert," Jessica said. "He set his coffee cup down on the carpet without spilling a drop."

The other two men watched for a few seconds, then resumed talking.

"Look how cool his friends stayed when he fell," Corky said.

"I'm so excited." Jessica gave the man a thumb's up sign as he looked her way. "Here I'm not an outsider because I'm sick. I feel like I'm part of this group already."

"I wish I had someone to talk to and meet with back home," Corky said as they entered the meeting room and sat where they had a good view of the projection screen.

"How many in your town?"

Corky shrugged. "About ten thousand, I guess."

"If you go by one in a thousand having narcolepsy, there should be about ten of you there. You may be the only one who's been diagnosed."

"Yeah." Corky's head was hanging almost to the tabletop.

"Try to find the others, Corky. Help them get diagnosed. Try to form a support group. If there isn't already one near where I live, I'm going to start one."

"You're what I'd call an activist," Corky said.

An activist. When she was in college, that's what non-activist students and faculty had called her and her friends. Some had haughtily asserted her idealistic efforts were symptoms of adolescence.

Her activist days now stood out in her mind as her best. The sit-ins on behalf of better housing for the indigent had actually raised money. President Bush had sent aid to the Iraqi Kurds after she and her friends had gotten many of the students and faculty to deluge the White House with letters. But since graduating six years ago, she hadn't helped any cause, except to occasionally send money to charities. No one would call her an activist now. She wondered if her cataplexy would allow her to change that.

The meeting got underway with a panel of doctors outlining current techniques for diagnosing and treating narcolepsy and cataplexy. Afterward, for more than an hour, they fielded questions on medications, success of treatments and ways of adjusting sleep hours. Jessica was impressed by how eager the narcoleptics were for information and how sharp their questions were.

She learned that all narcoleptics are not alike. Some sleep in short fits, some for as long as twelve hours at a time. Some respond to one medication, some to another, some to none. Some have short, vivid dreams just before they fall asleep, some have hallucinations when wide awake. Most have cataplexy, but a few do not. What triggers their cataplexy varies too: eating, exercising, performing on a stage and being startled are just a few. The only cataplexy trigger common to them all is laughter.

Jessica observed that most people were eager to talk to someone like themselves. Being alone, misunderstood and isolated was a problem they all shared.

From time to time, she saw people nod off, occasionally with their upper bodies and arms sprawled on a table. How reassuring and comfortable to see a room full of people behaving as she did. What a contrast to the meetings at work where she'd feared what others were thinking about her when she was sick.

They heard the webmaster of the Young Americans With Narcolepsy (YAWN) website speak. The site publishes information on medications and runs a chat room where young patients can talk about coping with school and other life issues. The Web was a miraculous boon for these young people.

By the time the afternoon session was over, Jessica's face was burning with the effort of concentrating. She'd taken copious notes she hoped she'd be able to digest later.

As the last speaker finished, Jessica and Corky headed for their rooms. An outdoor banquet would begin at six and they wanted to change clothes and wash up. Jessica felt as if she was auditioning for a place in the lives of these people and wanted to look sharp.

She'd brought a black, round-necked sweater and an above-the-knees black skirt with red and white patterns. Her gold pendant and gold hoop earrings would set off the black of the sweater nicely. And, of course, black flats. No spiked heels for her.

Just before dark, as candles were being lit, Jessica got a seat at one of the many linen-covered tables set up on a lawn. A cool, soggy breeze coming in from the ocean was strong enough to make the palm fronds swish and rattle overhead.

She was seated between Corky and Bea Noyes, a narcoleptic in her early forties, still in the clothes she'd worn when speaking at the meeting. The woman's facial muscles appeared to be sagging with exhaustion. But Jessica couldn't help herself—she just had to question Bea anyway.

What she learned was encouraging—narcolepsy and cataplexy hadn't prevented Bea from leading a full life. She'd written educational brochures for the Narcolepsy Network and helped organize national conferences. She taught biology at a community college and kept house for herself and her husband.

As shrimp cocktail was served and wine poured, Jessica got acquainted with the couple across from her. It was hard to tell how old Terry was, but his brown hair was thinning. He had isolated cataplexy and thought there weren't more than fifty like him and Jessica in the country. His wife, Ginger, a Chinese-American in a stunning gold and black brocaded jacket, told Jessica their twelve-year-old son had shown no sign of either narcolepsy or cataplexy.

"I'm really enjoying it here," Jessica said, donating her shrimp to Corky. "It's so nice not to be the only weirdo for a change."

Terry winced and fingered a scar on his chin. "It's been hard to learn to live with the way I look."

She wished she could take back her words. "No, no. I didn't mean you! I just meant we're all strange the way we drop off asleep and crumple onto tables."

Ginger took Terry's hand. "I keep telling you you're oversensitive, honey. No one thinks anything of those little nicks." She turned to Jessica. "He's an actor and had a lot of good TV parts until he had an attack and fell down a mall escalator. All the way. Every step cut his face. He hasn't looked for work since."

Terry scowled. "Work as what? Alien monster in a stupid sitcom? Not much market for a monster who crashes several times a rehearsal."

Cataplexy had cost him his career. She remembered the disabled woman news anchor who'd never gone back to TV news.

Just as it was getting very dark and a chill wind was rising, a gas heater above them popped on. With her next dose of clonazepam almost due, the pop was all it took. Jessica's circuits flipped and she barely got her salad plate shoved out of the way before her face hit the table.

Someone ran over and snapped a flash photo of her with her chin against the plate, one hand clutching a wine glass.

"No, no!" she shrieked. "I'll look like a drunk." She pulled herself partway up, then collapsed again.

Another flash went off and she melted and slid to the ground, face up.

"Come on everybody. Get in the picture," she called out. As long as she was the center of attention, she might as well make the most of it.

The official conference photographer took their picture. People, she didn't know who or how many, voluntarily or because their cataplexy had been triggered, got down on the grass and posed with her. With all the excitement, it was a long time before she was strong enough to be helped back into her chair.

"You made a big splash on your first night out," Bea said. "Next year everyone will remember you."

Jessica gave her mouth a wry twist. "Don't say big splash. I'll be falling into one of the pools next."

"Hello!" Terry called to someone behind Jessica. "Good to see you."

Jessica turned around to see two women with flutes of champagne sitting behind her. Bea turned too and soon the four of them were in a lively discussion about symptoms and medications. Bea said she could hardly wait to hear about the new experimental drugs—modafinil for narcolepsy and sodium oxy-something or other for cataplexy.

"Sodium what? What's that?" Jessica shouted over the babble.

Bea said that although sodium oxybate was only in clinical trials in the United States, it had been used for years in France to treat cataplexy. She doubted it would enable someone with cataplexy to be a dancer or tennis player, but you could live on your own, drive a car and go shopping.

Maybe these drugs were what George Elion had been hinting at. Helpful as clonazepam was, she was beginning to doubt it would ever totally free her of disability. No one here seemed to be. There probably was no perfect medication.

When Bea got up to table hop, a youngish man sat down in the seat beside Jessica. "Danny's my name," he said, reaching to shake her hand. He leaned into her, his big brown eyes and long eyelashes close to her cheek, and smiled. She couldn't tell if he was a little drunk or a little cataplectic or both.

"Danny!" Terry called from across the table.

She soon learned that Terry and Ginger knew Danny, a car salesman from Columbus, Ohio.

"I'm pretty good as long as I keep up with my meds," Danny said, suddenly serious. "My boss lets me take a couple of short naps during the day to make sure I don't drop off with a client."

On her mental scorecard, Jessica noted another narcoleptic with cataplexy who'd worked out a way to stay employed. Through Danny, she met a forklift operator fired for falling asleep on the job. He introduced her to a narcoleptic nurse who'd worked in an intensive care unit, but had been transferred to a geriatric ward, and a young woman who'd had to give up her ambition to become a concert violinist. It seemed everyone she met had had to make career compromises. Some had found work that paid decently and gave them satisfaction, some hadn't. Nobody, except possibly Terry, was as seriously cataplectic as she was.

Bea returned in time for the entrée and Danny left. While they ate, they listened to a sleep doctor speak on the latest clinical trials of modafinil and sodium oxybate. So far there had been no side effects or safety issues, unlike with clonazepam, which the speaker warned altered the mind and was addictive. Jessica became agitated because she felt he was being unjust to clonazepam.

It was midnight by the time the dinner broke up. There'd been no mention of the Las Flores breakthrough and no sign of George Elion.

"I wish I could stay with these people forever," Corky said as they made their way past illuminated palm trees. "But I can't believe I'm saying this. I never knew any of you 'til this morning."

Jessica nodded and breathed in the chilly night air. "We go deeper with each other in a few minutes than some people who've shared lives a long time."

"I think I'm going to break up with my boyfriend," Corky said. "He keeps trying to get me to stay home and not stress myself."

"I broke up with mine because he wanted to control everything I did. I think we attract guys like that because we look helpless."

"Lately, John wants to have sex while I'm having an attack. He says it gives him a thrill. Can you imagine?"

"Sick. Trade him in for a nice narcoleptic boy."

Corky giggled. "Like Danny?"

"Why not? You know what I'm going to do when I get home? I'm going to take a chance on a guy from where I worked. He's the one who sent me the roses in my room."

"Is he nice?"

"About as nice as me."

"Then go for it, Jessica."

"There are a few problems. We both find it hard to get close. Don't like to show our vulnerability. It's hard to get close to someone when you're holding them at arm's length." How surprising that she was revealing this to Corky, who'd been a stranger two days ago.

Jessica woke to the sound of splashing in the pool outside her room. Still in pajamas, she eased out of bed, shuffled to the sliding glass door and pulled open the drapes. It was still early. Sunlight was barely glowing from behind the mountains.

Dripping wet, George Elion was emerging from the pool. His glistening face and arms were the light tan of a blonde in summer. The rest of his pale skin covered a lean body Jessica would sooner identify with a grad student who rarely took time to eat rather than a guy who worked out a lot. She slid the door open and called to him.

"How are you?" His face lit up with pleasure at seeing her. He was so close he was dripping on the carpeted patio.

"Good. I've been here since yesterday."

He rolled his eyes. "I didn't get in until late. Had to make films of the dogs having attacks and they wouldn't perform."

"How's the water?"

"Brisk." He shivered. "Come on out while I do a few laps and then we'll have breakfast."

"I'll put on my suit and join you." The only suit she'd brought was a bikini. That should get his attention.

He stepped back and clutched his arms across his chest. "I'd rather you just watched. The water's pretty cold, might give you a shock."

Well, she'd rather not just watch. "Go on. Get back in the pool before you freeze. I'll be right out."

She went into the bathroom, swallowed a clonazepam and put on the bikini. Just watch him swim indeed!

In front of the full-length mirror in the bedroom, she took a close look. She'd lost weight, which was good for the butt, where she'd always been a bit heavy, but bad for the bust, where she was on the light side. She tightened the pink bra straps to lift her breasts and sucked in a stomach that, after cataplexy, had gone from flat and firm to a little flabby.

He was going to see how good she looked both out of the water and in it.

Grabbing a towel, she trotted out to the pool.

George was hanging on to the side of the pool at the deep end. "I hope you're not coming in."

She threw her towel onto a beach recliner, ran three steps and cannonballed him. Cold, it was really cold. She gasped for breath and felt the switches flipping.

George shook his head to clear the water from his face. "I can't believe you did that."

"Are you used to people doing what you tell them to do?" She was beginning to weaken.

"What happens if you have an attack in the water?"

"You're here. You'd save me if it came to that, wouldn't you?" She was about to need saving.

He took her hand and pulled her to the shallow end. "I'll help you out."

"I don't want to get out. I just got in." She was able to stand on the bottom step where the water came to her waist and supported her. She was twenty-six. No one was going to tell her when to get out of a swimming pool. She lay on her stomach where she could grab a step and flutter kick. It felt good to stretch out in the water.

Grim-faced, George sat on the edge of the pool and watched her cavort until the sun blazed down on them from over a motel rooftop.

"Breakfast time. I think I'll get dressed now," Jessica sang out.

After breakfast, where Jessica ignored George's lecture on how a cataplectic should conduct herself, she and Corky hurried to get seats near the front of the conference center auditorium. She saw George, gesturing as though making an emphatic point, stroll in with an attractive young woman. Whatever he was saying, the woman was soaking it up.

That was okay. Grateful as she was for what he'd done for narco-leptics, she knew George wasn't for her. She'd rather be with Kyle. He would have stayed in the pool with her, she just knew it.

The audience hushed as Terry walked to the podium. Anticipation was so high that no one needed to be told to be quiet. Jessica's eyes misted, seeing Terry up there facing an audience.

"I owe thanks to the remarkable dedication of the Las Flores re-searchers on this stage. As many of you know, I have a pretty bad case of cataplexy and my hopes for a better life are pinned on the work of people like them. Today the Las Flores Sleep Center will announce a major breakthrough in their research on narcolepsy and cataplexy."

Terry went on to introduce Rudy Maddox, the principal investiga-tor who would make the announcement; then post-doc George Elion and finally two graduate students who'd spent untold hours counting cells on slides.

Terry finished to wild applause and Maddox came to the podium. "The normal thing for a speaker like me is to begin with a joke," he said, "to liven up my audience. But in present company I'm afraid it would have the opposite effect."

The audience murmured polite chuckles, punctuated by a small number of shrieks as here and there someone slumped to the floor in a laughing spasm. Jessica went into a trance to distance herself from contagious laughter and managed to fight off an attack.

"Serendipity is alive and well," Maddox went on. Forcefully, and with obvious care given to his choice of words, he described experi-ments at a lab, not a sleep research center, on a newly discovered brain secretion called hypocretin, believed to regulate appetite. That lab had created "knockout" mice for the secretion—that is, they'd created mice without genes for making hypocretin—expecting the mice would be-come anorexic. Instead, they fell asleep at all times of day and night and experienced attacks of paralysis. Someone in their lab who'd once known a narcoleptic looked up sleep centers on the Web and reached Maddox at Las Flores.

After viewing a video of the mice, Maddox and his associates had concluded they appeared to be narcoleptic and cataplectic. They decided to investigate whether human narcoleptics had diminished hypocretin levels, possibly caused by autoimmune or autoinflammatory attacks on transmitters or receptors in the brain. Because anatomical studies had shown hypocretin was secreted in an area in the mouse hypothalamus, that was where they looked in humans.

"We had no living narcoleptic willing to volunteer for brain exploration," Maddox deadpanned. "So we had to round up deceased ones." He described how they'd obtained hypothalamus slices from six narcoleptics who'd willed their brains to Las Flores. Everyone in his lab who could be spared was enlisted in counting cells that had been destroyed before death and those that had not. On average, they found the narcoleptics had lost seventy percent of their hypocretin cells by the time they'd died. No damage was found in nearby brain cells, eliminating the possibility of general brain injury. The conclusion was that hypocretin cell destruction was the root cause of narcolepsy and cataplexy.

The audience broke into applause. Those who could gave a standing ovation.

Jessica immediately had an idea about how hypocretin worked. It must set priorities for neural switching assignments. Lots of neurons must be grabbed for vital functions such as digesting food and responding to startling noises and other potential threats. Narcoleptics and cataplectics like her had probably lost so many hypocretin cells there weren't enough left during these perceived emergencies for activating arms and legs, chewing and holding the head up. Or even staying awake, in the case of narcoleptics. She could sometimes hold off collapse, she surmised, by stalling the hypocretin-controlled switches.

And laughing? That was obvious. Her brain was wired so hypocretin cells gave the highest priority to laughing. They would disconnect anything for a good laugh. This was probably her own fault. All her life she'd been training her brain to put high value on humor. Now she might never feel free to laugh with abandon again.

God had done this to her. What a sense of humor He must have, seeing to it that her greatest strength became her greatest weakness. Was He sending her a message because He knew she'd appreciate the irony? Afflicting a selected person here and there so that laughter rendered them prostrate might be His way of reminding humanity of the power of humor.

But she could be way off base. God might not be involved here at all. The explanation might just be that she had an autoimmune illness where antibodies attacked certain cells in her body—were there such things as humor cells?—and made her sick. As Hatfield had said, causes have consequences, and that's the whole story.

"What does this discovery mean for patients?" Maddox said. "First, it holds out the hope of easy, reliable diagnosis—no more guesswork in ambiguous sleep studies that may or may not be able to capture an actual attack."

More cheering.

"Second, no more attributing symptoms to psychological problems or malingering."

Cheers rose to the domed ceiling, echoing downward like rain on the auditorium.

"We hope in the not too distant future to be able to draw samples of your hypocretin and compare them to the norm. Further in the future, we may be able to treat narcolepsy and cataplexy directly by inoculating the patient with natural or recombinant hypocretin."

The applause became so loud that Maddox held up his hand. "Many difficulties lie ahead. Gathering hypocretin from living animals is slow and hugely expensive and we don't yet know how to make it in a recombinant process. But the work will go on, I guarantee you."

Jessica's spirits soared. What a wonderful thing these researchers had done for the people in this room.

"I'll never forget this day," she said to Corky.

Corky had nodded off, but Jessica knew she'd heard.

That night the final dinner of the conference was outdoors again. A babble of voices—people here had a lot to talk about—nearly drowned out the sound of the surf and the rustle of palm fronds. The aromas of the meal they were about to share blended with the salty tang of ocean spray. In the glow of the overhead gas heaters Jessica saw many friends she'd made over the past two days.

Friends—what an inadequate word. Jessica looked around. Sitting next to her was Corky, head drooping in narcoleptic slumber. On her other side, like the night before, was Bea. Across the table Terry looked more relaxed today after his success at the podium. Danny was sitting down the table with Julia and Sally, the champagne drinkers.

"I'd like some more of those baked beans," Terry said. "Can I get you anything while I'm up, honey?"

"You don't have to get up," Ginger said. "Someone's coming around to help us."

"I don't need help," Terry said emphatically.

Ginger sighed. "It's such a thing with you. You don't have prove anything to us."

Jessica understood Terry's point of view; he wanted to show he could do what was needed for himself and his wife.

· "You're spoiling it for him." Danny waved a hand smeared with sauce. "He wants to help you. Let him do it."

Terry picked up his plate and baby toddled, lifting one foot at a time, toward the buffet. Jessica watched what others must have seen her do many times. No doubt about it—the walk looked strange on an adult.

"Jessica's going to write a story about us," Danny announced. He wiped his sauce-drenched hands on a large napkin and tucked it under his chin. "I'm going to make sure she doesn't write that Danny spilled barbecue sauce all over himself."

This morning Bea had asked her to write a newsletter article about the conference. She must have told the others.

"Write whatever you want," Julia giggled. "Write he smeared himself from head to foot and ear to ear and we threw him in the ocean to clean him off."

"I'll take you with me," Danny called out.

"I want you guys to write me when you get home," Jessica said. "Tell me what you want the outside world to know about us." They'd each been given a list of names with postal and e-mail addresses for everyone at the conference.

Danny turned serious. "I don't care about the rest of the world. All the people I care about are right here."

Corky woke up. "You will write to me, Jessica?" Jessica had learned that even when asleep and slumped over, Corky heard everything. Not everyone's narcolepsy left them conscious of what was going on around them. "You won't leave me all alone again."

"Of course I'll write. Constantly. Your e-mailbox will always be full."

Everyone at the table grew quiet. Now they'd done it; they'd talked about the time when they'd all go their separate ways. She wished they'd get noisy again. She didn't want to go through the pain of parting before she had to. A train passed, its whistle growing higher in pitch as it approached, then lower and finally trailing away.

Terry returned with a plate heaped with ribs and beans. He looked around at the quiet group as he sat down. "Looks like no one knows what to say when I'm not here."

"We could use a little cheering up," Jessica admitted.

"I have something cheerful to say. I have a joke," Julia called out from down the table. Sally, lips parted in anticipation, leaned across the table to listen. Jessica couldn't hear Julia, but saw Sally's mouth fly open and heard a shriek of laughter and surprise. Julia, who obviously had known what would happen, reached over and yanked away Sally's plate just in time to keep her face from landing in it. Everyone at the table fell silent as they watched a scene they fully understood.

"That must have been a good one," Terry said.

"Tell me, tell me," Danny begged. He was sitting next to Sally.

"Just a minute." Sally's face was pressed to the festive paper tablecloth, which muffled her voice. "This is so funny. I don't want to spoil it by mumbling." It took two or three minutes before she could sit up again.

She began whispering in Danny's ear. At first he looked puzzled, then screwed up his face in disbelief. At the very end he burst out laughing; Sally grabbed his plate of barbecued ribs away just before he crashed.

"The wave!" Everyone shouted as Danny went down.

"Now me. Tell me," Corky insisted.

Danny managed to raise himself partway, leaning on his elbows, and whispered the joke to Corky. She laughed hysterically as she too went down.

"The wave," Jessica shouted along with the others, shoving her dinnerware to the middle of the table. "I'm next."

At first it seemed Corky was telling a straight story, but just as the crazy joke ended, Jessica let out a whoop. Laughter gurgled in her throat. It took over her whole brain, leaving her with no control, lofting her beyond reach of all other sensations, forcing her body into neuron starvation until she flamed out and fell with her face flat on the table.

What a fantastic feeling! To experience the full force of it she hadn't tried to delay the switches at all.

And she'd worried that with cataplexy she would have to avoid laughing the rest of her life.

"The wave!" everyone was shouting. "The wave!"

Jessica reached out and grasped Corky's hand. She'd tell the world that no one has ever had a really good laugh until they've had it with a bunch of cataplectics.

Staring into the blackness that was the ocean beyond the cottages, Jessica lingered at the table beside Corky, who was still unable to get up. Others headed off to their rooms or to the lounge.

These were her people, her tribe. They slept, dreamed and shut down their dreaming arms and legs in the tribal way. They shared a bizarre neural anatomy unknown to outsiders. Perhaps their bonds went as deep as their genetic structure. She'd do anything for them.

The activist in Jessica sprang to life. Sit-ins and marches were out, but she could write about her new friends, the narcoleptics and cataplectics. Her head was stuffed with knowledge that could help a person struggling to get a rare disease diagnosed and treated. She could offer advice on how to live independently with the problems severe illness brought. She had a lot to say about where the medical system performs well and where it is deficient. First on her list would be turning out more articles, but then she'd write a memoir. She could develop a history of diagnostic science. And maybe a novel to make people more aware of the plight of the disabled. There was time for all of it.

Corky raised herself off the table. "You will write, won't you, Jessica? You won't forget me?"

"I'll write. I won't forget."